DAUGHTER OF
DARK RIVER FARM

1917. Kitty Maitland has found a safe and welcoming home at Dark River Farm, Devon, and is finally beginning on a path to recovery after her terrible ordeal in Flanders ... until the arrival of two very different visitors. One, a charming rogue, proves both a temptation and a mystery – but she soon discovers he's not a stranger to everyone. The other newcomer, a young woman with a past linked to the farm, sows seeds of mistrust. Between the two of them, and the choices Kitty has to make, Dark River becomes a place of fear, suspicion and danger. Can it ever return to the haven it once was?

DAUGHTER OF
DARK RIVER FARM

DAUGHTER OF DARK RIVER FARM

by

Terri Nixon

Magna Large Print Books
Long Preston, North Yorkshire,
BD23 4ND, England.

British Library Cataloguing in Publication Data.

A catalogue record of this book is
available from the British Library

ISBN 978-0-7505-4548-8

First published in Great Britain 2015 by Carina,
an imprint of Harlequin (UK) Limited

Published in Large Print 2018 by arrangement with
Harlequin Books S.A.

Magna Large Print is an imprint of Library Magna Books Ltd.

Printed and bound in Great Britain by
T.J. (International) Ltd., Cornwall, PL28 8RW

This book is dedicated to my family with love, and in deep gratitude for your support as always.

Chapter One

When the stranger came to Dark River Farm he was empty-handed, yet he brought with him something different for each of us. For me it was a chance to rediscover my lost childhood, the days when all had seemed possible and I had not yet felt the savage bite of pain and loss. For those I loved, perhaps his gifts were darker... Only time would tell.

Dark River Farm, Dartmoor, June 1917

'Go on, Kitty, it won't kill you.'

I squinted through the gathering dark at the glowing orange tip of the cigarette. The barn door was open and I looked nervously out at the encroaching night, and then at the door to the farmhouse across the yard. It remained closed, and I didn't know whether to be disappointed or relieved. Belinda drew my attention back by tapping the ash from the end of the cigarette with one grubby fingernail, and her eyebrows went up in mute encouragement. She held the cigarette closer, and I reached out and took it, and raised it to my lips.

Bel nodded. 'That's the way. Nice big pull, and hold it in. Try not to cough.'

Of course, as soon as she said that I felt the tickle

in my chest, even before I'd properly breathed in, but I concentrated on mimicking Belinda's effortlessly elegant method. How I wasn't instantly sick, I shall never know. It tasted terrible, and I felt smoke curling in the back of my mouth, back up into my nose, and burning everything in its path. I opened my mouth in dismay, and the cough that erupted from my throat hurt enough to bring stinging tears to my eyes.

'Don't drop it!' Belinda lunged forward to pluck the dangling cigarette out of my numbed fingers, while I coughed a bit more and blinked away the tears. I tried to speak, to tell her it was absolutely the most awful thing and I didn't know how or why she did it, but could make no real sound beyond a hoarse whistling.

'Here, have a drink,' Belinda said, not without sympathy, and handed me the bottle.

I greedily sucked down a big mouthful of wine, and waited until I could trust myself to speak without rasping too much before I said, 'Belinda Frier, you must have a throat made of stone.'

She chuckled, and drew on her cigarette again. 'It's just practice. You can try again in a minute.'

'No fear.'

She shrugged. 'Well, all the more for me then.' She looked around the barn, blowing smoke rings and watching with lazy amusement as they vanished into the gloom. I contented myself with swilling wine around my mouth, and welcomed the gradual fading of that awful, dry, burnt taste. Before I'd gone to Belgium I'd seldom had wine. Mother thought I was too young, and Father only drank brandy, and although there had usually been wine in the cupboard at Number Twelve, our little ambulance post near Dixmude, it was very diluted to make it last. But I'd begun to enjoy it; it helped me sleep when all else had failed. I could taste the difference between this and the thin, watery wine I was used to though, and my head had already started to hum quite pleasantly.

'Where did you get this?'

'It was a present,' Belinda said, and winked. I found myself smiling, although I wasn't really sure why, except I liked spending time with her; she made things seem like fun, and it was about time I had some of that again. I began to hum a little tune: Billy Murray's popular song from last year, 'Pretty Baby', and Bel picked up on it and joined in. Ordinarily I didn't like the song, although it was constantly in my head, but Bel kept getting the words wrong which made me laugh, and then she started to change them deliberately, just to make me laugh again. Soon we were singing quite loudly: she pausing to inhale more of that revolting smoke, me to swallow more of the delicious wine, and then she stubbed out the last of her gasper on the bottom of her shoe, and stood up.

'Let's dance!'

So, as the sun faded, and while we were supposed to be clearing the barn of last year's damp grain sacks, Bel and I held hands and danced; the wine was fizzing in my blood now, and I kept stumbling over my own feet, making Bel laugh harder.

'You'd better sit down, Skittles,' she said. The nickname cut through the pleasant haze, and I stopped dancing.

'Why did you call me that?'

'It's what Evie and the others call you, isn't it?'

'Yes, but–'

'I'm so sorry, I didn't realise it was reserved for your war chums,' Bel said, a little tightly, and I felt silly for my reaction; it had been in another life that I had found that name, and that life was gone now.

'It's all right,' I said. 'You can call me that too.'

As long as you don't call me Kittlington...

The thought came out of nowhere, and was accompanied by a real pang. I heard the name spoken in Archie Buchanan's soft, Scots-accented voice, and although I'd known that voice since I'd been a child, it had, for at least three years now, had the power to reach into my heart and warm me right through.

'Come on,' Bel said, her good humour returning as swiftly as ever. 'I thought we were dancing!'

I hadn't planned on opening up, to her of all people, but she saw my face, and led me back to the boxes where we'd been sitting before. The wood felt cold now, through the threadbare corduroy of my trousers, but it didn't matter. I picked up the wine again and took a long gulp. Bel still held my other hand, and she gave it a squeeze.

'I understand,' she said. 'Your handsome captain has gone.'

'He's not mine,' I said, removing my hand from hers and wiping my mouth on my sleeve. This time last year I had prayed for Archie to see me as a woman, as if I could throw a switch in his head that would make him blink, look at me properly, and realise I was more than his friend's

14

little sister. That stupid Billy Murray song had mocked me at every turn. I spoke the words again now, with a bitter tinge to my voice:

'You're just a baby to me.
Your cunning little dimples and your baby stare,
Your baby talk and baby walk and curly hair–'

'Well you do have curly hair,' Bel pointed out. 'Although you don't really talk like a baby, and ... anyway, babies can't walk, can they?'

I raised the bottle in acknowledgement of her logic. 'It's no longer the issue in any case,' I said, and took another drink. I would give anything now just to be 'Oli's little sister'. 'It's more than that now; you know that.' My voice sounded as if it came from a long way away. Another time, even.

Bel nodded, her face solemn. 'I know, darling, but–'

'And I can't change what happened, so what's the use?' I didn't want to talk about Archie any more; it hurt too much. 'Anyway, he's gone.'

'Back to the war, the big hero,' Bel said, and lit another cigarette. We sat quietly for a little while, I don't know what Belinda was thinking about, but my mind was, as usual, on Archie and his marriage proposal.

Archie had, on the last day of his last, too-short leave, taken me to one side and said what I had desperately longed, for three years, to hear him say. Feeling his big, warm hands grasp mine as his feelings tumbled into the empty air between us, I realised I had no idea how I was going to respond, and when I at last opened my mouth, it

15

was with utter dismay that I heard my own words and knew them to be the truth.

'I'm sorry, but no.'

Chapter Two

West Derby, Merseyside, September 1914

Oliver was at the window again, impatience leaking from every pore. He was beginning to tug at my nerves and, older brother or not, I was just about to tell him to sit down, when he gave a pleased exclamation and left the room. I peered out of the window but our overnight guest had already mounted the steps, and all I could see was a dark-clad shoulder as he waited by the front door, and a suitcase sitting on the step just behind.

Not having seen Archie Buchanan for nearly four years, I tried to remember what he looked like but could only come up with 'tall'. I had a clear memory of a Scottish accent though, warm and friendly, and that memory was attached to the vague outline of someone who had already reached adulthood and left me behind. I remembered he'd been very gentle, easy to talk to, and had always included me in conversations and day trips when he could, even though Oli had tried to persuade him I was too little to bother with. I'd crossly reminded Oli one day, that he himself was only two years older than me, and a good six years younger than Archie.

'Ah, but when two chaps are on the rugger field together, they depend on each other. There's a tight bond.' He demonstrated by linking his two hands together. 'Unbreakable.'

I'd rolled my eyes, as all good little sisters do, but enjoyed the fact of their unlikely friendship, as Archie began to spend more and more of his school holidays with us. We'd borrow ponies from friends of my father's, but although Oli could ride, he had little interest and it would often end up as just Archie and me. He seemed to spend most of his home life outdoors, and it had been easy to see that was where he was most comfortable. We'd both missed him when he left school and returned to Scotland, but his image had faded quickly and all I could recall now was the enjoyment I'd found in his company.

I smoothed down my new dress and stepped back from the window, steeling myself to play the perfect hostess, and relieved my lessons were being put to the test before an old friend, who would be too preoccupied catching up with Oli to notice my shortcomings as a well-bred young lady. Knowing Archie, if he did notice them he would only wink and make some joke to put me at my ease.

As I was forcing my unwilling body into a posture of elegant welcome – *Shoulders back, Katherine, chin up. Up!* – Oli marched back in, beaming. Behind him came Archie Buchanan, and the ready, familiar smile I'd prepared suddenly felt as if it sat on someone else's face. My expression must have looked frozen, but in truth I had no more control over it than I had over my suddenly hammering pulse. Had I forgotten, or was it just

17

that I'd never noticed, the beauty of those bold, strong features? The eyes of multi-toned greys that swirled and shifted with the late afternoon light from the window? The breadth of shoulder that gave his considerable height the perfect balance?

I had been twelve, I reminded myself. A child. But I wasn't twelve any longer, and the emerging woman in me felt a new, tingling sensation low in my stomach as Archie smiled at me and, ignoring my politely outstretched hand, took me into a hug instead. His suit was speckled with light drops of rain and I felt the little cold spots on my cheek, but more immediate was the press of his hands on my back, and the low murmur as he greeted me with the familiar words, 'Well, well, if it isn't young Kittlington.'

He drew back and held me at arm's length, and studied me carefully. I tried not to gaze into those extraordinary eyes as I waited for him to smile appreciatively at the way I'd grown, to apologise for his forwardness in pulling me into such a brotherly hug, and to kiss my hand instead.

He smiled, at least. 'You'll be a lovely young lady one day, darling.'

One day? I was already sixteen! Archie squeezed my upper arms and patted them, then let me go and turned to Oli, thankfully not noticing the way I slumped as he broke contact.

'Hard to believe I'm off out there tomorrow,' he said. 'I can't wait to get stuck in.'

And then he and Oli were off, talking about the war, and what it meant for Europe, and whether or not Oli would follow him into active service. It was as if I didn't exist. I retreated to the big chair by the window, finding my gaze drawn back time and time again to this confident, imposing-looking young man I'd known all these years and never really seen until now. He was quicker to laughter than I remembered. I think Oli brought that out in him, and I liked it; he had a low, rich laugh, showing white teeth that had a single crooked one at the side, and crinkling his eyes at the corners.

He looked uncomfortable in his suit though, being used to less restrictive clothes for his outdoor work on the grouse estate at home, but the jacket fit well across his shoulders, and his legs looked longer than ever in neatly pressed trousers. When he and Oli took the chairs opposite my position on the settee I found myself pulling in my stomach, and angling my legs where they crossed, so my ankles looked slimmer; I'd been eating far too well and not at all wisely lately. I made up my mind to eat only vegetables from now until he returned, but even as the thought crossed my mind I knew the resolution would last only until dinner. I was no gannet, but I did enjoy plenty of butter on my bread.

Archie was talking now, about where he was going. It all sounded so exciting, even Oli was beginning to wonder if he'd made the right choice. 'It's not that I don't want to follow Father into the firm,' he admitted, 'but I'd much rather be off fighting for king and country.'

'Then join up,' Archie said. 'Your studies will still be there when you get back.'

'Father won't hear of it. Sickening really.'

'I assume his partner's son is working at the company?'

19

'Alistair, yes.' Oliver glanced at me, not bothering to hide a little smirk, and I pulled a face.

Archie noticed, and grinned. 'Ah, I'd forgotten. Julian Corwood still insisting you marry the wee oik, is he?'

'Not if I have anything to say about it.'

'It's the only way to keep the business in both families,' Oliver said mildly. 'Even you can see the sense in it, surely?'

I stood up, all thoughts of vegetables and pudgy ankles vanishing. 'Oh? And if Mr Corwood had a daughter he wanted married off instead, would you have seen the sense in it then?'

'But he hasn't,' Oliver pointed out. 'He only has Alistair, and once you two are married and present Father and Julian with a couple of grandsons to steer through law school, I'll be off the hook and can do what I please.'

'I'm not a brood mare!'

This argument was not new to either of us, and was clearly amusing Archie who relented, seeing my mutinous expression.

'They can't force you. Anyway, that's a long way off.'

'I'm sixteen,' I told him, with some heat. 'How far off do you suppose it is, actually?'

Archie looked at me, and I once more became aware of my short, rounded stature. I coloured and drew myself a little taller, but his smile had gentled and I realised it made no difference; I was still a child to him.

'Don't fret, young Kittlington. This isn't the old days; no-one can make you marry against your will.'

'I'll run away,' I said, before realising that these words only reinforced the immaturity I was trying so hard to deny. 'I mean,' I went on, 'I'll get a job somewhere else, away from Ecclesley. Maybe I'll even join the Red Cross.'

Oli laughed. 'Can you imagine what Mother and Father will say to that?'

'I don't care.' I glared at him. 'Anyway, it's not as if the business *needs* a marriage to bind it. Father says it's doing terribly well.'

'And so it is, but only because the two families work so well together. Do you see now?'

'Stop talking to me as if I were a child!' I said it to Oli, but threw a glance at Archie, still hoping to see realisation cross his face, and some indication that our friendship had formed a solid basis for something deeper. There was nothing, just that infuriatingly gentle smile, and his low, soothing voice that just stopped short of patronising.

'Don't get yourself all het up, sweetheart. It's not worth it and I'm going to be leaving tomorrow so let's not spoil things.' He rose and straightened his jacket. 'I'm going to wash and change, if that's all right, Oli?'

'Of course, old chap. Dinner's at eight.'

Archie nodded to him, smiled at me, and left the room. His stride was long and easy, and so familiar, yet elicited different feelings now – watching him turn out of sight into the hallway left me oddly empty-feeling, and it wasn't simply because his dismissive, parting words had stung.

I dressed for dinner with more care than usual, choosing a dress that draped rather than clung, and smoothing my gloves neatly over my arms,

21

glad to have at least lost the dimples in my elbows and to have gained a more shapely outline. Archie wasn't what I'd heard described as a 'man of the world', but I had no doubt that, at twenty-four, and as handsome as I now realised he was, he would have been on the receiving end of a good deal of female attention.

I turned away and slipped into my shoes, wishing I were one of those people who could wear a kitten heel without feeling ridiculously overdressed, and went to the door. As I turned to pull it closed behind me I took another look around, suddenly hating all the frills and flounces I'd loved so much before. This was a child's room. Tomorrow I would speak to Mother about getting new bed coverings, and a real dressing table. It was time to grow up.

As a family, we were decently off and locally respected, but, much to my father's endless regret, not aristocracy, and our Ecclesley house, although large and well appointed, was not simply somewhere we stayed when we were in town, it was our home. We retained only a modest staff too, but they were always delighted when we welcomed guests, so even Archie, who they'd known from boyhood, was shown to the table as if he were visiting royalty.

'Ah, Buchanan,' Father said with approval. 'Good to see you again, lad.'

'And you, sir.'

'Or should I call you Captain Buchanan?'

Archie smiled. 'I'd like that very much; however, I'm commissioned only as a second lieutenant.'

'Only a matter of time, old chum,' Oli said, grinning. I couldn't help agreeing with him, but kept silent and enjoyed the faintly embarrassed look on Archie's face; it made him look a lot younger again.

'And how's your mother?' my own mother wanted to know. 'It must be terribly difficult all alone up there in the middle of nowhere.'

'She's well, thank you,' Archie said. 'She asks after your family all the time.'

I let the banalities wash over me as I ate. How's this person, and that person? Are you busy at work? Who'll be drafted in as beaters now most of the young estate workers had signed up? And: of course young Oliver is too keen on law and the family business to consider going off to war. That last one caused Archie and I to stop chewing, and to look from Father to Oli and back again.

Oli shrugged. 'Well, I'd be happy to go over to help out if they needed me.'

Father waved his hand. 'Storm in a teacup – be over before we know it. Not like Africa at all.' He pointed his knife at Archie. 'Now *that* was a campaign and a half. Your uncle could tell you all about that, young man.'

I saw a glint in Archie's eyes, and realised he was hiding a flash of anger at the easy dismissal of the very real danger into which he was going, although his voice did not betray it. 'Aye, so I understand. Uncle Jack doesn't talk about it much though. He was at Rooiwal near the end. Was that anywhere near you?'

Father coloured, but to do him credit, he didn't attempt to lie. 'Well, of course I'd have liked to have joined the party,' he said, 'but the business was just taking off. Couldn't go off and leave it. Too many people depending on it for a living. Do have some more wine, lad.'

Archie's mouth twitched as he held out his glass, and I was relieved to see his anger disappear in a barely suppressed grin at Father's discomfiture. 'Thank you, sir.'

Conversation moved on, and since no-one was the slightest bit interested in anything I might have to say, I used the time to study Archie more closely, to examine the response to him that had taken me so completely by surprise. The familiarity was still there. It wasn't as if he was someone else, but that I was, and along with our easy friendship I recognised the need to experience the warmth of a closer contact... Talking to him wasn't enough any more. I wanted to know how he felt about everything, and I wanted him to care how I felt too. I realised I had stopped eating now and was staring at him, and I looked quickly at Mother, but she was busy admonishing Oli for drinking his wine too quickly. If he had this effect on my appetite I needn't worry about fat ankles for much longer, anyway.

After dinner I sat with the others while they talked of times past and times to come, and looking at Oli's eager expression I knew he'd meant it when he'd told Archie he'd have preferred to sign up than go to law school. Archie loosened his tie as they all began to relax, and settled back into his chair with a glass of Father's best brandy, while I pretended to read but found my attention wandering from the page constantly, whether he was speaking or not.

He was starting to look tired; the journey from Scotland had been a long one, and he had to be up early to get the train from Liverpool to London. Yet despite his slightly edgy weariness, he had a compelling magnetism to him that drew my eyes again and again. The strong, clean features and ready smile were only part of it; his voice wrapped me in its soft-spoken tones. His hands, holding the brandy glass up to the light to peer through the amber depths, were steady and graceful, and I closed my eyes as I remembered the warmth of them pressing me to him in that brotherly hug.

Abruptly I tore my gaze away, and set my book aside. 'I'm going out for a walk.'

'But it's dark,' Mother protested.

'There are lights, and I need some fresh air.'

'You can't go out alone!'

'I'll only be a few minutes. No need to disturb anyone to come with me.'

Without waiting for a reply, I went out into the hall and plucked my coat from the hook, and once outside I half expected to hear the light raindrops sizzle as they landed on my face. I was more tangled, in thought and emotion, than I'd ever been before, and the culprit was sitting back there in our drawing room. Not a thought cast my way, not a care in his head except what he was going into tomorrow. And who could blame him for that?

I closed my eyes again and pictured those beautiful, strong hands holding, not a brandy glass, but a gun. Then I pictured his face, contorted in fear, pain, or both, and the abrupt reality of where he was going squeezed my heart until I thought it would collapse. France, or Belgium, or farther afield; wherever he ended up might not be so far in miles, but it was another world, and it might be a world from which he never returned.

I took a few steps down the deserted street, and realised I didn't have the strength to walk after all. Instead I found a bench and sat down, not caring about the puddles of rainwater that seeped through my coat and dress, and tried to give myself a good talking-to. It was silly to feel such panic and sorrow; Archie was volunteering for this and was proud to be doing so; he had made his own choice. But I desperately wished he would change his mind.

I remembered how my friends and I had gathered to watch some of the local lads as they marched off, and we'd cheered and thrown flowers, and thought how happy they all looked, how determined to get over there and sort things out where the governments had failed. We'd kissed as many boys as we could, telling them all how splendid they were, and waved them out of sight with a feeling of deep patriotism and satisfaction that all was happening just as it should.

But Archie... He might be well over six feet tall, he might be square of shoulder and strong in limb, but he was the calmest, most gentle man I'd ever known – the least likely to be goaded into real anger, the quickest to forgive. He shouldn't be going out there, no matter how proud it made him. I compared him to Alistair Corwood and almost laughed aloud, but it was no laughing matter.

It occurred to me that I was missing the last hour or so I would spend in his company, and, surprised at how much that thought hurt, I stood up to go back inside, and stopped; the silhouette coming towards me, with the easy, graceful walk I still recognised after four years, moved into a pool of light and my heart tripped over itself.

'Kitty!' He raised a hand and came closer, his smile lit by the overhead light and shining straight at me.

I smiled back. 'What are you doing out here? I thought you were talking to Oli and Father.'

'I needed to get away. The two of them have managed to get into a discussion about work. Deadly boring. Shall we walk?'

'That would be ... nice.' I was having trouble forming my words, and when Archie offered me his arm I took it, hoping he couldn't feel the wild trembling of my hand in the crook of his elbow. He was treating me like an adult at last, and I tried to behave like one, asking polite questions he had already answered during dinner, and keeping my pace slow and measured instead of running up and down the road, yelling with delight.

'Well, I've got an early start,' he said at last, and turned homewards once more. 'And you shouldn't be out here alone with a man, even if it's only me.'

Only him? But I wasn't ready to go back.

'Tell me a bit more about your uncle,' I said quickly. 'Jack, isn't it?'

'Aye, Jack Carlisle. Well, he's my mother's younger brother. We've not seen him in a good while but he writes now and again. He's a diplomat now, attached to the army and still holds the

27

rank of major, but he's not on active service any more.'

'Sounds exciting.' It sounded nothing of the sort, but I just wanted him to keep talking.

'Really?' Archie looked at me, a smile tugging at his lips.

'Does he live in Scotland too?'

'No, he's based in London and Liverpool mostly. And he spends most of his free time at the Creswells' place in Cheshire.'

'Are they rich?'

'They are. He was apparently very close to Lord Creswell. Henry. They fought together in Africa.'

'Unlike Father,' I dropped in, and Archie laughed.

'I'm not going to comment on that again. Anyway, Uncle Jack promised he'd take care of the family if Henry died in the war, which, sadly, he did. So Jack's sort of a father figure to Henry's two children now, and rumour has it he and Lily Creswell are a bit of an item.'

'A happy ending,' I said. 'Good!' Without thinking, I hugged his arm, then immediately let go in case he thought I'd meant anything by it. He gave me a faintly puzzled look, then accepted my withdrawal and put his hands in his pockets. We had arrived back at the house, and I had never been so displeased to see warm, welcoming lights at a window.

'I should get to bed,' he said. 'I really need to be up at first light.'

Sending my body into complete turmoil, he put his hands gently on my shoulders, and dropped a

28

kiss onto my forehead. With his jaw just inches away, it was as much as I could do not to turn my head to kiss him back, but I led the way indoors and said goodnight, making a meal of removing my coat, so he wouldn't see how my hands still shook. I watched him from the hallway as he went in to say goodnight to my family, and then went to my own room, trying to untangle my insides and take a single deep and calming breath. I couldn't do it. And then, as I lay there in the darkness, remembering the firmness of his lips on my skin, I decided I didn't want to. The ache was too sweet, too new and too full of possibility to push away.

The following morning I breakfasted early, and Archie had yet to make an appearance by the time I'd finished. The meal was still sitting like a lump in my stomach and I felt as if I hadn't chewed a single bite as I waited in the hall, pretending to be straightening my ever-annoying curls in the mirror, but every sense straining in anticipation.

At last I heard his footfall on the stairs, and my eyes went to the bag by the door before I looked up to see him for what might be the last time. He was pulling on his cap as he came round the bend in the stairs, and his uniform looked like part of him already, as though he'd been born to wear it. For a moment I had trouble recognising the Archie I'd known in this grown man, but then, as he always had as a boy, he took the last few stairs in a quick little run and was my old familiar friend again.

Watching him straighten his belt and reach for his coat, I saw the quick, assured movements of a man completely at ease, and felt some of the terror fall away; no-one who looked as comfortable and ready to go to war could possibly come to any harm. Second Lieutenant Archie Buchanan would come home safely in a month or two, having made his family, and me, the proudest we could be, and Europe would be safe thanks to him and those like him.

And then, perhaps, there would be time for us.

Chapter Three

11 November 1916

My nineteenth birthday. A chilly, grey day that nevertheless started out with a vague hope of celebration, then fell flat after breakfast, when I realised I'd be spending it completely alone, but by teatime had flung me headlong into a life I could never have imagined for myself.

Oliver had finally joined the army late last year, to our parents' aggravation, but just before the compulsory call-up, so at least they could tell people he'd volunteered. He was stationed at Nieuport, on the Belgian coast, and had kept this rare home visit as a birthday surprise – an even more joyful one when I saw he had brought Archie with him. He stood behind Oliver, smiling at me over the top of Oli's red curls, his own hat removed and tucked beneath his arm. When Oli had re-leased me from an unexpected, but not unwelcome brotherly embrace, Archie took my hand.

'Happy birthday, darling.' He bent and kissed my cheek, and I felt my skin glow where his lips had touched, firm and warm.

'You've been promoted,' I said, accepting a hug but trying not to linger too long in his arms. 'Congratulations, Captain Buchanan.'

'Aye, your father's an uncanny knack of predicting the future.'

'Except when it comes to this little two-year "storm in a teacup",' I pointed out, and he grinned.

'And how fare you, young Kittlington?'

I pulled a face. 'Bored, I'm ashamed to say. Can we go riding while you're here?'

'I'd have loved to but I can only stay tonight. I'm getting the early train up to Edinburgh, and then to Fort William. Mother's been waiting a while and she's not inclined to wait much longer – she keeps threatening to turn up at HQ just to make sure I'm cleaning m'teeth every night!'

I laughed, and hoped he couldn't see my ridiculous, crushing disappointment. Still, it wasn't to be helped; family came first. Which reminded me: 'Oliver, your timing is impeccable – did you somehow know Mother and Father would be out?'

'They've left you alone on your birthday?' Archie frowned, and I felt a rush of gratitude for his understanding. I'd spent the morning telling myself not to be silly, but it hurt anyway.

'Really? There's a bit of luck,' Oli said, and clapped Archie on the back. 'Come on, Arch, we've got time for some billiards before Father comes in and starts banging on.'

I followed them into the billiard room. Mother wasn't here to admonish me, and besides Oli hadn't been home for ages, and Archie was my friend. Why shouldn't I talk to them?

To my pleased surprise, not even Oli gave me his patented 'you should be off sewing things' look, and tolerated my presence. To begin with I just listened to them talking, of things I'd never understand in a million years, I was sure. Trenches I'd heard of, of course, and seen them on the newsreels, filled with cheerfully waving boys, but I'd had no idea there was so much mud and you certainly couldn't see it in those pictures. To hear Oli and Archie talk you'd think men lived in puddles for days at a time and never had the chance to change their socks. Archie talked of 'near misses' that made my fingers curl into the material of my dress, and Oli told him how a tunnel had been spotted by the enemy. Someone hadn't stopped digging when he ought, and the Germans had heard and blown it up. The explosion, he said, rattled the windows of the nearby town, and... He caught sight of my face and stopped. I think he'd been about to say something about the men who'd been down that tunnel, but thought better of it.

'Anyway,' he finished, 'that was the end of that. The sappers had to start again two days later and thirty yards farther up the line.' He spoke as if that had been the worst of it, but I could tell by the way his and Archie's expressions were matched in solemnity that this was far from the truth.

Archie sought to lighten the tone. 'So, what have you been up to, Kitty? Met a nice lad yet?'

I didn't want him to see how much that stung, so I just gave him a slightly withering look. 'How about you – the nurses falling at your feet, I suppose?'

He chuckled. 'Not that I've noticed. And thankfully I don't come into much contact with them. You've never wanted to go into that profession then?'

'I've done some training, but I don't really have the temperament for putting up with the dreadful snobbery of some of those nurses. Actually I've noticed that myself and one or two others tend to be kept away from the patients.'

He had bent over to take his shot, and stopped, looking at me over his cue, an amused smile playing about his lips. 'You remind me quite strongly of someone I've recently met,' he said. 'She's an independent out there. Ambulance driver. They're always looking for people like you.'

'Like me?' I found myself interested, despite the creeping horror their earlier descriptions had elicited. 'How do you mean?' Part of me admitted I just wanted to hear him say complimentary things, but another, bigger part, really did yearn to do some good.

'Level-headed, healthy, sensible.' He didn't notice my frustration, and it took all the self-control I had not to break his billiard cue over his stupid head. Was that all he could find to say about me? 'And,' he went on, lining up his shot again, 'preferably already a dab hand with the internal combustion engine, so they wouldn't have to waste time teaching.'

'How did you know I'd been learning that?' I

asked, slightly appeased. I was glad I hadn't told him myself, so it couldn't be interpreted as boastful.

'Your brother here's dead proud of you,' Archie said, by way of explanation, and Oliver snorted, but then looked at me and shrugged.

'Well, you're quite the little mechanic, Kitty. There's no denying it.'

There was a solid clack as the cue ball hit its target, and Archie straightened, satisfied. 'So, what about it? Would you like to learn more and maybe think about it?'

'Yes!'

Oliver was looking at me as if I'd just told him I planned to emigrate to Australia. 'But you told the parents you were going to stay in England. That's the only reason they let you train!'

'Don't you think it sounds perfect though?' I pleaded, desperate to claim him to my side; Mother and Father would find much less to argue about if I had his support. 'All that training with the Red Cross, and all I'm doing with it is cleaning floors and knitting socks!'

'Quite right too. You're doing valuable work right here in England. Why on earth would you want to go over to that hellhole?'

'At least it's nearer to you, Oli. They're sure to take that into account.' I turned to Archie. 'Who would I be working with?' It didn't matter; I already knew I would agree to anything he suggested. If he thought I could do it, then I could. I felt a complicated thrill of fear and excitement as he explained about the ambulance base, run, until recently, by Evie, one of the Cheshire Creswells he'd mentioned before.

'She's not there just at the minute,' he said. 'She's away home caring for her husband, who's lost his memory. I don't know when she'll be back, but there are others who'd look after you 'til then. You'd be working independently, but under the guidance of the Red Cross, and attached to my own regiment, which is stationed close by. Evie's partner, Barbara, is leaving to marry.'

I looked over at Oli, who was chalking his cue and concentrating so I couldn't tell what he thought. 'Oli? What do you think? I'd love to really have the chance to do something good.'

He eyed me then, and his face softened into a reluctant smile. 'You'll be wonderful out there, I'm sure of it. Just promise me you'll be careful, and do as you're told.'

I could have hugged him, but he was across the room and leaning down to take his shot. Archie had moved out of Oli's way and was standing very close to me; it felt as if another inch would allow me to feel the warmth radiating from him and from there it would be a short step to putting my arms around him instead, and frightening him senseless. I backed away a couple of paces, just in case.

He whistled in reluctant appreciation as Oliver's shot took him into the lead. 'Bloody good shot, Mr Maitland, sir.' Then he turned to me again, much to my gratification. 'What about your parents?'

'They'll try and stop me, I'm sure, but I'm nineteen. There's nothing they can do.' Even the sixteen-year-old I'd thought so worldly seemed a child now. I had no illusions about the work I'd be doing, especially after listening to them talking earlier, but I pushed away a niggle of uncertainty; there was a duty to be done, and what could possibly happen if we were under the Red Cross?

'You can go out and see how you get on,' Archie was saying now. 'Any help, even for a short while, will be invaluable out there. No-one will think badly of you if you don't stay.'

'Oh, I'd stay.' Determination often got the better of good sense with me, but I had the feeling this time my confidence was well founded.

Archie's smile of approval convinced me further. 'When can you come?'

'When can I start?'

He laughed. 'It'll take a month or so, but as soon as I get back I'll talk to Lieutenant Colonel Drewe about arranging your documents.'

And, just like that, everything changed.

Flanders, Belgium, December 1916

The lorry was empty but for myself, and my rather forlorn-looking suitcase, by the time we reached the little cottage known only as Number Twelve. The girls I'd travelled with from England had all disembarked at the hospital in Furnes, where they were greeted by a harried-looking sister and whisked away to change even before the driver had restarted the lorry.

I was not treated to even that dubious pleasure; the cottage stood apparently derelict, and as the driver lifted my bag down I wondered if we'd come to the right place. Suddenly sure we had not, I turned to say as much, but he had already climbed back behind the steering wheel, and before I could summon the words: 'wait a moment!' he was driving away, over the pitted and uneven road, back towards Furnes.

If the cottage seemed deserted, that road was not. Ambulances creaked and roared, coughing their way towards the large clearing station up the road, and the empty ones rattled past them towards Pervyse, where the driver had told me heavy fighting was taking place. That was where the Baroness de T'Serclaes and young Mairi Chisholm were, and I couldn't help feeling a little excited despite the gnawing fear. I wondered if we would see them, or even be called upon to help them – their work was famous at home, and their bravery the stuff of legend. Everyone I knew still called them Mrs Knocker and Miss Chisholm, but the newspapers called them The Madonnas of Pervyse – I could hardly believe they were so close by.

During the long drive from the ferry, even when we'd drawn closer to the fighting, I'd heard cracks and distant booms that didn't sound as if they could be signalling any real danger to me personally, but as I turned back now to the ancient-looking cottage, in the hopes of seeing some sign of life, a tremendous roar seemed to suck the breath out of me, and I dropped to my knees and tucked my head down.

'You'll get used to it,' a voice said. It sounded faintly amused, but friendly enough, and I lifted my head to see a slender, attractive girl with very blonde hair cut raggedly short. She held out her hand, both to pull me to my feet, and by way of introduction.

'I'm Evie Davies,' she said. 'I only got back myself two days ago. You must be Katherine Maitland.'

'Kitty,' I said, and shook her proffered hand. She wasn't at all what I expected; something had put a picture in my mind of a tall, capable-looking woman with a loud voice and a no-nonsense attitude. This girl looked hardly older than myself, and had smiling blue eyes and a clear voice. Well spoken, but with none of the 'frightfully Home Counties' accent I disliked so much, and which Mother seemed determined to adopt over our own north-western tones.

'I thought you'd be here a week or so ago,' she said, 'but I'm glad to be able to welcome you myself. I've only been back a day. Anne and Elise have gone back to their usual billet.'

'There was a hold-up with my parents,' I explained. 'They're not overly keen on me being here, I'm afraid.'

'We'll take good care of you. They needn't worry.' She saw me looking at her hair, and ran her hand through it, heedless of the grease and oil on her fingers. 'Dreadful, isn't it? I dare say I look an absolute fright.'

I wanted to say it actually suited her face rather well, but she pressed on. 'Lice are a terrible problem. I hope you'll be spared the need to do this, but be prepared for it. I'll check you every day, if you like.'

The notion of someone checking me for lice gave me a further jolt, but I tried not to look

38

horrified. 'Thank you.' I combed my fingers through my own red curls and hoped for the best, but if I had to cut them off I would, without hesitation. I wouldn't look anywhere near as boyishly pretty as Evie, but who was there to care here? The driver had told me Archie's headquarters were just a few miles to the east of Number Twelve, but he might as well be in France for all the chance I had of seeing him. Oli had applied to be transferred to Dixmude as well, and would soon learn if the request had been approved, but even so I'd rarely see him either. I was here to do a job, not to be coddled, and I pulled myself straight and fixed my mind on here and now, pushing daydreams to the back of my mind.

Evie sloshed her way through the icy mud to the ambulance, and I followed. 'We've only got the one bus at the moment,' she said, opening up the flap at the back. 'Boxy and I saved up and brought her over, but we're hoping for another one soon – we've raised some donations, and the Red Cross back home are awfully keen to help where they can. Meet Gertie.'

'Gertie?'

'Haven't you seen that postcard? The one with the pig?' I shook my head. 'Well anyway, Boxy said the ambulance snorted like a pig, and we should paint her pink.'

'She sounds fun,' I ventured.

'Oh, she is. We got on terribly well right from the off. As shall we, I'm sure,' she assured me, giving my already frozen hand a squeeze. 'Now, let's get you settled in, and I can tell you a little bit about what we do.' She gave me an encouraging smile, but her eyes seemed distant, as if her thoughts were anywhere but here. I remembered what I'd been told about her husband, and wondered if he was back with his unit, or if he'd even regained his memory ... but she would surely not be here if he hadn't. I couldn't imagine how she felt, knowing he was back in the lines. Archie spent a lot of time in the field with his men, but it was so much easier to think of him sitting at HQ with the other officers, discussing tactics, than out there facing the kind of explosions that had just driven me to my knees.

I followed Evie into the cottage, a tiny two-roomed affair. 'We'll share the bedroom,' she said. 'There are two beds, but luckily they're very narrow so there's room to get between them to dress. You'll sleep in your clothes most nights anyway, especially during winter. Have you got a flea bag?'

'A ... a what?'

'For sleeping in.'

'Oh, no, I haven't.'

'We'll see what we can find for you,' she said. 'It'll probably leave a lot to be desired in the hygiene department, but extra layers are not to be sneezed at.' She grinned, looking like a grubby child for a moment. 'And speaking of sneezing, you'll be doing plenty of that, too.'

It seemed as if having me to show around, to explain things to and put at my ease, was helping her too. She made us both a very welcome cup of cocoa, and as she talked about the work, and what we were and were not permitted to do, she gradually lost the slightly dazed and distant look and I began to see the real Evie beneath – re-

40

silient, determined and with a sense of adventure that could barely be suppressed, even here. Even as she spoke, the guns were continuing their raucous shout, and I flinched more than once, but she didn't seem to notice them.

'Don't they ever stop?' I asked, wondering how on earth we were supposed to sleep.

'Occasionally.' She sobered a little then. 'It's not always a good thing when they do though; it means the bombardment's stopped and our boys are ready to go out and try to regain some ground.'

'And do they?'

'The Front has barely moved in two and a half years. A few miles, that's all.'

I considered that for a moment, and looked around me, trying to imagine having lived here all that time. How much longer could it go on?

But I was starting to learn already, that Evie would not be solemn or reflective for long. 'Come on then,' she said briskly, standing up. She put her mug by the tiny sink. 'I'll show you the cellar.'

I jumped up too, eager to show my enthusiasm, but as I reached out to pick up my own half-finished cocoa I knocked the cup over, and sent brown muck spreading across the table.

'Oh! I'm so sorry,' I said, looking around for a cloth. She tossed me the greasy rag from her belt and I mopped up the drink, blushing furiously at my clumsiness. She didn't even blink as I tried again, and this time knocked the rolling cup to the floor. Luckily it was tin, and bounced instead of breaking.

Within a day I had earned the nickname that would stay with me for as long as Evie and I knew

41

each other. We'd had word that a convoy was expected at the station and I was to stay behind and ready the cellar, while Evie took Gertie and fetched out those men whose wounds might be treated easily here instead of weighing down the clearing stations and hospitals. We'd just had a hastily thrown-together shepherd's pie for dinner and I was clearing the plates, my heart thundering with renewed fear at the loudness of the guns now night had fallen. I turned from the table towards the sink, and, failing to notice Evie standing behind me buttoning her greatcoat, I cannoned into her. She staggered sideways, barely keeping her feet, and the plates crashed to the floor. They were the last of the crockery that had been left in the cottage before it had been evacuated, and Evie looked at the sharp-edged and useless pieces with a little sigh of disappointment.

Then she looked back at me, and to my enormous relief her mouth stretched into a grin. 'Everything's going down like ninepins since you've arrived. Going to have to start calling you Skittles.'

I closed my mouth, which had been hanging open in a kind of wordless and disbelieving dismay, and Evie kicked the pieces of china out of sight under the table and wiped the gravy off her coat with her sleeve. She flashed me a bright smile, jerked her head towards the cellar, and went out into the night alone. I knew then that, no matter how awful the job I'd be doing, Evie Davies was exactly the kind of person I'd want to be doing it with.

In February the Clearing Station just up the road from our ambulance base was badly hit by shellfire. Even after everything I'd seen and been horrified by in the past two months, that had a profound effect on me, that somewhere so clearly marked with the red cross of a recognised medical facility might be deliberately targeted; was there a line that must not be crossed? And if so, where was it?

In the meantime Oliver had still been trying to arrange his transfer to Dixmude, and it was only this that had persuaded our furious Father to abandon his intention of travelling out here to pull me back to Blighty by my hair. He'd managed it just a couple of days ago, and on the day after the Clearing Station was hit, he arrived in a general staff car with a friendly lieutenant colonel named Drewe, and, to my breathless delight, Archie.

We chatted for a while, although my nerves had resurfaced at the sight of a 'brass hat' in our little cottage, but Archie and Evie seemed to notice this and, between them, put me at my ease again. I watched Archie across the table as he chatted, and noticed new lines on his face I hadn't seen before, but he looked completely at ease here, and I gathered he'd been a regular visitor in the past – I wasn't sure how I felt about that, and saw his eyes linger on Evie a little more than I liked.

But she was deeply in love with her husband; I knew that. They talked about him today, and I was able to piece together what I hadn't felt able to ask Evie since I'd arrived: Private Will Davies had become detached from his battalion last summer, during the battle of High Wood, and reported missing, and Archie had been the one to bring him home. Evidently he'd been risking his life to do so, and although the pride I took in his courage felt wrong, I enjoyed it anyway.

Sadly Will's return to physical health was apparently not reflected in his emotional healing, and I gathered he and Evie were struggling. Oli, the great clot, ventured to say he was glad to hear that Will was back in active service, but Evie's uncharacteristically cool reply ended that conversation, and we sat in uncomfortable silence for a minute before I turned the subject around to why Evie did not wear a wedding ring. It seemed important to remind myself that she was married, and, although I disliked myself for thinking it, to remind Archie of that, too. Conversation moved on to my driving, and I felt bad for those unformed but suspicious thoughts, as Evie praised me with real warmth.

'You're more than ready to make the night run yourself now, Kitty.'

Gratified that Archie was there to hear her praise, I smiled, not knowing quite what to say.

Colonel Drewe patted my hand. 'Excellent! I'm sure you'll do a splendid job.'

'Thank you,' I said shyly. 'I'll be awfully pleased to be of some real help at last.'

'Watch out for shell holes,' Oliver put in. 'Those roads are abysmal.'

Soon after, Archie declared it time to leave, and Oli gave me a hug. For the first time, I felt he really cared for me as his sister and not some annoying little oik that kept hanging around, so I hugged him back, and I think we both felt a little bit tearful at that moment. I know I did.

'Look after yourself,' Archie said, and squeezed Evie's hand.

'And my sister,' Oli said to her. 'I'm relying on you.'

I tried to dismiss the pang of jealousy at the closeness that clearly existed between Evie and Archie; the time they had known each other had been short, but strange and emotional, and it was bound to have had an effect on them. This obsession was dangerous; I had to put him out of my mind and concentrate on learning the job, so I could do the night runs alone as soon as we received our new ambulance. There was no room for distraction or mistakes.

But as Archie snugged his hat down over his dark hair, and gave me one of his warm smiles, I felt my stomach turn over with longing, and knew that if I slept tonight it would be filled with dreams that would leave me feeling empty and hopeless in the morning.

It would only be a week before my dreams would become so intense, so terrifying and so filled with horror, that empty and hopeless would have been almost like a breath of joy.

Chapter Four

Dover, Kent, April 1917

Passengers were starting to board. Frances Adams and I stood on the dock looking up at the huge ferry, at the faces turned back towards loved ones for a last glimpse, and at the hands raised in tearful goodbye ... and I was suddenly unsure how to make my own farewell. Ever since I'd come back to Dark River Farm Mrs Adams had tried to be a mother to me, and it had touched me deeply every time I saw it, but I'd never been able to show my feelings towards her in the way others seemed to find so natural. If I suddenly tried to hug her it would feel awkward for us both.

'Well, maid,' she said, turning me to face her. 'It's time. Are you sure you're going to be all right?'

'Quite sure,' I said, trying to stop my voice from shaking, because how could I be? I was not only going back into the very heart of the war, but also facing the destruction of my future, the disgrace of my family, and worst of all, the likely death of my brother. But the pretence went on, and we both knew it for what it was. The loneliness that washed over me as I contemplated this journey made me feel hollow and cold. Mrs Adams saw it, and pulled me into a rough hug, ending my dilemma with one quick, welcome movement. Although spare-framed, her height was comforting, and the kiss she pressed to my temple even more so.

'You don't have to do this,' she reminded me.

'I do. Oli's life might depend on it.'

She held me tighter. 'Oh, love, I do hope you can make the difference.'

'Thank you for coming this far with me,' I mumbled into her shoulder.

'I wish I could come all the way,' she said, and I knew she meant it. 'If I wasn't needed back at Dark River, I'd be–'

'I know.' I drew back. 'You've been unbelievably kind to me.'

'Well–' she cleared her throat '–I seen something in you, young Kitty. You're a kind, decent girl, and you've had a terrible time. I know you've shown everyone you're a tough little thing, but you deserve someone to lean on. We can't always be tough, can we?' Her eyes shone for a moment, then she blinked and sniffed. She put one roughened hand either side of my face, and studied me carefully as if she was worried it might be the last time she saw me – I fought down a swell of fear at the thought. My mother had never looked at me with this intensity, not even when I'd left for Belgium last Christmas, and when Mrs Adams's long, tired face broke into a gentle smile I felt a twist of unexpectedly strong emotion in my churning stomach. I smiled back, and she blinked again. This time the tears would not so easily be banished, and while our smiles felt less forced now, both were accompanied by snatched, hiccupping breaths.

A honking sound made us both jump, and I

47

reluctantly let go of her and bent to pick up my case. 'I'll write, as soon as I have any news.'

'See that you do.' Mrs Adams touched my cheek again, and there was a look of real sorrow in her eyes now. 'I'll be thinking of you, maid. We all will. Take care, and don't do nothin' dangerous.'

'I won't be going back to the ambulance station,' I assured her. 'Evie says I'll be billeted in one of the hotels near HQ. Jack Carlisle will meet me off the ferry and take me there.'

Her words were jerky and unsteady as we were both bumped by the fresh surge of people moving towards the ferry to board. 'Just see you come back safe.'

'I will. I promise.'

Walking away and leaving her standing there, it was almost as if I were the older woman, and she the one who was little more than a child. Somehow that helped, and I lifted my free hand to wave, and even blew her a kiss. She nodded, and then she was gone from view, only the top of her hat visible; if she'd been of average height I would not even have been able to see that, and I kept glancing back for that small comfort as the waves of soldiers and nurses lifted me closer to the ferry, and to the horrors I would have given anything to be able to forget.

The water churned, choppy and grey beneath us, as we made our laborious, zigzagging way across the channel. Even knowing Jack waited for me at the other end, I felt that chilly loneliness again, and wished I could simply stay on the ferry for ever.

48

A couple of VADs tried to engage me in conversation, but they were fresh from training, and excited to be going overseas to help our boys. I knew if I began talking I would dampen their chatter, and turn them into what I myself had become. It wouldn't be fair. So, ignoring the look that passed between them, '*Well, we tried,*' I went to the front of the boat instead, and stared out at the nothingness ahead.

I had been just like them. Most of us had, and even once reality set in, and that happy anticipation had been crushed from us, we found strength in the minute-by-minute dealings with people whose lives depended on the pressing of a wound, the spotting of an incipient heart failure, the speed of transport to hospital. I hoped those two girls would find the same, but, for me, all Belgium held now was the shocking, painful memory of one brutal night.

Lieutenant Colonel Drewe, the friendliest, cheeriest of men – grandfatherly, kind, patient. A veteran of the Africa campaign, and a man known for his bravery. How could someone like that...

I turned away from the rail, my chest tight, and a phantom pain at the juncture of my thighs, as if the bruises he had given me were still there, his Webley revolver still rammed into my side. The decrepit ambulance parked haphazardly at the side of the road had been just one of any number of broken-down and abandoned vehicles. Evie said later that he'd known I would have sole charge of Gertie that night, and I shivered at the cold knowledge that I'd been exactly where he'd wanted me to be when I'd seen him stumbling up the centre of the road; if someone else had stopped, and had not been alone, it would have been nothing to him to wave them on and claim to be perfectly well.

But of course it was me who'd stopped. And I *was* alone, and he'd looked at me with those strangely skittering eyes and accepted my help to climb into the back. I'd spoken gently to him, settled him onto the stretcher and turned to pick up the first-aid box, before asking him where he was hurt. When I'd turned back to him the gun had been out of its leather holster. My breath stopped, and my numbed fingers fell open, and the box crashed to the floor. The only words he'd spoken had been a warning that Oliver would be the one to suffer if I spoke of this night, and then he had stood up, seized my arm with his free hand, and pushed me onto the stretcher-bed in his place.

The time that followed alternately flew by in seconds, and stretched into interminable hours; my horrified mind could still not place which. He had left me shaking, but not crying, too stunned and sick-feeling for tears, with my trousers wrapped around one ankle and trailing across the filthy floor. Fresh blood smeared the stretcher, mixing with the half-dried blood of the countless wounded Tommies I'd transported that night.

Archie found out what had happened, of course. Evie had promised not to tell him, and then told him anyway. I'd been beyond fury, screaming at her, and knowing I was wrong to do it. But I couldn't help it. The anger I couldn't hurl at Colonel Drewe was eating me alive, and I had to free it or go mad. Poor Evie bore the brunt of it, and she bore it with patience and with grief, but her sorrow, and her guilt at letting me go out on the road alone, only inflamed my anger – it was the most vicious of circles.

I hadn't seen Archie since he and Evie had driven away from Dark River Farm together, leaving me in the care of Frances, Lizzy and the others. His face, as he'd turned his attention to the long track up to the main road, was the last glimpse I'd had of him, and I treasured it even through the anger and betrayal I'd felt towards Evie. I'd lain in bed, once the pregnancy was made real, hating myself, and hating the baby. I never hated Evie, but my anger towards her didn't fade until Lizzy had lost her temper and pointed out a few home truths: I had *wanted* to drive alone; it was all I'd ever begged for; Evie had been doing it from the start; she had cared for me and taught me everything I needed to know; I had given her my blessing to go and talk to Will... It had taken that tiny, fierce girl, with her dark curly hair sticking up in all directions, her hands on her hips and her eyes flashing blue fire, to break the awful cycle of self-recrimination and despair. It wasn't hard to see why Jack Carlisle's heart had been captured by her, despite the rumours about Evie's mother. She had made me realise those truths, but by then Oliver had deserted, and faced death if he was found, and death if he was not, and it was all my fault. Now, when I raged, I raged against my own cowardice, my own weakness, and only in the privacy of my little room at Dark River Farm. I wept, and cursed the hand fate had dealt me. And I cursed the child I carried. The next night Colonel Drewe's unwanted yet innocent gift died in a wash of pain and blood, in the back of another ambulance.

What remained of my youth died with it.

Archie might have left, but the image of his calm grey eyes had stayed with me, behind the closed lids of my own, during that terrible time. The memories of our younger, carefree days had been more immediate to me than the shock of what had happened, his image more real than the rasp of the sheets against my skin and the cool water I drank to assuage a raging thirst. There was also a bitter irony in knowing it was helping our sheep deliver themselves of their young, that had killed my own. I knew it, yet the guilt lay heavy in my heart for those dark and desperate prayers that the child had never existed.

Frances had told me afterwards that I'd called out for Archie more than once, in my more feverish moments, but all I could remember was being certain it was *now* that was the dream – a bleak and terrifying nightmare – and that reality still encompassed those sweet, uncomplicated days when we would go out riding, and he would tell me all about Scotland. My overwrought mind became my dearest friend, giving me vivid and detailed remembrances I hadn't known I possessed until now; I could smell the horses' sweat; hear the thump of hooves on short, scrubby grass; feel sleek, powerful muscles beneath me; and I recalled, with a new and perfect clarity, the sound of Archie's voice as he described Fort Augustus and the Great Glen in which he lived.

Waking to find the fever once and for all broken

I had wept again, but now it was for the loss of that escape route into the past. For no longer being completely absorbed in the simple joy of Archie's company, still believing it to be the innocent love of a child for a brother. It was knowing I had lost him for ever.

As we neared France the sky was changing colour from pale blue to an overcast grey. Evening was creeping inexorably closer, and my insides twisted tighter and tighter as I accepted that there was no going back now; if we were lucky my testimony might possibly save Oliver's life, but the truth would come leaking out, like a rancid green sludge, to poison my own.

People around me were gathering up their belongings, calling to new friends to say a new set of goodbyes, and collecting together in groups in readiness for disembarking. Some, the quieter ones, would be returning to what they knew all too well already, others embarking on a new life for which no amount of warnings and descriptions could prepare them.

I craned my neck for sight of Jack Carlisle, but not knowing if he would be in uniform or not it was hard to pick him out of the crowd waiting on the dock. Then, as the crowd thinned, I saw him, with his back to me. For a second my heart was jolted into a helplessly excited rhythm; his hatless head was turned away and he looked, from this side view, so much like his nephew; they shared a height and broadness of shoulder, both had very dark hair, and both held themselves with the same alert readiness, as if they might be called into action at any second. From this distance, and to my untrained eye, the uniform might have been that of any officer, as likely a captain as Jack's own rank of major. I lost sight of him as I started forward, pushing through the crowd until I came up to stand behind him, and raised my voice to be heard over the hubbub of conversation, and of vehicles rumbling to life.

'Major Carlisle?'

Then he turned, and my knees faltered.

'Young Kittlington.'

'Archie!' That thundering in my chest again, my fingers losing their grip on the handle of my suitcase, dropping it to the ground at my feet, the treacherous way my arms rose, without my bidding, to encircle his waist ... the feel of his own arms wrapped about my shoulders. Buttons, hard beneath my cheek, the crowd disappearing from around us, melting away to leave us alone in a suddenly peaceful world. There was nothing else. There simply was nothing else.

Long after my heartbeat had returned to normal, and my short breaths had deepened once again, he released me. I stood back and looked up at him, his familiar face tired, but still so strong, so beautiful. I reached up to touch his jaw with trembling fingers, and only just stopped myself from tracing his lower lip with my thumb. I ached for him to lower that mouth to mine, and to put all my doubts to flight, but his expression was one of concern, nothing more.

'Sweetheart, how are you feeling? Is the fever gone? We must get you a hot drink.'

He stepped back, leaving me swaying slightly

with the loss of his touch, and bent to pick up my bag. He held out his free hand to me but I shook my head; to hold his hand as he wished, as a child, would be worse than not touching him at all, and my heart cracked a little. After all I'd been through, I was still Oli's little sister.

I followed him to the car. 'Why are you here, instead of Jack?' I wanted him to say it was his idea, that he'd asked to come particularly, but deep down I knew he hadn't.

'He thought it'd be easier for you, at least when you arrived,' Archie said. 'Someone you know a little better, after...' he cleared his throat '...well ... he thought maybe since–'

'He thought I'd be scared to be alone with *him?*' I couldn't keep the incredulousness out of my voice, and he smiled. It lifted my spirits to see it, despite everything.

'Aye, well the same thing occurred to Lizzy when you went missing. People care for you, Kitty,' he added softly. We'd reached the car, and his face turned solemn. 'We understand what this is going to do to you. To ... your reputation. How people will see you. And how it's going to bring back an awful thing you'd want to forget if you could. It's an amazing thing you're doing, and we'll do everything we can to–'

'Thank you,' I said, my tone inadvertently short. He was only trying to say the right thing, but the thought of whoever 'we' might be, sitting around discussing what a brave little soul I was for speaking out against Colonel Drewe, made me shrivel inside with mortification. I saw the miserable realisation on his face, and touched his arm. 'I'm

55

sorry,' I said. 'I'm just tired. I am grateful though. And it's so lovely to see you, Arch.'

'And you,' he said, relaxing a little, and opened the car door for me. 'Hold on tight, the roads haven't improved since you were here last.'

He was right; I remembered feeling queasy on my way to the ferry, and that had been worsened by the way the car had constantly swerved to avoid the bigger shell holes, but in the past month the roads must have taken quite a pounding, and the going was jolting and slow. We arrived in full dark, and I was taken to a small hotel just up the road from where Oli was being held.

'Can I see him?' I asked, when Archie pointed out the building, a large, dark blob against the night.

'Not tonight, darling.' The casual word, one he had used ever since I'd known him, now had the power to slice through me. But even if he'd meant it in the way I longed for, his earlier reminder that my reputation was about to be ruined told me once and for all that it was too late now. When he left me to return to HQ I accepted the light, brotherly kiss on my cheek, and told myself it was just as well he still thought of me as a child after all. I eventually fell asleep to the hollow boom of distant guns, and only realised when I was awoken by a lull, that I hadn't even noticed them.

The following morning Jack greeted me in the lobby. He rose from his seat, and automatically started to pull his uniform jacket straight, then his dark blue eyes met mine and he stopped fussing, came over and, without a moment's hesitation, put his arms around me. I almost sagged in relief, but held myself firm, accepting his comfort, and then smiled up at him.

'Evie's right about you,' I said, and he looked both pleased and slightly embarrassed.

'In that case I hope she's said something flattering.' Then his own smile faded, and his expression held echoes of Archie's solemn look from the night before. 'Kitty, I want to sit down and talk to you for a while, somewhere private. Would that be all right?'

'Of course. Where should we go?'

'There's an office at HQ we can use. It's just a few minutes away.' He glanced down at my footwear, as if he half expected me to be wearing kitten heels and stockings. But although I'd wanted to look smart, Frances and Lizzy had both said variations of the same thing: *you were working when it happened, and you weren't dressed to catch a man's eye then. Best not look like some flighty girl now, when it matters most.*

I tightened the belt on my coat, and knocked the flat heel of my boot on the floor. 'I can walk for miles,' I assured him, and his smile returned.

'Well then, shall we?' He held out his arm, and I took it, and together we walked out into the rubble-strewn street.

HQ was, in fact, another hotel, but much larger. However, the room Jack showed me into had clearly been a smallish storeroom of some kind in its past existence, and a tiny desk was pushed into the corner, with a typewriter parked precariously on the edge and a single upturned chair taking up the remaining room on it.

I looked at it doubtfully, but as I turned back to Jack, mouth open to ask where I should sit, I saw the reason for the squashed up arrangement of furniture: someone had jammed two tattered armchairs into the space behind the door. They sat arm-to-arm, but even that cramped space looked comfortable and, most important of all, friendly.

I felt a little tearful as I realised this had been Jack's doing, I could tell from his anxious expression, and from his relief when I nodded. He looked so much like Archie that I had to swallow a new lump in my throat as I sat down.

'If you'd rather not speak to me, you only have to say,' he said quietly. 'And if you feel like crying, don't hold back on my account. I can stay, or go, as you like.'

His voice was low, like Archie's, but his accent was firmly north-western. No hint of Scotland anywhere in it. It was close to my own accent, in fact, and that familiarity helped as he started to talk, to explain all he knew of Oliver's circumstances, and, finally, gently, to coax out of me the story of what had happened on the road that freezing February night.

It was hard at first. Every word felt like a tug on an un-anaesthetised tooth, but as I talked they began to come more easily. I told him how I'd been so excited about driving alone for the first time, how Evie had patiently gone over and over everything I would need to know... I felt the constant ache of guilt over the fury I had unleashed on her blameless head, and tried to say as

58

much to Jack, but he shook his head.

'She understood. But don't give her a thought just now. I want you to get the worst part of the story out of your head and into mine, here, where it doesn't matter. Once you've spoken it out loud it'll be easier next time.'

So I told him the rest, and when I explained how Drewe had pinned me to the filthy, blood-soaked bed in the back of the ambulance, his face took on a strange expression. Lizzy had told me he'd known Drewe many years before, had fought with him in Africa, and had respected the man he'd been. Now I could see dismay and regret at the man Drewe had become, and I wouldn't be the one to sit in judgement while he mourned the fall of a great man, but for me there was only anger.

'They must see Oli was provoked,' I said when I'd finished. 'He shouldn't have hit the colonel, but Evie said Drewe struck him first.'

'There's no proof of that,' Jack said. 'We must stick to the fact of provocation, and not muddy the waters with a self-defence plea.'

'Do you think it will work?' I asked, my voice coming out small and scared-sounding.

Jack reached out and took my hand. 'I'm going to do everything I can to see it does,' he said. 'Now, would you like me to take you to see your brother?'

Oliver was barely recognisable as the confident, cheerful boy I'd so often wanted to push into the river. He'd been allowed to shave, and his uniform was neat enough as he readied himself for this new trial, but his eyes had lost their light, and his face, always thin, now looked skeletal. I couldn't begin to imagine how it felt to have come so close to death, and then to have been reprieved, only to face the horror of it possibly happening again.

'Kitty!' He rose from his bunk and embraced me, and, with Jack standing quietly in the back of the tiny room, we sat down to talk. Evie had only been able to give me the bare bones of the story; immediately after she'd heard it herself she'd gone to France to find Will. She had wired again, as soon as the news came through that Drewe had not died as a result of being struck by Oli, and from that moment on my brother's life had rested in my hands.

'Is Archie going to be there?' Oliver directed this question at Jack, who glanced at me before answering.

'No, his unit's rotated forward; he's needed in the line.'

I felt cold all over, and Oli squeezed my hand. 'He'll be right as rain, Kitty; don't worry.'

'And so will you be,' I ventured, not knowing any such thing, but wanting it so strongly it felt like the truth.

He grinned, and seemed his old self again, in that moment. 'I should bloody hope so, after you traipsing all this way,' he said. 'And just imagine how cross the parents would be if I got shot tomorrow, on their wedding anniversary. It would really put a wrinkle in the celebrations.'

'Can't have that,' I agreed, trying not to flinch at the word *shot*, and feeling a faint pang at the thought of life continuing its familiar path in the house where I'd grown up. 'Although, when the story comes out about the ... the pregnancy...' I stumbled over the word '...I have a feeling that will more than wrinkle things. Don't you?'

There was nothing he could say to that, and he simply squeezed my hand again. After a moment's silence, Jack motioned to the door. 'It's time we were off, Kitty.'

I turned to Oli and put my arms around him. He felt small, suddenly, even to me. 'It will all be all right,' I whispered. 'Please don't worry. I love you.'

'I love you too,' he whispered back, and I was sure if he'd spoken the words any louder they would have cracked.

Jack was right; telling him my story first, in the quiet little office where only he could hear me, made it easier to speak out at the court martial. I could see people studying me intently – my dress, my shoes, my manner – and was grateful for the advice given by Lizzy and Frances. I was not slim and pretty, like Evie, my hair was a tangled mess of red curls despite my attempts to tame it, and my figure, although I'd lost weight since I'd joined up, was still more on the rounded side – I was clearly not a temptress, and therefore my words seemed to carry more weight. That shouldn't have been the case, and it angered me that it was, but it was a relief nevertheless. I kept looking around for Archie, hoping Jack's explanation that there was a push on had merely been preparing Oli for potential disappointment, but I didn't see him anywhere. His presence as I gave my evidence would have given me extra strength, but perhaps my timidity also worked in my favour.

Jack's own evidence as to Drewe's character was honest and raw; he told of his deep respect, and of the sadness as he'd watched Drewe slide into morphine dependency. To hear then, that that dependency had sunk deeper than any of them had realised, had shaken Jack, but the medical evidence was inarguable, and the post-mortem report bore out Evie's suspicions; Lieutenant Colonel Drewe had been on the verge of that heart attack for a long time, and it might have happened at any moment. The verdict was delivered quickly: not guilty of murder, but guilty of manslaughter. The circumstances would now be taken into account, and we sat in frozen silence while we waited for the sentence to be pronounced.

It did not take long. Oliver would be stripped of his commission and given a dishonourable discharge from the army, to serve a ten-year sentence in a civilian prison. Cashiered. Not shot. My heart hammered almost painfully as I felt all the strength drain out of me, and I slumped in my seat. The release of tension was making me shake, and all I could do was fix my eyes on the back of the seat in front, and listen to the chant echoing loudly in my head. *Thank God, thank God, thank God...*

I felt the gentle pressure of Jack's hand on my arm. 'Sit up straight, love, and give him a smile to see him back to Blighty.'

Somehow I did so, and realised Oli's attention had been fixed on me anxiously. He nodded as our eyes met, his face pale, but he returned my smile. 'Come and see me,' he mouthed, as he was led away.

Jack stood, and drew me to my feet. 'Come on, I can think of one or two people who'll want to hear this news.'

'Are we going to see Archie?' I heard my voice thicken as I spoke his name, and my pulse picked up in sudden hope, but he shook his head.

'He really is rotated forward,' he said. 'I wasn't just saying that for your brother's benefit. We'll wire him the verdict. What I am going to do now though, is take you back to France.'

'To the ferry? Already?' Disappointment broke over me, but Jack smiled.

'To Arras.'

The hospital at Arras, where Will was awaiting his own Blighty ticket, was an astonishing affair. Underground passages, wards and operating rooms, smartly turned out nurses and orderlies creating calm from chaos ... and although the smells and sounds brought back everything I thought I'd never experience again, with them came, not revulsion, as I'd expected, or even dark memories of trembling exhaustion, but a strange and aching sweep of nostalgia. For the first time I understood what Evie had meant, when she tried to explain how it had felt to be at her glorious Breckenhall home and wanting, more than anything, to be back here.

Tiredness was creeping over me now, and I was feeling a little light-headed and hot, but the thought of seeing Evie again, and meeting Will at last, kept me looking around with increasing interest.

'Uncle Jack!' The familiar, clear voice cut through the noise, and I turned to see Evie coming down the corridor towards us. She saw me at the same time, and gave a little cry and drew me into her embrace. 'Skittles! How are you, sweetheart?' Then she drew back, her breath catching as she belatedly realised why we were there. 'What happened? Is the trial over?'

'Yes, love,' Jack said. He caught my eye and suddenly, in the midst of this madness, the relief set in properly; the smiles on our faces filtered through Evie's tiredness, and she gave a shaky laugh.

'He's been acquitted?'

'No, not quite. But he's not going to face the guns.' Jack gave her a brief account of what had happened, and although her face shadowed at the news he would spend ten years in prison, she understood as well as we did how close he had come to losing his life.

'And what of young William?' Jack wanted to know. 'How's he doing?'

'He's bright enough. Cheerful as ever. Infection was a worry for a while but it won't be too long before he's fit to travel. Come in and see him.' She led the way to a crowded ward at the far end of the hospital, and we followed her to the bed halfway down one side, where a couple of nurses were standing at the foot, entranced by what they were watching.

'He's making things again,' Evie said, her smile lighting the room. 'People give him all the spare paper they can find.'

64

The two nurses caught sight of the sister approaching from the other end of the ward and scuttled away quickly, leaving a clear view of Will, his fingers twisting with dexterous concentration and unaware his audience had changed. Then he looked up and saw Evie, and my heart clenched at the look on his face. I'd seen a battered photograph Evie carried with her, and the man who sat propped against these pillows might have been someone else – that man's father perhaps. This man was older, thinner-faced, with deeper cut lines around his mouth and eyes – but the smile that curved his mouth stripped away those extra years, and his hand dropped the paper boat he'd been crafting and reached out to his wife.

She sat down on the bed and her free hand slipped around to cradle the back of his head, and as she kissed him, I could almost feel the touch of phantom lips on my own and it took no guesswork to understand whose they were. That, at least, answered a question that had hovered darkly in the back of my mind since the attack; would I ever be able to bear the intimate touch of a man on my skin? The answer was evidently yes, provided that man was Archie Buchanan.

I looked away, and saw Jack was doing the same as Evie and Will finished greeting one another, then Evie spoke, and the conversation went naturally to Oli and the verdict. Will did not know my brother, but he seemed genuinely delighted, and his smile was warm when he turned it on me.

'I'm glad,' he said, in his husky, slightly broken voice. 'It's not often justice gets done, but thanks to you, it has this time.'

'Thanks to Evie,' I pointed out, and Will looked back at her, and seemed to have trouble speaking again. Instead he just nodded, and swallowed hard. He shifted on his bed, and hissed a sharp breath, one hand pressed to his middle.

'Keep still,' Evie said in worried tones, but he found another smile.

'I'm fine. I just forget sometimes.'

'Well I'm going to keep reminding you,' she said crossly, and I exchanged another look with Will, who sighed.

'Was she like this with you?'

'Worse,' I told him, and Evie rolled her eyes, but her smile returned.

Will's other hand was still wrapped around hers, and he squeezed it. 'She couldn't even let me die in peace,' he said, and his tone was amused, but his eyes on Evie's were soft with awe. 'She followed me out into no man's land just so she could keep nagging me.'

'She *what?*' Jack's voice cut like a whip through the room, and several faces turned to us in aston-ishment and interest.

'Will!' Evie groaned. 'You weren't supposed to say anything about that.'

'Oh, hell.' He looked at Jack and then, apolo-getically, back at Evie. 'You didn't tell me it was a secret.'

'Secret be damned!' Jack growled at Evie. 'I *knew* there was something up, when you could hardly stand up the other day, getting out of the car.' His hands clenched at his sides, then abruptly relaxed, and he shook his head and gave her a wry smile. 'Evangeline Davies, you are going to be the death

66

of me.' He dragged a chair over and gestured to me to sit down, then leaned against the wall at the head of Will's bed, and folded his arms.

Evie sensed the worry behind the exasperation. 'I'm sorry, Uncle Jack. I hate keeping secrets from you, but that was ... well, quite a big one. Please don't tell Lizzy.'

'Don't be silly; of course I'm going to tell her! But I won't tell your mother.' He ran his hands through his hair and sighed, dropping his voice considerably. 'In all seriousness, love, don't let anyone else find out or Archie'll cop it.'

'He had no idea,' Evie protested, her own voice little more than a harsh whisper. *'I* didn't even know I was going to do it, so it wouldn't be fair to blame him.'

He looked at her steadily. 'We've just seen how close things can come to "not fair",' he reminded her. 'The point is you were in his care.'

'He helped me bring Will back,' Evie said. She turned to her husband again, who was clearly deeply regretting having spoken up. 'If it weren't for him Will would have died out there.'

'You're as bad as each other.' Jack shook his head again. 'Archie's a good lad, Evie. I'd hate to see him get into trouble over this.'

'He won't,' she assured him. 'We'll keep it to ourselves now.'

I couldn't imagine what had been going through Evie's mind to go out into no man's land, not after what we'd both seen. The thought of her and Archie out there in the dark, just a few feet away from the German lines, gave me chills, but I wanted to know everything. 'Will you tell me about it though, Evie?'

'Of course.' She glanced around us at the crowded ward. 'When we're back at Dark River. Speaking of which–' she brightened '–how's Lizzy?'

We chatted for a while longer, then I noticed Will was starting to sweat slightly, and his breathing was shorter. Evie noticed at the same time, and turned to look for a nurse. 'It must be time for your next injection,' she muttered. 'I'll go and find someone.'

'It's another hour yet.' He caught at her hand before she could rise. 'It's all right; they're very good. I'm never left waiting past my time.' He managed a brief smile. 'Don't want to get addicted to the stuff, do I?'

His words ricocheted around us, and Evie's face paled. 'Don't say that,' she said, her voice low and worried. 'You won't get addicted.'

It was only then he realised what he'd said. 'Of course I won't! Evie, please ... don't worry.'

'But look at you!' She was close to tears. 'You can barely breathe, you need *something*.'

'I've got something,' he said gently, and lifted their still-linked hands. 'Just sit with me? Don't mind if I drift a bit. Just ... sit with me.' He let out a slow, difficult breath and his eyes closed. I saw his jaw tighten against a small sound of pain, and Evie raised his hand to her lips and kept it there.

Jack and I murmured our goodbyes and started to drift away, but Evie caught up with us before we reached the door. 'He's sleeping already,' she said. 'He's so tired. Hopefully he'll sleep until it's time for his next injection.'

Jack put an arm around her. 'I was never certain I'd say this, but I think he's worthy of you, Evie.'

'I love him so much,' she said, choking on the words as she looked back to where Will slept. The lump of bandage beneath his pyjamas stretched right across his waist, and around his left side, and I guessed the surgery had been intensive, and more dangerous than Evie had wanted to say.

'He's going to need a lot of help to stay off morphine once he's out,' Jack said, and while I knew it had to be discussed, I thought he might have delayed a bit. But Evie was made of sterner stuff than me, and she nodded.

'But it's a good sign he didn't let me call the nurse over, isn't it?'

'It is. I think he knows how scared you are though, and if you're not careful he could go the other way.'

She gave him a horrified look. 'You think he'd actually deny himself pain relief?'

'He loves you, sweetheart,' Jack reminded her, and kissed her forehead. 'He'll do anything.'

'Are you all right, Skittles?' Evie asked me, and put a hand on my arm. I nodded, but I was starting to feel distanced again, as if I were watching from the other end of the tunnel.

'I'm just tired,' I told her, and smiled. 'A good sleep and I'll be right as a trivet.'

Five minutes later the three of us were outside, listening to the crump of guns and the shouts of men and a newly arrived convoy. Now the worry over Oli was eased, all I could think about was Archie. I could see Jack's mind had turned inward, and wondered if he too was thinking about his nephew.

'I'm going back to Belgium tonight,' he said to Evie, confirming it. 'I want to be there when the lad gets back.'

'Of course,' she said. 'Give him a hug from me, won't you?' She glanced at me as soon as the words were out of her mouth, but I smiled and gave a tiny shake of my head. If I'd had any remaining doubts about her love for Will, they'd have been dispelled as soon as I'd seen the couple together.

'Will you take me straight to the ferry, or am I coming back with you?' I asked Jack.

'I'm sure you'd like to see Oliver once more before he's shipped back, wouldn't you? I can take you to the hotel again if you like, and you can see him in the morning. I'm not sure you're up to a channel crossing by the looks of you anyway.'

'I'd feel better for sleeping in a bed,' I admitted, and Evie gave me a hug.

'You take care, sweetheart. You're still not back to your old self.'

We said our goodbyes, and while I sank with relief into Jack's passenger seat, Evie went, with equal relief, back down to spend another long night at Will's bedside.

We arrived back in Belgium in the early hours, and I fell into bed with deep gratitude. The travelling, the cold and the tension had all gradually chipped away at me, and I still felt a low ache in my belly but I couldn't tell if it was a physical pain or the emptiness of losing the baby. Frances had been appalled at the way I'd embraced the blame, and she denied any possibility that I deserved it, but I felt the truth wrap itself around my heart and it was a hard truth to forget.

Late in the morning I managed to spend ten minutes with Oliver before he was marched out, dressed in civilian clothes and looking so very young it made me want to run after him and hold him while we both cried. But I remembered Jack's words, and instead gave him the strongest smile I could muster, then returned to my hotel and collapsed into bed once more. I remained there all day, drifting in and out of a fitful sleep filled with fever-dreams, and during my lucid, waking moments, I told myself over and over again that Will was alive, that Oli was safe, and that Archie would be too. What more could any of us hope for?

In the early evening I rose, much recovered, to have a shallow, lukewarm bath, and to find something for dinner. The big guns were quiet tonight, and it wasn't until I went outside after my meal that I heard the light cracking of rifles. I tried to shut them out, to reduce them to the same background noise as they had been before, but the image of Will in that hospital bed wouldn't leave me. It seemed madness, after all the pain and injury I'd seen, that any one person could bring the horror home to me so completely, but he had. And now all I could think about was Archie out there in no man's land. What if *that* rifle shot had been the very one that signalled the end of his life? Or *that* one? A life was being taken for almost every single one. Why not his?

My hands trembled as I drew on my gloves

against the evening chill, and I was concentrating on smoothing them over my fingers, so it wasn't until he spoke my name that I saw him. He was covered in mud, his hat shoved under his arm, and there was a smudge of blood across his forehead, but he was smiling, and he was whole.

'Been playing in the dirt again?' I asked, trying to hide the surge of joy that cramped my insides.

'Aye. Lost our football and we had to go over and ask Jerry could we please have it back.'

I lost the battle, and laughed out loud, hearing my voice shaking in the evening air. 'I take it you've seen Jack?'

'I have. He told me about Oliver,' Archie said, and took a step towards me. He was looking at me oddly, and I couldn't work out what he was thinking. Then he reached out and gently lifted my hat off my head and dropped it to the ground, along with his own. Seizing my face in his two hands, he looked at me with a fierce, intense expression and then, finally, our lips touched, igniting a flare that shot through me from crown to toe. I heard my own gasp, and then his groan, and the touch grew firmer, his lips parting, and his tongue flickering along my teeth.

For what seemed like hours we remained locked together, my heart thundering, my hands finding their way into the thick hair at the back of his head and curling into the warmth there, and it took a while for me to realise I was pressing against him with my whole body. My gloved fingers caressed the back of his neck, and I could feel his thumbs brushing first my cheeks, and then my temples, before the kiss broke and he drew my head against his chest, holding me there as if there was a chance I might try to draw away.

'Oh, bloody hell, Kitty,' he murmured. 'What have I done?'

'You've come back safe,' I tried to say, but the tears were choking the words off in my throat, because the kiss had awakened everything I had been trying so hard to suppress. And it was too late.

I did draw back then, and wiped my eyes with my still-wrinkled gloves, belatedly feeling my face flame at the way I'd behaved. 'I'm glad you've come back,' I stammered. 'But I'm sorry for...' I waved a vague hand, unable to find the words to excuse my overeager response. My family would be mortified.

He straightened away from me. 'I'm sorry too,' he said. 'Strange, how we react to danger. I've been over, and made it back before, but this time it felt ... I don't know, like I had more to lose.'

I wanted to ask what, but no matter what he answered it would be wrong; to hear what I'd hoped to hear would hurt more than anything else.

'Well,' I said instead, 'it's understandable that we should have felt...' Again I couldn't find the words, but I went on. 'I mean, it's been a terrifying time. For all of us.'

'Aye.' His voice lost that confused, longing tone, and became brisk. 'Uncle Jack has asked me if I'd bring you back to England. But I can't get away.'

'No, of course.' I cleared my throat. 'That's... I wouldn't expect it.'

'I didn't want you to think we're abandoning you.'

'Don't worry. Really.'

'I'll arrange for a driver to take you to the ferry. I'll try and get some leave once Will's able to return.'

'That'll be nice.'

'Aye.'

'So, then,' I said, at the same time as he said, 'Right.' We looked at each other and smiled, a little hesitantly, but the smiles were real.

'I'll write,' he said, holding out his hand, then bent to pick up my hat and handed it to me. 'Sorry about this.'

I pushed away the thundering memory of how it had felt when he'd taken it off me, and took it, then looked back down at the ground, where his own cap still lay. 'Don't you want that?'

He picked it up, and gave it a pointless dusting-off, smearing the mud across the flat crown. He shrugged and grinned. 'Ah well, could be worse.'

'Archie?' He raised an eyebrow, and my voice was soft. 'Come back safe next time, too.'

'Nae bother,' he said, exaggerating his own accent, and this time the kiss was as chaste and brotherly as they had been all my life. 'Don't work too hard; you're not up to it yet.'

And he turned away, leaving me standing in the street with the memory of our first and last kiss tingling on my lips.

Chapter Five

Dark River Farm, May 1917

He did manage four days' leave, when Will came home, two of which were spent at the farm, and they had been two days filled with relief and happiness, and the warmth of our old friendship. But there was something new between us now as well, something beautiful and helpless, and doomed. Tomorrow morning would see him leaving again for Belgium and his other life, and while the largest part of me battled with the terror of it, and the longing for him to stay, some smaller, hidden part accepted the relief of knowing his attention was no longer on me. On what I could not give him.

Evie, Will and Lizzy were in the kitchen on this last evening, and I knew they'd start talking about us as soon as one of them glanced out of the window and saw Archie had come into the yard to find me. As always, I watched his approach with the same mixture of longing and apprehension, fixing a smile on my face and hoping I'd find the strength, once again, to resist touching him.

'Young Kittlington,' he said, and his voice was almost enough to break down that resistance; he sounded tired, exhausted even, and I knew this short leave had not provided the rest he needed. He'd spent most of his time helping Mrs Adams do various jobs, and the rest in talking to me – I was much the harder work of the two; I knew that. I also knew I was the reason he'd come here at all, instead of going home to Scotland.

'Captain Buchanan,' I returned, leaning slightly away to discourage contact, but broadening my smile to compensate. 'Are you all set?'

'Aye. Not much to pack,' he pointed out, and turned to lean on the fence. He seemed absorbed by the high-stepping chickens as they pecked at the food I'd just thrown them, and didn't speak for a moment, so I joined him at the fence; it was easier to stand beside him and not have to look at his face.

After a while he cleared his throat. 'Look, Kitty, I know you understand how my feelings for you have changed, grown into something else.'

'Archie–'

'No, wait. Please. All these years you've been Oli's sister. Sweet, but just a child. Even when Evie told me what had happened to you, who we thought did it, and I wanted to rip Drewe's driver limb from limb, I was feeling it as the shock of someone hurting my family. The anger blinded me to everything else. At first.'

'And what of your devotion to Evie?' I couldn't help saying. 'Did she feel like family too?'

A flush touched his neck. 'I thought I loved her. Perhaps I did, and perhaps I still do, but not in that way.' His voice dropped, became urgent. 'Kitty, that time I came to find you at the hotel, and I saw you concentrating so hard on your gloves, you looked so intense, but so sad. It hit me harder than I've ever thought possible, but I

76

couldn't accept it. It felt wrong, and I thought I'd frighten you if I told you how I felt – I know you've always looked on me as a brother. I'd have hated more than anything to lose your trust.' He sighed and rubbed his face with both hands, pressing his fingers to his closed eyes. 'That's why I lied, and arranged for someone else to bring you back when Uncle Jack asked me. It's why I let you come back alone, when all I wanted to do was take hold of you and never let you out of my sight again.' He dropped his hands away from his face and fixed his eyes on mine again. 'I have never felt so ... *fiercely,* about anyone, the way I feel about you. Now I've accepted it, and let it in, it actually hurts.'

'It does, doesn't it?' I whispered, without meaning to. I couldn't look away, but my eyes burned.

Archie searched my face, and finally asked, in almost a whisper, 'Do you think you could ever feel the same way about me?'

I couldn't speak. Didn't he realise? Didn't it blaze from my eyes, the way I felt it in every part of me? He caught my hands in his, and I was too startled to pull away.

'Will you wait for me, when all this is over?' He let out a ragged breath. 'Kitty Maitland, will you marry me?'

I could have wept for all the years I'd longed to hear him say it, and more than anything I wanted selfishly to entrust myself to those familiar arms which, I knew without a doubt now, would keep me safe for ever. But I never could, and I couldn't even tell him why; he would only persuade me I was wrong, and that would ruin him because I would believe him. His trembling uncertainty of my love for him formed the words I heard falling into the tense silence.

'I'm sorry, but no.'

The pain on his face was echoed in my heart, and I hated myself for putting it there. Almost more, I hated the fact that it was not a surprised pain; his face just paled, and his eyes closed briefly, and the resigned look that drew his brows together told of someone hearing what they'd already braced themselves to hear.

'I understand,' he said in a low voice, but he didn't let go of my hands. I wanted to tell him he didn't understand, not at all, not if he believed it was because my feelings were not every bit as fierce, and every bit as hopeless.

'We'll still be friends though, aye?' he said, and his mouth flickered into a smile, although his eyes remained shadowed.

'I hope so,' I said in a small voice. He touched my cheek, and while I fought every instinct I possessed not to lean into his hand, I told myself this was the right thing to do. He deserved some- one unspoilt and respectable, someone he could be proud of, someone bright and lively who could make him laugh... God knows he needed that, after all he'd seen. Yes, I was doing the right thing.

I wondered when I'd start to believe it.

Dark River Farm, June 1917

'What's that?' Belinda stubbed out her freshly lit cigarette on the floor of the barn, and I turned to

78

the door, my mind racing; if Mrs Adams caught us drinking and smoking we'd be given vile jobs to do tomorrow, but even worse, for me at least, would be her disapproval.

'Is someone out there?' I hissed.

A light cough confirmed it, and Bel went to the open door and peered across the yard towards the house. 'No-one's come out,' she called back in a low voice, while I patted around for the cork to stop up the wine bottle again. My fuzzy-headedness had faded quickly with the sudden shock of possible discovery, and I stood and picked up the long-handled broom with which I'd been beating rats out of the pile of sacks. Although who would believe we'd been working, when we could barely see to–

'Oh!' Bel turned, and in the near-complete darkness I saw the gleam of her teeth as she grinned. 'It's him!'

'Who?'

'The chap who gave me the wine! He's coming over. Quick, light the lamp.'

I stared, unable to move. A man was coming to the barn? And she knew him? 'Who is he?'

'I met him earlier today in town. We talked a bit but I didn't think he'd–'

'Well well,' a pleasant voice said, 'it's the beautiful blonde Belinda. Hello again. I was about to knock at, the house when I heard voices out here...' The man who appeared in the doorway was little more than a silhouette, but I saw him lean to look around Belinda and straight at me. 'Good evening, and what's your name?'

'The lamp!' Bel urged, and drew the stranger

79

into the barn. 'Mr Beresford, this is Kitty Maitland. She's sort of Land Army too.'

'Nice to meet you, Miss Maitland. Sort of Land Army?'

Belinda had given up waiting for me to light the paraffin lamp, and bent to do it herself. 'She's more like the family really.' She straightened and turned to me. 'I met Mr Beresford in town today, and in exchange for some advice on where to stay, he gave me that wine you're enjoying so much.'

'Ah, glad it's being put to good use anyway,' Mr Beresford said, and in the newly flickering light I noticed he was quite short, but exceptionally good-looking. He held out his hand to me, and, without thinking, I put mine in it ready to shake. But he lifted it to his lips instead.

'I'm actually rather glad I was unable to find room at the hotel you told me about, or I should never have come here and met two such stunning girls.'

I didn't know what to say, but it didn't matter; Bel was happy to chatter for both of us. She quickly ascertained that Mr Beresford was hoping to find accommodation under the roof of Mrs Adams, of whom he had heard such warm things. 'I'm more than happy to pay my way,' he said earnestly. 'It'd just be for a night or two, then I go back to France.'

'Wonderful!' Bel clapped her hands together. 'There's a spare room at the back of the house; it's where Mr Adams used to keep all his wet-weather clothing. It has a bed too. Only a camp bed, but–'

'That sounds perfect,' Mr Beresford said. 'I'm arranging for funds to be sent through to the bank, and I expect Mrs Adams would be glad of some extra money in a couple of days when it comes through. Besides, I don't eat much.' He patted his flat stomach and grinned. 'Have to stay fighting fit, after all.'

'Are you home on leave?' I asked, looking for his bags.

'Yes. I'm afraid I met with some regrettable thuggery on my journey though, and practically all my belongings were stolen.'

'Oh!' Belinda's face fell. 'That's terrible.'

'All they left me with was that bottle of wine I'd just bought, and what I carried in my pockets. I hope you understand now why I paid for your advice in wine rather than money?'

'Of course, why didn't you say so before?'

He shrugged, and smiled quite charmingly. 'Embarrassed, I suppose. A pretty girl smiles, all dressed for work and clearly as capable as they come, and it's hard to admit one has been overcome and unable to defend one's own property.'

'I'm sure Mrs Adams will be glad to put you up for a night or two,' I ventured, 'given your sad circumstances.'

'Best if you ask her, Kitty,' Bel said. 'She has such a soft spot for you. You can tell her he's perfectly all right, and she'll trust your judgement.'

I looked at Mr Beresford again, hoping I could trust hers. 'I don't know...'

She put her head on one side, a sign I recognised, and one that made me grimace. 'Come on,' she urged, 'you know how she's changed since you came to live here. She used to be so strict.'

'She still is!' But I surrendered, as we'd both

known I would. 'Oh, all right. I'll go in and talk to her.'

Reluctantly I stepped out into the dark, but half-way across the yard I hesitated and almost turned back, my stomach suddenly churning as I realised I'd left her alone in there with a strange man ... but Belinda was a grown woman, and a supremely confident one. I sighed. I had to stop trying to wrap the rest of the world in my own fears.

I found Mrs Adams in the creamery, a low light in the corner glowing while she shaped and patted butter into blocks.

'All done?' She looked beyond me. 'Where's Belinda?'

'We've almost finished, Mrs Adams,' I lied, hoping she wouldn't come out to the barn to check. I explained briefly about Mr Beresford's bad fortune, and his request for paid accommodation until it was time for him to return to his unit.

Mrs Adams pursed her lips. 'He's a friend of Belinda's, you say?'

'It seems so.' There didn't seem any point mentioning that Bel had only met him once; he was friendly, he'd be here two nights at the most, and then he'd move on. 'Maybe he can help out with one or two things around the place,' I added.

'Well, it'll mean Will can stop looking around as if he feels he should be doing them,' Mrs Adams said grimly. 'Poor boy'd do himself a mischief if we took our eye off him for five minutes.'

'So shall I bring Mr Beresford in to meet you? Then you can make up your own mind.'

'Yes, all right,' she said. 'Show him into the sitting room. I'll be out in a few minutes. Oh, before you go back?'

'Yes?'

'When are you going to start calling me Frances? Evie and Will do.'

'They're guests,' I said. 'I work here.'

Mrs Adams looked sad rather than exasperated. 'You *live* here, my girl. You're my daughter now, to all intents and purposes.'

'I do have a mother,' I reminded her, as gently as the words allowed. She raised an eyebrow, but said nothing. She didn't have to.

About two weeks after I'd returned from giving evidence at Oliver's trial a letter had arrived, routed through Elise at Number Twenty-Two, the ambulance station to which Evie had moved after our own little cottage had been shelled. I'd opened it with trembling fingers, recognising the handwriting immediately, but any hope that my ordeal had touched my mother's heart was dashed as soon as I began to read.

Katherine,

News has now reached us of the events surrounding your brother's arrest and court martial. I wish that word had come from your hand, but of course we had to hear it by way of gossip and newspapers. To learn that you are responsible for Oliver's downfall does not lessen our shame in his actions, it merely serves to throw some understanding upon it.

Likewise I can understand how a girl like you would be flattered by the attentions of an officer, but even if you did not make it clear to him that you had come to your senses, you are, after all, a sturdy girl and cannot have been so incapacitated that you could

83

not protect yourself. I'm sure if you think back you will realise the truth of this. Such a man would never force himself upon a wholly unwilling partner.

Word of your ruin is already spreading among those upon whom we depend for the continuation of the family's successful business, and those whose good opinion we value. I can only hope you are able to redeem yourself in their eyes, in the course of your chosen war duties – Oliver has no further opportunity to cover himself in glory, but you, at least, have the chance to expunge the shame you and your brother have brought on your family.

I'd lowered the letter, my face burning, my heart smashing against my ribs and making me feel hot and dizzy. Her words were stark enough, but the meaning I read behind them stole my breath; did she hope for me to be wounded in action? Perhaps I was imagining it. Surely I was? I lifted the letter and continued reading, and the words blurred in front of my eyes.

Your father and I both feel that any leave you take for the foreseeable future would be better spent away from Ecclesley, perhaps with the families of your new set of friends. This would give us the chance to ease your path back into society after the war, if you have not already muddied it too thoroughly. (Should this be the case I am certain you will see the wisdom of making a new life, better suited to your rather rebellious nature, and of finding a husband to whom purity and good name are secondary considerations.)

I felt sick now, remembering that letter and how

84

devastated I had been to read it. Mrs Adams knew of it, but not what it said. I'd showed it to no-one; the shame had burned too brightly. For days I had wrestled with the guilt of lying, of letting them believe I was still in Belgium. I had taken up a pen countless times between then and now, poised to write the letter that would tell them the truth and cut my last hopeful tie with them, but as long as I returned home a plucky war heroine, with any luck even wounded in the service of others, my future as an Ecclesley Maitland would be assured. When I eventually wrote back, sending the letter to Elise so she could post it again from Dixmude, I found my pen had written words I couldn't bear to hear in my own head: that I understood, and hoped that one day Mother and Father would learn to forgive me. By then I'd known there was nothing to forgive. Those who truly loved me had helped me believe that, but I felt that as long as I begged, pleaded and generally sounded like the old Kitty, Mother and Father might remember their little girl, and realise how dreadful their pronouncement had been.

Standing in the creamery at Dark River Farm I thought of my parents in their large, comfortable house in Ecclesley, and I felt an odd lightening sensation, an almost dizzying change of view. From nothing more than habit, and a fear of change, I'd been longing for a forgiveness that would never come, hoping, with a child's yearning heart, for acceptance. It dawned on me now that I'd found that acceptance, just not in the arms of the parents who had raised me. I was wanted here, as soiled and broken as I was. I looked around, taking in the familiar warmth, the sweet smells, and the overall sense of peace that pervaded every corner of this draughty old farmhouse, and then I looked at Mrs Adams.

'I'll show him into in the sitting room. Frances.'

She nodded, and turned wordlessly back to her work, but her smile stayed with me all the way across the yard.

'You won't have cause to regret it, Mrs Adams,' Mr Beresford said, his own smile wide with relief and gratitude. Now I could see him properly I couldn't help being taken by the warmth of his hazel eyes, and the way he looked so earnestly at whoever he was talking to, whether it was the pretty and vivacious Belinda, the stern, inquisitive Frances, or even me.

'I'm sure I won't,' Frances said. 'Now, I'm told you don't have anything to unpack, but maybe we can find something for you to change into amongst my Harry's old things. He was a lot taller than you, but we have scissors, and Sally's a decent enough hand with a needle.'

'You're too kind,' Mr Beresford said, and as Frances took him off upstairs to search for something that might fit well enough, he glanced back and winked. Not at Belinda, at me. I pretended not to notice, and Bel didn't say anything, but I thought I saw her eyes narrow anyway, and tried to think of a way to revive the companionship of our dance in the barn. But before I could, the sitting room door opened and Evie came in.

Driving the city's ambulances between docks and hospital had given her some purpose, but it was not the same as it had been in Belgium, and I could still see the yearning in her eyes every time someone mentioned life at the Front. She would go back as soon as Will was recovered, I was sure of it. As would he. For now though, while he fought to regain his strength, and Frances kept her beady eye on him all the while, Evie worked hard doing the thing she was best at: driving.

Evie looked around her now, as she came in, her blonde hair grown back to its pre-war curls, her face tired but smiling. 'Good evening, girls. Where is he, then?'

'Upstairs with Mrs Adams,' Bel said.

Evie blinked. 'What's he doing up there?'

'She means Will, you idiot,' I said to Bel. 'He's finishing some odd jobs in the bathroom, Evie. He won't be long.'

'I wish he wouldn't try to do so much,' Evie said, trying to sound merely exasperated, but I could hear the worry in her voice. She sat down in the chair by the window. 'Who did you think I was talking about?' she asked Belinda.

'We have a house guest, just for one or two nights. A rather dashing young man called Mr Beresford.'

Evie grinned. 'Typical. I expect you managed to charm him into thinking he needed a room.'

Bel, who worshipped both Evie and Lizzy, looked pleased but adopted a tone of indignation. 'I did not! He was the one who smiled first, when I was in the bank. The poor man had just had his belongings stolen. Can you imagine? Anyway, we got talking, but I didn't know about the robbery until just now. He was embarrassed to admit it to me, and just said he was looking for a place to stay.'

'And you batted those long eyelashes at him, and offered him a room for the night?'

'Certainly not!' Bel said, still wearing a look of reproach. 'I told him of a hotel in town. As it turned out he was unable to get funds right away so he couldn't go there, but he remembered the name of the farm, and came here instead.'

'Well, it'll be good for Frances to have someone to help her out,' Evie said, and smothered a yawn. 'It's a little bit late for an early night, but I shan't be up long so I hope Will comes down soon, or I'll be off to bed without seeing him at all today.'

The two of them chatted for a while, and I wanted to join in but I was starting to feel the effects of the wine again. Out in the barn it had given me a little burst of energy and amusement, but in this warm, cosily lit sitting room, with full dark fallen outside, it made me feel oddly distanced from everything. Evie and Bel's quiet talk washed over me, and I thought fuzzily ahead to tomorrow, and the jobs I needed to do. I should really get up and go to bed, but I was too comfortable, and it was nice listening to my friends' voices and occasional laughter.

I dozed a little in the chair, but jerked awake again as Frances and Mr Beresford came in. He smiled around at everyone, but as his eyes lit on Evie his expression changed, and the smile, when it reappeared, became faintly mocking. 'Well. How very nice to see you again, My Lady.'

Chapter Six

Evie stared at him, her face blank with astonishment. Finally she found her voice, and it was low and hard. 'What are *you* doing here?'

'Do you know this gentleman then?' Frances looked from one to the other. 'Evie? Are you all right? Should I ask him to leave?'

'She'll be fine, Mrs Adams,' Mr Beresford said smoothly. He cleared his throat and frowned, tapping lightly at his chest. 'It's just been a while since we saw each other – '15, I believe. We didn't part on the best of terms, I'm sorry to say. Not for want of trying, I might add, though, was it?' He said this last to Evie, whose hands were clenched tight on her knees.

'Why are you here?' she repeated.

'I was lucky enough this time to bump into *this* lovely young lady.' He gestured at Belinda, who was looking as if she wanted the chair in which she sat to swallow her up. 'She has far better manners than you. She mentioned the name of the farm, and here I am.'

'Coincidence, I suppose?'

'I know it's not flattering to accept, but I have not spent the past two years yearning after your rather sour-faced company.'

'No,' she said, letting out a breath. 'Of course not.' She looked at Frances. 'Forgive me, this is your home. I had no right to demand an explan-

89

ation.' She struggled to adopt a more friendly tone. 'I met Mr ... Beresford, was it? in Brecken-hall when I was on leave at one time, and I'm afraid I *was* rather dismissive and rude.'

'That's not like you,' Frances said.

Evie gave her a grateful smile and turned back to the visitor. 'Mr Beresford, you must understand you were asking an awful lot of questions about my husband's location, and there's a war on.'

'Ah. I see. You thought I might be a spy?'

Her lips tightened at his amused smile. 'It's a possibility; you must admit.'

'Of course,' he said smoothly. 'However, I can assure you it's not the case. Your apology is accepted.' I could see Evie open her mouth to point out that it was Frances she had apologised to, not him, but she closed it again with an effort, and instead inclined her head graciously.

The atmosphere in the room relaxed a little, and Mr Beresford sat in the empty chair opposite me while Frances went out to the kitchen to make some Bovril. He turned once again to Evie.

'So, these two lovely girls are working hard for this new Land Army thing. What's your contri-bution to the war effort?' She narrowed her eyes, but his smile was pleasant and interested, and she evidently decided she'd imagined the slightly antagonistic tone of the question.

'I do a bit of driving. For the hospitals.'

Belinda piped up at once. 'Oh, come off it! Evie's an absolute heroine,' she said to Mr Beres-ford. 'Been driving ambulances all over the Front, dodging bullets and shells and all sorts.'

'Jolly brave,' he murmured. 'And why are you

here now?'

'My husband is convalescing,' she said. 'Frances offered to let us stay here in the country, until Will's recovered enough to rejoin his unit, but that won't be for some time yet.'

Mr Beresford frowned, and his faintly patronising manner altered to one of genuine concern. 'I'm sorry. Was he badly wounded?'

'Badly enough.'

'What happened?'

But Evie clearly didn't seem to want to say any more, so I stepped in with some questions about Mr Beresford's own wartime background. He told us he held the rank of lieutenant, and was stationed near Amiens, but all the time he spoke he kept shooting glances at Evie. She avoided eye contact, and I could see she was listening out for Will's step on the stairs. When it came I saw her relax, and a smile painted the edges of her lips. The door opened and Mr Beresford jumped to his feet, cutting me off mid-question, and he looked tense, suddenly, and a little uncertain as he faced the doorway.

Will saw him, and the warm greeting he'd had ready for us died. Pale, he stared at the visitor as if he thought he might be dreaming. His lips parted but no words came out, and Belinda and I exchanged a glance and waited with breathless astonishment.

Mr Beresford spoke softly, and there was no mocking in his tone this time. 'Good to see you again, Will.'

'Dear God ... *Nathan?*'

'That same bad penny,' Mr Beresford said, and

to my astonishment I saw he had tears in his eyes.

Evie was on her feet now, too, and had moved to Will's side. She slipped her hand through his arm, and turned to face Mr Beresford, plainly furious. 'Why didn't you tell me who you were?'

'I didn't know what he'd told you about me,' he said, and his voice shook. All his previous confidence, and slightly sardonic coolness, had vanished. 'I thought you might send me away, and I couldn't blame you if you did. But ... Will, I had to see you.'

Will gently extricated himself from Evie's grasp, and squeezed her hand before crossing to stand before Mr Beresford. His voice was quiet, but tight-sounding, as if it was an effort for him to say anything at all. 'You ruined me.'

'I know.' Mr Beresford lowered his gaze, unable to look up into Will's face. 'I'm so sorry. I didn't know what to do ... I had to leave.'

'No letters?' Will's voice hardened now, and I saw a flicker of relief on Evie's face that he wasn't just going to brush whatever this man had done aside and welcome him back into his life.

'I wrote, Will! That's the truth. You must have already moved on.'

'I had no choice, thanks to you!'

'I know, and I'm sorry,' Mr Beresford said again. 'I hadn't planned to stay away so long, but by the time I realised I couldn't come back it was too late.'

Frances chose that moment to bring in a tray of warm drinks, and looked from Evie, to Will and Mr Beresford, and back again. 'Not again! What's *happening* tonight? Will, are you all right, lad?'

92

'Yes,' he said. 'Thank you, Frances, I'm fine.' But he didn't sound it.

Mr Beresford ignored everyone else and gripped Will's arm. 'I wrote to you, I swear. And to your family. They must have ignored my letters, or not been able to find you to pass them on. Look, let's talk, just you and me. Like we used to. What do you say?'

Will studied him for a moment, then nodded. 'Tomorrow.' He was standing awkwardly, slightly hunched, and I guessed he'd been overdoing things again.

Evie noticed it too, and laid a gentle hand on his back. 'Now Nathan's here, he can do some of those jobs you keep pretending you're not doing,' she said, trying to make him smile.

Will didn't take his eyes off Mr Beresford. 'Oh, I think he owes me at least that much,' he said softly. 'Tomorrow,' he repeated, and Mr Beresford nodded.

'I'll explain everything.'

'Yes.' Then, to everyone's surprise, not least of all Mr Beresford's, Will pulled the man into a rough hug. Slowly, Mr Beresford's arms came up to return it, taking great care not to grasp Will too tightly.

'I'm so sorry,' he said again, and he sounded as if he were fighting tears. I glanced at Evie, who was observing her husband with a mixture of exasperation and deep, almost painful affection, and she gave me a watery smile and shrugged. When Will and Mr Beresford broke apart, I looked again at the visitor's face. Nothing about his sudden emotional response seemed forced. His eyes were reddened, but they followed Will and Evie as they left the room, and his breath was shaky as he raised a hand to bid them goodnight. He coughed again, and I wondered how long he had been on the road to have caught a chill like that in the summer.

'How do you know Will, Mr Beresford?' I asked, to break the silence that followed their departure.

'We're old friends,' he said, still looking at the closed door. Then he turned away and looked at both of us in turn. 'I should think you ought to call me Nathan now, don't you?' He bestowed his warm smile on Belinda, who straightened in her seat, and his voice returned to its previous lightness, his manner once more the charming, well-bred young man – it was as if someone somewhere had thrown a switch. 'Such extraordinary luck to have bumped into you. You must allow me to buy you something pretty when I get my money.'

'Oh, there's no need,' she said, although her smile made it clear a gift would not be rebuffed. 'How long is it since you've seen Will?'

But Nathan shook his head. 'I want to talk to him first; it's not fair that I should discuss it with anyone else until I have.'

'You really didn't know he was here?' I asked.

Nathan looked at me shrewdly, his lips pursed. 'Tomorrow,' he said, echoing Will. And he would say no more on the subject.

The following morning, neither Belinda nor I wanted to leave the house; we were both desperate to hear the story behind this stranger and his con-

94

nection with our Will. It was clearly a complicated friendship they shared, but one deep enough to allow the unlikely gesture of a warm embrace and tears, amidst the shock and suspicion of their re-acquaintance. Especially in a room full of women. But Frances quickly tired of us finding excuses to remain in the kitchen and, knowing full well the reason behind it, gave us a job to do safely away from the farmhouse.

'Jane's replacement arrives today, and will need collecting from the station.'

Belinda saw a chance to stall further. 'What's she called? And is she nice?'

'She's called Jessie. Well, Frances Jessica, but she likes to be known by Jessie. And yes, of course she's nice. She's the daughter of an old friend of mine.'

'Another Frances? Where's she coming from?'

'Stop chattering! I know you're only trying to fill time. Anyway, Jessie's finished her training, and arrives in Princetown on the mid-morning train. You're to take the trap and fetch her.'

'Which one of us?' I asked, hoping it would be Belinda. She was hoping it would be me.

'Both of you,' Frances said firmly. 'I want young Will and his friend to have time to talk things over, without the likes of you silly girls poking your noses in. I'm sure Evie will tell you all she feels you need to know, later on.'

'But we don't *both* need to go!' Belinda protested, and Frances shrugged.

'All right then. Kitty can take the trap, and you can finish out in the barn since I notice you've still got two corners to clear.'

I saw Bel weighing up the options of a ride out to Princetown, fresh air, and a first glimpse at the new girl, against the gloom of an old barn, spiders, and the smell of damp hessian and droppings.

'Perhaps her bags will be heavy,' I said helpfully. 'I'm not sure I could manage alone.'

'Oh all right,' Belinda agreed. 'I'll come and help.'

Frances gave one of her rare chuckles. 'Speaking of bags, don't forget to take something to tie them down with. You don't want them flying off in the road. If you get the trap ready now you'll be in plenty of time to meet the train.'

Belinda and I escaped with sighs of relief, and later, as we drove up to Princetown, I speculated on the new arrival. 'She's had some training then. Did you have any?'

'I did, yes, but it's only four weeks in any case,' Belinda pointed out. 'You can't learn a lot in that time, and you don't really know what you're doing until you've seen a full year on a farm. Then again, if she already knows Mrs Adams she won't have to worry about getting into bother over mistakes.'

Her slightly gloomy tone told me she was thinking of her own numerous instances of *bother,* and I smiled in sympathy and changed the subject. 'Was Jane sad to leave?'

She nodded. 'She did like it here, but one of us had to take care of Mother, and Jane's got far more about her than I have. More patience too. I wonder if this new girl really wanted to do this, or if she'd rather have been off nursing or something.'

'Like you would?'

96

Belinda had made it quite obvious she'd have loved to have taken my place in Flanders when Evie had gone back there earlier in the year, despite her general squeamishness. 'Do you think you'd have made a good nurse?'

'Probably not,' she said. 'But I'm sure I'd have made a rattling good ambulance driver.'

I looked at her, guiding the pony with a practised, elegant hand, and wondered what she believed it was like out there. Did she think we sat quietly behind the wheel while we were loaded up, then drove up the road and waited again, chatting with orderlies and doctors while they lifted out the quiet, smilingly grateful soldiers? I shook my head, and she saw me from the corner of her eye.

'You may think I'm a bit silly,' she said, a little tightly, 'but I can drive, at least.'

'There's more to ambulance driving than driving ambulances,' I said. 'It's truly awful out there, Bel. You should think yourself lucky to be here.' I waved to encompass the hedges, the fields and the uneven, but relatively smooth road.

'Evie doesn't feel a bit lucky,' Belinda said. 'She hates it here; she can't wait to get back.'

'It's different for her,' I said quietly. For a moment we drove on in silence, then Belinda cleared her throat.

'Look, it's a lovely day. We've practically been banned from the house... Why don't we have some fun while we're out? We've ages before the train.'

I perked up. 'What kind of fun?'

'While you were harnessing Pippin I went into the barn, to get some rope for Jessie's bags.' She glanced over her shoulder into the trap. 'Found something else as well.' I followed her gaze and saw a bag, wedged upright in the corner, and the clear outline of a bottle inside it. 'Go on,' she said. 'There's plenty left.'

'Frances will be furious!' I breathed in dark delight.

'Not with you,' Belinda said wryly. 'You can't do anything wrong for her. She won't find out anyway.'

'What if she does?' Frances had a way of just *knowing* things. It was uncanny.

'She won't! All right, if she does, we'll have to say it was your idea, then neither of us will take a strafing.'

I remembered feeling woozy and uncomfortable last night, but as I started to say so, a breeze lifted my hair, and almost took my hat off, and I also remembered I'd only felt horrible once I'd gone indoors. A moment later I scrambled into the back and seized the bottle.

'Salut,' I said, and pulled the cork out with my teeth. I climbed back onto the front seat, and took a drink before passing the bottle over.

'Cheers,' Belinda said, and did likewise. 'Almost there, better drink up before someone sees us.'

After a minute she took the bottle off me, and peered into it with an expression of disappointment. 'You drank more last night than I thought,' she complained. 'Either that, or you've drunk a lot more now.' She threw the bottle back over her shoulder, where it landed on the floor of the trap and rolled under the seat. 'There. Out of sight, out of mind. We must be sure to tell Nathan it went down well.'

'What do you think of him?' I asked, curious. 'I mean, I know he's good-looking, but Evie obviously doesn't rate him, and she's met him before.'

'I tend to trust a man who's not afraid to cry in front of strangers. And besides, Evie didn't know who he was. It's Will he's hurt, and if Will forgives him, who are we to judge?'

'You're right.' The pleasant part of the wine-hum was back now, and I squinted through the midday sunshine at the grey little village. 'It's lovely here.'

She gave me an amused look. 'Drunk a lot more now,' she decided, and I aimed a light blow at her arm.

'All right, it's not pretty, but it's very dramatic. Especially compared to Ecclesley.'

'Will you ever go back there, d'you think?'

I shrugged. The wine had loosened my tongue or I would never have said, 'Perhaps. I miss my family, even though they don't miss me.' Then I cleared my throat, hurrying on before she could press me any further. 'Slow down – station ahead on the left.'

'I know. I was born here!' But instead of turning in, she urged Pippin on with a flick of the reins. 'I want to show you something first.'

As we passed out of the village my gaze was drawn down to our right, where the fields fell away to meet the stone wall that housed the massive and notorious Dartmoor Prison. Although since the prisoners had all been freed for service, they called it the Princetown Work Centre. Small figures still worked in the fields just outside the wall – a party

99

of conscientious objectors. I thought, with a twist of sorrow, about Oliver in his London prison, with none of this stark but beautiful landscape to take some of the grim loneliness away from his days.

But Bel wasn't interested in the prison. She drew to a stop, instead, just beyond the sawmill on the outskirts of the village. 'Look, what do you see there?' She pointed into the field that lay immediately behind the smaller one by the road, and I squinted.

'A horse.'

'Not just a *horse!* Look again.'

I did so, and realised I was looking at something altogether more special than a lumber-lugging workhorse. The animal grazed, calmly unaware of his audience, and the smooth, clean legs shifted slightly in the grass as he moved to a fresh clump. It was hard to look away again.

'I come here all the time to look at the horses,' Belinda said, and her voice had dropped. 'But now most of them have been called up there're usually just workhorses left. I saw this one when I dropped Jane back home last week.'

'Where did he come from then?' I realised my voice had taken on the same hushed tones, as if we stood right next to the animal and didn't want to startle him.

'According to Jane it's on loan from the ARS.'

'The what?'

'The Army Remount Service. It's a stud.' She paused, and her expression altered subtly, but tellingly. 'I used to ride Mrs Adams's horses, you know, before they were called up. I miss it.'

I looked at her with dawning suspicion. 'You're

not suggesting you try and ride that thorough-bred. Are you completely mad?'

In answer, Belinda threw Pippin's reins to me, and climbed into the trap to start rummaging under the seat. She pulled out the rope we'd brought with us to tie down Jessie's bags, around twenty feet of it, and shoved a few sacks out of the way to make a space on the floor of the trap. She looked at it for a moment, considering, and swiftly tied two simple knots around a foot apart along its length; I could feel my eyes narrow, recognising the technique but hoping I was wrong. Then she knelt down, and, with her tongue firmly locked be-tween her teeth, she laid the rope out, and began tying a series of further, more intricate knots.

I resigned myself to the fact that I'd been right, and sighed. 'You're making a halter.'

Belinda looked up briefly, and grinned. 'Come on, Kitty! I said we should have some fun!'

'But that horse is huge!' I looked over at the field again and tried to guess just how huge. 'Probably at least seventeen hands.'

'Ah, you know about horses.'

'I used to ride. I didn't have my own horse, like Evie did, but some friends of my parents used to let Oli and me ride theirs.' I couldn't bring myself to mention that Archie had been my more fre-quent companion, and that he was the most natural horseman I had ever seen – it had been a joy, even before I'd acknowledged my more mature feelings for him, to watch him on horse-back. 'I've never ridden anything bigger than fif-teen hands though,' I said, 'and never bareback.'

'Then it's high time you did.' Belinda looked

critically at the mess of rope in front of her, then she picked up an end, threaded it over and under one of the bigger knots in the middle, and the tangled rope seemed to melt into the right shape. 'There!' She took Pippin's reins out of my hands and hooked them securely over the fence post. Her voice turned wistful. 'Embrace life, Kitty. Find the fun where you can. God knows it's grim enough the rest of the time.'

She was right. I looked from her to the field, and felt the wine doing its dangerous work again. Suddenly I didn't care. 'Come on then!'

Chapter Seven

Belinda and I ran, crouched low and laughing, across the field that lay alongside the yard of the sawmill, and, hugging the hedgerow, we followed it to the wall at the top. Belinda went up first, finding handholds easily in the stones, and dropping down the other side. My head was still buzzing a little, but rather than hindering me, it seemed to take away my hesitation and tension, and before I realised it I was thudding to the ground beside her.

The stallion raised his head and sniffed the air, but did not appear likely to bolt. I took a moment to appreciate the splendour of him; his chestnut coat gave off waves of light that changed from minute to minute, flashes of deep red against the brown, and I imagined how it would feel to be up there on his back, feeling him respond to my movements...

'Watch the house,' Belinda whispered.

My blood thrumming, I glanced behind us but there was no movement from the yard of the timber mill. When I looked back Belinda was carefully walking towards the horse, letting him see her but keeping the halter down at her side; she was clearly an expert, and I relaxed as she ran a practised hand down the stallion's long nose, then stepped up to stand alongside him, patting his neck. He stamped and snorted, and I turned to check the yard again, but no-one came out of any of the large sheds to investigate. Somewhere in my clouded thoughts I wondered what the time was, and how long we had been here, but I was distracted by the little thrill of shared triumph as Belinda slipped the halter beneath the stallion's head, and, in one quick movement, drew it over his nose and cheek.

To our surprise, he stood stock-still as soon as he felt the touch of the rope, and Belinda turned to me with a grin of delight and gestured me over. 'Slow,' she cautioned, but she hadn't needed to warn me. I was used to far more skittish horses. Standing this close to the thoroughbred made me realise just how huge he really was; straddling his back seemed an impossibility, and I didn't know how Belinda would manage, but when I glanced to the side I saw her stooping to make a stirrup with her hands.

'Me? I'm not going first!'

'Yes, you are, come on.'

I didn't give myself time to think. I just slipped

my foot into her linked hands, and she boosted me up until I was able to throw my right leg over the stallion's back. He shifted again, and his head dropped, but he didn't sidestep, or make a sound, and the memories came sweeping back as I picked up the makeshift rein, feeling my fingers move to let the rough rope slide into place.

Belinda's face, turned up to me, was shining. She looked like a child at that moment, and her excitement found its echo in me ... I was nineteen, not ninety; I'd missed out on so much fun, and the war showed no signs of ending; this might be my last chance for a long time. Maybe ever.

Belinda must have seen something of this in my face, because she nodded and stepped back. 'I'll keep watch. Go on; just don't let him jump the gate into the road.'

'We have to name him,' I said, 'just for today.'

She thought for a moment, then glanced at the timber yard and smiled. 'Woody?'

'Perfect!' I sat up straight, missing the solid feel of a stirrup beneath my feet, and gently pressed with my knees. Nothing happened. I pressed harder, still nothing, then I brought my heels in, and Woody took off.

The field flew by beneath us, and before I had time to realise what had happened, we had reached the top corner, and I could feel Woody's strides shortening, and the muscles beneath my legs bunching. At least it wasn't the gate at the bottom of the field, but this wall was no small thing either and, panicked, I gripped tighter with my knees, wondering why on earth I'd thought I could do this without a saddle. My fingers let go of the rope and instead twisted into Woody's mane, and I fought the urge to lie down over his neck and wrap my arms around him, and then we were up, and over. As we landed I felt my grip slipping, and my breath stopped until I settled into the rhythm again. I slowly sat up straight and let go of Woody's mane, relaxing and letting myself once more enjoy the sensation of grace and power afforded me by this unexpected and thrilling experience.

This field currently housed a few sheep, who raised their heads and stared at us thundering towards them, before slowly bunching together and shuffling off out of the way. I laughed aloud at their casual, almost resigned acceptance of the intrusion, and I liked the way that laughter sounded, combined with the thudding of hooves on summer-thick grass. I couldn't pretend I had any real control over Woody's flight, but I could tell both of us were enjoying it. I'd once been carried off by a frightened pony, and that sensation had been completely different; the pony had faltered and jerked, its head was down, and I'd had the feeling that at any moment it might have stopped dead, sending me sailing over its head. Woody, however, was stretching his long legs out, and his canter was smooth and easy, loping over the grass, rounding the field at the top and following the wall along to the far corner.

The last remnants of a strong wine drunk too quickly had faded as soon as we'd begun moving, and everything was pushed to the back of my mind: worry about being seen, worry that we'd be late picking up the new girl, even the ache of missing Archie – such a constant companion now, that I barely noticed it – all fled beneath the appreciation of sharing this all-too-brief moment of utter freedom with this glorious, highly trained animal.

The merest touch with my left hand brought him around to face back down the field, and this time, when he took the wall, I was ready and leaned into his neck as he gathered himself and sailed over. Landing in his own field, with Belinda standing such a short distance away, it felt as if playtime was over. We had only been a few minutes, and I felt a shaft of resentment at having to stop so soon – what could she do if we just went around again, after all? I could pretend he'd just taken off. She'd never know...

But with great reluctance I eased Woody's canter gently back into a trot. We stopped in exactly the same place we'd started, and I made myself slide down, resenting the feel of solid ground under my boots again. Belinda was gazing at me with a deep admiration that only made it worse; I wanted to keep that look fixed on me, but it would soon fade now I was just Kitty again – frightened of everything, unable to face going back to Flanders, and not even particularly good at farmwork.

For now though, she was smiling. 'My turn. Boost me up – hurry, before someone comes!'

I tried to curb the lance of jealousy as I saw her settle into place on Woody's back, and gave him a last pat before I stood back. My heart was still pounding with exhilaration, but now it was mixed with trepidation as I heard a door slam in the distance. A moment later, an outraged yell cut

106

across the still air, and Belinda and I both jerked in shock; she must have pulled back on the rope halter, and Woody's head came back, colliding with hers as she leaned forward to grip his mane just as I had done. She screamed in pain, and as I reached out to grasp the halter, Woody's hoof scraped down my shin and my shout startled him further. He backed up, unseating Belinda, who toppled off to land on the ground on his other side.

It all happened within seconds, and both the fear of discovery, and the burning pain in my shin, faded into unimportance as Woody trotted away, allowing me to see Belinda properly. Her face was covered with blood, and the tiny bits of skin that showed through the grisly mask were absolutely white. A glance at her foot showed why; it was still turned awkwardly beneath her where she'd landed, and from its position it must surely be broken.

'Bel,' I breathed in horror. 'Don't move!'

'Not likely,' she said through gritted teeth. I limped over to her, relieved to note that Woody was now pulling up grass once more, as if nothing had happened. Only the halter he wore gave away our activity, and I wondered if I could get to it and take it off before the sawmill owner reached us.

Belinda guessed what I was thinking. 'Leave it,' she mumbled. 'They know anyway.'

'We need to get help for you,' I said. 'Does your face hurt?'

'Not much. It's numb.' She looked up at me and, to my astonishment, actually smiled. With

107

the blood in her teeth it was a gruesome sight, but the smile was genuine. 'Just my luck, isn't it?' she said. 'A nice-looking bloke comes to stay, and here's me with a flattened nose.'

'And probably a broken ankle,' I pointed out, and she swallowed, the smile fading. She looked as if she might be sick.

'I don't want to move,' she said. 'Never again. Can I just stay here? Will you bring me food?'

I gave a little laugh. 'Maybe this man will have some sympathy when he sees you,' I said, gesturing at the figure, who had now come through the gate and was marching towards us. But it was a short-lived hope.

'You bloody little idiots!' he threw at us, as he walked straight past and went to Woody. 'You could have crippled him!'

'What about Be ... my friend?' I retorted.

'You needn't be shy about saying her name,' the man fumed. 'I know you're from Dark River Farm. It's written down the side of your bloody trap!'

'Well what about her? Aren't you going to help her?'

'Not yet,' he grunted. 'Not 'til I've checked you 'aven't done any damage to this 'orse.'

I watched, with grudging admiration, as he thoroughly checked each of Woody's legs, running his hands down each one, and all the while talking in a quiet, soothing murmur. Then he took hold of the home-made halter and led Woody up and down for a few minutes, his eyes missing nothing as he watched the placement of each hoof. Finally he slipped off the halter and

108

came back to stand in front of us.

'Which one of you made this?'

I remembered Belinda's idea that I should take the blame for any trouble, since I was a favourite of Frances. 'It was me,' I said. 'It was all my idea, I'm sorry. You can't blame Bel.'

The man turned pale blue eyes on me, and, now the immediate worry of injury to the loaned stallion was ruled out, he seemed to relax, if only a little. He wasn't much older than us, which surprised me. We weren't used to seeing men of fighting age around any more – at least, no-one who wasn't dressed in hospital blues. This man was probably between twenty-five and thirty, blunt-featured, with the ruddy complexion of an outdoorsman, and a rather scruffy head of sandy-coloured hair. I guessed his occupation must have exempted him from call-up, because he certainly looked healthy enough.

'This is a good little 'alter,' he said. I shot a glance at Belinda, but she didn't seem to care that I was taking the credit for her handiwork. Her head was down, her hair loosened from its pins and hanging in a pale curtain over her eyes, and she barely seemed aware there was anyone else here.

'Look, my friend is hurt,' I said. 'Please, can you help me get her back to the trap, and I'll take her home.'

The man shook his head, and now he looked annoyed again. 'Bring 'er into the 'ouse, and we'll see what's what.'

'I can't carry her, and she can't walk!'

He sighed, handed me the halter, then stooped

109

to lift Belinda. She gave a little yelp as her foot left the ground and swung free for a moment, before he settled her more comfortably and set off back towards the mill. I followed, my mind frantically searching for a reasonable explanation as to why we had seen fit to risk Woody's health, but of course there wasn't one. Frances would be furious with me when she found out, despite what Belinda seemed to think.

In the house, the man set Belinda down on the couch, and I was finally able to gather my scattered thoughts and set to work. I checked her ankle first, and after a few minutes' careful examination, I sat back on my heels. 'I don't think it is broken, after all.'

Belinda let her breath out in a shaky sigh of relief. 'What about my nose?'

'Hard to say. I'll clean it up in a moment, but first of all we need to stabilise your foot.'

'You a nurse?' the man said.

'No. But I'm Red Cross trained.' I thought, for a moment, that my efficiency had impressed him enough to have cooled his anger, but it hadn't. He merely handed me the things I asked for, without comment, and when I'd fixed a makeshift splint onto Belinda's ankle, and wiped her face clean of blood, he began his tirade all over again.

'You could've killed that 'orse! Do you have any idea how much he's worth? What the army would've said? Not to mention 'aving to go through the bloody process of a loan all over again, to get Lady in foal!' He continued in this vein for quite some time, before I glanced at the clock, and groaned, abandoning any notion of

110

tending to my own scraped shin.

'The train'll have been and gone by now. Jessie will be waiting.'

'Did you hear a word of what I just said?'

'Yes, and I'm sorry. But we're supposed to be picking someone up from the station. We have to go. Bel, can you walk if you lean on me?'

'I think so.' She looked at the mill owner, her eyes worried above her puffed and swollen nose. 'Will you be telling Mrs Adams?'

'I expect so,' he said. 'You 'ave to understand how dangerous it was, what you did.'

'We do!' I begged. 'Please, we don't have any horses at Dark River any more – just Pippin.'

'That don't make you special,' he said, his brows lowered. 'They took ours too, all except them that was needed. We 'ad some beauties, but the army've got 'em now, or they're more likely dead. Don't mean you can go around stealing rides when the fancy takes you.'

'No,' I said quietly. 'We understand that. It was just a silly idea and we've learned our lesson.'

But he was in full flow now. 'I mean, how would it look if I came over your place, and took your best cow just 'cos we ain't got any milk?'

I was beginning to lose my patience now. 'Look, Mr...?'

'Pearce.'

'Mr Pearce, we're sorry. We really are. If you do tell Mrs Adams, be sure and tell her it was my fault. But we have to go *now!* That poor girl we're collecting will think she's been forgotten.'

'And you are?'

'Kitty Maitland.'

'Kitty's fault. Right you are.'

I looked at him for a moment, unsure if he was teasing, but his face was grim. Well, nothing to be done now; I'd tried my best. 'Bel, come on.'

Belinda stood up, leaning on me, and took the halter from Mr Pearce. He followed us out to the trap, and I helped Belinda to climb onto the seat, where she loosened the knots in the halter with a few quick movements, and threw the rope back into the trap. I saw Mr Pearce's watching, one eyebrow arched slightly, but before he could say anything I picked up the reins and wheeled the cart around to drive back towards the station.

The platform was empty, as was the turntable; the train had long since begun its return journey, and the passengers dispersed.

'Well where on earth is she?' Belinda said. Her voice was starting to sound very nasal, and when I looked at her I saw her nose was even more swollen now. I winced, but didn't mention it; it would only upset her more.

'She knows the farm. Do you think she might have begun to walk?'

'She must have.' Belinda sighed. 'This is all we need. She's bound to be really cross, and blab to Mrs Adams.'

'She might not. She might be very sweet,' I said, turning Pippin around once more. I hoped I was right; we were in enough trouble as it was. 'Mr Pearce knows full well it was you who made the halter,' I added idly, as we set off back to the farm. 'I saw him looking at you dismantling it.'

'I didn't really mean for you to take the blame

112

anyway,' Belinda said. 'I only said that when I thought nothing could possibly go wrong.'

'Whereas actually, nothing has gone right,' I pointed out, and we continued in gloomy silence until, up ahead, we spotted a dark-clad figure with two cases, one particularly heavy-looking. 'There!'

We rattled up alongside the girl, who looked up at us, then at the name on the side of the cart. A smile broke across a pleasant, heart-shaped face. 'Oh, I'm so pleased to see you. I thought no-one had remembered I was coming!'

Belinda and I slumped in relief, and the girl passed up the lightest of her cases, before taking my proffered hand and climbing up to sit in the back, dragging the heavy one up behind her.

'I'm Kitty Maitland,' I said, 'and this is Belinda Frier.'

'So nice to meet you, I'm Jessie Goulding. What on earth's happened to your nose?'

Belinda and I looked at one another and I pulled a face; we hadn't even considered what we'd say when the inevitable questions started. If we told the truth we'd get into awful trouble for sure, but that might be unnecessary trouble, and avoided by a little white lie. Without knowing whether Mr Pearce was going to tell Frances what we'd done, could we risk having that misdemeanour to add to our list if the truth did come out?

Jessie smiled. 'Were you doing something you shouldn't have been?' Again, we looked at each other and said nothing. 'It's all right,' Jessie said. 'I won't tell. I promise. Frances can be a bit strict, can't she?'

I felt a surprising jolt of jealousy at the casual

113

way this girl spoke about Frances, and wondered how close they really were. 'Thank you,' I said, shooting a pointed look at Bel, who tried to smile, but her poor face really did look swollen now and she couldn't be blamed for the grimace that had to suffice.

As we drew nearer the farm I glanced into the back of the trap, and noticed Jessie sitting more upright. Her face had lit up, and she looked lively and interesting as she twisted and turned her head as if trying to take in all the familiar things at once. She caught me looking, and smiled again, and I smiled back; perhaps we'd become friends. We seemed to be of an age after all. A best friend could be closer than a sister, I'd heard, but having had neither I could only wonder. Evie, while I loved and admired her, was a crucial few years older and married, and in any case she had Lizzy – our brief closeness in Flanders was from another time, another world.

As for Belinda, I had fun with her, and had even opened up a little when I'd been drunk, but we were chums, not close friends. I liked her enormously, but didn't wholly trust her to be the kind of person I could rely on. Perhaps then, Jessie Goulding and I were destined to find that kind of unbreakable friendship... I settled against the hard seat back, hoping that would be the case, and making up my mind to do all I could to bring it about.

I pulled Pippin to a stop in the yard, and caught sight of two figures walking up through the field towards the wood. One taller, but walking stiffly and a little hunched, the shorter one very straight-

114

backed, and gesturing with his hands, clearly agitated in his speech. Curiosity burned as I remembered that strange, emotional exchange last night; what on earth had Nathan done to Will all those years ago?

'It looks exactly the same as I remember it,' Jessie said, with quiet satisfaction.

I turned back to see her climbing down from the trap. 'When were you here last?'

'I suppose I must have been around ten or eleven. Frances usually visits us instead, but I do remember coming here when my mother wasn't well.'

'And how old are you now?'

'I'm twenty-one.'

'Can you two stop chattering,' Belinda said through gritted teeth, 'and bloody well help me down off this seat? My ankle has seized up.'

We took Bel's hands, helping her to slide off the seat and land more lightly than she would have been able to otherwise. Then she put an arm around my shoulder, and I shot Jessie an apologetic look as I left her to carry both her own bags again, and helped Bel into the kitchen. Jessie didn't complain, simply picked up her belongings and followed us indoors where Lizzy and Sally were preparing lunch.

'Gracious!' Lizzy put down her vegetable knife in alarm, and came over to help Bel into a seat. 'What *have* you been doing? Are you all right?'

'Quite all right, thank you,' Bel mumbled, sounding more nasal than ever.

'It's my fault,' Jessie put in quickly, and smiled and held out her hand. 'You must be Lizzy. Frances has told me so much about you. I'm Jessie Goulding.' She sighed. 'I'm afraid Belinda slipped and fell from the trap while she was helping me to load my bags. I feel awful about the whole thing.'

Belinda's mouth dropped open, but she nodded quickly. 'Don't worry. It wasn't your fault at all. I was in too much of a rush to get home.'

'You're always in too much of a rush about everything,' Lizzy scolded gently, and tilted Belinda's face up to catch the light from the window. 'You've managed to give yourself quite a wallop there. Kitty, could you fetch a wet cloth? Bel's nose is bleeding a bit.'

'It's better than it was,' I said, dampening a cloth at the sink. 'We cleaned it up, but I expect the jolting of the trap started it off again.'

'How about that foot?' Lizzy wanted to know, frowning at the splint I'd put on. 'Is it broken? We'll have to get Dr Nichols over.'

'It's not broken,' I said, and passed the cloth to her. 'I thought it was but I had a good look at it, and I'm sure it's just sprained.'

'Well you'd know,' Lizzy said, smiling at me with a warmth that made me feel clever again, for a minute. She could always do that. 'Well done, Kitty.'

I blushed, and glanced at Jessie, who was eyeing me with a new speculation in her expression. Perhaps Lizzy's words had given her a good impression of me; I hoped so. I tried to send her a look of gratitude for her quick thinking, but I don't know if she read it correctly, and we were both soon distracted by Belinda's little whimpers as Lizzy gently wiped the fresh blood from her face.

'I'll show you to your room,' I said to Jessie, and picked up one of her cases. It turned out to be the heavy one and I grunted with surprise. She picked up the other, and followed me upstairs to the room we knew as the dorm. Jane had left her part of the three-bed room as neat as Bel's was scruffy. The bed was stripped down, and the cupboard by its side was polished, the little jug and bowl set just so in the centre of the linen square, the drawers freshly lined with paper ready for Jessie's possessions. Reflecting that Jane was, indeed, the best person to be taking care of hers and Bel's mother, I put Jessie's case on the bed and bent to unbuckle the straps.

'There, I'll just leave you to–'

'This isn't my room.'

I blinked. 'Um, well, this is where Jane slept, and since you're replacing Jane I thought–'

'Whenever I come to stay I sleep in the room next door. The yellow room.'

'Oh, but that's...' It was on the tip of my tongue to tell her it was my room, but she did have a prior claim after all. And it might be quite fun to share with Sally and Bel. 'I'll move my things in here then,' I said instead.

'Thanks lots,' Jessie said, and smiled again. 'It's only what I'm used to, d'you see?'

'Of course.' I buckled up the case again and slid it off the bed. How on earth had she managed to carry the blessed things so far before we caught up with her? This one felt as if it were filled with rocks.

'I'll help you change the bedding after lunch,' I offered, and she nodded her thanks. 'What's in this

117

case?' I asked, before realising how that sounded. 'I'm sorry. That was quite rude of me.'

'That's all right,' she said. 'I should have carried that one. It's far heavier than this. It's got my books in it.'

'You like to read? I do, too.' I was itching to see what books she had, hopeful of the kind of conversations I'd often had with Lizzy's younger sister, Emily, but she had turned away, so I just took some clothes from the drawer and carried them next door to the dorm.

On my way past the yellow room again I poked my head around the door. 'I'll see you downstairs. I'm going to help with lunch.'

In fact I was intending to slip out of the front and follow the path Will and Nathan had taken up to the woods. Jessie would be a while sorting her things out, and the others were busy in the kitchen. It was the perfect time to seize some of that excitement that still bubbled around inside me. I was desperate to find out the truth behind Nathan's past, and even better, to be able to tell Belinda before she found out for herself. If either of the men saw me I could always pretend to be looking for Frances.

But as my foot crossed the threshold, and my heart started to speed up in anticipation, I heard Jessie's voice cut through the small hallway from halfway down the stairs.

'Oh, there you are, Kitty!'

I stopped, hissing a quick, impatient breath, before turning back. 'Yes, here I am. Are you settled?'

'Oh, nowhere near,' she said cheerfully, 'but we

have plenty of time for that. I was hoping to see Frances first.'

'She'll be out clipping sheep,' I said. 'Would you like to sit down with a cup of tea? I'll go and find her for you.' The perfect excuse. Now I was on the outside step, feeling the sun and the breeze, with freedom just a door slam away.

'Will she be back for lunch?' Jessie wanted to know.

'Probably not. While the weather's this good she'll want to see it through. Shall I go and find her then?'

Jessie shook her head, looking disappointed. 'Not on my account. I'm keen to see how Belinda is though, aren't you?'

I hesitated, then sighed. 'Yes, of course.' I stepped reluctantly back over the threshold. 'It was good of you to say what you did. You know, about her falling off the cart.'

Jessie turned back with a smile. 'Oh, I could tell you two had been up to something,' she said. 'I bet it was fun. Perhaps you'll tell me later?'

'I will,' I promised, hopes of a friendship re-kindled, and quashing my sense of mild annoy-ance at being turfed out of my room.

In the kitchen Belinda was sitting with a cold cloth pressed to her nose, and with her foot propped on a chair piled high with cushions. Lizzy and Sally were cleaning up the lunch preparations, and Jessie sat down while I went to the cutlery drawer.

'Does Frances have help now that Harry's ... gone?' she asked.

'She still has Colin Trebilcock, him who

119

collects the milk,' Lizzy said. 'He was too old to join up, but he's healthy enough, and he comes over to help with some of the heavier work. Other than that, she's learned to ask now and again in the village.'

'Swallowed her pride then,' Jessie said. 'Well people will be quite happy to help. Harry was a popular man.'

I felt that tug of jealousy again. She had only been here half an hour, if that, and already it was clear she knew more about the farm than I did. I was starting to feel edged out again, despite Frances's heartfelt declaration that I was family now. I shook myself mentally; there was room for both of us, after all.

'How was your training?' I asked, meaning to sound friendly and interested, but too late I realised I had merely sounded exactly the way I was feeling about myself – making the point that she was the new girl here. I could have kicked myself, particularly when Jessie's embarrassed look told me she'd heard it in just that way.

'We didn't really learn very much,' she said, 'not in the time we were given. But I've learned enough about safety to be reasonably sure I won't chop off any limbs, or...' she flicked a sudden grin at Belinda '...fall out of a pony trap and break my nose.'

Lizzy snorted laughter, and the faintly strained atmosphere was broken. 'I should hope not,' she said. 'Right, Bel, that cloth should have done the trick now. Kitty, run and fetch some water, please. Jessie, if you wouldn't mind, perhaps you could take the plates out of the aga? Sally, the vegetables

120

should be ready for straining now.'

Within moments the kitchen was a mass of activity, and Jessie moved quickly, and without question, to carry out the task assigned her. There was something about Lizzy's calm authority that had the same effect on almost everyone who met her, and even Belinda obeyed her without pause, with the result that, five minutes later, we were all sitting down to a hot, beautifully cooked midday meal.

'Which bedroom is yours?' Jessie asked Lizzy, tearing off a chunk of bread and dipping it into the rich, dark gravy on her plate.

'I live a little way down the road, nearer the village,' Lizzy said. 'I did live here for a while, but I moved back into Ma's house with her, Emily and the twins.'

'And what do they do?'

'Adie and Albert are only little still, so they're at school. When it's not being closed down,' she added with a sigh. 'Emily, that's my sister, works at Devonport Technical School.'

'Is she a teacher?' Jessie looked impressed, but Lizzy shook her head, smiling.

'No, it's been taken over to put shell casings together. That's what she's doing.'

'I didn't realise they were making bombs there,' I said with a little shudder, hearing the phantom sounds of Flanders.

'It's only the casings,' Lizzy reiterated. 'They get sent to Bristol for the charges and fuses and things. I know which end I'd rather be working at.'

I nodded agreement. 'What about your mother?'

121

We hardly ever talked about Lizzy's family, and it had been Jessie who'd led the way. I felt bad about that and determined to make up for it.

'Ma's just started working up at Princetown, at the moss-drying plant.'

'Boss?' Belinda asked, and frowned, trying again. 'Mm-moss?'

I tried not to giggle, but she caught my expression and flicked a pea off her fork at me.

'Belinda!' Lizzy cuffed her arm, and Belinda glared at me, but I saw her mouth twitch. She knew how funny it sounded, and she poked her tongue at me out to hide the smile.

'Sphagnum moss,' Lizzy said. 'For field dressings.'

Jessie lit up with interest. 'What a brilliant thing! How do they get it dried out?'

Lizzy began to explain the process, and I listened too, quite interested until the door opened and Will and Nathan came in. Belinda and I exchanged wide-eyed looks, and she grabbed her napkin and lifted it to cover her nose while I turned my attention back to them. Will was looking tired, and his hand was wrapped across his waist – I was glad Evie wasn't here to see that. But Lizzy was, which was the next worst thing.

She was on her feet in seconds. 'Will, sit down.'

He dropped a kiss on her forehead. 'I'm well; don't worry. Just walked a bit too far.' He nevertheless eased himself into the vacated seat, and let out a slow, careful breath. He was always taken by surprise that he wasn't able to move with his former vigour.

'Don't tell Evie,' he pleaded, and Lizzy looked

at him for a long moment, then her cross, worried expression faded.

'I won't, if you'll promise to let him–' she nodded at Nathan '–take on the lion's share now.'

'Agreed,' Will said, and grinned. It was easy to see why Evie had fallen for him when he did that, and Belinda even took her eyes off Nathan for a moment and responded with a tiny smile of her own, visible above the napkin that still covered her swollen nose.

Abruptly Archie's face floated to the front of my mind, and I saw his own grin – slightly lopsided, shaping his face to something unique and beautiful ... eyes of an unusually changing grey, with his bold, dark eyebrows making them appear all the more piercing. I remembered the look in those eyes when I'd turned him down, and the pain that shot through me almost made me gasp out loud and I took a hurried gulp of water.

'So, did you two sort things out?' Belinda asked, impatient for details.

Nathan leaned against the door, and nodded, but his eyes were on me. 'I've explained everything,' he said, 'and Will understands. I hope that means you'll take his word that I'm no rogue?'

'Oh, you're a rogue all right,' Will said, 'but I do understand a bit more now.'

'What did he do? Tell us!'

'Bel! It's not for us to ask that.' I felt the weight of Nathan's gaze again and let my eyes rise, until they met his. I saw a glint in them as his lips curved into a smile, then he shifted his gaze to Belinda, and raised a questioning eyebrow. Belinda gave a resigned sigh, and lowered the napkin.

'Hell's bells!' Will exclaimed, and Lizzy chuckled.

'Bel's hell, perhaps. Poor girl fell out of the pony trap.'

I winced, thinking it made Belinda sound a bit foolish. 'She *was* only trying to help,' I said quickly. 'It was Pippin's fault. The silly thing wouldn't keep still.'

'Exactly,' Belinda said. 'And I'll have you know I'm really quite badly hurt.'

'You poor thing,' Nathan murmured, and she gave him a gratified look.

'You need to keep that foot raised,' Lizzy said. 'As soon as you've finished lunch, go to your room and lie down. Kitty can bring you some cushions to rest your ankle on.'

'But I don't want to spend the afternoon up there,' Belinda protested. Her eyes flicked from Will to Nathan and back again, and it was obvious she thought she'd be missing something.

'It's either that or finish off out in the barn,' Lizzy said. In Frances's absence she slipped easily and naturally into the role of leader, and Bel subsided with a disappointed, but thankfully not grumpy look. Belinda disappointed was one thing, and easy enough to remedy, but Belinda grumpy turned everything grey.

'I'm moving my things into your room too,' I told her, hoping it would cheer her up.

'Why?'

'Because Jessie always has the yellow room when she comes here.' Too late I realised I'd once again picked the wrong thing to say, and I groaned inwardly.

124

Predictably, and momentarily forgetting how Jessie had spoken up in her favour, Belinda scowled. 'That's hardly fair, Jessie. You've not been here for about ten years.'

'That's enough, Belinda,' Lizzy broke in. She looked at the three of us – myself wondering if I'd spoken out of turn, Belinda looking cross on my behalf, and Jessie blushing and clearly wishing she'd said nothing about the bedroom at all.

In another attempt to steer the conversation onto something pleasant, I told Lizzy that Jessie had brought lots of books with her. 'Perhaps she and Emily might like to look at each other's collections,' I said. 'Lizzy's sister is a great reader too, Jessie.'

'That would be lovely, if Jessie doesn't mind.' Lizzy smiled at the new girl. 'Emily is about your age, Jessie. I'm sure you'd get on very well.'

Jessie smiled back. 'I'd like to meet her.'

'She's not home today. She's taken a trip down to Cornwall, but that probably means she'll come back with even more books for you to look at. There's a bookshop down there that she loves.'

'I've never been to Cornwall,' I put in, 'but it would be nice to visit one day with Emily. We got along famously the last time I was here. I think she mentioned the shop then. Something to do with an attic?'

'Penhaligon's Attic.' Lizzy nodded. 'It's in Caernoweth. Lovely place. I'd like to go down there again myself sometime. Jack would love it.' Her expression lost some of its lively enthusiasm for a second, but it soon returned. 'Perhaps we can all go down there together, after the harvest is in. I'd

125

like to see Freya again too, the girl who lives there.'

'That would be wonderful,' Jessie said. 'I adore Cornwall.'

'Evie and I would like that too,' Will said, and Nathan's face darkened slightly. I wondered, at first, if it was the mention of Evie. Perhaps Nathan's antagonism towards her was disguising the fact that he had once carried a torch for her? Then I realised it would more likely because we were speaking of things that must, by necessity, happen after he returned to the fighting. Harvest wouldn't be for another few months yet. He would be long gone from Dark River by then and it must be an awful thought for him.

I told Jessie I'd help her with the rest of her things as soon as she was ready. 'Just let me know when,' I said, hopeful of a more pleasant relationship with this oddly unsettling girl now we'd found a common interest.

'I still think it's wrong that you've been turfed out of your room,' Belinda said.

I shot her an annoyed look. 'It's all right, Bel, really. I don't mind. Jessie's known Frances much longer, after all.'

Jessie's expression sharpened, and her smile dropped, and I recognised the same vague and formless sense of rivalry I'd felt in myself earlier. It must have simply been because I'd used Frances's first name. I swallowed a sigh; any path to possible friendship between us would clearly not be as smooth as I'd hoped.

Chapter Eight

'We're moving those old wet sacks out, and spreading them in the yard to dry.' I handed Jessie a broom. 'Hit them first, to send the rats running.'

'Rats?' Jessie looked doubtfully at the big pile in the corner of the barn.

'There aren't many,' I assured her. 'I suppose you were too young to help out when you were here before?'

'I collected the eggs,' she said, 'and fed the hens. And sometimes helped sweep out the henhouses.'

'Well ... just look on this as sweeping out a very large henhouse, and imagine the hens are small and brown, with long tails.'

She gave me an amused look, and lifted her broom, bringing it down on the top of the pile without hesitation. Nothing stirred within, and she nudged it with her foot. 'I think we're hen-free here.'

I laughed, and set to work on the opposite corner, watching her from the corner of my eye. I still couldn't decide how I felt about her; one minute she seemed keen and eager to help, friendly and a little shy, but there was clearly a wire running through her that twanged, as jarringly as mine, whenever her sense of belonging was challenged. This was made very apparent around half an hour later, when we'd emptied the barn of damp and frayed sacks, and were kneeling out in

127

the yard, spreading them to dry in the afternoon sun.

'Well, at work already, Jessie?' Frances pushed open the gate that led from the field, and we both looked up to see her face creased in a welcoming smile. Jessie crossed the yard between them at a run, and flung her arms around Frances who looked startled, but pleased, as she returned the embrace.

I tried to remember how long it had been since anyone held me like that, with the pure joy of seeing someone and not the sadness of impending goodbye, or with the helpless sympathy of one who wants to give comfort but has no words. I couldn't. I swallowed past a painful lump in my throat, and felt my eyes start to sting. What was wrong with me? This woman had taken me to her heart within hours of meeting me, and yet she'd had to beg me to call her by her first name. Evie had tried so hard to help me after the attack by Colonel Drewe, and I had pushed her away. Belinda only wanted to teach me to have fun, but I couldn't bring myself look on her as a confidante. And Archie ... but I choked that thought off.

'Well done, Kitty, sweetheart,' Frances said, keeping her arm around Jessie as they walked back towards me. 'But why isn't Belinda helping you?'

'She's hurt her foot,' I said, avoiding Jessie's eyes.

'Oh, that girl! What on earth has she done now?' She held up a hand as I began fumbling with the story. 'Never mind, I'll see her in a minute. I must say you've both done a wonderful job here.'

Frances let go of Jessie to reach out and remove a stray thread of sacking from where it had become caught in my curls. It was a small gesture, but an intimate one, and I hoped my smile reflected the surge of affection and gratitude I felt.

'Right, time to catch up, young lady,' she said to Jessie, who took her proffered hand but with a suddenly clouded expression. I couldn't deny my pleasure at the way Frances so obviously favoured me more highly than she might a regular Land Army girl, but I honestly tried to make it more about Frances and me than about Jessie and me. I remembered the moment on the ferry dock, her work-roughened hands either side of my face, the smile that broke through tears that had startled and moved me ... and I resolved to stop questioning my right to that sense of belonging. Frances had never given me cause to doubt her affection, so why had I always done so?

Relaxing into this new resolution, I left Frances and Jessie to their talk and went upstairs to see how Bel was getting on. Her foot was still obediently propped on the cushions I'd placed for her, but she clutched the little mirror she'd asked for, and when she saw me she raised it and looked at her swollen face again.

She sighed. 'Honestly, Kitty, why now?'

'Now?' I sat down on her bed, and gently checked the makeshift splint on her ankle. 'As opposed to when?'

'Well, for one thing, when there isn't a new girl just starting. I look like a freestyle wrestler.'

'And for another thing?' I looked at her sideways, with a knowing little smile, but she was still

129

gloomily gazing at her reflection. 'I'm sure Nathan remembers you quite well as the pretty girl he met in town,' I said comfortingly, and she flushed and lowered the mirror.

'Well naturally I'd like him to find me interesting and attractive,' she said, 'but knowing he tricked me into inviting him here has made me think twice about how attractive a person he is.'

'You deserve better,' I agreed. 'He's charming all right, but then so are a lot of men.'

'Absolutely.' She took a deep breath and let it out, effectively closing the subject. 'So, how is Jessie at farmwork?'

We talked for a while about our first impressions, and I mentioned Jessie's closeness to Frances.

Bel still frowned at the way I had been summarily removed from my own room, simply because the new girl might have used it once or twice as a child. 'She presumes an awful lot. I wouldn't expect to have my own room, and nor would Sally, but you're different. You're more like family.'

'Jessie doesn't know that,' I pointed out reasonably.

'Then perhaps she ought to. She and I should have a little chat; she's as much here to work as I am.'

'Gosh, Bel, you sound quite fierce!'

'Well, you're my friend, and while I'm stuck up here I'm not there to look out for you. Just don't let her push you around.'

'I won't,' I said, touched. 'Are you coming down for dinner?'

'Try and stop me. I'm bored as blazes up here. And–' she brightened '–we might find out why

130

Nathan has come here looking for Will.'

I smiled at her characteristic return to perkiness. 'I'll call you when we're ready.' I left her to her mirror, and as I closed the door I saw her prodding mournfully at her puffy nose, and wincing. Poor Bel! Still, at least she was no longer caught up in Nathan's spell; she was far too nice for him.

I was just finishing clearing the yard when Evie returned from work. I hadn't even heard the lorry that dropped her off at the top of the road. I had been too preoccupied thinking about Oliver; he'd be allowed to write and receive letters soon, and I was mentally preparing what I would say to him, how I would describe this new life, and whether or not I should ask him if he'd heard from 'the parents', as he called them. I didn't want to open any wounds that might be beginning to heal over.

I looked up as Evie came into the yard, her bag across her shoulder, her hat off, and her sleeves rolled back against the evening warmth. She put the bag down and came over to help me put away the last of the sacks, stacking them neatly in the now-swept corner of the barn.

'How's the new girl settling in?' she asked, as she closed the barn door.

'Well, I think. She and Frances are very close.'

'Yes, Lizzy was telling me. Frances knew Jessie's mother, quite some time ago when they were both living in Gloucester. Your trousers are filthy, by the way.'

I dusted them down. 'I thought Frances was from Tavistock?'

'She was, originally. Then again neither of us is

from Devon are we? Yet here we are. They met when they both worked at the same hotel.'

'Jessie doesn't say much about her mother. Perhaps they had a falling out?'

'Perhaps.' Evie took my arm as we walked back to the house. 'Have you seen Will today?'

'He and Nathan joined us for lunch. They went for a long walk in the woods, I think. They seem to have talked things through and reached some understanding.'

Evie looked across the yard towards the woodland path. Her expression was guarded, but I could see her blue eyes narrowing slightly, and it wasn't in reaction to the early evening sun. I followed her gaze.

I frowned, unsure if I'd said too much. 'Are you worried?'

She didn't answer at first, then seemed to shake off the shadow. 'No, not worried. Sad for Will, though.'

'What happened between them?' I asked softly.

'It doesn't sound so awful really,' Evie said, 'not when you compare it to everything that's happened since.' She guided me towards the low wall that kept the pigs in their sty, and we sat down. Evie ran her hands through her dishevelled hair and tried to tug it back into order, but quickly gave up. 'When they were very young, and lived in Blackpool, they were the best of friends. Nathan inherited an attic room in Breckenhall and asked Will if he wanted to go with him, to set themselves up an art studio.'

'I love Will's work,' I broke in, and Evie smiled, pride and love glowing in her expression.

132

'He's incredible,' she said quietly, and for a moment I thought I'd lost her; her eyes seemed focused on a different place, and a different time. Then she swam back. 'Nathan's very talented too. He's a painter. But no-one bought his work, and Will's small sales at market weren't enough to sustain them. One morning Will woke up to find Nathan had gone. No word, no note.'

'That's horrible.' I knew how it felt when someone close just vanished from your life. Betrayed and hurt barely scratched the surface.

'The real trouble was he'd left an unmanageable pile of debts,' Evie went on. 'He'd sold the studio, without telling Will, and so Will had to try and find work to pay off those debts, but he also had to leave the studio and find another home. That's when he took the job with the butcher.'

'Didn't you say his family were butchers too?'

'Yes.' Evie smiled suddenly, as if that question had brought back some private memory, but I didn't press her to share it.

'So Nathan didn't write, or come back at all?'

'Not until now,' Evie said, her smile dropping away. 'Which makes me wonder why. And how did he find us down here?'

'Maybe someone at Oaklands told him.'

'They wouldn't, I'm sure. More likely it was Martin, the boy who took over from Will as Mr Markham's apprentice when Will joined up.' She stood up and held out her hand. 'Anyway, Skittles, that's the whole sordid, but not very exciting story. Now, have you heard from Archie lately?'

'He writes,' I said, feeling my throat tighten when I thought about those letters – light-hearted,

133

even funny, confident and matter-of-fact. I loved to look at his slightly scrawly handwriting, yet it hurt a little too. Worse was the way I could actually hear the words, spoken in his softly accented voice. He had never again asked me to consider waiting for him, but now and again he would say something that made me realise we must talk; I had to tell him how it must be between us now, because while he had accepted that I didn't love him in the same way he loved me, he still believed we could be good friends. But I wasn't sure I could do it. How could I bear to be that close to him and not be touching him? Or watch him fall in love with someone else and have to stand by and smile, offering congratulations while my heart splintered as I knew it would? I had to decide whether to break from him completely, or to hold on to as much of him as I could without ruining his life.

I left Evie to wash and change out of her uniform, and almost went into my old room out of habit, before remembering Jessie. I longed for privacy, to lie down and let my mind reach out for Archie, but if I went to my new room I would have poor, bored Bel talking to me. So I went back out to sit in the barn, half my attention on waiting for Frances's call for help preparing the evening meal, the rest of it fading away, replaced by the memory of Archie's hand on mine, and his grey eyes glinting with humour and warmth. Before I'd told him no.

I was jolted out of a happy dream-state some time later, by the sound of the door creaking open. I sat very still, not yet ready to move and dispel the

134

pleasant warmth of the dream that lingered, and waited for either Sally's or Jessie's voice to drag me back to this tired reality. Instead I heard the flare of a match and, a moment later, a long, relieved exhalation.

'Bel?' I sat forward, peering around the hayloft ladder, blinking in the shadows. But it wasn't Belinda who looked back at me; it was Nathan.

He removed the cigarette from his lips with his finger and thumb, and squinted at me through the smoke. 'Why, it's pretty Kitty.'

I flushed. 'No, just plain Kitty.'

'Nothing plain about you, sweetheart,' Nathan insisted, and crossed the barn to where I sat. He was still not particularly close, but I didn't like the feeling of him looming over me, and stood up quickly. I immediately felt a little more in control, and my heartbeat settled a little bit.

I nodded at the cigarette. 'It's dangerous to do that in here.'

He looked at the glowing tip, then put it back in his mouth, speaking around it. 'You and Belinda didn't seem to mind last night.'

'That wasn't me; that was just Bel. Besides, your cough won't get any better if you keep smoking.'

He shrugged, and took a long pull. 'Want some?'

'No, thank you. Why are you here?'

'Here as in the barn, or here as in the farm?'

'Either. Both.'

'I'm at the farm because, as you know, I have amends to make for someone I once wronged. And I'm *here*...' he looked around us, at the high roof arcing over our heads, and at the dark corners

135

filled with farm tools and implements, and those freshly dried sacks '...because someone mentioned peeling potatoes, and I have a strong aversion to that kind of thing.'

I couldn't help laughing at that, and was rewarded by a slightly quizzical smile in return. 'You're hard to read, Miss Maitland. One moment all blushes and turning away, the next rather attractively cross, and then ... then that laugh.'

'What laugh? It's just a laugh.'

He dropped the barely smoked cigarette on the floor and, following the direction of my eyes he carefully twisted his boot onto it to put it out. 'Oh no, it's not,' he said softly. 'Your laugh is like...' he waved a hand '...trickling water. Cool and fresh on a hot day.'

'Don't be ridiculous!' I spluttered, trying not to laugh again in case he thought I was doing it on purpose. But he sounded so earnest it was hard not to. 'You're a charmer, Mr Beresford. I'm sure you've been told that more than once.'

'I have,' he admitted. 'But that doesn't mean I'm not saying what I really think.'

A silence dropped between us, and I found I didn't know what to do with my hands so I folded my arms.

'Ouch,' he said.

'What?'

He grinned. 'When a pretty girl folds her arms at you, you know you're in trouble.'

'Stop calling me pretty! Evie's pretty, and so is Lizzy. Belinda definitely is. But I know what I am, and I know what I'm not.'

'So you think it insulting, that I see you in a way

136

you see others but not in the way you see your-self?'

I didn't know how to answer that, so I dropped my arms back to my sides. 'There, is that better?'

'Much,' he said, and took a step closer. He brushed one finger down the length of my arm. 'Strong arms, but beautifully shaped,' he mused. 'You're a hard worker, Miss Maitland. Tell me...' he stepped away again, leaving me feeling a little light-headed '...is there someone you're waiting for? A handsome soldier, perhaps, holding your promise like a talisman to keep him safe?'

Again, I couldn't answer, but this time it was because my breath had caught so hard, and so tight in my chest, that it hurt to breathe. My heart screamed at me to tell him yes, my handsome soldier was Captain Archie Buchanan. He was strong, brave and loyal, he loved me and I loved him, and I would wait for him for ever ... but the word that echoed in the barn now was the same one that had cut his future loose from mine. 'No.'

'Good,' Nathan breathed. He moved closer again, and I looked at his warm, hazel eyes, the smile that put deep laughter lines around those eyes despite his youth, and his wide, generous mouth. That mouth drifted closer to mine, and, without thinking, I raised my face to his. This man was undoubtedly a scoundrel. His past and mine were both littered with casualties of our poor choices: my parents, Will, my lost child... We were a match, of sorts, the two of us, and if I didn't deserve a good man like Archie, then Nathan only deserved me.

As our lips met I pushed away the image of

Archie's smile, and the memory of our kiss, but as Nathan's hand rose to touch my breast I was suddenly not in the barn any longer, but in the back of a stinking ambulance. With a sharply indrawn breath that stuck in my throat, I stepped back, my blood racing, my hands bunched into fists. There was no gun in my side now, and the man in front of me was as far from Colonel Drewe as a man could be, but pushing Archie away had pushed away the only barrier between me and that dark, shocking memory.

'Don't be scared, little Kitty,' Nathan said softly, and reached out to take my tightly clenched hand. He didn't say any more, but gently began loosening my fist, finger by finger, while my breathing slowed and I searched deep inside myself for a way to accept the touch of another man; I couldn't live my life like this! I had to do it... Drewe would not destroy this part of my life as he had destroyed my family, and my work.

So I removed my hand from Nathan's, and placed it on his chest, then I kissed him. Firmly, without further hesitation, and with my lips parting beneath his to accept his gently probing tongue. It was an experiment, nothing more. The kiss held none of the heart-staggering joy of kissing Archie, and Nathan's slight body, so close to mine, felt almost like that of a boy when I compared it to the height and strength of the man I truly loved. But if there was no passion, and no deep, burning need to stay there for ever, at least there were no more flashes of horrific memory, no instinctive revulsion, no self-loathing for my weakness.

I felt Nathan's hands at my waist, and I raised my own to rest on his shoulders. I tried not to think of the way it had felt to slide my hands around the back of Archie's neck and touch the warm skin there, how his thick, soft hair had felt to my questing fingers, how his mouth had tasted of rum from the tot his company had shared in celebration of their safe return. But I remembered the feeling of his chest swelling with the breath we'd shared, the sweet frustration of not being able to press myself close enough to him, and how I'd wanted to touch every part of him at once.

I had no desire to explore Nathan's body further, and his tongue was starting to prod too far into my mouth – his mouth was wider than Archie's, and his lips less firm. His hand went to my breast again, squeezing gently, and this time I didn't pull away, not until I became aware that tears were sliding down my cheeks, and more were clogging my throat. At the same time I realised that, I heard an outraged shout that froze my blood.

'Kitty!'

Nathan thrust me away and I stumbled back, and we both turned to look at the doorway. Belinda stood there, resting heavily on a broom, the head of it cushioned beneath her arm.

'Bel? Are you... I'm–'

'Mrs Adams asked me to come and find you for dinner,' she said in a chilly voice, and turned and hobbled away.

'It was just a kiss, sweetheart,' Nathan said. 'You didn't do anything wrong.'

I didn't say anything, but flung him a dark look and hurried after Belinda. She was moving quite quickly, despite the awkwardness of using the broom as a walking stick, but I caught her up halfway across the yard. 'Bel, wait!'

'I don't care what you do,' she said, without turning. 'I just think that he's the wrong one to be doing it with.'

'I know!'

'Then why do it?' She stopped then, and swung around to face me. 'We've both agreed he's a rotten egg, haven't we?'

'I had to,' I said miserably.

She caught her breath, and her voice lowered to a whisper. 'What? You don't mean–'

'No,' I said quickly, 'not like that. I mean ... I didn't know if I could, you know, let a man touch me. I had to find out.' I hadn't told her about the kiss in Belgium. It was mine to hold and to remember.

'With *him?*'

'Who else is there? And it made me feel good that he wanted to.' I sighed. 'I didn't really enjoy it, but...'

'But it didn't make you scared,' she guessed, and reached out with her useful hand to take mine. 'I understand. But he's not to be trusted, darling. You know that.'

'I know. I won't do it again.'

'Does he know that?' She jerked her head in the direction of the barn.

I shrugged. 'I don't know, but he'll soon find out.'

Belinda looked at me, and gave a laugh that was more like a snort. 'That's my girl. Come on, Mrs Adams needs some help.'

After dinner, when Sally had gone to close up the hens for the night, and Lizzy had gone home, Belinda, myself, Evie and Frances finished our chores and sat chatting quietly in the sitting room until bedtime. I cherished times like these – they didn't happen every day; usually one or more of us would be working until it grew too dark, and we would often simply melt away to our beds without even seeing any of the others. But tonight was one of those nights where we all found ourselves in the sitting room at the same time, and a companionable peace was settling over us all. Jessie came in, and I gave her a little smile, which she returned before plucking a book from the shelf and curling up in the corner of the settee.

'Where's Will?' I asked Evie. She was sitting in her favourite spot by the window, and she looked strangely incomplete. I hadn't seen Will at dinner, nor Nathan, and assumed they'd been talking again. But that was hours ago.

'He went to bed,' Evie said, a shadow crossing her face. 'He was in the loft trying to fetch something down, and he slipped. He didn't fall, but it ... pulled something.' Her hand went to her own stomach, and I winced.

'Why was he doing it alone?'

'He shouldn't have been,' Frances said, her voice sharp. 'I told him to wait until Mr Beresford could help.'

'And where was he?' Evie said coldly. I felt my face heat up, and met Belinda's eyes across the room. I gave a tiny, pleading shake of my head, hoping no-one else had seen. She looked at me steadily for a moment, then her gaze shifted deliberately to Evie, who was clearly distraught at her husband's pain. I understood what Bel was trying to say, and Nathan's words about avoiding peeling potatoes suddenly sounded mocking and hollow in my head. But if Frances discovered what I'd been doing...

'I think he was helping Kitty finish up in the barn,' Belinda said. 'I saw him stacking tools when I went to fetch her for dinner.' I shot her a look of gratitude, and she replied with a slight nod. 'I expect he would have gone right up to help Will when he'd finished, but it was too late.'

'And where is he now?' Frances wanted to know.

None of us had an answer, and the silence grew less companionable, and more awkward. Then, bless her heart for ever, Belinda brightened.

'Evie! I forgot to tell you, a letter arrived for you.' She hobbled over to the fireplace and reached behind the clock for a grubby-looking envelope.

Evie looked at the handwriting and the concern for Will was hidden by a smile. 'It's from my brother.' She smoothed the letter out, and after a moment the smile widened into a grin. 'I hope Mother doesn't find this! He says:

"Dearest Evie,

I just wanted to let you know I've been granted home leave for ten days from the fourth to the fourteenth of July, and I'm asking you, no, *begging* you, to please come to Oaklands and save me from Mother! In all seriousness, I'm longing to see you and Will – I was devastated to hear of

142

what happened – and would be so pleased if you could come home for a few days, at least. I understand if Will is not able to travel so far just yet, in which case please tell him I'm thinking of him and wishing him well, and I will take a few days out of my time to come to you instead.

Your ever-loving brother

Lawrence".'

'I do hope you plan to go,' Frances said.

Evie looked hopeful. 'I'd love to, and I think it would do Will the power of good too.'

'He won't be tempted to go lugging things about in attics,' I agreed. 'Oh, Evie, how lovely for you both!'

'I'll apply for leave myself, first thing tomorrow,' Evie said, folding the letter again, the smile still on her face. 'And despite what that ghastly boy says, it will be nice to see everyone again, including Mother!'

I felt a twinge of envy at that, and looked at Frances, who was looking at Jessie. The envy grew.

Evie reached into her bag and withdrew her little notebook to put the letter safely between its pages. She glanced at the last page, then up at me. 'I forgot how close you lived to Uncle Jack all those years.' She read it again. 'How close to Formby is Ecclesley?'

I pondered. 'Ecclesley's in West Derby, so it's about fifteen miles I think. Not far at all.'

'Funny to think of that; it's a small world after all.' She put the book back in her bag, but kept glancing at it with a little smile, remembering her brother's letter.

'What's Oaklands like?' I asked. In all the time we'd worked together, she'd never really talked about it. I saw Jessie lower her book, and Frances sat forward in sudden interest too. Even Belinda looked curious; it was easy to forget Evie was aristocracy. She was so hard-working, and so ... normal. She blushed a little at the attention, but it was good to see her mind taken off Will for a moment, and encouraging her to talk about her family home seemed the right thing to do.

'Is it a very big house?' I prompted.

'It is.'

'How many rooms? And are they all beautifully decorated? Do you have stables?'

She laughed and held up a hand. 'Stables, yes. I knew that would be one of your questions!'

'Of course, you have a hunter, don't you?'

'I did. Orion. But he broke a leg just after the start of the war, and it wouldn't heal properly. We had to have him put down.' She sighed, but her smile returned as she began to describe the gardens, and the Cheshire countryside around her house. Particularly the quarry. I wondered what could have captured her attention in what must have been quite a dirty, noisy quarry, when she was otherwise surrounded by lush greenery. I supposed though, with her love of machinery it made sense.

'Breckenhall's a lovely town,' she said. 'It's not very big, but it had a wonderful market. I don't know if it still has, what with rationing and everything, but the town's pretty anyway.'

'I'd love to see it.' I gave a wistful little sigh. 'The manor sounds so grand, and the parties

144

must have been wonderful. Lizzy told me how she sat on the back stairs and listened in at your birthday party, Evie.'

'If all you want are parties and grand occasions, I can't think why you're here at all,' Jessie said, out of the blue. I blinked at her, surprised, but she had lifted her book again and flicked a page.

'It's *not* all I want,' I protested. 'But you have to admit, it does sound an exciting place to be.'

'Haven't you had your share of excitement, Skittles?' Evie smiled. 'I would have thought this quiet life here was perfect for you, after being in the thick of things in Flanders.'

'Oh, I do love the farm,' I said. 'It's just that I've never been to any really big parties. I didn't have a coming out ball, or anything.'

She grimaced. 'You've not missed anything there; don't worry.'

'But I would love to hear all about yours.'

Evie also glanced at Jessie, then at Frances, and then turned back to me. 'Another time, sweet-heart.' Her thoughts turned inward again, and I glared at Jessie's bowed head.

'I'd like to hear about it too, someday,' Frances said gently, and it was only then that I realised what lay behind Evie's reluctance to talk about her wealthy family. I felt awful, but didn't know what to say without sounding patronising, so I said nothing and hoped Frances hadn't heard my words the same way Jessie had. I didn't think she would begrudge another family their wealth, but it couldn't be nice to be reminded of it. Luckily Evie was a better person than I was.

I stood up. 'Jessie, I didn't get around to helping you with your bedding after lunch, like I promised. Would you like help now?'

She looked surprised, but nodded. 'Thank you, yes.'

Upstairs I found some clean sheets, which I carried into my old room and opened out ready to lay them over the mattress. Jessie caught the other end, and I searched for a way to break the ice.

'What's your home like?' I'd done it again; it was the wrong thing to ask. Her expression tightened and she jerked the sheet taut between us, nearly pulling it out of my hands.

I sighed. 'Now what have I said?'

'Don't you ever talk about anything except what other people have, or don't have?'

'That's not what I–'

'I sort of like you, Kitty, but at the same time I wonder why on earth you're here? Why are you accepting Frances's home as your own when you already have a perfectly good one?'

'Ah, there we have it.' I flapped the sheet, harder than necessary, and we glared at each other while we smoothed it onto the bed.

'There we have what?'

'You're jealous!'

'Jealous?'

'That Frances treats me like family instead of a land girl.'

'Don't be ridiculous!'

I turned away to take a pillow slip off the pile, and roughly stuffed the pillow into it. 'I could ask you the same thing, about why you're here. Is it to work, like the rest of us?'

146

'Or what?'

'Or to claim a place as a daughter of the farm.'

She stopped tucking in her corner, and straightened, fixing me with an incredulous stare. I met it, and went on, 'After all, *you* have another home too.'

'How dare you presume to know me!'

'It's only what you've said to me,' I said, angered further by my own defensiveness. 'You haven't the slightest notion what I've been through, and yet you think you can march in here and try to drive a wedge between me and the woman who has cared for me through it all?'

'What *wedge?*'

'Oh, I heard you downstairs. All the things you didn't say, wrapped up in a bland little comment about me wanting parties and grand occasions!'

'What didn't I say?'

'That I'm ungrateful, that I shouldn't go on about fancy things in front of Frances and hurt her feelings ... I was just trying to take Evie's mind off Will, if you must know.'

'You were not *just* trying to do that at all,' Jessie snapped back. 'Frances has been through some terrible times too. You're not the only one, and you have no idea what she's suffered. She has taken you in, given you a roof and a job, and all you can do is sit there with a look of utter lust on your face, trying to get Evie to talk about bloody chandeliers and silk!'

I stared at her in dismay; part of me knew she was right, but the anger I felt at myself was too big, and I had to fire it back. 'And you come in here,' I shouted, 'throw me out of my own room

147

because you once slept in it ten years ago, and expect everyone to fall over themselves to be nice to you!'

'I kept your silly secret about Belinda!'

'You don't *know* our "silly secret"!'

'I know you have one.'

'Well tell Frances, then. See how she feels about you having lied to her too.'

That stopped her, and she seized the quilt, without waiting to see if I'd help her. 'I didn't have to lie on your behalf,' she muttered, but the spark had gone out of her. Still, she had sprung to our rescue, and I wanted to thank her again, hoping that perhaps it would ease things between us. But she carried on, 'I just think it'd be better all round if you made up with your own mother and went home. Then you could have all the fun you want.'

That did it. I dropped the pillow on the floor and stalked out, and in the dorm I sat on my new bed, fighting tears of frustrated anger. The worst of it was, I really did want fun. I didn't *want* to want it. I wanted to look around me here, to appreciate the pretty window with its view of the fields and the woods along the river. I wanted to need nothing more than this tranquil, hard-working life, and the woman who'd given it to me when I'd lost my own.

But the memory of laughter, and of dancing with Bel in the barn, and the giddy sense of displacement the wine had given me ... and most of all the feeling of freedom and joy when I'd ridden Woody, had all served to remind me of what I was missing. My youth had been stolen before I'd

148

had the chance to turn my nose up at parties, like Evie could, before I'd really learned anything about what young women enjoyed, and before I'd felt the sweet anticipation of the kiss of someone I loved; by the time Archie had kissed me I'd already lost him.

That reminded me of Nathan, of course, and when I thought of how close I had come to Frances finding out, I went cold. Thank God for Belinda. When she came in, a few minutes later, she looked at my reddened face and the way my hands were clutching my shirt into clumps, and sat down on her own bed.

'Have you and Jessie had a row?'

'How did you know?'

'She just came downstairs in a proper funk, and left some of your things on the kitchen table. There had to be a reason she didn't just pop them in here instead.'

I sighed. 'She told me I should go home.'

'Why on earth did she say that?'

'Because she thinks I take advantage of Frances. That I'm ungrateful, and that I don't deserve what I've been given here.'

Belinda sat up straight, outraged. 'She said all that?'

'No, but it's what she was getting at. You heard her downstairs.'

'Hmm.' Belinda subsided again. 'She doesn't know you yet, that's all. You just need to get used to each other, and to what you both mean to Frances. It'll all be fine soon, you'll see. Now, promise me you won't be alone with Nathan Beresford again, and I'll sleep more easily.'

I gave her a sheepish grin. 'I promise. You can have him.'

'I don't want him!' she huffed. 'I just don't want you getting involved. He's an utter cad and will only break your heart. Archie's the one for you, and the sooner you accept that, the better for everyone. Especially poor Arch.'

Poor Arch. Sleep that night was fitful, and filled with snippets of bizarre dreams, in which Jessie and Archie sat at either end of a huge table, and they both kept almost disappearing. I was frantically trying to answer their demands for service before they faded away altogether, and when I woke in the morning I was exhausted before the day's work had even begun.

Nathan was in the kitchen when I went down blearily rubbing my eyes and blinking against the bright light that streamed through the east-facing window. 'Good morning, pretty Kitty.'

I felt anything but pretty at the best of times, but today I knew I looked my worst, and I blushed. 'Just because it rhymes doesn't make it true,' I said.

He grinned, and struck a pose. 'But, my dear, it *is* true,

That is how I see you,

With your red hair so curly... Forgive me; it's early.'

I stared at him, mouth open, and then burst into laughter. I couldn't help it. His smile widened, and he nodded at the teapot. 'Can I interest you in a cup?'

I waited to see if he was going to follow it with

another rhyme, but he didn't. I felt a flicker of disappointment, but sat down, forgetting, for a moment, that I was supposed to be the one making breakfast today. 'That was very clever.'

'Ah, I'm quick of wit – always have been.' He put a mug of tea in front of me, and sat down opposite, fixing me with his disturbingly lovely eyes, a smile still lurking at the corners of his mouth. I started to return it, then abruptly remembered last night.

'Why didn't you help Will, up in the loft? If you'd been there he wouldn't have slipped and hurt himself.'

He frowned. 'I know. I can't tell you how dreadful I feel about that. I really didn't think he'd do it all by himself. I just needed to take a moment to think about ... things. That's why I came to the barn. Seeing you there was a pleasant surprise though.' He reached across the table and touched my hand where it clutched the mug. I jerked away, spilling a brown puddle onto the clean table, and jumped up to get a cloth, glad of an excuse to break away from his steady gaze. I thought back to his kiss... Had it really been so uninteresting? Surreptitiously I glanced at him as I mopped up the spill; he was so good-looking, how could it have been? Perhaps I had been too wrapped up in memories of Archie to really appreciate what had happened?

'Kitty, tell me: what do you think of me?'

The question surprised me, and I took a moment to consider my reply. 'I think you really do care about Will,' I said thoughtfully, 'and I also think you're hiding something. But beyond

151

that I really don't know.'

'Not what you think I *might* be,' he insisted. 'What do you think of what you see, who you're talking to, right now?'

'A charmer,' I said drily, and he chuckled.

'Well, that I can live with.'

'I think you're funny, and clever. I don't think you're at all trustworthy, but ... I like talking to you.'

'Good,' he said softly. 'Because I find your reticence fascinating.' He touched my hand again, but this time I didn't pull away. 'I don't know you any better than you know me. I suspect we both have secrets, things we'd rather forget.' His expression clouded, but his hand tightened on mine. 'But life's for living right now. Don't you agree?'

'Wh-what do you mean?'

'I mean, pretty Kitty, that I want to make those gorgeous green eyes flash, and laugh back at me again. I want that lovely mouth laughing too. I want your sweet, rough little hands touching me just for the devilment of it. Let's not fool ourselves–' he stood up, still holding my hand, and came around the table to crouch at my side '–we're never going to be anything more to each other than we are right now, but let's make right now worthwhile, eh?'

He rose, swiftly enough to bring me to my own feet without thinking, and before I knew what had happened, his arm had gone around my back and he had pushed me back against the table. My chest tightened with panic; he wasn't tall, and he wasn't even particularly well built, but he had me in a grip I couldn't break. His lips took mine with

152

eagerness, and no hint of violence, yet I couldn't breathe...

My foot came down on his. Hard. Nathan yelped and stumbled away, wiping the back of his hand across his mouth. I slid out from between him and the table, trying to get my sickeningly racing heart under control again, and went to stand by the window, my arms folded, and my hands clenched into fists beneath them.

'I'm never doing that again,' I told Nathan without looking at him. 'And you mustn't try to make me.' At least my voice wasn't shaking the way my insides were.

'Are you sure?'

I turned and saw a tiny, hopeful smile on his lips, but I didn't need to reply. The smile faded, and he shook his head. 'I just thought...' he shrugged '...never mind. I was wrong. I'm sorry.'

'I like you,' I told him, feeling safer now we had a few feet between us, 'but not in that way. Never in that way.'

He studied me for a moment, and he looked very serious for once. 'Never is a long, long way away,' he said. 'And life is short. Remember that.'

Chapter Nine

Dear Katherine,

I have received a letter, from someone who has chosen not to give their name, telling me you are no longer in Dixmude at all, but at the address at which this letter now finds you. I cannot begin to tell you how disappointed we are to find you have been lying to us for so long, and we feel it was quite sly of you to go to all the trouble of having your letter posted to us from Belgium, just to maintain that deceit.

We have decided that, despite what we said before, your planned marriage to Alistair Corwood might in fact serve in two ways. It would strengthen Corn-wood, Maitland and Sons as a business, and also enable you to re-enter society with some semblance of dignity. To that end we have discussed matters with Mr Corwood, and he has agreed. I am writing now to tell you I have made arrangements to bring you home, and will be arriving in Plymouth on the fifth, at three o'clock. I trust you will provide transport to the farm from there. Please also ask Mrs Adams if she would be so kind as to grant her hospitality for one night, and ensure your things are packed ready for your return to Merseyside on the sixth.

Mother

I let the letter fall into my lap, and rested my forehead in my muddy hands. 'Oh, Bel, I just can't believe she'd do this!'

'Well, she is your mother,' Belinda said, picking up the letter and skimming it. 'Of course she'd only want–'

'Not her, Jessie!'

'Jessie?'

'Who else would bother to write and tell mother where I was? Evie wouldn't, you wouldn't, Lizzy wouldn't!' Nathan's face flashed into my mind, but I rejected that too; he wouldn't be so petty. 'Neither Will, nor Sally nor Frances would. But

154

Jessie hates me, and even said she thinks I should go home.'

'I suppose she got the address from Evie's book,' Belinda said, and handed me back the letter.

I snatched it and reread it, groaning as I got to the part about returning to Merseyside. 'I can't go back.'

'Would it really be that bad?' Belinda ventured. Her face was much less swollen now, and I could see a vague optimism in her re-emerging features.

I still couldn't tell her about my parents' hints that I hadn't fought hard enough, that some part of me, deep down, had welcomed Drewe's advances. 'It would be dreadful,' was all I said, realising how limp that sounded. 'Father will never forgive me for going to Flanders, and Mother will blame me for Oli, and for the family's reputation being so bashed about... What can I do?'

'But you'll see more life there, won't you? Parties and suchlike?' She sounded hopeful.

'Not likely. I'm the lesser of the two evil children, but I'll still be the black secret everyone knows about and no-one will mention.' I struggled to find a bright side, but I wasn't as good at that as Belinda, and we sat in silence for a few minutes, until our gloomy reverie was interrupted by the clattering sound of a cart in the yard. Bel got up and limped to the window, and a moment later turned to me with a look of horror. 'It's the man from the sawmill. Oh, Kitty, I thought he'd decided not to tell after all!'

I felt a cold, creeping nausea at what Frances would say – for our ten minutes of wine-induced fun, we had endangered not only the life and health of a hugely expensive horse, but also the future chance of the ARS loaning any more animals, which meant financial strife for the company, and even meant fewer horses for the Front... Thinking of the ongoing trouble we might have caused made me feel sicker than ever.

'What are we going to do?' Bel echoed my earlier plea, but no answer was forthcoming now, either.

'We'll just have to tell the truth, I suppose,' I said at length. 'Why on earth didn't we tell Frances sooner? It will be the lies that decide our punishment now, and she hates lies more than anything.'

'I'm going upstairs,' Belinda said, and a moment later I was alone in the kitchen, and listening out for the knock on the front door that would echo the frantic hammering of my heart against my ribs.

The knock was answered by Lizzy, who'd just come down the stairs herself, with a pile of clothes to wash. I heard her clearly, her voice drifting in through the half-open kitchen door. 'Can I help you?'

'My name's Seth Pearce. Are you Mrs Adams?'

'No. Mrs Adams is out working at the moment,' Lizzy said. 'Perhaps there's something I can help with?'

I crept to the window and looked out, squinting sideways so I could just about see Mr Pearce, his hat in his hand, and his feet scuffing the front step.

'I'm the owner of the sawmills, up't Princetown.' He sounded rather as if he were unsure of what to say, which was odd if he had come to make a complaint. 'I just wanted to, uh, enquire after the young lady.'

'Young lady?'

'The pret ... the one with the light hair, her who hurt her foot last week.'

'Oh, Belinda? She's much recovered, thank you. Might I ask how you met her?'

My fingers twisted in the curtain, and I held my breath.

'I, um, I came upon her and her friend after some ... misfortune befell her.'

'Before she fell from the cart, you mean?'

'Yes!' It was the sudden grasping at a lifeline. 'That's it. I saw the name of your farm on the cart. She looked to be in a bit of a bad way, and I think I might have, well, not been awful sympathetic. At the time, like.'

I felt my lips press together in a suppressed grin of relief and realisation. Bless him! He'd probably spent the best part of the last week gathering the courage to come here.

'Anyway,' he went on, 'I remembered something she said, about your 'orses having been taken, for the lads at the Front.'

'Yes, that's true. Would you like to come in, Mr Pearce?'

'Thank you, miss.'

I dropped the curtain and went quickly to the sink, where I was engaged in swilling water around a jug as Lizzy led Mr Pearce into the kitchen.

'Mr Pearce,' I said, trying to send him a look of gratitude that wouldn't be intercepted as such by the keen-eyed Lizzy. 'How lovely to see you.'

He gave me a look that made him almost attractive for a moment, an amused, more relaxed look – probably glad I wasn't Belinda, and therefore lacked the power to make him embarrassingly tongue-tied. Lizzy offered him a drink, but he declined, becoming nervous again as he looked around – I recognised the half hope, half dread of longing to see someone but being scared to death they might actually appear.

'Now, Mr Pearce,' Lizzy prompted. 'You were asking about Mrs Adams's horses?'

'Oh. Yes. Well no, not really asking. You see, what I had in mind would be a little ... arrangement, whereby I give you the loan of one of my own horses, for work you've need of that's too much for your trap pony. The harvest, an' suchlike. And for riding, of course. Pirate likes a good gallop but we ain't really got the time to exercise him right. Do him good.'

Lizzy and I both stared at him in surprise, then Lizzy shook her head. 'I'm sorry, Mr Pearce, but we couldn't pay you.'

'No, I was thinking ... maybe instead of payment, you might pass a little bit of your fresh produce my way. Not a lot, just perhaps some butter, and some milk. And I hear you make your own honey too. I do understand that would still cost you,' he hurried on, 'but it wouldn't be a set amount, just ... what you can, when you can.' He stopped for breath at last, and I had the feeling it was the longest speech he'd made in a long time. 'Do you think Mrs Adams would be interested?'

'That's a very generous offer, Mr Pearce,' Lizzy mused. I knew she didn't need to ask him what lay behind it; she was even quicker to read people than I was, and her own eyes strayed to the door, as if Belinda might walk through at any moment. 'Let me talk to Mrs Adams about it. I'll send one of the girls over to see you. Is that all right?'

'Perfectly, thank you.'

'Not at all,' Lizzy said. 'Thank *you*. And it's very kind of you to ask after Belinda. I'll be sure to let her know.'

As soon as the front door had closed behind Mr Pearce, Lizzy came back in and fixed me with a look I recognised with a sinking heart. 'Now, Miss Maitland, let's hear it. What really happened to Belinda's foot?'

Shortly afterwards I was sitting on my bed, and Belinda was looking at me in dismay. 'Do you think I'll be expected to ... accept his advances, in return for the loan of a horse?'

'Of course not!' I shook my head. 'What do you take Lizzy for? And Frances would never expect it either, silly! But isn't it good? We'll be able to go riding whenever we like ... well, whenever work allows. And Mr Pearce will never tell your secret!'

'Our secret,' she reminded me, a little tartly. 'You were the one riding Woody. I never got the chance, remember?'

But in my mind I was already off, galloping over the moors. 'I wonder what Pirate's like?' I heard the dreaminess in my own tone, and it made me smile.

'Kitty! We don't even know if Mrs Adams will accept the offer yet. And I am not the slightest bit attracted to Mr Pearce, so if he does expect me to—'

'He won't.' I waved a dismissive hand.

'At least it's taken your mind off that letter,' Belinda said.

I came back to reality with a snap. 'Oh no! I don't want to leave, especially now!'

'Because of the horse?' Her eyes were on me shrewdly.

'Why else?' I was relieved I'd managed to stay clear of Nathan for the past few days. I'd expected him to have left by now but it couldn't be long... It occurred to me that Frances's little family would be sadly depleted within a few weeks, and that our lives, always altering in small ways, would soon be very, very different. Going back to Merseyside meant I'd probably never see Evie again, either, and that thought gave me a surprisingly heavy ache.

I went in search of Will the moment I was freed from the morning's chores, and found him slowly gathering some of his sculpting tools ready for packing. He looked at ease and contented.

'Skittles! How nice.' I didn't mind him calling me that – he and Evie were one, in my mind.

'How are you feeling today?' I asked, helping him fold a large cloth that he used to catch wood shavings in.

'A bit silly after the fall, but happy to say I'm a lot better today.'

'Did you let Evie give you some morphine?'

He shook his head. 'I just had a lie down, and actually went to sleep. By the time I woke up things had settled down a bit and I've been taking it very easy this past week.' He began rolling his knives together in their leather wrap.

'You've got a dreadful habit of trying to do too much.'

'It's taking a while to heal,' he admitted, press-

160

ing gently at the place where the bullet had struck him, in his left side. It had travelled halfway across his body, and I remembered the thick bandages I'd seen across his waist in the hospital at Arras. They must have had to open him right up to make the kind of miraculous repairs he'd needed. It was no wonder he still hurt.

'Still, I'm under orders to continue to rest,' he went on, 'and I'm looking forward to going back to Breckenhall.' He shot me a little grin. 'Not so sure about Oaklands itself, but I think I'll get a decent enough welcome.'

'What's Evie's mother really like?'

He stopped packing for a moment, and straightened with a little wince. 'Well now. I remember giving Evie a bit of a talking to when she was complaining about her, but I could certainly see where the complaints came from. Having said that, when I'd lost my memory Lady Creswell accepted me into the house without the slightest hesitation, or disapproval when my manners fell short of what she'd have liked. I was, I'm ashamed to say, often very difficult. In fact she was not only the perfect hostess, but she was also ... kind.' He paused, then nodded, looking surprised at his own choice of words. 'Yes, kind.'

Not something anyone had ever said about my mother, as far as I knew. It seemed to be true then, that the established aristocracy often differed from 'new money' in more ways than simply titles in the family lineage. Lily Creswell sounded formidable, but Evie herself, even in her most frustrated moments, had never once suggested a lack of love on her mother's part, or of her not wanting the

161

best for her children.

'Lady Creswell sounds complicated,' I said, with a certain wistfulness.

'She's as complicated as her daughter is straightforward,' Will said, his voice warm with affection. 'But I'm sure you didn't come to find me just to ask about Lady Creswell.'

'No. I came to tell you I probably have to leave.'

'Leave? Whatever for? This is your home, Kitty.'

'I can't think how to avoid it. Listen.' I took the letter out of my pocket and read it to him. When I'd finished, my voice had begun trembling and he gently took the letter out of my hand and glanced over it.

'You know what you should do with this?'

I sighed. 'Throw it away, I suppose, but—'

'No. You should do this.' I watched the letter become a blur of twisted paper and strong, agile fingers, and when the movement stopped Will held a tiny paper box. 'Here.' He handed it to me. 'Put something nice in it, and give it back to your mother.'

'Something nice?'

'Something that'll remind her of her harsh words, and show her that you're better than she's painting you. That you're still her daughter,' he said. Then he smiled. 'I once told Evie something very similar, and she had to admit I was right, in the end. You might just about have room for a lock of that gorgeous red hair. I wouldn't mind betting she's forgotten how much she loves it. And you.'

I looked down at the box and saw parts of the neatly written words 'society,' and 'Mother,' and I recalled, with a nauseous clarity, the letter she'd

162

sent after Oliver's trial. A lock of my hair would not make her remember how much she loved me, because I don't think she ever really had, or she wouldn't have said those terrible things.

'Evie should be home in a little while,' Will said gently, seeing my face. I could see he felt bad that he hadn't been able to make me feel better after all.

'You are lovely,' I told him. 'You just don't know my mother, and I'm glad you don't.'

'She'd probably hate me,' he agreed with a little grin. I couldn't help responding; those dimples brought back his youthful appearance, and softened the harsh lines carved into his face. I had trouble believing anyone could hate him, but if anyone could it was Harriet Maitland; she'd see a man of little means latching onto an easily led young woman, using his charm to persuade her to marry him, then deserting his post in France and bringing shame to her and her family. Perhaps that was unfair of me; I had no real way of knowing what she'd think, but she seemed determined to think the worst of me, and I was her daughter. She had never shied away from making snap judgements.

To change the subject, I told him about the offer Seth Pearce had made Frances, and we talked for a while about what had happened. I enjoyed making him laugh, and we passed the time pleasantly enough until, around half an hour later, Evie came looking for him. Just in from work, she looked tired, but pleased to report she had been granted the leave she'd requested.

'We'll be able to see Lawrence, and you'll be

163

able to visit Martin,' she said.

I tried not to acknowledge the twinge of envy at her pleasure. 'Is Martin the one you mentioned before, the one who probably told Nathan where you were?'

'That's the one. He and Mary were witnesses at our wedding.' She caught sight of the little paper box on the table, and picked it up. 'What's this?'

I told her about the letter, and I could see she was itching to undo Will's folding in order to read it, so tried to tell her as much of what it contained as I could. When I'd finished, she frowned.

'Perhaps Will's right,' she said. 'Your mother will probably be trying to build bridges, now she's had time for the shock to wear off.'

'Then why hasn't she taken back what she said?' I blurted, distressed beyond thinking straight.

Evie's eyes narrowed. 'Why, what did she say?'

I just looked at her, then at Will, who looked curious but concerned. 'It was another letter she sent me, just after Oli's trial. I've never told anyone; it was too awful. But I couldn't throw it away either. I was worried I might forget, and forgive her.'

'Fetch it then,' Evie said grimly, and touched my arm to show me her expression was not directed at me.

I did so, and watched their faces as they read it together. I could tell Evie was reading fastest, by the way her breath caught, and her eyes widened, a split second before Will's did. 'You've reached that bit then?' I said quietly.

'"You are, after all, a sturdy girl and cannot have been so incapacitated that you could not

164

protect yourself."' Evie read aloud, slowly. She lifted her eyes to mine, then gripped the letter more firmly and read on. When they had both finished, she put the letter down and came over to me and folded me into her arms.

'You mustn't go with her, Skittles darling,' she said in a low voice. 'Neither of you is ready for that yet.' Then she pulled back, and glanced over at Will. 'She must come with us, don't you think?'

'To Oaklands?' I stared at her in sudden hope.

'Yes. Mother would be pleased to have you as a guest. I'm certain of it.'

'Are you sure?'

'Quite sure. And if not, well, the house belongs to Lawrence anyway, and even if he thought you were the worst person in the entire world, which he certainly won't, he wouldn't refuse you hospitality.'

'I should hate to stay where I wasn't wanted,' I began, but Evie smiled.

'You most certainly *are* wanted. Now, go and tell Frances. She'll need to share your duties out among the others for a while.'

'Bel will be so pleased about that!' I grinned, relief making me a little giddy. 'How long shall I say we'll be gone?'

'Two weeks,' Evie said. 'That should be plenty for all of us, I imagine, especially Mother.'

I left her and Will alone, both still smiling at me, but as I closed the door I saw their expressions slip into identical scowls, and through the wood I heard Evie's voice, clear and furious.

'That woman had better not set foot on this

farm, not while I'm here and can reach a bloody pitchfork!'

I put my hand flat against the door in a silent gesture of gratitude, and felt the fear and tension fall away; my own family might not want me, but I had Evie and Will on my side, and I had Frances. Maybe soon I would also have Lily Creswell.

Chapter Ten

If my first sight of Oaklands Manor had filled me with awe and admiration, then my anticipation of meeting Lady Creswell had taken my insides and replaced them with rocks. I couldn't fully enjoy, for more than a moment, the turreted, many-balconied house, the huge oaks that dotted the lawn, the tantalising sight of the walled garden just beyond the drive, because I now realised I'd forgotten every last piece of instruction I'd ever received about meeting aristocracy. Evie didn't count, of course, but I could see even her standing straighter and reaching for Will's hand.

He took it, his fingers folding over hers, and I saw him squeeze gently and receive a grateful smile in return. My own hand curled, and if I let myself drift ever-so-slightly away from reality I could almost imagine Archie standing beside me, but that flash of comfort was gone a second later, leaving me emptier than before.

The front door opened, and the butler came out looking like the lord of the manor himself, but Evie greeted him like an old friend, and he unbuttoned slightly, giving her a smile that looked as though it rarely saw the light of day. He greeted Will and me with more formal politeness, then picked up our three bags as if they weighed no more than paper and led the way into the huge hall. I had no time to stare at the paintings that graced the walls, or the carvings that danced across the high ceiling, before a door opened at the other end and Lady Lily Creswell came out.

My stomach knotted instantly, and I realised I had absolutely no idea if she knew of my circumstances; in the flurry of packing, and the excitement and relief of leaving Dark River, I hadn't thought to ask Evie. I shot her an alarmed look, hoping for a reassuring smile or a slight shake of the head ... anything to tell me what to expect, but her attention was on her mother. I turned back to watch the lady herself cross the hall, and swallowed hard.

'Evangeline, darling,' Lady Creswell said, and took her daughter's hands. She kissed Evie's cheek, and it was a real kiss, not that awkward and pointless brushing of the air near a person's face that my own mother had perfected. Then she took Will's hand and pressed it. 'William, I'm glad to hear you're much improved.'

He gave her a sort of half bow and smiled. 'I am, Lady Creswell, thank you. It's good to see you again.'

'You must rest while you're here. Lawrence is so looking forward to seeing you. He's out at the moment but will be back for dinner.' Then she turned to me. 'And you must be Kitty,' she said, with surprising warmth. I felt my knees unlock as she took my hand, and she saw my nervousness and gave me a gentle smile. 'Don't look so frightened, child. I'm delighted you were able to come. Evie has told me so much about you, and about your immense courage out in Belgium.'

I felt the blush rise from my neck, and found a smile creeping across my face. 'Thank you, Lady Creswell.'

'You must tell me all about it at dinner. Now, Dodsworth will show you to your rooms.' She turned to Evie. 'You and Will are to have the same room as Will had before, and Kitty can have your old rooms.'

'Where's Lawrence gone?' Evie asked.

'Just for a walk.' Lily smiled at me. 'My son has always had a fondness for walking, but since he's enlisted it's become something of a need for him. He does it whenever he can. Must be to do with being cramped up in those ghastly tanks. Do you enjoy walking?'

'I do,' I said. 'There are lots of lovely walks on the farm, and you can go down through the woods, along the riv...' I stopped, my eyes going to the wide, richly carpeted staircase that swept up to the upper floors, and then to the many doors leading off into rooms that were no doubt even more ornate than this enormous hall. Lily saw me looking, and touched my hand again.

'Don't be ashamed of where you live,' she said gently. 'It has no lesser value than this house, believe me.'

I couldn't think of anything to say, but hoped my gratitude showed in my face.

168

'Come on, Skittles,' Evie said. 'My old room has a bath, and you'll be glad to get the travel dust off you I expect.' She followed Mr Dodsworth up the stairs, her hand still holding tightly to Will's, and as I brought up the rear I glanced back down and saw Lady Creswell still standing in the centre of the hallway. She raised a hand to me, and I smiled back, but as I turned to face the front again all I could think about was how small and alone she looked.

Lawrence, or rather Lord Lawrence, did indeed return in time for dinner. He strolled into the sitting room where we'd gathered for a drink, and his smile, so like Evie's, cut across the room and lit on each of us in turn. Evie had said he was just one year older than me, but had held the rank of lieutenant for at least a year now, and I could see Lily's eyes on him with pride and affection as his presence broke down the slight uncertainty of our little group. As blond as his sister, with light blue eyes and an open, friendly face, he held himself very straight even in a relaxed situation such as this, but when I tried to address him using his rightful title he broke into laughter and flatly forbade me to do it again.

Dinner, therefore, was not the taut, nerve-wracking experience I'd dreaded. Lawrence sat next to me and kept up a lively chatter with all of us. He and Will were close; I already knew that. Evie had told me they'd been friends for years, but they'd spent last Christmas, after Will had been traumatised at High Wood, almost constantly in one another's company. Lawrence had been the only

169

one who could truly begin to understand what Will had been through, and it was clear that Evie welcomed the bond between them.

But tonight there was no talk of war. Tonight there was just a family group, and for once I didn't feel as if I hovered at the outside edge of it. Lawrence teased stories out of me I thought I'd never tell, and even Lily laughed aloud at my telling of the illicit horse-riding incident. Everyone winced at the description of Belinda's fall, but I thought it best not to add that her main concern was that her nose was all swollen just when she was trying to look glamorous for Mr Nathan Beresford. I even managed not to think about Archie for most of the evening, until much later, when Lily asked Evie how he was. Evie shot a glance at me before answering, but after all, Lily had no idea Archie and I even knew each other; it was natural she would ask her daughter.

'He's doing well, I think,' Evie said. 'Kitty knows him very well, and has done since they were children.'

'Oh?' Lily raised an eyebrow and I wondered if I was imagining the slight cooling of her manner. 'Are you close?'

'We were once,' I said, feeling an ache crawl through me at my own words. 'But, well, you know. People lose touch.'

'Indeed,' Lily said, and relaxed a little. 'Lawrence, darling, Kitty enjoys walking too. Perhaps you'd like to show her the grounds tomorrow, while the summer's still treating us kindly?'

'Of course,' he said, smiling at me. 'The garden's at its best just now, Kitty. We'll go early, if that's all right? It can get a bit hot.'

I nodded agreement, then caught Lily's satisfied look, and understood. Of course, why hadn't I realised? It also answered my still-niggling question about whether or not she was aware of what had happened to me in the spring; only the purest of wives would be good enough for the heir to Oaklands Manor, and she evidently believed me to be worthy, on that score at least.

'I'm very tired,' I said, putting my glass down. 'If I'm going to be out walking early tomorrow, I think I should go to bed.' I stood up, and thanked Lily for her warmth and hospitality, and after also bidding goodnight to Evie, Will and Lawrence, I fled to the sanctuary of my room, where I lay down and let out a groan. Lawrence was sweet and very easy to be with, but even if we found one another remotely attractive, which we clearly didn't, Lily would find out sooner or later what had happened and would be all the more furious with both Evie and myself for hiding it.

Her instant suspicion about Archie rankled, too. That she saw him as a threat to her intentions for her own son gave me a surge of defensiveness, and a determination to protect the friendship I'd been half prepared, so recently, to throw away; she had no idea how deep that friendship went, and it was none of her business. I closed my eyes and beckoned him forward, and he came, his grey eyes made sombre by those straight, dark brows, but the mouth parted in a smile that belied that solemnity. 'Young Kittlington,' his voice breathed into me, and this time it took no effort at all to feel his presence close beside me, and his large, warm hand in mine. I went to sleep with him next to me, as I had countless times before, and would time and time again – knowing he was beyond my reach out there in the world of noise and light, but here, in the secrecy and darkness of my sleep, he could be mine again.

The following morning Lawrence gave me the promised tour of the gardens. Evie stayed back at the house with Will, who was stiff and uncomfortable after the long train journey the day before.

Lawrence looked behind at the house with a faint frown, as they waved us off and we started down the avenue. 'I know he was badly hurt,' he said, 'but surely he should be improving more quickly?'

'He was, but he slipped a few days before we left the farm, trying to move something without help.' I felt another flicker of annoyance towards Nathan. 'He didn't fall, but it didn't help his recovery, and he's still in a lot of pain – he won't take morphine; he's terrified of becoming dependent.'

'Poor chap,' he said softly, then cleared his throat. 'Right, we'll start at the far end and work our way back. Sound all right?'

'Sounds perfect.'

My first morning at Oaklands passed in a surprisingly easy, pleasant way. Lawrence showed me the orchard, and the walled garden, and then the place where Jack Carlisle had planted two apple trees. One of them had been planted in honour of some friends he had known long ago and there were some initials on the little stone: AJD. It was odd not to know the names behind

172

those letters, and the people behind the names, while someone familiar to me had loved them enough to sweat and toil in their memory.

The other tree was older, and instead of a stone at its foot it had a framed photograph. Carefully wrapped against the weather, and hard to see clearly because of that, I nevertheless recognised Jack himself; he'd have been the same age as Archie when it was taken, and the resemblance, always strong, was uncanny enough to make me break out in goose bumps. The two men in the picture were in uniform, and it might have been a formal picture but their closeness was evident in their relaxed attitudes and easy smiles.

'Is the other man your father?' I asked quietly.

Lawrence nodded, sobering for the first time since we'd left Will behind at the house. 'They were the absolute best of friends. Uncle Jack planted this tree just after father died, and every time he came here he tended it. Our gardener, Shackleton, did his best, but he had so much more to do, and he didn't have the same devotion to these two trees as Uncle Jack did.'

I remembered the garden at Lizzy's mother's cottage near the farm, and that Jack had taken it over while he'd been staying there. 'He's got green fingers, all right,' I said with a smile. 'Not the sort of thing you'd expect from a man like him.'

'He always had an air of mystery,' Lawrence agreed, 'but we were lucky enough to see the other side of him too. I'm glad he's happy.'

'With your old scullery maid, so I understand. Does your mother know that?'

'Pretty sure she doesn't, actually. Evie did ask

me not to tell her. I'm happy for him, though. Can't see him married to that Wingfield woman he was engaged to before. But Lizzy...' He looked uncomfortable suddenly, and I thought perhaps an unwelcome memory had resurfaced, then he shook it off. 'Anyway, Evie says they're happy, and that's all that matters.'

'Funny how things turn out,' I mused. 'Who can guess where lives will lead?'

'Who indeed?' he smiled back. But there was nothing behind the smile that suggested our own lives, be they separate or together, were on his mind just at that moment, and I turned to go back up the path, breathing a little sigh of relief.

'I should like to show you Breckenhall,' Lawrence said, catching me up after clearing away some dead leaves from the two trees. 'They still have a market there sometimes. Perhaps when Will is recovered a little more we could all walk in together. Would you like that?'

'I would, thank you.' We walked quietly for a few minutes, then I broached something that had been on my mind since I'd arrived. 'Lawrence, has your mother ever considered opening the house?'

'Opening it?'

'As a convalescent home. You know, for soldiers.'

He looked surprised that the thought had never occurred to him. 'No, I don't think so. Jolly good idea though, and one I might take up with her.'

'Well you...' I trailed off, hesitant to take him onto my path of thought, having known him such a short time.

'Well what? Come on, you might as well ask,' he said, then saved me the bother. 'Oh, you're think-

174

ing that, as heir to Oaklands it's actually my decision?'

'Well, isn't it? I've never been too sure about the way these things go down through families,' I confessed. 'But if *you* choose to do it, surely that's an end to discussion?'

He thought about it, blond brow furrowed. 'I think you're right, as it goes.'

'And you agreed it would be a good idea.'

'I did, didn't I?' He grinned at me, and caught hold of my hand. I didn't pull away, but neither did I feel the way I did when Archie did the same. It was like holding my brother's hand – comforting and friendly, but utterly lacking in anything deeper. Nevertheless I smiled back, and, as we walked up to the house I hoped Lily would be looking out of her morning-room window; her approval meant a great deal, and I wasn't ready for that suddenly chilly glance to fall on me again just yet.

Inside Oaklands, Lawrence led me upstairs to the first floor, and down a long corridor. We stopped at the last-but-one door, and he pushed it open. 'Father's study,' he told me.

'What are we doing here?' I looked around nervously; despite my own assertion that this was Lawrence's house, it still felt wrong to be standing in the study of his deceased father. The room was surprisingly cosy, with two chairs by the empty fireplace, and a large, clean desk in front of the window. I wandered over to the window and moved the heavy curtain farther aside, letting more light in. Beyond the French window was a large, wide balcony; I'd seen it from outside and wondered what lay behind it, and now I knew. I felt a tickle on the hand that had remained on the edge of the curtain and jerked away, visions of spiders making me shudder. But it was only a piece of string. My eyes followed the string upwards, saw how it ran across the ceiling, and hung equally free at the other end, swinging down beside the door. What on earth was that for?

'Aha!' Lawrence's exclamation swept the mild puzzlement from my mind, and I turned to see him holding up an envelope.

'What's that?'

'Father's will.'

I smiled. 'Are you really thinking about it, then?'

'It's the only thing we *should* be doing with Oaklands. I really have no idea why it's never been mentioned before. Embarrassing, really, that I didn't think of it myself.' He pulled out the document and spread it on his father's desk. I didn't speak, while he absorbed its contents, and just continued to look around the room and out across the wide sweep of lawn. After a few minutes, he beckoned me over.

'You're right. It looks rather as if the decision's mine.' He stepped back so I could read the will and, despite not having known the man, to see the words and wishes of one who had once been happy, vibrant and loving, set up a strange, sad echo in my heart.

'Well that's good news, then,' I said, trying to smile, but Lawrence caught the tremble in my voice, and touched my arm.

'Uncle Jack has always been more of a father to

176

me than Henry Creswell,' he said quietly. 'I was very young when Father died, but Jack was here ... even when he wasn't. If you understand what I mean.'

'I do, yes. I don't know Jack very well, but I do know his nephew Archie. Evie says they're very alike, in more than appearance.'

'Well that's the best compliment your friend Archie could hope for,' Lawrence said. 'Evie worships Uncle Jack, even more than I do if that were possible.'

'Archie has that same way of ... just being with you, when he can't be,' I ploughed on, and as I talked I felt some of the weight peeling off my shoulders. Speaking his name aloud, telling someone who didn't know him how his gentleness equalled his strength, how he could make me laugh by the way he twisted people's names around, how he sat a horse with effortless grace, and rode with the skilled abandon of a wild west cowboy... It all came spilling out and I barely heard my own voice as Archie solidified in the room with us. Eventually I stopped for breath, and I saw Lawrence looking at me with his mouth open. Abruptly my face flamed and I cast about for something to say, but everything I thought of sounded limp and pointless. So I just shrugged.

'How long have you loved him?' Lawrence asked gently.

'For ever, I think,' I admitted. 'Hopeless, isn't it?'

'On the contrary, sweetheart.' Lawrence put his arm around me. 'If there's one thing I've learned in the past two years, it's that you must seize every speck of joy that drifts your way. Provided

177

the one you love hasn't placed their heart else-where, there is no reason, *no* reason, why you should deprive one another of that joy.'

He sounded sombre again now, and I wondered who he'd fallen in love with, who had given her heart to another. I felt him take a deep breath, and let it out slowly. Then he gave my shoulder a squeeze and let me go.

'I don't understand why mother is so insistent on us hitting it off,' he said, his face twisting in a wry smile. 'It's not as if it makes a jot of difference now, whether or not I have children.'

So he'd guessed as well, then. It was a relief not to have to bring the subject up. 'How do you mean?'

'Well, now the Kalteng Star is gone.'

'The Kal ... what star?'

'Ah, you haven't heard of the Kalteng Star? Good!'

'Why good?'

'Because now I shall have a fascinating story to tell you, and it will make you forget how you've just opened your soul to a complete stranger.'

I laughed. 'Let's hope so.' In truth, although I should have been embarrassed, I wasn't. It had been more than a relief to talk about Archie. It had allowed a trickle of the deep pleasure and pride I held in knowing him to seep through the cold parts inside me.

'The Kalteng Star was, is, a blue diamond,' Lawrence said. 'It was stolen several years ago. They thought it was Lizzy who took it. Jack's Lizzy, who works at Dark River Farm now,' he clarified, seeing my stunned expression. 'She went

178

to prison for it. Ah, I see you didn't know that.'

'No!' *Lizzy in prison?* 'Who really stole it?'

'Chap named Markham. At least, he made his girlfriend do it. It's a long story, and actually it's mostly not very nice, but I'm sure Evie will tell you the details. She knows much more about it than I do.'

'What has that got to do with whether or not you have children?'

'The will stipulates that the diamond goes with the eldest daughter of the house, but only until the Creswell line ends, when it's to be returned to Borneo. I'm the last Creswell, so, no daughter, no Kalteng Star.'

'But your mother still seems very keen to see us together.'

'Yes, doesn't she? Embarrassingly so. Presumably now it's just for the same reason as anyone normal: because she wants grandchildren.'

I could understand that, but apart from Lizzy's part in it, it all seemed rather trivial when held up against what was going on all over Europe, all the people who had married at the start of the war but would never have children, never mind grandchildren. I wasn't prepared to give up my life to fulfil Lily's wish, any more than I was prepared to do it to fulfil my mother's.

'Well,' I said, 'Evie and Will are sure to give her heirs, once he's recovered, and since there's no diamond it doesn't matter if they're called Creswell or Davies does it?'

'Absolutely right,' Lawrence said with a smile of approval. 'And I would adore to be an uncle, so much less aggravation than being a parent, I

179

would think. Come on.' He put the document back in the drawer, and held out his hand. 'Let's go and see if Mrs Hannah's made any cakes. Oh! That reminds me, I must tell you what poor Lizzy did to my sister's birthday cake.'

The days passed by too quickly. Several visitors, curious family members for the most part, called in, claiming they were 'just passing', in order to get a closer look at the man who had caused Evie to defy convention and marry so far beneath her. I could see them eyeing him, and, while they outwardly acknowledged his courageous acts in France, I could see them making their judgements. Evie could too; her face would often tighten, and I'd see a muscle flickering in her jaw as she fought to keep her tone even in response to questions about his peacetime occupation. Will himself was every bit as aware, but his was the soothing hand on her arm, the quiet voice in her ear and the smile that so often held her eyes and earned her smile in return, just when I thought she was about to say something terrible. I ached for the two of them after everything they had been through, and more than once I too had to restrain myself from speaking out, but I took my lead, as always, from Evie, and managed to avoid disgracing myself on their behalf.

More than once, too, I was touched, and, it must be said, a little envious, as Lady Creswell herself spoke up in Will's favour, silencing the more vocal critics. I remembered his insistence that she had been kind to him before, and wondered why my own mother could not bring herself to show the same sensibilities with my situation. But the letter I'd sent, in reply to her orders for my return, had been polite, apologetic, but firm. And remained unanswered.

On the day before Lawrence was due to go back to Courcelette, I went into the sitting room to see him pouring himself a hefty dram from the whisky decanter. His hand shook, although he smiled at me and saluted me with his tumbler before taking a large gulp.

'Ah, here's sweet Kitty,' he said, and I realised that wasn't his first drink of the day. Not that he could be blamed. 'Would you like to join me?' He waved at the decanter, and I shook my head.

'I was going to ask if you wanted to take that walk into Breckenhall.'

'Splendid idea!'

'Shall I ask Evie if she and Will would like to come?' I half turned to leave the room again, but Lawrence surprised me.

'No. I'm sure they've got other things to do.'

'I know Evie wanted to visit the market,' I said, 'And Will's doing ever so much better. I think he'd like to pop in and see Martin. His best man,' I added, seeing the blank look on Lawrence's face.

'I see. Well, then yes, of course. I'll wait out the front. Join me when you're ready.' He swallowed the rest of the drink down. The fresh air and exercise would do him good, and I was glad I'd sought him out, or he might have spent his last day in a stupor and suffered for it the following morning. I hurried upstairs to tell Evie our plans.

'Lovely. We'll be downstairs in ten minutes,' she said. 'Tell Lawrence he'll have to walk slowly though. I know what he's like.'

I waited by the front door, and kept Lawrence chatting about anything except the war. It was hard, ignoring what so clearly occupied his thoughts, but I managed to make him smile, and to recall some of his childhood adventures.

'There was an amazing fight, right there on the lawn,' he pointed. 'With my cousins David and Robert Wingfield. That was the night the diamond was stolen. We got absolutely drenched in mud, and Lizzy was the one who broke it up.' He sighed. 'I wasn't very helpful to her when they accused her of stealing the Star, I'm afraid. Most of the evidence against her was down to where she'd been when that fight took place.'

That explained his discomfited expression when we were looking at the trees and talking about Jack and Lizzy. I tried to imagine Lizzy breaking up a fight between three sturdy young men, and it only took the memory of her tearing me off a strip for my treatment of Evie to convince me she could have done it quite easily.

Lawrence was smiling again now. 'In a minute I'll show you where Will crashed the butcher's van. We'll be walking past the very spot.'

'He *crashed* it?'

'Tipped the bally thing right over on its side. Evie was with him. I should have realised then that something was afoot, but I was only fifteen. That was the first time he spoke to me, and come to think of it, the rogue wasn't nearly humble enough, considering I was such a fancy little lordling at the time.'

'You never were!' Evie said, coming across the

182

threshold on Will's arm. 'You pretended to be, but you were nothing but a sweetheart.'

'Hush, Evangeline, I'm trying to live up to expectation,' Lawrence grinned. The cool air seemed to have helped dissipate some of the whisky-induced high humour, and now his smile seemed more natural. 'Right, Private Davies, set the pace. I don't want to push you.'

Evie and Will moved ahead, and Lawrence offered me his own arm, which made me smile. I took it, and together we walked down the long, straight avenue to the stone gateway at the bottom, and then turned left towards Breckenhall.

After a few minutes Lawrence pointed to the side of the road. 'There.'

Will turned and saw where he was indicating, and started to laugh. 'You remembered the exact place!'

'Of course, my friend, of course,' Lawrence said. 'I saw the van on its side, and thought Mr Markham must be driving it. But of course it wasn't him. And, innocent child that I was, I couldn't think what my sister was doing there, until they spun me some yarn about him–' he pointed to Will '–swerving to avoid hitting her.'

'It wasn't some yarn,' Will protested. 'I did swerve. It's just that it was my own fault in the first place for getting distracted.'

He looked down at Evie, whose hand slid from the crook of his elbow down to his wrist, and from there they linked hands, still looking at each other. Will smiled and Evie, clearly moved by instinct beyond thought, stretched up on tiptoe and kissed him. It was a brief touch of the lips, but Lawrence turned away and muttered from the corner of his mouth, 'I do wish they wouldn't.'

'No-one's here to see,' I assured him. 'I like that they're so clearly in love. They've earned it, don't you think?'

'More than anyone I know,' he agreed. Then he winked. 'I don't know Archie though, do I? So you don't count.'

Evie and Will broke their moment, and continued walking, and Lawrence began larking about, playing the landed gentry to the hilt, and pretending I was his lady. In this way we arrived in Breckenhall in high spirits, and I could see those people of the town who recognised Lawrence glancing at one another and then nodding knowingly in our direction. That made me laugh even harder, and I was still giggling when we arrived outside the butcher's shop where Will had been apprenticed before the war.

'I'm going to nip in and say how d'you do to Martin,' Will said.

Evie gave him a shrewd look. 'And ask him if he's the one who told Nathan where you were?'

'That too,' he admitted. 'Are you coming in?'

'Let's all go in,' Lawrence said. 'Make his shop look terribly popular, so all the locals will flock to see what the fuss is about. May as well make ourselves useful for once.'

Will pushed open the shop door, but the rest of us hung back while he greeted Martin and they exchanged a warm handshake. After a few minutes, during which time Martin admitted, shamefaced, that he had become friendly with Nathan and had indeed told him where Will was convalescing, he nodded at the door at the back of the shop.

'Reckon there's someone upstairs who'd like to see you, too,' he said quietly. 'Should I call him down?'

Will followed the gesture, and his eyes widened. 'I thought he'd gone to London.'

'He did. He came back two nights ago. Shall I fetch him?'

Evie gave Will a searching look, then shrugged. 'It's your decision.'

'He was a decent man,' Will said gently. 'He just ... lost himself a bit.'

'I'm not going to see him,' Evie said. 'Come and find me in the market when you're ready.' But her words were softened by the look she gave him, and by the way her hand brushed his as she passed on her way to the door.

I glanced back towards the shop as we walked towards the market square. 'Who's Will going to see?'

'Frank Markham,' Evie said. 'He was the one Will was apprenticed to. He gave him the job after Nathan left him in that mess.' She moved away to look at something more closely, and I blinked in recognition.

'Wait...' I turned to Lawrence. 'Markham? Isn't that the one you said stole the...' I floundered '...the Tingtang Star?'

'Kalteng!' Lawrence smiled, and nodded. 'Yes, that's him. That's why Evie is none too keen to pass the time of day, I should think.'

'But Will still likes him.'

'Will has a generous soul. Markham saved him

185

from ruin. I assume he feels he owes him five minutes of his time, at least. They've both been invalided out of service, Markham for good since he's lost half his arm.'

I winced. 'And he's a butcher. How does he keep working?'

Evie came back, overhearing the last part of the exchange. 'Martin's a good apprentice. Now stop talking and come and look at these fabrics. This is the stall where I found the material Mary used for my wedding gown.'

We had made our way around half of the market, and I was once more on Lawrence's arm, when we heard Will shout Evie's name. We all turned, and saw Will hurrying towards us, and Evie went to meet him, her face creased in concern.

'Will! Be careful, you're–'

'It's Frank. Bloody hell, Evie, you have to come and talk to him!'

Chapter Eleven

Lawrence and I watched them disappear into the shop, then looked at one another in amazement.

'Well what in blazes was that all about?' Lawrence wondered.

I shook my head. 'Will looked as though he hadn't a clue what to say, or do.'

'Not like him. Decisive bloke, normally. One of the least flappable chaps I know.'

We started to walk again, slowly, and I kept glancing back until the shop doorway was out of sight, but there was no sign of either Will or Evie. Lawrence was becoming quieter and quieter. The earlier fun had gone out of the day, and I knew he was thinking about what tomorrow would bring.

I'd heard him talking to Will about his unit, the Machine Gun Corps, and where they'd likely be going next. There was talk of the Heavy Branch, the tanks, being split from the rest of the regiment and given its own designation of Tank Corps, and I'd longed to ask more questions about what it was like to drive one of those great beasts, or even to ride in one, but Lawrence's voice had held no enthusiasm, and even Will's interested conversation had drifted away when he'd sensed that too.

Asking those questions now would have been even harder, so we walked around the market more or less in silence. When we'd circled the remaining stalls, and watched many of the stallholders packing their wares away, the increasing emptiness of the market seemed to echo the shadow that had crept across Lawrence's mood. We sat down at the edge of the square, in sight of Markham's shop, to await the return of the others. Lawrence sighed. It was a long, shaky sigh, and a high note escaped his throat unbidden, reminding me he was still only a boy.

'You'll be safe,' I told him quietly, not looking at him. I knew he'd be embarrassed at having made the sound that was almost, but not quite, weeping.

187

'How can you say that, you of all people?'

'Because you have to be. You have to turn Oak-lands into a convalescent home, remember?'

He gave a little laugh, then sniffed and wiped his hand across his eyes. 'Perhaps I'll be the first customer.'

'Perhaps,' I allowed. It would be patronising and pointless to pretend that, at least, wasn't possible. 'Either way, you'll be in the right place, with the right people. And just think of the preferential treatment you'd get!'

He smiled, and was about to answer when we both heard the tinkle of Markham's shop door-bell. Evie came out first, saw us and waved, and turned to take Will's arm and it was immediately obvious that she was not merely being affection-ate; Will's walk was hesitant and his free hand was wrapped across his waist. I gasped in sudden pain as Lawrence's hand clamped down on my arm, and turned to tell him he was hurting me ... but the words didn't come.

Instead I followed his hard, anguished gaze to where Will had stopped to catch his breath, and everything suddenly became very clear. He felt my eyes on him and looked down at me, swallow-ing a denial, and just gave me a sad, hopeless little shrug. So that was the way of it ... the one he loved, whose heart belonged to another.

'Oh, Lawrence,' I breathed, and he managed a watery smile.

'Hush, Kitty. I'm trying to live up to expect-ation,' he said, and I felt like weeping along with him.

Evie found us in the sitting room much later. I'd accepted a glass of whisky, to keep Lawrence company, but the taste of it just reminded me of the first time I'd tried it – just a few hours before I'd discovered Colonel Drewe had left me with more than bruises and nightmares. The glass sat on the little table beside the settee, untouched but for that first sip. Lawrence sat beside me, tense and worried, and his own glass rolled between his hands more often than it was raised to his lips, for which I was grateful. His fear of leaving for the Front in the morning had been momentarily eased aside by worry for Will, but Evie smiled, although her face was pale.

'The doctor's gone,' she said, 'and Will's under orders to remain in bed. I think that slip in the loft was the last straw. I don't think there's any bleeding, his blood pressure hasn't dropped enough for that, but he ought to stay as still as possible now, and give himself a chance to heal.' She poured her own drink, and sat down opposite us, closing her eyes as she took her first sip. I felt Lawrence slump in his seat beside me, but I don't think Evie had noticed any more than the general relief she would expect from a close friend and brother-in-law.

I remembered what had made Will exert himself to find us in the market. 'What was wrong with Mr Markham, anyway?'

Evie opened her eyes again, and I saw her thoughts come back into focus. 'It wasn't him, so much as his daughter.'

'His daughter?'

'He got a girl in the family way a few years ago. The kitchen maid, Ruth Wilkins. Ruth was dismissed, of course, and went back to London. I think she was hoping to find her old family, but from what I've heard they didn't want any extra mouths to feed. Frank went to find her when he was invalided out of the army last year, and last week he did.'

'What's the matter with the child?' Lawrence asked.

'Nothing. At the moment. But Frank has stolen her from her mother, and brought her back here. He has her hidden away in his rooms above the shop.'

I could feel my eyes growing round and wide. 'Why?'

'Well, because...' She fixed me with a troubled look, and sighed. 'Ruth is working the streets. There are men who ... manage her. Amy's only just four now, but it won't be too many years before she'll be in danger of being used in the same way as her mother.' I went cold at the thought, and my hands clenched painfully tight.

'I'm certain Ruth would have been happy to let Amy go with Frank,' Evie went on, 'but it's not up to her. The kind of men who control her wouldn't want to lose a potential moneymaker. The benefits, to them, would outweigh the cost.'

A nasty, greasy, queasy feeling squirmed in my stomach. 'I just... I can't even–'

'Unthinkable,' Evie agreed quietly. 'Frank evidently agrees, so when he found out where she was staying he went in there, grabbed Amy, and ran. I gather there was a struggle with one of the men standing over Ruth, but Frank's quite a big chap, and even one-handed it seems he didn't

190

have too much trouble. Besides, it wasn't Ruth he was after.'

'What will they do to *her?*' I whispered, horrified for this girl I'd never known, but even more so at the thought of what might have happened to the poor child.

Evie shook her head. 'I don't know, love.'

'But Amy's safe?'

'For now, as I said. But Ruth knows where Frank lives, and she might send them after him and Amy. From her point of view she'd be sensible to do it because, to be brutal about it, it might buy her life.' She put down her glass. 'I think you should get some sleep now, Skittles. It's been a long afternoon. You too,' she said to Lawrence, and her expression was filled with sadness. 'You need to be away early tomorrow, after all.'

'I'm not going to bed,' Lawrence said quietly. 'The sooner I go to bed, the sooner it'll be time to leave.' His voice hitched suddenly, and when he looked up his eyes were brimming with unshed tears. 'Evie ... I don't think I can bear it again.'

A second later Evie was at his other side, taking him in her arms and drawing his head to her shoulder. I waited for a moment, unsure what to do, then laid a gentle hand on his shuddering back, and left brother and sister alone.

I came awake, gasping, swamped in a darkness so heavy I couldn't even tell if my eyes were open. My heart was thudding against my ribs and I could feel sweat trickling down beneath my nightgown, pasting the thin material to my back and buttocks. My thighs were trembling, as if the

191

muscles there had been tightly clenched, and I felt the ghosts of hard fingers pressing into the flesh, the echo of a once-trusted voice telling me to relax ... the cool relief of tears at the corners of my hot, swollen eyes.

I sat up in bed, these familiar sensations gradually easing away into the peace and silence of Evie's childhood bedroom, and drew my knees up to rest my forehead on them. This dream was not new, so why had this time been so much worse? I made myself recall as much as I could, exploring what had been different about this one, biting the back of my hand against a sob when the dream became solid memory, as I'd known it would once I poked around in its depths. But I couldn't fathom what it was that, this time, had brought me awake in the darkness, barely able to breathe.

I lay back down, closed my eyes and, as always, found the only path back to sleep – Archie Buchanan. I didn't want my imagination to claim the honour of putting this nightmare to flight. I needed it to be as much a memory as the one that had led me here, so I put myself in the road outside the hotel in Dixmude, I put Archie in front of me, and I let my heart do the rest. My hat dropped to the ground to lie beside his, his hands gently tilted my face upwards, and his mouth came down on mine. This time the tears that coursed down my temples to soak my pillow carried my terror and despair with them, and left me feeling calm and able to sleep, with Archie's hands cradling my head to his chest, and his breath ruffling the fine hair at my crown.

When I awoke again Lawrence had gone. I found Evie sitting alone in the library, a note crumpled on the table beside her. 'He left in the middle of the night. I convinced him to get a few hours' sleep, and he promised he would, just so I would go to bed. Then he ... just left.'

'He probably hates goodbyes,' I said, feeling an emptiness that surprised me; we got along well, but after all we'd only known each other a week. 'I would have liked the chance to see him away.'

She nodded. 'Well, he writes often, so I'm sure we'll hear from him soon, and then we can give him a sound telling-off for sneaking away like that.'

'Your mother must be beside herself. And how is Will today?'

'He's awfully fed up. I keep nagging at him to lie still, and he's just not used to it.' She swallowed hard, and in her face I saw the battle she fought day after day. 'I sometimes feel like forcing him to take that blessed morphine,' she admitted. 'But at the same time I know why he doesn't, and it... Oh, Kitty, if it were possible to love him more, I would now.'

'He'll never turn into what Colonel Drewe became,' I said softly. 'It's just not in him.'

'But he sees my fear of it,' Evie said. 'And he won't risk it.'

'He's a very courageous man,' I said, and she gave me a distracted smile, her mind on her husband, and his struggle towards recovery without pain relief.

I couldn't bear to see her distraught, and

193

shifted the subject slightly. 'Has he got something to read?'

'One or two things.' Her smile became more natural then. 'I daren't give him any of our really valuable books. He's more likely to rip the pages out and re-create the Taj Mahal. Oh!' She remembered something, and went to a bureau in the corner of the room. 'Remember I showed you that stall, where I bought my wedding gown material?'

'Yes. I'd love to see the dress itself, if you have time?'

'It's packed away, but this is what I was going to show you,' she pulled out a book of photographs, and flicked through the heavy pages for a moment. 'Here. Our wedding day.'

There were only three photographs. One wasn't fixed properly, and slid out as I lifted the tissue paper away, and Evie caught it before it fell to the floor. She passed it to me, and I caught my breath.

'Evie, it's beautiful!'

'*He's* beautiful,' she pointed out softly, and I looked again. Although I'd seen him every day for two months, I'd never seen him completely free of pain. In this picture, taken the very day before he'd left England in 1914, he was standing tall and straight beside his new wife, lit with pride, his hair ruffled by the wind and his face unmarked by the experiences that would so soon change him for ever. He was, as she said, beautiful. I looked up in time to see her wipe her eye with the back of her hand.

I looked more closely, trying to pick out the design of her dress, and noticed a rather grey,

194

shabby-looking something, scrunched up at her belt. 'What's that?'

She took the picture to see what I was talking about, and smiled. 'That, young Skittles, is the rose Will made me out of newspaper before the war. The rose I took to Flanders, and the rose that led me to your brother when he was hiding out in Number Twelve and probably saved his life.' I fought back a familiar pang at the thought of what Oli had gone through, and she saw it.

She touched my hand gently. 'Do give him my love when you write to him. And let me know how he is when you hear back.'

I nodded, and there was a quiet moment – I don't know whether Evie's thoughts were with Will or Oli at that moment, but mine had taken an unexpected turn towards Frank Markham and his daughter. With that turn came a sudden idea that made me sit up very straight, and I opened my mouth, but before I could say anything the door opened and Lily came in, an odd look on her face.

I assumed it was sorrow at the way Lawrence had left, but Evie read the look, accurately, as shock rather than sadness. She led her mother to the biggest of the armchairs and made her sit down, then sat down herself, on the arm. 'What is it?' Her voice shook; there were so many things that could put that look on someone's face nowadays.

'It's Samuel Wingfield,' Lily said, sounding as if her lips were too numb to speak properly. 'They've found his body. In Germany.'

The name rang a faint bell with me, but neither

Evie nor her mother wore any hint of grief as their eyes met. Lily still looked stunned, but Evie's face was carefully expressionless, although I saw her hands wrap around each other on her lap.

'How did he die?'

Lily blinked and looked away. 'I, uh, I don't know. It was a telegram. Matthew is coming to explain.' She cleared her throat, and stood up, fussily smoothing down her skirt. 'He'll be here this afternoon. Evie, call Mrs Cavendish if you would, please? Tell her we'll be one more for dinner.'

'Mother,' Evie rose and stopped Lily as she reached the door. 'Has this upset you?'

Lily opened and shut her mouth once or twice, then shook her head. 'You know I have never taken to Samuel,' she said finally. 'I despise the man, and always have.'

'Then why...' Evie made a vague gesture with her hand, to encompass Lily's arrival, and her stunned inability to think straight.

'It's... I... Evie, he was going to give it back!'

'What?' Evie froze, and now her face too was white and shocked-looking.

'The Kalt ... the... He sent me a letter. I agreed to pay him. He was going to give it back,' she repeated, 'and now it's gone for ever.' I looked from one to the other in slowly dawning realisation. No wonder she had still been so keen to see Lawrence and me together.

'The diamond?' I said, just to be sure. They both turned to me with identical looks of surprise that just as quickly melted as they faced one another again. I was effectively shut out, which suited me well for now, but they didn't ask me to leave.

'Mother, tell me everything, and then I'll tell you what I know,' Evie said, and I could hear her struggling to stay calm.

Lily frowned slightly at that, but returned to her chair, smoothing her dress down almost obsessively as she explained, 'He wrote to me last year. I'm surprised you didn't find the letter. It arrived when you were home on leave. I had only just opened it when you came into the morning room.'

A glance at Evie showed startled recollection. 'I saw you push something away under your blotter. But then the telegram came to say Will had been exonerated, and it completely went out of my mind.'

'The letter said ... it said...' Lily stopped, her lip trembling too much to continue. I'd never seen her so unsure of herself, and now there were tears at the corners of her eyes too, and Evie was moved to crouch at her knee and take her hand.

'Just let me read the letter, Mother. We'll talk later.'

Lily nodded. 'It's in my room, in a box at the top of the wardrobe.' As Evie rose to leave, Lily caught at her arm. 'I'll be in the garden, I need some fresh air.'

Evie gestured to me to follow, and together we almost ran upstairs to Lily's room. I had a moment to appreciate the clean, plain beauty of it, so huge, white and ruffle-free, but with heavy red velvet curtains and a deeply plush carpet of the same colour, and then Evie had pulled down the box from the wardrobe. Together we sat on the bed, and she pulled out an envelope, with Lily's name printed on it in extremely neat handwriting. She read the letter aloud.

"'My dear Lily,

"'I find myself in possession of something you misplaced in the first few hours of 1913. I would very much like to return it to you but cannot possibly offer it gratis, and the cost of such a thing might, I understand, be seen as prohibitive. However, I am prepared to wait one full year, in order to allow you time to gather the necessary funds. The return of your lost item will, over time, more than enable you to recoup your losses.

"'To assist you in your decision I must tell you I have certain knowledge of your late husband that would, should it be revealed, cause deep concern. Naturally I would hate for anything to come to light that would absolutely and without doubt ruin the Creswells as a family of note, and I trust that you and I will come to some arrangement regarding the aforementioned item, in order to re-establish cordial relations.

"'Do not trouble yourself to try and reply. I have not supplied a return address and instead will write to you again in one year with suggested arrangements. Should I receive any unwanted attention in the meantime you must consider this mutually beneficial offer withdrawn, and all my personal goodwill towards the family with it.

"'SW'"

'What knowledge was he talking about?' I asked, in a kind of awed horror. If I had hoped for excitement at Oaklands, this was certainly above and beyond my expectations, and far more than I might have wished for. At the same time, fascination had me in its cool, impersonal grip, and I wanted to know everything.

But Evie shook her head. 'It doesn't matter.

198

What matters is that he's dead now, and Father's secret with him. But I suspect we haven't seen the last of that damnable stone after all, more's the pity.'

I looked at her for a moment, suspicion dawning at the way she kept her eyes averted. 'What do you know about this, Evie?' I kept my voice even, but I heard a firmness in it that surprised us both. She looked at me briefly, then back down at the letter.

'I know what Samuel's talking about, and I know who killed him. At least I think I do.'

'Who?'

'Uncle Jack.' For a moment I thought I'd misheard, but a look at her face told me I hadn't. She looked sickly pale, almost green, and I knew my face would be the same. *Jack?*

I cleared my throat, barely trusting myself to speak. 'But he's not that... I mean, he's...'

'Kind? Dependable?' Evie said. 'Honest?'

'Yes! Like Archie.'

'He's all those things, darling, but he's not like Archie. Not all the way through.' She closed her eyes and swallowed hard, and her voice trembled when she said, 'I've learned a lot about him in the past year, Kitty.'

'What things?'

But she shook her head. 'Not now. The important thing is I trust him, and I love him. Probably more than ever. But I truly believe he killed Samuel Wingfield, and I believe he now has the Kalteng Star.'

I couldn't take it in. It was too big, too horrific to consider. I concentrated, instead, on what I

199

knew. 'He went to Germany, right after the trial. Was this the reason?'

She nodded. 'I overheard him and Lizzy talking about it one night. He'd seen Samuel when he was there last. Lizzy was frightened. She didn't want him to go, but he insisted. For me. And most of all, I think, for my father. He'd promised to protect our family, and this was his way of doing it.'

'I saw the tree he planted for your father,' I ventured, after a little silence. Then I had to ask, 'Will you tell your mother Samuel's secret, whatever it is?'

She shook her head. 'Uncle Jack risked everything to protect it, and my mother.'

'But don't you think she has a right to know whatever it is Wingfield was hiding?' Lawrence's anguished expression as he'd looked at Will came to mind, and I pressed on. 'If you know something, surely you ought to tell the person it affects the most?'

'Not if it's not going to change anything,' Evie said, 'and especially not if it's just going to cause hurt. There's enough of that in the world just at the moment, don't you agree? What would be the use?'

I thought about it; my knowledge of Lawrence's feelings for Will had not changed them, nor would Will's or Evie's. I looked up at her, but she was staring across the room, seeing only she knew what. She was right; what good would it do?

I touched her hand and she came back with a jump. 'Evie, your mother will be in the garden, waiting for you. Do you want me to come too?'

'No, I'd like to be alone with her. Perhaps you

might go and check on Will? Tell him I won't be long.'

I knocked at Will's door, and he sounded alert and cheerful as he called for me to come in. It felt as if I hadn't smiled for days, but I did so now, at the sight of him propped up against his pillows, looking rested and comfortable.

'You really are a dreadful layabout,' I said, sitting down on the bed. 'Evie just asked me to pop in and let you know she's talking to her mother, but she won't be long.'

'Thank you.'

'How are you feeling?'

'A lot better. I've been threatened with all sorts of things I shouldn't trouble a young lady with, if I try and get out of bed without help.'

I laughed. 'Good!'

'I gather Lawrence has already left,' he said. Something about his voice made me look at him sharply, but his face gave nothing away.

'He went in the middle of the night,' I said. 'You've been friends quite a while, haven't you?'

'Since the day the van went over, I suppose.'

'He probably thought you were quite worldly. To a young boy, you would be.'

His blue eyes narrowed slightly as he met my deliberately steady gaze. Then he sighed, and I could hear the relief in it. 'Just don't say anything to Evie. Please.'

'So you know then?'

'I might not be a special kind of genius, but I'm not daft. I've seen the way he looks at me sometimes, although I pretend not to.' Then he added

201

softly, 'It's the same way Archie Buchanan looks at you.'

My head jerked as if someone had tugged my hair, and when I looked at Will I saw the gentlest of smiles on his face. 'We're not talking about Archie,' I muttered.

'Why not? I don't want to talk about Lawrence. I want to know why you've turned Archie down when you clearly love him every bit as deeply as he loves you.'

'It's because I do love him.' I remembered my conversation with Lawrence, and how it had lifted me to be able to speak of my feelings, and I wanted that feeling of relief again, as temporary as it was. So I told Will everything that had weighed my heart down for so long, but this time there was no relief in the words I spoke; each one was a spike in my throat.

'It matters to me that he has the life he deserves,' I finished. 'And he deserves someone he can be proud of.'

'And it doesn't matter to you whether he's happy?'

'Of course it does!'

'*You* make him happy, Skittles. I could see it at the farm. We all could.' He squeezed my hand and made me look at him. 'Take it from one who knows... You have to grab every chance you can.'

'That's what Lawrence said.'

'Well, he's clearly a man of good sense. Not to mention impeccable taste.' Will gave a wry smile, and let go of my hand in order to brace himself and shift his position against the pillows. 'Can't you at least give him a chance?'

'Lawrence?' I quipped, and he rolled his eyes, making me smile.

'Look, I understand why you did it, but really, don't you think it's up to him to decide whether you're "worthy" of him?'

'I do sound rather as if I'm playing the martyr, don't I?'

'Not at all, sweetheart. Your family have proved how important it is. To them, at least. But Archie's ... well, he's different. He won't set any store by something as ridiculous and changeable as circumstance.'

'I know, but—'

'Look at Jack and Lizzy. When Lizzy met Jack she was seventeen, and as innocent as could be. She was twenty-two when they finally got together, and just out of prison. No more her fault than what happened to you was yours. We all know that, despite what your parents said.' He took my hand again. 'Do you think Archie's a lesser man than Jack? Or Lizzy more of a woman than you?'

'But Lizzy's wonderf—'

'And so are you. You should credit Archie with the same ability to see the truth as his uncle.'

My heart began to pick up pace as I thought about what he'd said. He was right. I'd been draping my family's prejudices over Archie, dressing him with that same ugly, opaque cloth and not daring to listen when he'd tried to cast it away. I'd done the same with him as I'd done with Evie, Frances and Belinda – heard their declarations of love and friendship, and searched so hard for a way to convince myself they meant it that I'd talked myself out of believing in it.

I felt a new, hopeful smile creep across my face. 'I'll do it. I'll write to him.' Then I hesitated. 'What if he's already changed his mind though?'

'Then you must change it back,' Will said. He closed his eyes and his voice dropped. 'Best do it today.'

'I'll have Evie chasing me up hill and down dale if I tire you out,' I said, standing up. 'I'll leave you to sleep now.' I leaned over and kissed him lightly on the forehead. 'Thank you, Will. I miss Oli dreadfully, but you're the perfect big brother.'

'Happy to oblige,' he murmured. 'Now off you go and tell Archie what a little idiot you are.'

The Matthew who had sent the telegram was, I was surprised to learn, Samuel Wingfield's son. I would never have guessed it from the warmth of the greeting extended by both Lily and Evie; I'd understood the enmity between the two families to be severe, yet Evie clearly trusted him, and Lily liked him. I gathered he was the only member of the Wingfield family who had earned himself the epithet of 'uncle', with the Creswell children.

'How is Constance?' Evie asked, as we went in to dinner. No-one had yet mentioned Samuel; it seemed everyone, including his son, was reluctant to bring his name out and turn the evening sour.

'Constance is Uncle Matthew's sister,' Evie explained, seeing me trying to keep up with it all. 'And, to make things more confusing, she was once engaged to marry Uncle Jack.'

'Now there's a chap I always respected,' Mr Wingfield said, and by the way he looked at Evie I

204

guessed he knew more about Jack than Lily did, and was aware that Evie knew it too. Presumably then, he would be the one to confirm her suspicions, although the more I thought about that, the less likely it seemed. Jack Carlisle was impressive, imposing even, and there was a distinct sense that he knew a great many influential people, but when I thought of the man who'd taken such pains to put me at my ease during Oli's trial; the man who'd moved mountains, and furniture, to ensure I'd be as comfortable with him as I could be; the man who loved the same people I did... How could anyone imagine he was capable of murder?

By dessert, Evie had had enough of tiptoeing around the subject, and as soon as Dodsworth had left the room she turned to Mr Wingfield. 'Uncle Matthew, you said you would explain how your father died. That is, if you're not too–'

'Not at all, dear.' Mr Wingfield patted his mouth with the thick napkin, and replaced it on the table next to him, deliberately arranging it, and using the time to gather his thoughts.

'My father's body was found close to the Swiss border,' he said. 'He'd been shot, once. A clean shot, between the eyes.'

'An assassin's shot,' Lily murmured, and I was jolted by the phrase.

Evie saw my expression, and although her face had paled, her voice was steady. 'It's what my father used to call snipers. Both our side and the enemy's. Uncle Jack hated it. He always said it was an assassin when it was them, but a marksman when it was our side.'

'You won't have any love to share for snipers,

Evie,' Mr Wingfield said gently. 'Let's not talk about that now; it's not helping.'

'So why do you think your father was killed?' Evie asked.

'He'd been carrying ... papers, evidently. Classified papers.' He cast a look at Lily, and I read uncertainty in it. 'Lily, I'm not sure if you knew this, but my father was a spy.'

I nearly dropped my fork. Part of me was fizzing with excitement at the thought of all I'd have to tell Belinda, but a colder part of me realised the implication, and I caught Evie's eye. She gave the slightest, warning shake of her head, and I dropped my gaze back to my food, pulse racing. Jack was a spy as well, then ... and Archie?

My breath caught at the thought, and I began to choke. Eyes streaming, I turned to Lily for help, and she absently handed me a glass of water before turning her stunned attention back on Samuel. I was able to force a tiny dribble down the frighteningly small passage of my constricted throat, and made myself breathe very slowly, swallowing time and time again until I could feel the air moving more easily. By then Mr Wingfield had finished talking, and there was a heavy silence lying over the table. He rose and poured Lily's wine for her himself. Lily drank half the glass down at once, and set it back on the table with a trembling hand.

Mr Wingfield reached for that hand, and it lay unresponsive in his, as he spoke very gently. 'Jack's a spy, too, Lily. But Samuel was working for the Germans, and Jack's one of ours.'

'Hush!' Lily glanced over at Evie, as if to indicate

this was not the time to reveal such devastating news. But Evie looked away, expressionless, and Lily's face tightened. 'You knew, Evangeline?'

'Yes.'

'For how long?'

'Does it matter?'

'Yes!'

'Last year. When Samuel took the Kalteng Star and Lizzy was hurt.'

Lily's face wore an expression of one for whom many different puzzle pieces were slotting into place all at once. She kept opening her mouth to say something, remembering something else, and subsiding. In the end she picked up her glass again and finished her drink before standing up. 'I'm going for a walk,' she said in an oddly calm voice. 'I'd very much like to be left alone for a while.'

When she had left the room, a piece of that puzzle slipped into place for me, too, but I didn't want to voice it in front of Matthew Wingfield, just in case he was not the kindly man he appeared to be. After all, he was Samuel's son. I looked at Evie, who nodded. Her father had also been a spy – the secret Jack had been protecting.

The question that burned in my mind now, and wouldn't be quenched by any amount of wine, was whether Archie was who he seemed to be after all.

Chapter Twelve

Up and down the country, every country, lives and families were being torn apart. Changed, reshaped, misshaped, broken. Telegrams, lists on post-office walls and windows, and in the newspapers – a crookedly typed name that, to most people would be simply two words, eliciting vague sorrow, but unrecognised and unremembered. Reluctant eyes the whole world over scanned those lists, relief building with every unfamiliar name that passed ... and then that one. The one that stopped the breath in the throat, impersonal black marks on a piece of paper that those suddenly burning, blurring eyes fixed upon, willing them to change, to be the trick of a cruel imagination. A lie.

Oaklands Manor, with its fairy-tale turrets and beautiful grounds, with its sense of peace and its quiet strength, was not spared. The news of Lawrence's death fell over us, a cold, heavy blanket, smothering all talk. Eyes would not make contact. Stunned faces remained blank in the view of others, but low sobs and disbelieving cries echoed through the house as fresh grief took hold somewhere, in someone. Lily moved through the rooms in dazed incomprehension, and Evie was torn between tending to her, and to her husband. Will remained in his room and I could only imagine the thoughts that claimed him; there was nothing else to think about.

I spent most of those days in the walled garden. I sat by the two apple trees, planted with such love, and in such deep grief, and I remembered Lawrence's fond memories of the man who had planted them, and nurtured them when he could. Caring for them as he had done for his friend's children, and now the youngest of those children was gone. For days I fought the pain, and then, on the day of Lawrence's memorial service at the little church in Breckenhall, I stopped fighting it and let it take over. Sweet Lawrence, so young... His blue eyes should have been filled with fun, with excitement and mischief, but in the short time I'd known him they'd been shadowed with fear, and with the knowledge of a love that could never be returned.

He'd been terrified of going back, but I'd told him he would be safe. It was what you said to ward off the fear, and the bad luck that seemed like a living being, dogging your footsteps unless you found some kind of talisman to give you courage. Lawrence's talisman was speaking aloud the fear of injury; if he said it, it wouldn't happen.

But within two days of his return to France, his tank unit had pushed through the enemy lines – a time of celebration and of triumph, until a lone German, courageously refusing to leave his gun, managed to load and fire his mortar directly beneath Lawrence's machine. I tried to shut my ears to the phantom screams that tore through my head when I imagined how it must have been, and to close my eyes against the horror... It was *Lawrence*.

The service, where the names of too many other boys and men were read out, marked the beginning of some kind of acceptance in Lawrence's family, too. There was no body to lay to rest, not even over in France, but still, somehow, we managed to feel we were saying goodbye. Afterwards we all returned to Oaklands, still quiet, but now and again finding some anecdote that earned a flicker of a smile, blurred by tears, but a smile nevertheless. We were a small group, united in grief, and there existed between us a kind of bond, forged by darkness, but not held prisoner by it.

It was only two days later that everything changed again.

Mr Dodsworth came to find me after breakfast on the last day of July. 'Her Ladyship would like to speak to you, Miss Maitland. In the morning room.'

I followed him from the library, through the hall, and waited at the door of Lily's favourite room, while he knocked and waited to be called in. Then he left with without a word, leaving me standing, rather adrift, in the middle of a large, rather cluttered room. The summer sunshine spilled through the huge windows onto the desk, at which Lily sat, her fingers twiddling with her pen. She looked up and I was struck by the hollowness of her expression. The light had retreated from her eyes until they seemed nothing but darkened caves in the pale perfection of her face. Her voice, too, had lost its strength, and it was because of this that the harshness of her words did not at first sink in. Then I realised what she'd said.

'You must leave us now, Kitty. Tomorrow will be quite all right, but I'd like you to be gone by mid-morning at the latest.'

I wasn't sure what to say; I was a visitor, it was true, but we were all of the understanding that, with all that had happened, I was welcome to stay until Will was strong enough to return to Dark River Farm. I started to say as much, in a stammering voice, but Lily held up a hand, effectively cutting me off after only a few words.

'Will is family. You are not.'

'You wanted me to be!' I flashed back, without thinking. Had I really felt I belonged here, after all?

Lily focused first on my shocked face, then on the way my hands clasped one another in an attempt to hide the trembling betrayal. Then she looked away. 'I was prepared to accept you,' she corrected.

'What do you mean by that?' But I realised, and went cold. 'Lady Creswell...'

She rose and turned to look out of the window. 'Your reputation would have been difficult to reconcile, but our family name was strong enough to have withstood it.'

'And now it isn't?'

'Strength is no longer the question,' Lily said bleakly. 'The name, and the family, will soon be gone. Everything is ruined.'

'Because of the diamond.'

'Yes!' she shouted, and I jumped as she banged her hand flat on the desk. 'Because of the diamond! Evangeline always hated it, but she was happy enough to live off what it gave us!'

211

'She seems content enough living at the farm,' I said. 'She never needed all this,' I waved my hand at the room in general, and at the glorious, incongruously summery garden beyond the French window, contrasting so sharply with the icy atmosphere in the room. 'She was even happier in Flanders. I used to wonder why, when she could live in luxury like this. She nearly always cried with relief when she came back to the mess we lived in out there.'

'And now you have *such* a deep knowledge of our family.'

The sarcasm was so thick it buried my good sense, and before I knew what had happened I had blurted out, 'I know more about some of it than you do!'

She sat down again, her elegant hands clenched into fists, the knuckles bone-white. 'What are you talking about? What do you know?'

'I ... nothing.' I could have slapped myself, but the words were out now, and hung between us. 'It doesn't matter.'

'Oh, I think it does,' she said softly, then shrugged. 'I'll get the truth out of Evangeline, anyway. I assume that's where you learned it, whatever it is. I know she's hiding something about Jack Carlisle.'

'You'll hurt her if you do,' I said. 'Is that what you want to do?'

'Of course not! Whatever you may think, I love my childr...' she swallowed hard '...I love Evie.'

I felt wretched already, and now I had to tell her something that would stop her dragging the terrible truth about her husband, out of her griev-

212

ing, and still confused daughter. 'It's not about Evie, or Jack,' I said quietly. 'It's about Lawrence.'

She paled even further. 'What about him?'

I took a deep breath and sent a silent apology to Lawrence. At least it couldn't hurt him now. 'He would never have married me, or given you a grandson.'

'He might have had a daughter.' Her voice shook, and she cleared her throat. 'A daughter would have kept us for another generation, at least.'

'No. He ... he was in love with someone else.'

'Then he would have married her instead! In the absence of anyone else, Katherine, you were merely a convenient–'

'It was Will!' She was struggling to find something to say, but I went on, 'Your son was in love with your daughter's husband.'

There was a long silence. Then she spoke, in hardly more than a whisper. 'Get out.'

'It's not Will's fault; he doesn't know–'

'Now.'

I left, my heart hammering and my hands slick with sweat. It was true it couldn't hurt Lawrence, and it would save Evie the anguish of having to reveal the truth about her father, but what had I done to Lily?

The next morning my dreams woke me once more, but this time the sun was already creeping under the heavy curtain, throwing shadows across the floor. I stared at them while the panic gradually subsided... Just as before, the familiar dream had left me with more than the usual tightness in my belly, and with a deeper sense of terror. More than anything though, there was a white-hot fury that still licked through me even now, minutes after re-establishing myself in my safe surroundings. But now I knew why.

This time, in the back of the ambulance, there had been someone else besides myself and Lieutenant Colonel Drewe. A small shadow, crouching by the other stretcher, trying to sink into the floor. A child. I'd tried to tell her to push aside the canvas flap and climb out, but my words were coming out as jumbled nonsense, and with no volume no matter how loudly I tried to scream. Then a hand was across my mouth – a memory hand, not a dream one – and all I could do was try to reach the girl with my mind; she had to get away, before he finished with me and turned to her...

Amy. Of course it was Amy. Evie's words echoed insistently in my mind. Her fears had become mine and now they would not go away. I remembered the idea that had hit me moments before Lily had come into the library with the news about Samuel Wingfield, but it was too late to mention it now. Bringing the child back here was out of the question. My eyes went to the suitcase that lay on the ottoman at the foot of the bed, open and awaiting only my nightclothes and toiletries. I had packed it at Dark River with such high hopes, such relief and such excitement, and now look at me.

Evie had expressed disappointment at what I'd told her had been my decision – whether or not Lily set the story straight later didn't matter; I

214

just didn't want the two of them to argue over it – but she had given me money for the train fare.

'Travel safely, Skittles. Will and I should be back home soon.'

Home. She was right; Dark River had been dancing on the edge of my mind at first, but my time here had first been too exciting, and then too emotionally draining, to spare the Dartmoor farm more than a fleeting thought, and I felt a pang of guilt as I realised I hadn't even put pen to paper since I'd arrived at Oaklands.

I dressed in my travelling clothes once more, and closed my suitcase, the dream still tugging at my memory and distracting me from my preparations. The idea came again, altered, and it made me stop everything and sit down for a minute, mulling it over. I looked at the clock. There was time, if I left now, and I seized my suitcase; breakfast would have to fall by the wayside today, but it would be worth it ... if I wasn't too late.

Lily had arranged for the car to take me to the station. She came out of the morning room and saw Mr Dodsworth handing my bag to the gardener, who did duty as a driver whenever necessary.

'Kitty,' she called, and I stopped in my tracks. She came over, and hesitantly touched my arm. 'What you said yesterday, about Lawrence–'

'Don't worry,' I said. 'No-one else knows.'

'I'm sorry if I was ... harsh,' she said. I looked at her closely, wondering if this was simply her way of sweetening things between us so I wouldn't tell anyone. But she did look sorry, and her face, always pale, now also looked much older. The

215

combined loss of her treasured son and her comfortable life had taken a strong, beautiful woman, and added at least ten harsh years in the space of a few weeks.

'I'm sorry too,' I said. However much it had hurt to have this woman I respected look at me with the same condemning eyes as my own family, I'd rubbed salt in her still-raw wounds. That it had been a necessary cruelty, to protect her from even worse pain, did not matter; I had been the one to inflict it so how could I blame her for still wanting me to go? 'I understand everything, truly. It's been an honour to meet you, Lady Creswell, and I'm only sorry it has ended like this.'

She nodded her acceptance, and turned away quickly, as if worried I might take her olive branch as an invitation to stay after all. But we both knew my days at Oaklands Manor were at an end, and I followed Dodsworth out to the car, and didn't look back as we turned onto the main road into town. It was only when we passed the spot where a young and besotted Will had overturned the butcher's van, and Lawrence had experienced the first, bittersweet pangs of love, that I felt a tear sliding slowly down my cheek.

I asked Shackleton to let me out in the town centre rather than at the railway station, and as the car faded into the distance, leaving me alone in the road with only my suitcase and a small purse, I wondered if I was doing the sensible thing after all. Then I remembered the dream, and turned to go into Frank Markham's shop.

Martin gave me the distracted smile of a shopkeeper who vaguely recognises a customer, but cannot remember their name, then went back to serving the woman at the counter. His manner altered when I stepped behind the counter and pushed open the door that led to the back.

'Hey, miss! You can't... That's not...'

'It's all right,' I said. 'I'm a friend of Evie and Will's.'

He blinked at me, and nodded his recognition, then quickly shook his head again. 'That may be, but, miss, that there's private!'

'Is Mr Markham home?'

'Miss!' Martin was across the floor in two strides, and put his hand across the doorway to prevent me from going through. 'I mean it. He'll have my hide if I let anyone up!'

He looked really worried, not just annoyed, and I suddenly realised why. 'Don't worry,' I said. 'I know, and I'm here to help. Will sent me.'

The lie gave him pause, and he stared back at me for a moment, then stepped away. 'I hope to goodness he did,' he muttered, and turned back to his customer.

I went up the narrow staircase, and found a tiny landing with a door leading off it. I knocked, and after a moment heard a hesitant voice from within. 'Who is it?'

'My name's Kitty. I'm a friend of Will's.' There was no reply, and I dropped my voice. 'Please, Mr Markham, I want to help, if I can.'

There was another pause, then the dragging sound of a bolt being pulled back. The door opened and the man who looked out frowned, but the frown cleared as he looked beyond me and saw

217

I was alone. He stepped back and gestured me in. There was a bright electric light inside, and I blinked after the dimness of the landing and stairwell. When I was able to look at him properly I could see a tall man, with a shock of grey hair surrounding a face that might have been appealing once, and eyes of the same colour as his hair. Not like Archie's always-shifting, many-shaded grey, these were one, cool and hard colour, and narrowed now in suspicion.

'What can you do to help? If you're thinking of calling the authorities, I won't–'

'No. It's not that. I'm offering to take her away to Devon with me. Just for a little while, until you can find somewhere safe for her.'

'There in't nowhere safe, stupid girl!' But it was fear that had sharpened his voice, and I didn't flinch.

'Maybe not in Breckenhall,' I allowed, 'but ... you have family, don't you?'

'My adoptive parents are in Canada now. And the McKrevies won't have her, if that's what you're getting at.'

I frowned, confused; hadn't Evie said he was a Wingfield? 'Who are the McKrevies?'

'My father's family. They'll turn her away on sight, poor thing.' He twisted to look at a door I assumed must be his bedroom.

'Is she in there?' I asked quietly. 'And is she all right?'

He turned back, quick and angry, but then relaxed. 'Yes.'

'Might I see her?'

'Do I have a choice?' he said in a broken voice.

218

'I've got to let you take her, haven't I?' He gestured at his left arm, and I saw the sleeve was pinned back just below the elbow. 'I can't take care of her. I knew that when I took her.' He looked at me with a pleading expression. 'But I had to do it anyway. You see that, don't you?'

I nodded, unable to speak for a moment; if this unknown child could invade my dreams, and her future become entwined with my past, I couldn't even begin to imagine how her father must feel. Frank moved past me and pushed open the door with surprising gentleness. I wondered if Amy was sleeping, but she sat in the middle of his narrow bed, a silver spoon clutched in her hand, and deep in concentration as she stared into it. She looked up and saw us, a bright-eyed four-year-old, her almost white-blonde hair a tangled mess, her clothes torn and dirty, but her face scrubbed clean, and solemn. She was terribly thin.

'I did my best to clean her up,' Frank muttered, 'but she kept wriggling and I didn't want to hurt her. She's eaten though,' he said quickly. 'Don't go thinking I haven't fed her.'

'Don't worry. It'll take a while to fatten her up.' I sat down on the bed. 'Do you like your spoon, Amy?' Amy nodded and held it up to her face again, going slightly cross-eyed as she stared into it.

I looked up at Frank, who seemed unable to take his eyes off his daughter. 'She's sweet. Why are you so sure the McKrevies will turn her away?'

'Why would they offer a home to the daughter of a prostitute, and a cripple they'd never wanted to begin with?'

'They never wanted you?'

'My mother married into their family out of spite over ... some old, forgotten feud. I don't know.' He flicked a dismissive hand. 'But she died having me, so they had me adopted out. No obligation once my mother was gone.'

'What about *her* family?'

'The Wingfields?' He gave a short laugh. 'To be truthful to you... What's your name again?'

'Kitty.'

'To be truthful, Kitty, I'd almost rather Amy stayed with her mother than join that band of thieves and liars.'

I was as taken aback by the coldness in his voice as much as by his words, but didn't comment. The Wingfield name was enough to tell me he had his reasons. 'Where are the McKrevies?'

'Blackpool.'

'That's not far. Have you written to them?'

'No.' He sighed. 'I've told you they won't have her. Ballentyne McKrevie's a hard old sod. He'll never have anything to do with me.'

'But you have to try!'

'What's lady for?' Amy piped up, brandishing her spoon at me.

'Lady is talking about helping us,' Frank said. 'Hush now. Daddy and the lady are going to go and talk some more, out there. Call me if you want me, but call quiet, see?'

She nodded. She had clearly become used to secrecy and subterfuge. Her wide blue eyes followed Frank and me, as we gave her little finger-waves by the door and then stepped back out into the front room.

'You must at least try,' I said again, sitting down without being invited. Frank fixed me with a long look, realised I wasn't going anywhere, and sighed again.

'Can I make you a cup of tea?'

'Please.' I looked around for the clock, but it was too late now to worry about catching the train back to Devon. I'd already decided what I was going to do. 'I'll take her.'

'So you said, and I don't want you to think I'm not grateful, but you can't just—'

'No, I mean I'll take her to Blackpool. To the McKrevies. I'm certain if they see her they'll want to help her.'

'I've told you, girl, they won't!'

'What if they don't know who she is?'

'If they...' He stopped spooning tea into the pot, and turned to stare at me. 'Have you lost your wits? If they won't take a child they know, why would they take a stranger?'

I hadn't thought that far ahead. The idea was only just unravelling itself in my head and I held up my hand, and then gestured for him to continue with what he was doing while I thought about it. In the end I gave up, but the idea still sat firmly in place, and I shrugged. 'What have you got to lose if they do turn her away?' I was so certain that one sight of the tow-headed child would be enough to melt the hardest heart that I was prepared to simply march up to the front door and throw her on this unknown family's compassion. 'If they see her, and are completely unmoved, which I can't imagine they will be, I'll just take her with me back to Devon, as I said in the first place.'

221

'So either way, she'd be safe,' Frank said, pouring hot water onto the tea in the pot. 'Away from me.'

'Don't see it like that,' I urged, feeling his anguish from across the room. 'I would look after her, and where I live isn't wealthy, but it's beautiful. It's in the country, and she could stay with me until you can make an arrangement to take her somewhere Ruth doesn't know about, where she can't send anyone after you both.'

'Why?' he asked suddenly. He put a cup of tea on the table at my elbow, and fixed his cool grey eyes on mine. 'Why does it matter so much to you? You don't know me, or Amy. You say you're a friend of Miss Creswell's, but I did her a terrible wrong. So come on, Miss Kitty, I want the truth, now. You trying to trick me into giving her up, so you can take her back to London?'

'No!'

He stared at my face a moment longer, gauging my honesty before subsiding, and sitting down opposite me.

'Well then?'

He was a stranger. I couldn't tell him about my experience with Colonel Drewe, even if I'd felt able to discuss my worries for Amy's future, which I couldn't. I didn't need to, in any case; those worries were echoed in the way he had risked so much to snatch her from her mother. That I could imagine it more vividly than he could was not something to be discussed, and made little difference anyway.

'My family turned me out,' I said at last. 'The lady at Dark River Farm, Frances Adams, took

222

me into her home, and made me her daughter. I feel I have a real home now.' I glanced at the bedroom door again, feeling tears prickling at my eyes. 'I want the same thing for Amy, Mr Markham. It's just … not fair.'

'Why did your family disown you?' His voice was softer now, and I believed he had accepted my reason.

'I can't tell you. It's not important, anyway.' I took a sip of tea and that helped to steady my voice. 'But you can trust me. It wasn't anything dishonest. I'm not a liar or a thief, like the Wingfields.'

'And you wouldn't take payment for what you're doing?'

'No. Well,' I hesitated, 'perhaps just the cost of the train tickets to Blackpool. I have the money to get to Devon myself; I was going back there today anyway, but–'

'I'll give you the money,' he said, a little gruffly. 'Don't think I'm mean. I just know that if you weren't genuine about helping you'd more than likely demand some kind of … recompense for your trouble, shall we say?'

'I promise you, Mr Markham, I only want to help. Truly.'

'When would you leave?'

'The sooner the better. But first I think we should try and smarten her up a little bit. Would you allow me to bathe her and wash her hair?' His lower lip trembled and clamped his top teeth into it to stop it. I looked away. 'I'll be very gentle,' I said quietly. When I looked back, he had himself under control again, and was nodding.

'I'll fetch the few things I've managed to get for her off the market,' he said. 'A few shirts and things on the thrift stalls is all.'

'That will be enough,' I said. 'Perhaps you could come in and explain to her what's happening, so she's not frightened?'

To my surprise Amy sat still for me, not even moving when I accidentally tugged at a tangle and yanked her head back, and that happened more than once; it was obvious her hair had not been brushed for a long time. The only time she reacted was when I reached out to take the spoon from her so I could work her too-thin little arms into the sleeve of her blouse. The shriek ripped through the room and brought Frank running, his face pale.

'It's all right,' I said quickly, relinquishing my hold on the spoon. 'Don't worry, Mr Markham. She's not hurt.'

''Poon!' Amy said, clutching it to her chest and looking at me with such a look of betrayal I found it hard not to laugh. Frank's face too, flickered into a smile, and he crouched beside his daughter.

'Sweetheart, the lady isn't going to take it away; she just wants to look at it. Will you let her see how pretty it is?'

Amy's face rose to mine, her eyes brimming with tears, but she held the spoon out to me. I took it, swallowing a rush of emotion that made my voice husky. 'Thank you.' I wasn't sure if I was grateful to Amy or Frank, or just for the chance to help these two mismatched and lost people. Neither did I know how I'd feel when it was time to part them.

We attracted no untoward attention at the railway station. Frank was well known in the town, and drew some interest at being seen with a young woman and a little girl, but he fixed a broad smile on his face and introduced us as family from the West Country. I was just preparing myself for the saddest of goodbyes, when I saw he was holding a ticket for himself. He saw me glance at it, and shrugged.

'It's not that I don't trust you,' he began, a little embarrassed, but I smiled.

'I'd expect nothing less.' I looked down at Amy, barely recognisable as the shaggy-haired child of this morning. She held my hand without hesitation; I wanted to believe it was because she trusted me already, but the realistic part of me knew she'd spent her entire young life being handed from person to person, and I was simply another in a long line of strangers into whose care she had been put. I saw Frank gently brush at the newly washed, dead-straight hair that hung beneath her bonnet, and looked away. The parting, when it eventually came, would hurt a great deal, but it wouldn't be Amy who felt the pain.

'It's number eighty-four.'

We stood at the top of an impossibly long street in Great Marton, on the outskirts of Blackpool. It looked as if the road would lead all the way through the heart of the city, right out to the coast, if we followed it; even though it was perfectly straight I couldn't see the end.

'The road's miles long,' I said, looking down at

Amy doubtfully. 'Will she be able to walk all that way?'

'It's only halfway down,' he said, and I wondered how many times he'd been back here, eyeing the wealth that would have been his were it not for ancient family feuds. 'On the left of the street. She'll be fine.' He crouched beside her, holding her arm with his one good hand. 'You be good, little one, and maybe you'll have a fine bedroom of your own tonight. Lots of toys. Would you like that?'

She nodded, but gripped her spoon tightly, as if reassuring herself that, no matter how many new toys she might somehow be given, she would always have that one.

'Why is she so attached to it?' I asked.

'I don't know. Shiny, I suppose. She had it when I found her, and when I tried to take it off her, to put it in my own pocket so she wouldn't lose it, she yelled to split the roof, just like she did with you.' He smiled and straightened, but as he turned away I could see his jaw quilt with suppressed emotion. 'I'll be waiting down there, in the park.' He pointed. 'I'll look after your case so's you can carry Amy's. Take as much time as you need, only...' he cleared his throat '...come and tell me. Whatever happens.'

'I will.'

He bent to pick up my suitcase, and I waited to see if he would actually say goodbye to his daughter, but when it became clear he wouldn't I took a firmer hold on Amy's hand, and drew her away down the street.

I still didn't know what I was going to say. I had

been wracking my brains on the train journey, to no avail, and it was only as we passed a small Anglican church, set back from the road, that an idea took hold. I bent and checked Amy's appearance, then led her to the door of the church. It was empty, but the back door stood open and, going through it into the small churchyard at the rear of the church, away from the road, I saw the vicar pulling up weeds from around an old, heavily leaning headstone.

'Excuse me,' I called. The vicar turned and straightened, eyeing the two of us with curiosity. Amy's hair colour and mine were both so vivid, yet very different. It was unlikely we were mother and daughter so it was best not to pretend we were.

'How can I help?' He threw the pile of weeds he'd been clutching onto a heap by the church wall, and wiped his hands on his trousers as he came over, prior to offering a handshake.

'I was wondering if you might know of a generous family,' I began, and saw his face cloud. 'I'm not looking for money, but for a safe home for my ... my sister's little girl.'

'Where's her real home?' He bent and looked closely at Amy, presumably searching for any sign of fear or ill-treatment. I was glad for his concern – it boded well – but hoped Amy wouldn't choose this moment to react poorly to strangers, or to break her customary silence and blurt out the truth. And I also hoped, fervently, that the kindly, middle-aged man wouldn't try to have a closer look at the silver spoon.

'Her mother, my sister, is unwell, and her

father...' I let myself tail off, hoping he would make the logical assumption without making me lie. I found it hard enough to spin a tale to a man of the cloth, but I didn't want to invoke a dark fate by speaking of death, not here in this churchyard.

'And have you no other family?'

'None, sir. I am about to leave for Flanders. Red Cross, you know. And my sister is terrified her child will be taken to an orphanage. She will be well again soon, we hope, and able to care for her daughter.' Again, I allowed doubt to enter my voice, and the vicar's expression clouded as he reached the conclusion I'd been hoping for.

He pursed his lips. 'A generous family, you say?'

'Generous-hearted, I should have said.'

'What brings you to this street?'

I floundered then, but decided to push my luck a little farther. 'My sister told me of a well-off family who she once worked for, and told me Great Marton was where they lived, but I'm afraid I'm not certain where to begin looking. Since we have no reason to believe they would take Amy anyway, I thought it best, when I saw your church, to see if you knew of *any* home where Amy might be safe and comfortable for a little while.'

His local curiosity was piqued. 'What family?'

I pretended to stumble over the name; I didn't want to put the words into his mouth. 'I'm afraid it's been a difficult time... I think perhaps it was MacKenzie?'

'McKrevie?'

I found it hard not to smile with relief. 'Oh. Yes, perhaps that was it.'

The vicar frowned. 'Well, I'd never thought of them as generous-hearted, as such, but they do contribute financially to the upkeep of the church. Although—' he brightened slightly '—Mr Mc-Krevie's two granddaughters are in town presently. They're both certainly kind enough to sweeten the old ... uh...' He stopped, blushing slightly. 'They live at number eighty-four. The big house with the courtyard, and the sycamores by the gate.'

I knew it was pushing things too far to hope he might agree to accompany me, so I said the next best thing. 'Could I ask your name, sir, so they know I've spoken to you?'

'You can tell them Father Steven sent you. And good luck, young lady. Young *ladies*.' He doffed an imaginary cap, and I smiled.

'Thank you so much, Father Steven.'

Armed now with a story, and the name of a respectable referee, I rang the bell of number eighty-four, and waited with a thundering heart.

Chapter Thirteen

'There's no Mrs McKrevie,' the butler told me, eyeing Amy with ill-concealed curiosity.

'Mr McKrevie then?'

'Which one?'

I thought back, and somehow came up with the name: 'Mr Ballentyne McKrevie?'

After a moment I was shown to the sitting room

of the large, though certainly not Oaklands-sized house. It was more like the type of house in which I'd grown up – a respectable and fairly impressive town house. The furniture was plain, which I liked, but there were no feminine touches that I could see, which meant I couldn't hope for a woman's sympathy. My story suddenly rested on very thin ice. I had no time to think up another, however; the door opened and a tall, thin man came in. His face was craggy and lined, and his eyes, sitting above puffy pockets, gleamed with sharp intelligence.

I stood up immediately, keeping the still-silent Amy's hand firmly in mine. Behind Mr Mc-Krevie I saw two girls, one around Evie's age, one perhaps sixteen. They were both pretty, but the younger girl, black-haired and blue-eyed, had a liveliness about her that was evident from the outset; she didn't sit politely, like the other one, but drifted about the room, paying little attention to either Amy or myself, or, indeed, the man I guessed was her grandfather.

He opened his mouth to speak to me, then, distracted and irritated, turned to her. 'For crying out loud, girl, sit down!' His accent was strongly Scottish, and although it was nothing like Archie's gentle accent it gave me an unexpectedly sharp pain.

'Sorry, Grandfather,' the girl said, and came to sit beside her sister, who was looking from me to Amy as if trying to guess what I would say before I said it.

I brought the story out again, seeing the younger sister soften as I hinted at Amy's tragic circum-

230

stances, and made sure to mention Father Steven. 'He said you were very generous-hearted, and always contributed to the upkeep of the church,' I half lied.

'Did he now? And that makes you think you can just walk in and drop your wee cast-off here?'

'She's not mine,' I repeated calmly. 'I'm just trying to do someone a service.'

'What did you say her parents were called?'

I faltered, then decided on names I'd remember, so I wouldn't trip myself up later. 'Her mother's Evie, and her father's William.'

'Can you prove you knew these people? Have you any photographs of you with them? Or with her? How do I know you haven't just snatched her off the street?'

To what purpose? I wanted to ask, but didn't. 'No, I have no photographs with me, I'm sorry.'

'Grandfather, it's only for a little while,' the younger girl said. 'We have the room to spare, and she wouldn't be any trouble, I'm sure.'

'She wouldn't,' I said eagerly, shooting her a grateful look. 'And Evie would collect her just as soon as she recovered.'

'Open the child's bag,' McKrevie said.

My patience with his games was growing short; either he would consider taking the child under his roof or he wouldn't. 'May I ask why?'

'I want to see what kind of provision your sister has made for her daughter,' he said bluntly. 'If there's care taken over what she's provided, I might believe your tale.'

I swallowed an angry retort. After all I was the liar here. He was perfectly right to disbelieve me.

231

But I could see now why Frank had known Amy would not be welcome here. He knew his father's reputation well. I opened Amy's small bag, and McKrevie hooked it towards him with his foot. He pulled out the few, clearly old and ill-fitting blouses, dresses and items of footwear, laying them surprisingly neatly on the floor beside him. I watched, with growing despair, as I saw exactly what he was seeing.

'None of these will fit that girl properly,' he said at last. 'You've just picked these off a market stall.'

'I haven't!' That, at least, was the truth.

'Grandfather, the little girl's sweet,' said the older girl. 'And look, she's very well behaved.'

'She's not a toy,' McKrevie snapped, 'and you're too old to be gushing over a stranger's child, Louise. If you had one of your own you wouldn't need to.'

'It's not my fault you frighten everyone away!' Louise snapped, and stood up, smoothing down her dress. 'No wonder Mother refused to come down with us. I'm going out for a walk.' She turned to her sister. 'Are you coming?'

The younger girl sent me an apologetic shrug, and followed Louise from the room. I saw McKrevie watching them with a look of exasperated affection on his face that was wiped away as soon as he turned back to me.

I bent and picked up the clothes Frank had found for Amy, and put them back in her bag. 'Am I to understand that, despite what Father Steven said, you're not–'

'Don't use that tone with me, girl,' McKrevie said. 'And it's got nothing to do with Father

232

Steven. This is *my* house, not his, and I won't have you making me out to be the one at fault.' He sat back in his chair and regarded me calmly. 'Furthermore, I don't believe that child has any connection with you, and I don't believe you're trying to find her a home because you're going out to France, either.'

'Belgium,' I said. I thought back to my first few nights at our little ambulance station, Number Twelve. 'I'm going to be attached to a unit just outside Dixmude. You can call and check in a few days, if you like. Ask to speak to a Captain Buchanan. My name is Katherine Maitland. You can describe me.' I held my head up and let McKrevie have a good look, but I knew all he'd remember would be 'short, plumpish and red-headed.' It would be enough; Archie would realise something was afoot, and would back up my story even if he didn't understand it.

I felt a twist of longing for him that hurt, and turned away from McKrevie so those shrewd eyes would not spot any of the pain in my face. 'I don't know what you think I'd have gained by—'

'Gained? What I think you'd have gained, girl, is the right to call back in a week, or a month, or even a year, when that child is firmly established under my roof, and in the hearts of my family, and demand some kind of payment for letting her remain here. And you know you'd get it.'

I saw how it looked then, and my resentment fled. 'I understand. You're wrong, but I understand. I won't trouble you any further, Mr McKrevie. Thank you for hearing my request.'

He stood up. 'Cardew will show you out.' Then,

to my surprise, he held out his hand. 'Perhaps your motives are pure after all, in which case I wish you and the child well. But you must understand I cannot open my house to every waif and orphan that comes calling. And many do, especially since the war started.'

I shook the hand he offered, remaining cool by reminding myself he'd just turned us out without any idea that I had anywhere else to go. But I did have somewhere. I would take Amy to Dark River as I'd planned, and we would look after her until Frank had found the means to take her away somewhere ... anywhere. She couldn't go back to her mother, to that life. It would be no life at all.

I was almost at the park, and wondering how Frank would feel when he saw his daughter again – he was sure to have mixed emotions – when I heard a timid voice just behind me.

'Miss?' I turned to see the McKrevie girls, looking a little embarrassed, but quite friendly.

I nodded in greeting, and smiled. 'Don't worry. I quite understand your grandfather's position. We're strangers to him.'

'Aye, he's not a bad man,' Louise said. 'I think, because of his job, and the house, people think he's richer than he is. But it's an old family home. We're no that rich really.'

'What is it your grandfather does?' I didn't like to ask about their father; he would be fighting age.

The girls looked at each other, and I saw Louise give a tiny shake of her head. With my thoughts on Archie, the first thing that came into my mind was secret war work, but that wouldn't have made sense, if people were trading on his job to coax favours. It wasn't my business though, and I could feel Amy tugging at my hand – she'd seen the open parkland just ahead.

'Thank you for speaking up for me,' I said to the younger girl. I realised they'd not been introduced by name, but it didn't matter now.

'But where will ye go?' She sounded genuinely concerned, and I bit my lip. The lie was in danger of spiralling too far; Amy was sure to run to Frank as soon as she saw him, and the love he held for her would be impossible to hide.

'I'm going to meet my brother,' I said. 'He's been helping me care for Amy since he came home from France.'

'A soldier?' Louise asked, and I saw the familiar flash of excitement I saw everywhere, in girls who'd had no experience of the truth of war.

'Yes. He lost an arm, so if you come along please don't stare.'

'Och, I'll no trespass on your time with your brother,' Louise said. 'And you shouldn't either, Helen,' she added. 'Come away now. It's been nice meeting you, miss,' she said to me, 'and I wish you well.'

'I don't want to come back yet,' Helen said. 'Might I please walk with you a while, miss?'

I fought down a frustrated groan, and made myself smile. 'Of course.'

'I'll be home in a wee while,' she said to Louise. 'Dinna look at me like that; I'm no going to embarrass myself.'

Amy let go of my hand the moment her feet

touched the grass, and she looked up at me, her eyes huge in her pale little face.

'Why it's as if she's never seen grass before,' Helen said, as Amy stooped to pat the ground with a bemused but fascinated expression.

'She's lived in the city all her life,' I said. 'Run along, Amy. It's all right; I'm right behind you.'

'Amy!' A man's voice cut across the space between us and a bench several yards away, and I looked up to see Frank scooping her up, the expected mingling of happiness and disappointment on his face. He looked over at me, and I knew I had to stop him from saying anything, but before I could speak, the McKrevie girl shielded her eyes and pointed with her closed parasol.

'Is that your suitcase?'

'Yes.'

'Is your uniform in there?' she asked, looking interested. I wondered if another year or two of war would see her going out there herself. She seemed to have too much energy to be cooped up at home.

I shook my head. 'No, we'll get those when we arrive.' More lies, but I took solace in the fact that I *had* served, at least. 'Anyway,' I said briskly, 'time is getting away from me, and we have to catch a train.'

'Where will you go?' she asked again.

'I have one more hope of a place for Amy; Evie told me of a kind lady in Devon.' As I spoke the words I felt the longing for it sweep through me, so fierce it was an ache. 'Dark River Farm, near Plymouth.'

'Plymouth!' she exclaimed, then blushed. 'Is it

236

pretty there?'

'The moors aren't what you'd call pretty, but it's certainly as beautiful as parts of Scotland, I should think. Very dramatic, and quite bleak in places.' I picked up my suitcase.

'I miss Scotland,' she said. 'Mother won't leave it, and Grandfather says we'll all maybe go back there to live someday.'

'Why are you living with him, anyway?'

'His health wasn't too good for a little while, and Mother thought it would help to have someone living in, since he can't seem to keep a housekeeper for more than a month.'

Small wonder, if the way he'd spoken to me was any indication. 'Do you like it here?'

'I like it better than Glasgow,' she said. 'And Grandfather's no so bad as he seems. I miss my father though.'

'Is he away fighting?' I asked gently.

She looked at me steadily, then glanced around to make sure no-one was listening. 'No. He's a … a conscientious objector. He's at the Princetown Work Centre on Dartmoor. Used to be the prison, aye?'

'I know it,' I said slowly, astonished that she would tell me, a relative stranger, such a grim family snippet. That explained her reaction to my telling her where I was going. I searched for a way to take the sad look from her face. 'They work outside, you know, on the moors. And they're not locked away like prisoners.' *Like Oli.*

'Oh, aye, I know. I'm no worrit about him. It's just … people say things, you know? He's no a coward though. He's what they call an absolutist:

237

willnae do a stroke of work that'll further the war effort.'

'And how do you feel about that?' I asked. My tone had become sharp. 'When you see brave men like him—' I nodded at Frank '—who might be pleased of some help. Soldiers, who would welcome someone who's safely tucked away at home to make them strong boots to keep out the mud. That wouldn't be a bad thing, surely?'

'Nowhere's safe,' Helen said, echoing Frank's words. Her eyes went to the skies and I felt a familiar shiver of fear; the air raids had changed of late, but not for the better; there fewer of those ugly, cigar-shaped Zeppelins now, and more bomber aircraft – only a short while ago an enemy attack on the Millwall Docks had gone shockingly awry, and had hit a nearby school instead. Eighteen children had died; few of them had been over the age of six. I looked over at Amy and my heart clenched tighter; already I knew I would be ready to kill for her.

'They bombed Edinburgh in April, you know,' Helen said, and then repeated, more quietly, 'Nowhere's safe.'

'But we're safer here than out there,' I pointed out, 'and those boys don't ask much of us. It's our duty to do what we can for them.'

Helen bit her lip. 'If my father willnae do anything that'll help to kill another human being, surely he can't be held to account for that? He didnae choose the war.'

'So he stays here, helping no-one.' All I could think about was the men I'd nursed, those who'd died, and those who were maimed... The war

238

marched on, and the boys fell, and this girl's father spent his days breaking rocks. 'I really should go,' I said, disappointed at the way the conversation had turned sour. 'Thank you again.'

'I hope the Devon lady takes yon wee girl in,' she said, nodding at Amy, who was coming towards us with a handful of daisies. She looked at me again. 'He's no a coward,' she repeated, and I touched her arm in mute apology for my harshness.

'It's all right,' she said. 'Not many people understand. At least you're not one of those women who can't pass a man of fighting age in the street wi'out handing out judgement along wi' their white feathers.'

'It's just... I've seen...' I gave up and shook my head. 'You're right. I don't understand, but that doesn't make it wrong, I suppose. I hope you see your father again soon.'

'And I hope you see the one you're missing.'

'Missing?'

She smiled then, and seemed older, even older than her sister. 'The one hidin' in your head, makin' you want to be fighting at his side,' she said. 'There is one, aye?'

'Yes,' I managed, my throat suddenly tight. 'How did you know?'

'Because of the way ye looked when ye talked about fighting men, and what they need from us. Has he been away long?'

'Since the start.' I wiped furiously at the tears that had sprung to my eyes. 'His name's Archie. He's a Scot, too.'

'Then he'll be fierce when he has to be, and careful when he must,' she said. 'You'd better get your train. It was nice meetin' you, Miss Maitland.'

'And you,' I said, getting myself under control again with an effort. I watched her walk away, back to the grand house that wasn't a home, and turned my thoughts away from Archie with difficulty and reluctance.

'Well,' I said to Frank as he drew level. 'I tried.'

'Yes,' he said, and let go of Amy's hand so he could touch mine. 'I'm grateful; don't think I'm not.'

'But?' I looked at him warily.

'But I don't know that I can let her go. Not all that way.'

I couldn't believe it. His face was tightly drawn, his mouth a thin line and his eyes cast down, away from mine. He had the most determined look on his face I'd ever seen, yet I could sense in him the longing to be convinced.

'Mr Markham,' I said gently, instead of giving him the sharp truths that sprang to my lips, 'please think about what you're saying. If Amy stays here, with you, it will only be a matter of time before Ruth sends her...' I cast about for the word, but failed to find it '...her men, up here. She can give them an address. They'll take her. You know they will.' I gestured to his left arm, not liking myself for drawing attention to it, but there was no help for it. 'You've said yourself, you can't properly care for her, so how will you protect her?'

'I ... I don't...' He took a short, ragged breath, then looked at me, finally. 'I'll find somewhere.'

'Look, let me take her just for a little while. Until you do find somewhere. You'd be welcome to come and visit her at any time, and you'll see she's in a wonderful, wonderful place. She'll love it. I promise you.'

He wavered. 'And it's a proper farm?'

I smiled. 'It's a proper farm. With cows and sheep and chickens. And even a pony and trap. I'll give you the address.' I saw both relief and acceptance in his face, and took his arm. 'Come on, we need to find the time of the next train to Plymouth.'

Frank paid for the tickets, although I still had the money Evie had given me. 'Keep it. You may find yourselves hungry later.'

Gratefully, I slipped the money back into my purse; in truth I hadn't even considered food; I'd had enough – put quietly into my bag by Mrs Hannah – for the trip back to Devon, but Amy and I had shared that on our way to Blackpool. We had another hour to wait for the train, and I told Frank he needn't wait, but he insisted.

We sat in the waiting room, Amy clutching her spoon and oblivious to the smiles she drew from the other waiting passengers, and Frank withdrawing further and further into himself as the minutes ticked by. He'd only known her for a week, but it was easy to see how she had become part of his life already; she felt like part of mine after only a few hours.

Seeing Frank's returning doubts, I began to talk to Amy about where she was going, and what she would see. 'Lots of animals,' I said. I had guessed, by now, that she was a long way behind in her development – she was more like a toddler.

241

'Do you like animals?'

'Mulls?'

'Like sheep. Ba-a-a-a. Do you know what a sheep is?' She shook her head doubtfully. 'They're white, and woolly, and a little bit silly. They live in the fields and give us their wool to make our clothes. Warm and cosy.' I snuggled her close and she giggled, and I looked at her in amazement; it was the first time, apart from when I'd reached for her spoon, that I'd seen anything but blank acceptance of her surroundings on her face. A glance at Frank told me I was actually making things worse; her laughter hurt him, knowing he had no idea when he might hear it again. I cleared my throat, and sat Amy upright again so I could watch her face.

'There are lots of people to care for you there.' I directed my words at the little girl, but I was saying it for Frank's benefit. 'Mrs Adams, who's the farmer. Then there's me, of course, and Belinda. And there's Sally and Lizzy too.' I didn't mention Jessie; I still bubbled with anger at the way she'd betrayed me to my mother. 'You'll especially like Lizzy,' I went on, 'she's very kind. And Evie will be home soon.'

Frank sat upright then. 'Evie Creswell that was? Will's wife?'

'Yes, of course.'

'I didn't know they were living down there too. Will didn't say.' He looked more relaxed. 'And this Lizzy? She's Evie's friend?'

'Yes. She used to be her maid, before the war.'

Now his mood was unmistakeably lighter. 'I'll be blowed,' he said quietly. 'Lizzy...' He frowned, trying to remember. 'Parkins? Parker!'

'You know her?'

'I do. She may not think too highly of me,' he said, and his expression was clear and warm now. He looked as he must have done in his carefree days. 'But she's all right in my book.'

'High praise,' I said, somewhat drily, and he grinned.

'She's a good girl, from what I remember. The last time we met I frightened her quite a bit, but she was kinder to me than she'd reason to be.' His voice lowered again, and trailed away in remembrance, then he looked up at the sound of the whistle. 'I'm glad we at least tried to get Amy back to her real family,' he said. 'It'll be something to tell her later on. But if I'm completely honest I'm happier seeing her off with you, and staying with Miss Creswell and Lizzy, than I would have been to see her here, never mind the posh frocks and fancy-mannered folk.'

'Are you saying Evangeline Creswell-that-was doesn't have good manners?'

Frank looked embarrassed, then caught sight of my raised eyebrow, and smiled. The train was pulling into the station now, and he sobered, looking down at his daughter. 'I've been thinking, sat here,' he said. 'When the war's over, I'll sell the shop, and I'll come for Amy. I can take her to Canada, to my parents.'

'That might not be for years,' I said. 'She'd be well settled by then, and Canada's a long way.'

'Then I'll move to bloody Devon,' he said grimly. 'Either way, I'm selling up the minute I can.'

'I'll write to you with the address,' I said. 'I haven't got anything to write it on here.'

He nodded. 'And I'll send money whenever I have it.'

A sudden, long-missed feeling of well-being crept over me. This man might have been something of a rogue in the past, and even a thief, but he loved his daughter and would clearly do anything to keep her safe. To me, and to Amy, that was all that mattered. I waved goodbye as the guard's whistle sounded, settled Amy on the seat next to me, sent a silent wish for peace to poor, sweet Lawrence, and turned my thoughts towards home.

Chapter Fourteen

We alighted from the train in the predawn, and slept for a couple of hours, huddled together in a field. Then Amy let me carry her most of the rest of the way to arrive at Dark River before the sun had properly risen. We were footsore and exhausted. Frances took one look at the two of us and asked no questions, but whisked Amy away to bathe and feed her.

'Bed,' she flung back over her shoulder at me, in her usual, no-words-wasted way, but I almost wept to hear her voice. I gave her a watery smile of gratitude, and fell, fully clothed into my bed five minutes later just as Belinda was getting up to start work. She too left her questions, for which I was grateful, and had simply bent to whisper, 'Welcome back,' and pat my shoulder, before leaving the room with a quiet, blessedly familiar click of the door latch.

Much later I blinked awake and glanced at the window; the sun had already moved around to the front of the house, which meant it was almost teatime. I couldn't remember sleeping so long, so deeply, with neither disturbance nor dreams. A sudden, very loud shriek from downstairs made me jump, then smile, and I washed quickly and changed my clothes, pulling the first thing I could find from the suitcase Frances had brought up sometime during the day and left opened on Sally's bed. It was one of my favourite skirts, taken to Oaklands to wear with pride at dinner, but had never been taken out of the case. Here at the farm it had seemed smart and respectable, as it had even in Ecclesley, but at Oaklands it had merely looked shabby and even embarrassing. I tucked in my blouse and fastened the belt, and smiled at my reflection.

'Welcome back,' I echoed Belinda's words, and went downstairs to see who had tried to take Amy's spoon away.

Lizzy looked up as I went into the kitchen. She had Amy on her lap, and a strange smile on her face. 'Everyone's dying to know who this is, you know,' she said.

'But not you?'

'I know perfectly well who it is. We've met, haven't we, Amy?' She was rewarded with a shy smile, and I felt something in me melt. 'I'm just

245

curious as to what on earth she's doing here.'

'When Frances comes in, I'll tell you,' I said, checking the teapot. 'It's a long story.'

'Pour me one please, if you wouldn't mind,' Lizzy said. She lifted Amy off her lap and stood up. 'I'm glad you're back; we're short-handed now. Sorry to say this when you've just got up, but Sally's left.'

'Left? Why?' I hadn't been particularly close to Sally, but she was a quiet, dependable sort, a familiar face, and I'd miss her calm, hard-working and friendly presence around the farm.

'She went to train as a nurse after her brother was badly hurt,' Lizzy said. 'Brought it all home to her a bit, I think.'

'Oh that's awful. Is he all right?'

'They think he will be, but it'll take an awfully long time. He lost both legs, and part of his jaw, but they can work such miracles now. He's convalescing at Exeter.' Her voice trembled a little as she went on, 'Evie wrote to tell me about Lawrence.'

I felt the sting of tears again. 'He was angelic,' I said quietly. 'A lovely, lovely boy.'

'He was. Evie once said, before the war of course, that he wasn't the bravest of soldiers. Just a turn of phrase, but it stuck in my mind when I heard he'd joined up.'

'He once told me he'd not been of particular help to you when you needed him.'

'It wasn't his fault. How's Will about it? He and Lawrence were always good friends.'

'I didn't see him much before I left,' I said. I hated keeping things from Lizzy, but I'd done enough damage. 'He'd been confined to bed. I think they're planning on coming back soon.'

'Yes, I understand Lady Creswell is going to stay with her parents for a while,' Lizzy said, accepting her tea and taking a sip. 'Oh, that's lovely, thank you. I don't know how, but Belinda always manages to make it taste of wet compost, even when all she's done is pour what's already made.'

I laughed, and the solemnity retreated. 'And how is Bel?'

'Still trying to avoid Seth Pearce.' Lizzy grinned. 'He's completely smitten, the poor lad.' She looked over at Amy, who was wandering towards the door. I started towards her, but Lizzy held up a hand and spoke quietly. 'Let her go, Skittles. She can't hurt herself. This is the first interest she's shown in looking around.'

'She's an odd little thing,' I said. 'I suppose it's because of the life she's led. Perfectly fine whoever she's with, but hardly a smile to be seen.'

'She's started to smile since she woke up earlier,' Lizzy said. 'Not much, but she seems to have relaxed a little bit.'

'As long as she has her spoon,' I pointed out, and Lizzy nodded.

'Ah, yes. That gave me quite a jolt, but it was the way I recognised her for certain.'

I looked at her questioningly, and, with one eye on the small, stockinged foot that was stretching experimentally over the threshold, she explained. 'Ruth came back to Oaklands last year, trying to sell information about...' She stopped herself, but I shook my head.

'I know about the Tingtang Star.'

247

'Kalteng!' she said, just as Lawrence had, and I smiled, but swallowed a sudden lump in my throat. 'Well, anyway, she brought Amy with her – though I didn't know that was her name until Frank told me – and Ruth was getting above herself with her demands, so I gave Amy that spoon, just to show her how easy it would be to have her accused of theft. Slightly underhand, I grant you, but since it was Ruth who'd seen me in prison for her crime I felt it was justified.'

'And you let her take it away?'

Lizzy shrugged. 'It was just a spoon, and the child seemed to like it.'

'Do you think she remembers you?' I craned my neck around, tensing as I saw the second foot follow the first, and Amy's little hand relinquish its hold on the doorjamb.

'I shouldn't think so. All I did was give her some bread and honey, and that spoon, and then they were gone again. I saw Frank not long afterwards, and he told me Ruth had refused to let him see her.'

I gave up trying not to worry, and followed Amy out into the yard. Lizzy came too. 'Frank remembers you fondly, you know,' I said.

'Does he now?' She looked bemused. 'I broke into his home and hid under the stairs. I can't think why he'd think well of me!'

'He said you were kind to him.'

Amy was walking more quickly now, and her unshod feet didn't flinch from the stony ground of the yard. I couldn't help wondering how often she'd gone without shoes before, and how toughened up her little feet must be. And if her feet were tough, what about her heart? I ached at the thought of what she must have seen and lived through. The sudden and familiar low call of a wood pigeon made me look up, and I took in the view of the brown-and-green moors, the huge, open sky, and the woodland in the distance. When I looked back at Amy again she was stooping to pick up a handful of dirt and study it, and the ache turned into a little squeezing feeling of relief that she would have the chance to put it all behind her, and that her future no longer held the same threat it had only yesterday.

'I think this will be a good place for her,' I said. 'You do think Frances will let her stay, don't you?'

'If you're the one who's asking?' Lizzy said with a faint smile. 'Of course she will.' She hesitated then, and cleared her throat. 'Sweetheart, I know why you're doing this.' She came closer and hooked her arm through mine. 'It's not something you ever need to talk about, but...' she hugged my arm '...I know, that's all.'

I was about to reply, when I noticed Amy lifting the dirt, inevitably, to her mouth. 'Amy! No!'

Startled, she dropped the dirt, but she didn't cry. Instead she sank silently to her heels and put her arms over her head. I'd taken two steps towards her, and was about to seize her grubby hand but just stopped myself in time. I shoved my hands beneath my own armpits, and turned helplessly back to Lizzy, who bit her lip, and I could see her eyes glistening.

'She'll be fine, in time,' she said gently. 'Don't worry, Kitty. You did the right thing bringing her here, but it'll take a while.'

'I must write to Frank, and tell him the address. He's promised to send money when he can, but he's also trying to put aside enough to be able to take her somewhere safe.'

'Give the letter to me and I'll post it for you in the morning. I'm going to the village myself.'

I smiled my thanks and turned back to Amy, who was slowly dropping her arms from their protective position, and had looked around, relieved to see Lizzy and I talking amongst ourselves and apparently paying her no further attention. She remained squatting, her spoon still clutched in her hand, and began to dig at the loose layer of soil and small stones, soon absorbed in her game.

'Look at that,' Lizzy mused with a smile. 'Best Creswell silver too.' I gave a little snort, and Lizzy turned to go back indoors. 'I'll keep an eye on Amy from indoors, but give Belinda a shout, would you? She's supposed to be cleaning off the tools in the barn.'

'Supposed to be?'

'She should have finished ages ago, and I've seen neither hide nor hair of her all afternoon.' Lizzy raised her eyes briefly to the sky and tutted, and I smiled, enjoying the familiarity of it all.

'I'll send her in.'

Crossing the yard, I turned back to check Amy was still happily engrossed in digging, and my attention was caught by a movement by the fence. Nathan! What in blazes was he still doing here? We'd been longer at Oaklands than we'd planned, and he should have left Devon long ago; no-one's Blighty leave was this long. I made up my mind to ask Belinda, but as I pushed open the

250

barn door I was distracted and amused by the sight of a guilty Belinda leaping to her feet from the pile of now-cleaned sacks.

'I'm just... Oh, it's you.'

'Yes, it's me. Lizzy wanted me to call you. Surely not dozing, were you?'

She looked sheepish. 'I was disturbed in the early hours,' she reminded me. Then she grinned and came over, flinging her arms around me and dancing me around in a little circle. I couldn't help laughing. 'Come on, I've got Amy to see to!'

'Oh, yes! You must tell me all about her,' she said, letting go of me and picking up her discarded pullover.

'Bel, why is–'

'Oh. Wait. Why does Lizzy want me?' she asked, cutting off my question about Nathan.

I blinked. 'Uh, I don't know. She just asked me to call you.'

We emerged into the late afternoon sunshine, and I found my eyes immediately seeking out Amy despite Lizzy's promise to watch her from the kitchen window; instinct was quick to take hold.

'Did she say anything about going out?' Belinda persisted.

'Out where?'

'The sawmills.'

'No, I told you she didn't say why she wanted you.'

'I bet she wants me to go,' she muttered. 'Why can't you go?'

'I'd be happy to,' I said, 'if I knew what you were talking about.'

Bel draped her jumper over her face and

251

groaned. 'She's always trying to get me to go. It's because of Seth.'

'Seth now, is it?' I said, amused. Then I remembered something, and brightened. 'Does this mean Frances agreed to that suggestion of his? Bel ... have we got a horse now?'

'You could say that,' she grunted, still from beneath her pullover. 'He's more or less ours whenever we want him, except we haven't borrowed him yet. *I'm* not going out there again, and Jessie can't ride. Now we're to start paying him, and Lizzy's got such a romantic soul she's bound to make *me* go.'

We'd drawn level with Amy now, and I stooped to take her hand. 'What's wrong with that? It's better than cleaning muddy old tools, surely?'

'No it's not.' Belinda snatched her jumper off her head, flinging it over her arm instead. Amy watched her with solemn, interested eyes. 'I don't find him the slightest bit attractive, Kitty! But he's sweet, so I feel bad when he gets all tongue-tied.'

'Well tell him! Then you won't have to spend your days avoiding Lizzy.'

'Will you offer to go instead? The little girl would love a ride in the trap.' She beamed at Amy.

I sighed. 'If it turns out that's what she wants you for, I'll offer,' I promised. We stopped at the door to knock grass and earth off our boots, and Amy banged her foot on the floor too, in imitation. Then she looked up at me, and gave me the sunniest, happiest smile I'd ever seen, and I walked into the house on air.

Jessie was in the kitchen too now, and had

252

clearly been told of my return, and the new addition to our Dark River family. 'Welcome back,' she said, and I couldn't read her mood, so I just thanked her, hoping she wouldn't be jealous of Amy now, too. Lizzy had pushed a box across the table towards her and I could see it held two packets of butter, a biscuit tin – probably containing some of Lizzy's home-made biscuits – and a large dewar bottle of milk. Beside these, she wedged a jar of farm honey.

'If you go now, you'll be home by teatime,' she said. Jessie nodded and stood up, both hands on the box. She looked expectantly at Belinda, then back at Lizzy, who nodded. 'And you, Bel. You know Frances doesn't like to send you girls out alone, not since your accident.'

She turned back to pick up something else, and Bel shot me a look and mouthed, 'You promised!'

I groaned; the last thing I wanted was to spend the next hour in the company of Jessie Goulding. Bel's look turned pleading, and I sighed. 'I'll go instead of Bel,' I said. 'I think Amy would enjoy the ride in the trap.'

Lizzy put two large brown eggs in the box, and tucked the spare bit of lining cloth around them. Her lips twitched in a little smile as she flicked a glance at Belinda. 'Why do you sound as if you're reading that from a piece of paper, Kitty? Go on, then, I don't mind who goes.'

Amy sat between us on the seat, and Jessie took the reins while I slipped an arm around the little girl. 'Animals,' I said, pointing to the little trap pony. I wondered if she'd remember.

'Mulls,' she repeated. 'Seep.'

'Pony,' I said.

She looked back at Pippin. 'Pony?'

'Good girl.' I hugged her again, then we moved off, and I felt her tense and grab at the seat. Again I was reminded that she hadn't had the encouragement and the example most other four year-olds had been blessed with. Gradually, as she became used to the rocking sensation, her grip eased, and by the time we were on the main road to Princetown, her little hands were linked in her lap. She looked up at me proudly, and I smiled and hugged her again; not even Jessie's silence could darken this moment for me.

'Why is Nathan still here?' I asked, when that silence had, after all, become embarrassing.

'Why shouldn't he be? He works hard enough now.'

'Well, shouldn't he have gone back by now? You know, to the war? He said he was on leave.'

She gave me a shrewd look. 'He also said he found us by chance,' she reminded me. 'Neglected to mention that chance involved finding our address from Will's friend, and making his way here deliberately.'

'Do you think he went absent without leave?' I thought about Oli, and went cold.

'No, I don't think he's run away. He takes the trap out quite a lot, drumming up portrait-painting business, and he'd be worried about being seen I would think.'

We were nearing what had once been Dartmoor Prison, and I looked at the men in the grounds and remembered the younger McKrevie girl. 'Do

254

you think he might be a conchie?'

Jessie leaned over the side of the trap, and spat neatly on the ground. I was shocked. 'Jessie!'

'What? Ladies don't spit, I suppose.'

'Well, no.'

'And men don't shirk.' She pointed to the figures in the distance. 'Except they do.'

'Have you ever given anyone a white feather?' I asked, uncomfortable to see such an extreme version of my own sentiments. Spitting in the street!

'A few,' she said. 'Back in Gloucester.'

'And how did you know they weren't Blighty cases, or just home on leave?'

'I think one of them was, actually. He threw the feather back at me.'

'Handing out judgement along with white feathers,' I repeated softly, and gave Jessie a look I hoped conveyed how I felt. 'You can't tell, you know,' I said. 'I've sent men home who didn't look as if they had a scratch on them. Particularly when they had their clothes on. I mean, look at Will.' I turned back to face the road, and said again, 'You can't tell.'

'That's why I stopped doing it,' she admitted. 'When that man threw the feather back he had such a look of contempt on his face, I could almost see him thinking, *What do you know?*' She flicked the reins, urging Pippin to go faster. 'I realised I didn't. I couldn't. So I stopped handing out feathers.' Her gaze lingered on the stone walls of the Work Centre as we passed. 'But those, they're not Blighty cases, are they? *They're* not home on leave. They're shirkers.'

'And if they have genuine reason to object?'

255

Jessie turned back to me. 'You, of all people, shouldn't accept that. Not after what you've seen.'

'Maybe what I've seen qualifies me better than you,' I said, not realising I was thinking it until the words fell out. Her words had echoed Lawrence's, questioning my belief that he would be safe, and the loss snatched at my breath again. He'd known, somehow... This time, he'd known. And I'd given him some nonsense about turning Oaklands into a convalescent home. I looked down at Amy's white-blonde hair, streaming out from under her hat in the evening breeze, and I thought about her father, his arm gone from the elbow down, his livelihood ruined. I thought of Will, his courage and his pain ... and of Evie's selfless, terrifying dash across no man's land, believing him to be dead yet unable to leave him alone out there.

And then I thought of Archie. Where he might be now, what he might be doing, whether he was even still alive. None of us had chosen the war, but we were in it, and everyone was part of it. We didn't choose the weather, but when it was stormy we helped those caught in the worst of it. We didn't choose sickness, but we sacrificed what we had to help those who suffered. I looked again at the diminishing figures of men swinging picks at rocks, and wondered what possible purpose was served by punishing those men who took the absolutist stance. What good was it doing, to deprive their families of an income? To make pariahs and outcasts of those families, and to cause those men to sicken and, even die?

I didn't voice these thoughts. It wasn't something I wanted Amy listening to. If the war continued she would be able to form her own opinions, but for now we had the peaceful evening, and the gentle sound of Pippin's hooves and the rolling wheels beneath us, and that was what I wanted her to remember tonight, when she lay her head down to sleep in her new home.

Seth Pearce was talking to his two remaining workers, and washing his hands at the outside tap, when we rolled into the yard. He looked up, and for a moment his face was lit and seemed almost handsome, but then he saw it was only us, and he turned back to finish, taking his time and twisting the tap with unnecessary force. Disappointment manifested itself in many ways.

'Good afternoon,' I called out, deliberately cheerfully. 'We've brought you some things from the farm.'

'Right you are,' he said, rubbing his hands on his mucky trousers to dry. I wondered why he'd bothered washing them.

'Wait here, sweetheart,' I said to Amy, and climbed into the back to hand the box down to Seth. 'I never got the chance to say thank you, Mr Pearce.'

His smile returned, but it was a mere trace of amusement, not the hopeful light of before. 'For what?' he said, 'the arrangement with Pirate, or for not telling the truth about what happened?'

I shot a glance at Jessie, who didn't look back. I didn't know if she'd heard. 'For your kindness to Belinda,' I said carefully, watching his face soften slightly. 'She much recovered now, thank you.'

He nodded. 'Right you are,' he said again. He looked into the box and his smile widened. 'This looks 'andsome. Wait there while I empty your bottle and rinse it out, then you can take it back with you.'

He went into the house that stood alongside the sawmill, the box I had struggled with sitting easily on his shoulder, and I looked around, wondering if, by any miracle, Woody was still here. The field was empty, but the stable door was half open, and a large, strong-looking horse stood with his head poking inquisitively out at the strangers to his yard. His long face was white, but a black splotch over his left eye told me who he was. I hopped down off the back of the cart and went to him.

'Nice to meet you, Pirate,' I said quietly, stroking his nose. He whickered and nudged my hand, but I had nothing to give him. 'How's things then, eh, old boy?' I ran a hand down as much of his neck as I could reach through the door, and he stood steady, his breath blowing my hair where it had escaped my hat.

'Mulls?' Amy called, and I turned with a smile.

'Big pony,' I said. 'Horse.'

'Pony.'

'All right.' No need to confuse things now. 'He's called Pirate,' I said. 'Do you like him?' She shrugged and went back to playing with her spoon. I turned back to Pirate. 'I'll come and fetch you soon. We can work together. How'd you like that?'

'Whenever you like,' Seth said, appearing with Frances's now-washed dewar bottle, 'Exercise'll

258

be good for him, but take it easy with him if you can; things will get busy here soon, ready for the winter. I need him fit and healthy.'

'Don't worry. I won't work him too hard. We'll be starting to get the hay in, in a day or two. He'll be perfect for that. It'll mean we can use the big cart and get it done in half the time.'

'Right you are.' He handed me the bottle, and I gave Pirate a last pat. 'Thank you. I'll call for him in a few days, if that's all right?'

'Will you, uh...' he looked past me at Jessie, sitting with Pippin's reins ready to flick him into motion '...will you be bringing the other miss? I'd like to see how she's faring, you know.'

'I don't know,' I said truthfully, and made up my mind to get Belinda here no matter what, even if it was just to put Mr Pearce straight about her intentions. Or lack of them. 'It depends who's free at the time.'

He nodded, then abruptly changed the subject. 'Are you ladies keeping your barns locked?'

'I ... I don't know,' I said, and turned to Jessie. 'Are we?'

'Not that I know of,' she said, equally puzzled. 'Why?'

'Oh, best lock 'em. Tell Mrs Adams to get a good sturdy padlock. I'll fix it for her if she can't find anyone to 'elp.'

'Mrs Adams is quite capable of doing that her-self.' Jessie replied, somewhat sharply.

'Why is it necessary?' I asked, embarrassed; Mr Pearce had only been offering help, after all.

'Some folks round 'ere have found tools gone missing. Fetch a good price they do, on the mar-

259

kets up Exeter way, where no-one recognises them.'

'I'll tell her,' I promised, and climbed back onto the front seat next to Amy.

'How do you know?' Jessie asked, before we pulled away.

'Beg pardon, miss?'

'How do you know they fetch a good price in Exeter?'

He fixed her with a steady look, and his helpful manner slipped away. 'Because I bloody well searched everywhere until I found them, that's how.'

We were almost back at Dark River before Jessie spoke. 'You know why Belinda's not interested in Mr Pearce, of course.'

I didn't like her knowing tone, and my own voice was more than a little frosty. 'No, how could I? How could *you* know?'

'It's because of Nathan.'

'Bel's not interested in Nathan.'

'She told you that, I take it.'

'She did. And I believe her.'

Jessie chuckled. It was a surprisingly, and annoyingly, pleasant sound. 'That must have been before you went away, then.'

'It was.' I had a nasty feeling, and a glance at Jessie confirmed it.

She turned to me with a little quirk to her mouth. 'They're spending an awful lot of time together, for someone who's not interested.'

We were coming up on the entrance to the long track that led to Dark River now, and she slowed

260

Pippin's trot, ready for the turn. One of her hands came out and steadied Amy on the seat, and I wanted to shove it away. I was supposed to be the one who protected the child. Then I felt a lurch of shame; was I really just as suspicious and jealous as she was?

'Belinda's flighty,' I said, putting my own hand on Amy's back. 'She's just looking for fun, that's all. And he's a charmer.'

'If you say so. But I'd say she was more interested in him than vice versa. Hold tight, lovey,' she said to Amy, and the cart wobbled onto the rough track, giving me that warm sense of homecoming again and pushing thoughts of Belinda and Nathan to the back of my mind.

It was three days later that Jessie's words came back to me. I chose a time when she was unavoidably busy with Frances, and asked Belinda to come with me to pick up Pirate. 'You can ride him back, if you like,' I offered. 'I'll bring the cart.'

Amy looked up from her scribbling paper, and I saw it was covered only with thick black lines. 'I comin' too?'

'Of course,' I said, and held out my hand. 'Come with me. We'll tell Miss Lizzy where we're going.' She put down her pencil and checked her spoon still hung on the ribbon Frances had fastened to her pinafore. I couldn't believe the solution had been so simple – no more screams. As long as she had it, she was happy, and could use two hands. She slid down from her chair and ran ahead of me to the stairs.

Belinda had stopped, with one arm in her

jacket sleeve. 'I don't want to go out there; you know that.'

'Don't be soft,' I said briskly. 'All you have to do is make it quite clear you have no feelings for Mr Pearce, then we can all stop treading on eggshells around him, and you won't have to keep finding excuses to disappear whenever there's an errand to be run.'

'You bring Pirate back then,' she said. 'I'll take you to the yard, but that's all.'

'You are making a mountain out of a molehill,' I grumbled, and went upstairs to tell Lizzy we were going out.

As good as her word, Belinda stopped at the gate of the sawmill, and barely waited until I had climbed down before urging Pippin to turn around. 'Hop in the back, love,' she said to Amy, and Amy obediently scrambled into the back to sit on the pile of blankets and sacks we used to cover whatever we were carrying in wet weather. I couldn't help feeling a twinge of disappointment when she didn't look back at me as they moved off.

Mr Pearce had heard us arrive, and came out of the house with a look of hopeful expectation. I felt awful. 'I'm sorry,' I said quickly, 'Bel wanted to stop and chat, but Amy's fussing.' A less fussy child I'd never known, but he wasn't to know that.

'Right you are,' he said. He gestured to the stable. 'I've saddled him up already. Saddle soap and whatnot's in this bag, and if your friend had waited a moment I'd have put some oats in the back of your cart. I'll bring them over later, instead.'

'Thank you,' I said, unable to hide a little smile when I thought about telling Bel she hadn't avoided him after all. 'That's really kind.'

'Not at all,' he said. 'The butter and milk's fresh as you like, and tasty. And the honey's 'andsome too. I'll, uh, I'll fetch the biscuit tin over to you later, when I bring the oats.'

Riding down the grass verge, with the comfort of a saddle beneath me and proper tack, I let my mind drift back over everything that had happened lately. Testing the memory of Lieutenant Colonel Drewe, and of Oli, and of the loss of my child, I realised there was still pain there but it was fading. Oliver would write soon, and then I would be able to write back; Drewe was dead... Only the loss of the baby still tore a little more deeply, and Amy was going some way towards easing that. Part of me knew that was foolish but for now it was something I could hold on to, and I would worry about losing her too, if and when it happened.

Then there was Archie. The familiar ache tugged at the pit of my stomach, and I wondered what he was doing right now. It hurt to think of him so far away, but it hurt worse to remember his kiss, and my swift end to his hopes that had come so soon afterwards. And why? Why had I done it? What had Lawrence said? His words, and his voice, seemed to speak directly into my heart: *you must seize every speck of joy that drifts your way*... But he had been unable to seize his own, after all. His sadness at the hopeless love he held for Will had dogged his last days, and he'd never

263

had the opportunity to find something to chase that sorrow away; death had stolen that chance. I'd promised Will I'd write to Archie, and only hesitated when I'd learned the truth about Jack Carlisle, but what if I did discover Archie was a spy too? What difference would it make? I sat up straight and urged Pirate into a canter, the wind in my face whipping away the short laugh that escaped into the air, and filling me with energy and excitement. On the heels of Lawrence's sad proclamation, I heard Nathan's words.

Never is a long, long way away, and life is short. Remember that.

I took Pirate the long way around, through the woods, and across the field. Coming back down to the yard I saw the cart, with Pippin still standing patiently in the traces, and no sign of Belinda. I jumped down off Pirate, hooking his reins over the fence post; Belinda would catch it for sure if Frances was around, and I sighed with exasperation as I began to unhook the cart myself. I eased Pippin forward, and was about to lead him to the water trough, when I heard a tinkling sound from the back of the cart.

I patted Pippin, confident that he would stand steady while I investigated, and went around to the back end of the cart and lowered the flap. To my horror I saw Amy, surrounded by grubby tools, and worse, broken glass. She grinned when she saw me, and lifted the tool she'd used to smash the glass with. I climbed up quickly, my eyes flashing over her for signs of red where there shouldn't be any, but, miraculously, she hadn't cut herself. It

264

must have been just one blow, and what was glass doing in the back of the cart anyway?

I looked closer and groaned; the wine bottle we'd so cheerfully emptied before our little misadventure with Woody. Bel had tossed it back here, and it had rolled under the seat to be forgotten. Until now.

I held my hand out to Amy, hoping she hadn't formed an attachment to the tool she'd found, as she had with the silver spoon Lizzy had given her. She hadn't, and handed me the dibble. Small, but sturdy enough to break through the stoniest earth to make holes for seeds and bulbs, it had made short work of the wine bottle, and the spade-like handle had helped Amy grip it with both hands. A fraction off-centre and it would have slid off the glass and into her leg. A chill swept over me when I thought what might have happened, and I thought I might actually be sick. Where in blazes was Belinda?

I helped Amy step over the broken glass, and took her to the kitchen door, trying to keep my voice calm. 'Lizzy, I'm just putting the horses away. Can you watch Amy?'

'Of course,' she said, shutting the oven. 'Come on, Amy, love. Sit and finish the drawing you were doing before, and tell me about the new horse.'

'Big,' Amy said, letting go of my hand and climbing onto the chair. 'Mulls. Not seep.'

'No, not sheep,' Lizzy said, and waved me away.

I quickly cleaned up the broken glass, wrapping it in one of the smaller blankets, and then put the dirty tools back in their box ready for cleaning. Then I turned Pirate and Pippin out together into

265

the field; I'd clean them down and feed them when I'd found Belinda, and she could blasted well help me!

I was about to go into the house when I remembered the tools, and sighed, turning back to the cart. The box was heavy; they were mostly small, handheld tools, but made of metal, and there were several of them. I hooked open the door with my foot, glad Frances had not yet bought a padlock for it, and lugged the box inside. Nathan was in there, working, and Belinda was there too. They were a perfectly respectable distance from one another, which made me think of Jessie's assertion that Bel was keener than Nathan, but they both looked guilty when they saw me.

'Kitty! I was just about to put Pippin away,' Bel said, jumping up from her comfortable seat on an upturned tea chest.

'He's in the field,' I told her coldly, dropping the box where I stood. 'He needs feeding.'

'Of course,' she said, then her face went slack with horror. 'Oh! Amy!'

'Oh, Amy,' I agreed. 'Don't worry; she's safe, no thanks to you.'

'Kitty–'

'I don't care,' I said, and turned to go. 'You're clearly more interested in spending time with your beau than anything else, so I don't want to listen to anything you have to say.'

She followed me out into the sunlight again, but her guilt had faded. 'Is that what you're more worried about?'

'What?'

'Me being with Nathan. It seems to me that's

266

what's got you so upset, not that I left Amy alone in the cart for a few minutes.'

I rounded on her furiously. 'A few minutes! When I found her she had smashed that old wine bottle to bits with a dibble! It's a wonder she didn't cut herself, or worse!'

'And still the only thing you can think of to say is that I'm spending time with my beau!'

'Bel, you told me you weren't interested. What's upset me, apart from Amy, is that you lied about it. To me! What did you think I'd say?'

'I'm sorry,' she said, subsiding slightly. 'If it's any consolation, he really couldn't care less about me. I'm not nearly worldly enough. Look, I'm sorry about Amy too, I'll clear up everything that—'

'I've done it.'

'Well. Thank you.' She saw I was still angry, and became defensive again. 'Look, it's all right for you, Maitland. You went off to the big posh house, got invited to parties, had all your fun. What was I left with?'

'Fun?' I was vaguely aware of someone coming out of the kitchen and going to the compost pile, but my blood was boiling now and I didn't care. 'If your idea of fun is being made to feel like a poor acquaintance – tolerated, manipulated, and then thrown out, then you're welcome to it!'

'Thrown out?'

'When Lawrence died, and I was no further use, yes. I was told to leave. And...' I stopped, my voice hitching as I remembered the awful scene '...Lady Creswell knew what had happened in Belgium. She knew it all along.'

'Oh, darling,' Belinda took me into a hug, and

267

I let her, feeling all my anger ebb away. She was infuriating, but she had such a good heart it was difficult to stay angry with her for long. 'Don't let her upset you,' she murmured. 'Frances loves you more than anyone, and she's overjoyed to have you back.'

We both heard the kitchen door slam; it must have been Jessie putting the vegetable peelings out. I drew back and my eyes met Belinda's, and she lifted hers to the heavens. We both laughed, and the last bit of tension faded.

'Some things will never improve,' I said, 'and she's one of them. But—' I fixed her with a stern look '—you, Belinda Frier, are not. Go and sort the horses out, and I won't tell Frances you were gallivanting with our guest in the barn.'

'If only he'd let me!'

'Oh, and Bel?' She turned back on her way to the field, and I gave her another grin, this time a sly one. 'Speaking of gallivanting, Seth Pearce is coming over later. Better make yourself beautiful.'

I ignored her comical look of dismay and went indoors. I had a letter to write.

Chapter Fifteen

Evie and Will were due home, at last. I'd had a long day in the fields, trying to finish everything so I'd have tomorrow morning free; we were sure to stay up late talking tonight, and Frances might get out her best whisky again. I still didn't enjoy the taste, but I enjoyed the feeling of sitting with everyone and sipping it, nevertheless – it made me feel part of everything. Will would be pleased with me too; I'd sent my letter off to Archie two days ago, and he'd have it within the week – every time I thought about it I felt a low, sweet tingle, part excitement and part apprehension, and I wondered how I'd keep my mind occupied with other things until I received his reply. It would feel like a year.

Singing softly under my breath, I cleaned the mud and sweat off Pirate, sluicing him down with fresh water and wishing someone could do the same for me. But I felt good. Better than good. Frances and I had shifted the last of the bales to the haystacks, hitching Pirate up to the bigger cart, which he pulled with ease, and Nathan and Jessie had covered the haystacks against the threatening thunderstorm. It was a wonderful sight to see it all dry and safe. Frances had gone inside to help Lizzy ready our evening meal, and I was taking what pleasure I could in the trickling of cool water running up my arms as I finished grooming Pirate, before bedding him down for the night. Tomorrow I'd take him for one last ride, then deliver him back to Mr Pearce for a short rest before his winter work at the sawmill.

I stopped outside the kitchen door to kick my boots off, and blew my hair off my forehead, looking forward to splashing some cold water on my sweating face. Voices drifted out from the kitchen, and I felt the thrill of anticipation; it would be so good to see Evie and Will again. Before I went in for the night I stopped long enough to enjoy my new habit – looking out across the moor and filling my mind with the scenery before moving inside, into warmth and comfort and company.

The sun was just beginning to dip, and was turning more orange than golden; flies drifted lazily around my head, and I heard the distant shout of a neighbouring farmer as he took his cows in for their evening milking. I could feel my shirt sticking to my back, and an ominous heaviness in the air, but a sense of peace, helped by the pleasant ache of muscles with a good day's work behind them, put a smile on my face that I was still wearing as I went into the kitchen.

Five people were sitting at the table. They all looked up as I came in, but one of them stood, scraping his chair back so fast it fell over. I looked rather stupidly at it, and then my hand was seized.

'Do excuse us,' Archie said, and whirled me about, pulling me behind him as he marched out through the door. I barely had time to wonder at his even being there, when he'd stopped, turned me to face him, and started to speak. I didn't even hear what he was saying, not properly. I was transfixed by the sight of a fly that had landed in his open shirt collar and was marching, unheeded, along his collarbone. I felt dizzy and swimmy-headed as Archie spoke the words he had carried with him from France, the vibration of his low, fierce voice almost a visible thing.

'Yes,' I said. The voice stopped. I looked up at his face for the first time, seeing his dark eyebrows lowered, his striking grey eyes unusually still, their shifting colours darkened to one, intense shade, his jaw tense.

'Yes,' I said again, solemnly, but I could feel my grin dislodging a piece of dried grass that had stuck to my eyebrow. He gently plucked it loose, and gave it an inordinate amount of attention before flicking it away and looking back at me.

'You're sure?' He no longer sounded fierce; his voice had dropped to almost a whisper.

'I was always sure. For me.'

'What does that mean?'

'We'll talk later,' I said. For now I just wanted to lose myself in the fact of his presence. 'I've always loved you, Archie.'

'But you said–'

'Later,' I repeated, and moved closer, touching my lips to his throat and feeling the sigh escape him. His arms came around me, to lock at the small of my back and pull me even closer, and my hands rose to caress the back of his neck. I tipped my head back to smile at him, and a second later his lips had claimed mine. For a brief moment we were back in the road at Dixmude, but this time there were no hats lying in the mud, and no people lying about their feelings; this time there was honesty and relief in every touch, and when we broke apart, his familiar, lopsided smile was enough to tell me I'd finally done the right thing. For both of us. He dipped his head for one final, brief kiss, and something playful I'd never known I possessed moved me to catch his lower lip between my teeth, and tug gently.

A splash of rain hit the back of his neck, wetting my fingers, and the skin between them became suddenly slick. Another hit his shoulder, and then one splashed onto my forehead.

Archie drew back and squinted at the sky. 'I think it might be Scotland ... uh, I mean raining.'

'I think you might be right.' I tilted my head back to follow his gaze. 'That would explain the water, don't you think?'

A low rumble trembled somewhere in the distance, and the rain came down faster. It was so deliciously cool on my work-heated skin, and Archie looked so young and carefree, with water dripping off his nose, I would have been happy to stay there all night. But the window opened, and Frances's voice cut through the pattering of the rain.

'That's all very romantic, and we're all delighted, but for goodness' sake come indoors. We'll have to dry those clothes somehow!'

Archie gave a low chuckle. 'That's us told,' he murmured directly into my ear. His arm went around my shoulder as we turned to go back into the farmhouse, and he grew serious as he pulled me to a stop. 'Before we go in... You might never understand what you've given me, but I hope you'll let me give it back as well as I can.'

I wrapped my own arm around his waist, feeling his warmth through the rough shirt, and loving the strength in his powerful frame all the more for the gentleness it disguised. 'You already have. I've been an idiot.'

'Well luckily for you I'm partial to idiots.' He ducked his head to pass through the door, and when the four remaining faces turned to us, they were all smiling. Evie crossed the kitchen and took me into a warm hug.

'It's so good to see you. And I can't tell you how sorry I am about those things my mother–'

'Don't,' I said. 'I understand, she was speaking from grief. And I'm happy.'

'Of course.' She drew back and smiled at us both. 'It's about time. The two of you have wanted your heads banging together.'

'Hey, it's not down to me,' Archie protested, tugging at my hair gently. 'I tried. More than once, if you'll remember.'

'Leave them alone,' Frances scolded, but her warm expression belied her tone. 'Kitty, go and wash. Archie, sit and finish your tea.' She gave a happy kind of sigh, one I hadn't really heard before. 'Lizzy is going to be thrilled to bits when she comes up tomorrow.'

'I can't wait to see her,' Evie said. 'She'll be every bit as pleased as we are. I knew, as soon as we met Archie at Crewe, that there was something he wasn't telling us about why he wanted to come here.' She smiled at me. 'I should have realised it would have something to do with you, Skittles.'

'Ooh, won't Lizzy be sort of your aunt now, Kitty?' Belinda added.

I hadn't thought that far. 'I suppose so, now you mention it. I'm going,' I assured Frances, who looked about to banish me once again to tidy myself.

Upstairs, after a good wash and having changed into clean, dry trousers and blouse, I looked at myself in the minor. For just a moment I found my old, traitorous doubts floating to the surface; why on earth would someone as handsome, kind and

273

clever as Archie Buchanan want me? I was still more rounded than I wanted to be, despite the physically demanding farmwork; my face wasn't anything like the girls on the Land Army posters; my hair did whatever it wanted to do, which was usually the opposite of what *I* wanted it to... In that I was more like Lizzy, I supposed. Perhaps the Carlisle men were naturally drawn to messy-haired women.

I heard laughter drifting up from downstairs, almost as if they had caught my thoughts and were sharing my amusement, and then Archie's voice rose above the others, protesting once again as he was good-naturedly scolded. When I turned back to the mirror to check my blouse was buttoned correctly, I saw my own smile and it widened. I deserved Archie, because he loved me. And he deserved me because I loved him. What else was there?

Jessie didn't come down for dinner, and neither did we see Nathan, who was out painting in the barn. I was glad; with just the six of us it felt like family, and with the constant awareness of Archie at my side I felt relaxed, and happier than I could remember. I missed Amy though. She had gone to bed already. At least tomorrow, now the hay was in, I would have time to spend with her – perhaps the three of us could go for a long walk if the rain had stopped.

The low rumbling of thunder had crept closer throughout the evening, and now, with the sky darkened, the increasingly frequent flashes were more vivid at the windows. Before we retired to the sitting room, however, Frances set stubs of half-melted candles in saucers and took her whisky bottle out, as I'd hoped.

'We've got a toast or two to make, before we take our comfort,' she said, her voice solemn. 'It's only right we should do it now, while we're all together.' She poured a tot into each glass and handed them around, then took a deep breath. 'Name your fallen, here among your loved ones,' she said, her voice shaking a little, 'and we'll wish them our peace.'

I felt Archie tense beside me, then pick up his glass. Everyone did the same, and spoke the names of those we'd lost. Some I didn't know: Belinda named an uncle and one of her cousins; Archie said the name of his battalion commander, who'd died at his side a year ago; Frances whispered her late husband's name; Will raised his glass to the man he'd fought alongside, and tried to save: Barry Glenn; and Evie closed her eyes and said, 'Lawrence Creswell.'

There was a silence while she struggled with her emotions, then she raised her head, cleared her throat, and tilted her glass in salute. 'Peace also to Billy Duncan, stable boy. Joe Shackleton, hall boy. And Boxy Wood, my courageous and desperately missed friend.' Evie had so many to mourn; surely she deserved an end to it now? It wasn't until then that I realised, with a mixture of gratitude and superstitious fear that I had no-one special to name. Not yet. I looked at Archie, a chill brushing the nape of my neck; what if that meant that one day I would find myself naming him? I cast about in panic. 'Anne Ashby,' I said at last, remembering the Red Cross girl who'd helped us so often at Number Twelve, and who'd died there in the same explosion that had wounded Evie.

No-one seemed to realise I'd plucked the name from the air. Each was lost in their own memories and grief. Oliver's life had been spared, and as of now, the only deaths I had encountered had been those poor boys who had passed through my hands during my duties in Belgium. I'd felt a responsibility to them, and a deep and aching sadness when they'd passed on, but let other people speak the names of those dead. Let their families and friends raise their glasses to them... Everyone I had ever really loved was here in England. Safe. I couldn't feel anything except passionate gratitude for that.

Shortly after we'd settled in the sitting room we heard footsteps on the stairs, and the door opened timidly to admit Jessie. She exchanged warm greetings with Evie and Will, and then her gaze took in Archie and me. We were sitting in separate chairs, but our hands were linked, and her face went blank with surprise. I'd never even mentioned Archie to her, and it seemed no-one else had, either. He rose to his feet, and I had to hide a smile in my curled hand when I saw her eyes follow the graceful way he uncoiled from his chair, to stand straight and tall in front of her.

'Jessie Goulding, this is Captain Archie Buchanan,' I said, enjoying her look of awe and, it was obvious to all of us, impressed appreciation. 'We've been friends since childhood.'

'Aye, and now she's agreed to keep me out of

mischief for the rest of our lives,' he added, turning to smile at me, and earning my everlasting gratitude on top of everything else. He turned back. 'Good to meet you, Jessie.'

'Likewise, Captain Buchanan,' she said, shaking his hand, and looking past him at me, with a hint of disbelief in her expression. She sat down in the last spare seat on the settee, and waited while Archie reseated himself at my side. 'Are you here long?'

'Not nearly long enough,' he said, reaching out to grasp my hand again. 'I'm on loan from the army for a week. Government business.' My heart lurched; government business could mean anything. He must have felt my hand twitch in his, because he looked over. 'Nothing dangerous, darling. I promise.'

The endearment, and his words, went a long way towards soothing the low-key panic that had started up inside me, but did not wholly extinguish it. 'Glad to hear it,' I said, a little uncertainly.

Conversation soon started up again, mostly about the farm, the way we'd worked in the past few days to get the hay safely in, how incredible that we'd done it with hours to spare... Then it went quiet again as the outer kitchen door opened. We heard Nathan come in, kicking off his wet boots, and a minute later he poked his head around the sitting room door, and smiled.

'Will! I heard you were coming back today.' He nodded at Evie – there was still reservation there – and then his gaze lit on Archie, sitting in Harry Adams's old chair as if he belonged there. He said nothing, but nodded, then his smile slid onto me and widened noticeably. I felt Archie's fingers tighten on mine, but squeezed back gently in silent reassurance. He had nothing to be concerned about there.

'You must be Nathan,' he said, rising again. 'Archie Buchanan.'

'Archie.' Nathan took the proffered hand and shook it firmly.

'Good of you to stay and help Frances. When d'you rejoin your unit?'

Nathan's smile faded. He looked up at Archie steadily, and I saw him coming to a decision. He turned to Frances then, who shrugged and nodded, a sympathetic look on her face, and I sat up, suddenly interested. What did she know that we didn't?

Nathan folded his arms across his chest. 'I'm afraid I've not been truthful with you all,' he said in a low voice. 'I never joined up; I'm exempt. Pneumonia. Scarring in both lungs.'

There was a silence in the room, while I thought about that cough he'd never quite managed to lose. Then I asked, quietly because I had the feeling I knew the answer, 'How do you feel about it?'

He looked at me with a strange little self-mocking smile. 'Pathetic, if you must know.' He looked over at Will. 'Especially in front of you.'

'But why didn't you tell the truth?' Will asked. 'We've known each other long enough, surely?'

Nathan sat down in the window seat and rubbed his hands on his thighs, trying to stop them shaking. 'How could I? Here's you, out there from the off, traumatised, yet still going back–'

'How did you know that?' Evie said, but Nathan

278

ignored her and continued talking only to Will.

'I was jealous of you, you know. Out there, doing your bit. I was turned down for active service when I first applied, then, when conscription came in I thought, great! They're going to need me at last.'

'But?'

'Turned down again, then given permanent exemption.' He tapped at his chest. 'The lungs don't work properly, never will.'

'So what have you been doing?'

He grimaced. 'Menial work. Grocery boy mostly. I saved a bit of money and bought those art materials, was able to get some portrait commissions but not much. Then I heard Will had married well. And that he was wounded.' He dropped his gaze to the floor. 'I swear to you, Will, I didn't realise the injury was so serious,' he said. 'I thought you were the lucky one. All the glory, a little bit of pain, and now back home safe, with his rich wife. But as soon as I saw you again, I felt the worst kind of heel. Just ... an awful, awful person.' He raised his eyes to his old friend, and I remembered the way they'd shone with tears at the sight of Will in such obvious pain. 'I might have come here with the purpose of begging from you and your wife, but I promise you that since that first night the thought has not crossed my mind. I've not let it.'

'Right, he's told you the truth now,' Frances put in, her voice a little rough. 'He was good enough to tell me about the exemption when I asked, but I agreed not to tell the rest of you. He feels badly. Now that should be an end to it.'

But Will wasn't ready to let it drop. 'How *were* you able to persuade Martin to tell you where we were?' He sat forward, his elbows on his thighs and his hands clasped tightly enough to make the knuckles white. 'How did you get him to betray me, Nathan?' His face was expressionless and I couldn't tell if he was simply numb from the lies, or furious with Martin.

'We both ... we talked,' Nathan said. 'Him and me, we got quite close after a while. His wife's away in London with the Red Cross, so I'd go to his house and we'd share a drink. Both of us felt...' He shrugged, but Evie stepped in.

'Rejected?'

He looked surprised at her understanding, then sighed. 'Yes.'

'I know Martin was disappointed not to be going,' she said, and reached for Will's hand. 'Do you remember, just before the wedding?'

Will nodded. 'His foot. He told me he was sure they'd relax the rules someday, and he was still waiting for that call-up. But it never came.' He turned to Nathan. 'I can understand why the two of you would have wanted to be out there, but believe me, and believe him–' he gestured to Archie '–you ought to be glad you never were. Thank your stars, Nathan. I've told Martin the same. Thank your bloody stars, mate.' He levered himself out of his chair, and left the room, and Evie gave us all a quick, nervous smile, and followed him.

'He'll be all right,' she said, and closed the door quietly behind her.

'I'm sorry,' Nathan said in a low voice. 'Tonight was supposed to be a happy time.'

'And so it is,' Frances said, with determined cheerfulness. 'We've got the hay in before the rain, Archie's home for a few days, and young Kitty's woken up at last.' She smiled at me, and Archie's hand found mine again. When I looked at him it took all my self-control not to lean across the gap between our chairs and wrap myself around him, right in front of everyone.

I turned away, with an effort. 'So how long will you stay here, now the truth is out?' I said to Nathan.

'As long as Mrs Adams will have me. At least until Will's fully recovered, if that's all right?' He looked at Frances, who inclined her head in agreement.

'You're cheap to feed,' she said, 'and you work hard. When you're not off painting your pictures. You'll take the pressure off young Will.'

He nodded. 'I don't want him to risk hurting himself again. I've ruined enough of his life.'

'You won't get an argument from me,' Evie said, coming back into the room. 'He'll be back in a while. He's gone for a little walk.'

'In this rain?' Frances groaned. 'How am I going to get those clothes dry?'

Her familiar complaint cut through the last of the tension, and we all smiled. No doubt that was her intention; I noticed a little smile on her lips as she rose to fetch the biscuit tin, and a happy warmth crept through me at the thought of this life I had found. I jumped as I felt a soft breath on my cheek, and realised Archie had done what I had somehow refrained from doing, and closed the gap between us. His lips brushed my ear, and his teeth closed gently on the lobe, making me tingle.

'I'd like to go for a walk too,' he said in a voice low enough so only I could hear. 'Just to talk. Can we, later?'

I turned towards him, my lips hovering over his. 'When everyone's gone to bed,' I murmured.

His smile almost made me groan out loud; I'd never seen such strong, intensely male beauty up so close – his thick dark eyelashes were almost touching mine, his breath was still grazing the corner of my mouth, and the pulse in his throat beat strong and steady beneath my fingers as I took his jaw in my hands, heedless of everyone else in the room. We didn't kiss, our lips barely touched, but the nearness of him almost stole my ability to think straight.

'I wish they'd all go to bed,' I whispered, and he was unable to prevent a little laugh escaping. Then he withdrew, and I realised everyone was deliberately looking anywhere but at us. Belinda was chatting to Evie, both of them turned away showing exaggerated interest in the contents of the Welsh dresser that stood by the door, Frances was wrestling with the lid of a tin I knew very well needed only a blunt fingernail inserted beneath the rim to release it, and Nathan had picked up an ornamental pig and was paying it close attention. Even Jessie was staring at her indoor shoes, as though they held some deep secret they wouldn't give up.

I swapped another glance with Archie, and he grinned and sat back in his own seat. Then he looked at the table where Frances had finally put the tin, and put his head in his hands in mock horror. 'Och no, Frances... Tell me those aren't Lizzy's biscuits?'

'You leave Lizzy alone,' Frances said. 'Those biscuits are ... well, they're...'

'Yes,' Evie agreed, her mouth twitching. 'Don't be rude, Archie. The birds enjoy them.'

'Aye, perfect for building a good, solid nest,' Archie agreed. Even Frances laughed then.

'Don't be horrid,' I said, feeling bad for poor Lizzy. 'It's not nice to laugh at her behind her back.'

'Oh, it's not behind her back,' Evie assured me. 'We've talked about this before, and I've begged her to give up, but she's determined to keep at it until she gets it right. She considers it our punishment to eat the practice ones.'

'Punishment?'

'For poking fun. Don't feel sorry for her, Skittles. She's perfectly aware of what she's doing to us. I've seen her grinning when someone new tries one and has to find something nice to say about it.'

'Anyway,' Frances said, 'we gave hers to Seth Pearce. He's too polite to turn them down.'

'That reminds me,' I said, 'have you managed to get a padlock yet, for the barn door?'

'Not yet. Colin Trebilcock says he may have an old one he doesn't need any more though.'

'Padlock?' Nathan asked, also reaching over to the tin.

'Apparently some people are getting desperate,' I said. 'Breaking in, stealing tools and selling them on, so Mr Pearce told us.'

'I'll fit the lock for you, if Colin brings one,' Nathan told Frances.

'I can do it,' she said, echoing Jessie, 'but thank you.'

As talk turned to the lengths people would go to, now that rationing was so severe, I found my attention straying once more to the man beside me. Had he changed too? I watched his strong, lean fingers holding his whisky glass, rolling it in the light of the nearest candle and studying the tawny liquid as he had three years ago, on the eve of his departure, occasionally lifting it to take a sip. My eyes went to the breadth of his shoulders beneath his uniform shirt, and the deep swell of his ribcage, rising and falling as he laughed at something Belinda was saying. Then my gaze travelled down his long, powerful legs, one ankle resting casually on the opposite knee – no elegant crossing of his legs here. He was comfortable and at ease. My fingers itched to slide onto his thigh and trace the shape of the muscles that flexed there when he moved, and to travel up across his hip and rest at his waist, to feel him breathing...

I yawned widely and looked at the clock, hoping others would take my lead. 'It's been a long day,' I said. 'I'm so tired.'

'Rest tomorrow,' Frances promised. 'Perhaps you and Archie would like to take Amy for a picnic?'

'Amy?' Archie said, but Evie's eyes opened wide. 'Kitty! You didn't!'

'What else could I have done?' I asked.

'Who's Amy?' Archie wanted to know. I glumly watched our evening walk fade further into the

284

realm of unlikelihood, as I started to explain, in as few words as I could and leaving out the details of the McKrevie incident.

'So here she is,' I finished. 'Mr Markham is going to fetch her when he can take her away somewhere safe.'

Before I could add any more, or Evie could express what she thought of the idea, Will came back in. Nathan tensed slightly, and Evie looked at her husband closely, gauging his mood, but we knew he was back to his usual self as he stretched a hand towards the biscuit tin, then hesitated, drew it back, and looked at Frances.

'They're not Lizzy's, are they?'

A short while later Jessie too gave a jaw-cracking yawn. I could have hugged her. Even more so when I saw Archie flick his attention to me, suppressing a smile. I wanted to ask him where he would be sleeping that night, just so I could imagine him in his bed and know how far away he was from me, but it would sound dreadful. So I did the next best thing.

'Are Evie and Will in their old room?' I asked Frances. 'Because I'm happy to bunk in with Amy if we're short of beds.'

'Don't worry about that,' Frances said. She ticked off on her fingers. 'Four bedrooms and Harry's storeroom: Nathan in the store, Evie and Will in their old room, you, Amy and Belinda in yours, and Archie will stay in mine. I'll move in with Jessie; it's only a couple of nights.'

'My bed's quite big enough,' Jessie put in, glancing at me, and the urge to hug her fell away;

there was no need to have been so pointed about it. I knew that bed perfectly well; Evie and I had shared it earlier in the year, when it was mine. But the resentment was faint, and short-lived. I had too much to be happy about. And now I'd be able to picture Archie too, in the room just two doors down the corridor from mine.

Before long everyone had decided the time had come to turn in for the night. Evie and Will had been travelling for a good part of it, and Evie was still concerned enough about Will to flatly ban him from sitting and catching up with Archie.

'Plenty of time tomorrow,' she said. Then she glanced from me to Archie, and I saw her lips close on a smile. 'Goodnight,' she said, and led an unprotesting Will out into the hall. They were quickly followed by Bel, Nathan, Jessie and Frances, and then at last Archie and I were alone.

He looked out of the window. 'Do you still want to go for that walk? Or do you want to talk here?'

'Let's walk,' I said. My skin was flushed, and the idea of a cool breeze, and even the rain, was extraordinarily appealing. 'If you're not too tired?'

Archie stood up for the third time, and this time he pulled me with him. His hands looped loosely around my waist, and his chin rested on top of my head. 'I'm bloody exhausted, but if you try and convince me not to go out there with you, right now, I can't promise I won't drag you out by the heels.'

Chapter Sixteen

The rain had stopped, and the thunder long since died away. The smell outside was fresh and sharp, a combination of hay and animals, and clean, clear air. Archie had slipped his greatcoat on, but he left it open when he realised the storm had well and truly passed. I too wore my coat open, and we walked side by side across the yard towards the little field where Pirate usually stayed. He was in the stable tonight, however, clean and comfortable after his busy few days. I heard a whicker from his stall, and the swish of his tail as he turned at our approach, and then his long white nose was poking over the half-door.

Archie stepped up to him, his voice low and appreciative. 'So, *you're* the one doing all the hard work here, aye?' I poked him in the ribs, and he chuckled. 'Well, I grant you have to harness him up, Kittlington, but after that it's plain sailing for you.'

'What are you talking about?' I protested. 'Those bales don't lift themselves into the cart, you know. Frances and I spent...' Then I saw him laughing silently, and prodded him again, this time less gently. He gave Pirate a last pat on the neck, then turned to me, putting his hands firmly on my shoulders,

'All right,' he said, his voice serious now, 'I want to know why it was you said you didn't love me.'

'I didn't,' I began, but of course it had sounded like that to him, with no explanation.

'Please,' he said. 'I'd thought maybe you didn't, but I hadn't wanted to believe it. Then, when you turned me down I felt...' He broke off, letting go of me and turning back to Pirate, as if he could find the words more easily if he didn't look at me. 'I felt lost. I'd had this incredible revelation of m'own feelings for you, and I'd thought about it, and thought about it, and then after that kiss in Dixmude I was sure you felt the same. When I realised you didn't, I–'

'I did!' I reached out to him, touching his shoulder, and he turned back again. I could feel the tension in him. 'Archie, I've loved you far longer than you've loved me. But after what happened, my reputation... You deserved better than me.'

'Reputation?' he repeated, nonplussed. 'We're not stuck in the dark ages! Why on earth would I care what anyone had to say about something they don't understand?'

'I know that now,' I said, struggling to find the right words. 'But at the time all I could think about was how my family had reacted, and how yours would hate me for destroying you. Even if it didn't matter to you it would end up making you miserable, and resentful–'

'My family will love you,' he said softly. He pulled me close to him, with both arms tight around my shoulders, so I couldn't pull back even if I'd wanted to. 'Uncle Jack already adores you, and whoever Uncle Jack adores, my mother adores.'

'And what about you?' I asked. Relief was making me want to tease a little bit, but I wasn't the only one, and I felt him shrug.

'Aye well, you're okay I suppose. You'll do for housework.'

I sagged against him in mock protest, but couldn't help laughing. To my surprise, he didn't hoist me up again, but instead dropped to a crouch with me, holding me away from the ground so I stared up at him in the almost-full darkness. His finger traced my cheek, and all the playfulness went out of me as I felt my skin burn beneath his touch. The trail of heat continued down the side of my neck, and with his thumb brushing my jaw, and his other hand sliding beneath my shoulders, he lifted me slightly and brought his mouth down. The kiss was deep, and searching, alternately warm and cool, and my hand came up to curve around the back of his head, holding him there. My other hand supported me at first, until I realised his hold on me was strong and steady, and then it lifted to slide beneath his coat. I could feel his breathing quicken, and let my fingers explore the contours of his broad back, tightening my hold so my hand curved around his side, where the hardness of bone gave way to the firmness of muscle.

I don't know how long we remained there, locked together in the chilly evening air, but when we finally parted I had no strength left. He shifted, dropping one knee to the ground to steady himself, and pressed his lips to my forehead. 'Ah, Kitty,' he murmured, sounding as breathless as I felt. He didn't say anything more, but as my eyes adjusted to the darkness I saw his own, and they were closed. He breathed slowly, and I copied him and felt my heartbeat returning to a normal rhythm, the trembling in my limbs easing. Eventually I stood up, but he remained on the ground, his head lowered. When I crouched down in front of him, he opened his eyes and smiled sadly.

'It's going to be so hard to leave you,' he said, touching my face, and let out a trembling breath. 'God, it's going to hurt.'

His words sliced deep, but I couldn't think about it now. 'We're just going to have to make the most of the time you have here.' I urged him to his feet. 'Come on, stand up. Let's go for that walk.'

He put his hand in mine and allowed me to pretend I'd pulled him upright, and by the time we'd walked to the bottom of the lane that strange burst of melancholy had faded, and he was making me laugh again. His hand was in mine, and we swung them like children, not even turning back as a fresh, cool rain began to fall again.

'Frances will have your hide,' he warned me, 'gettin' your clothes all wet.'

'Yours too,' I pointed out, 'and you've got to explain that muddy knee.'

'Ah, she'll not be rough on me,' he said confidently. 'I'm a guest. You're the daughter.'

That reminded me. 'I wonder if Mother has finally given up on getting me to go back to Ecclesley?'

'Oh, I'd forgotten. You're to marry wee Aleister Crowley.'

I giggled, a little bit shocked. 'Alistair Corwood!'

'Aye, him.' He raised my hand to his lips and kissed it. 'Don't worry, young Kittlington, I will-nae let the wicked witch steal you away to wed the evil heir to the Corwood-Maitland empire.'

'It should be Oli who inherits,' I pointed out.

He sobered. 'It should. But it isn't, and we must remember how it could have gone. He's lucky to be alive.'

'Thanks to Evie and your Uncle Jack.'

'And you.'

'Well, if it wasn't for me he'd never have–'

'Oh, no you don't!' He put a playful hand over my mouth, but I stiffened, and he snatched it away quickly. 'God, I'm sorry, I didn't think...'

'It's all right,' I said quickly. 'You just took me by surprise.'

We stopped walking, and he turned to face me. 'Promise you'll tell me if anything I do makes you ... uncomfortable, or scared.'

'I will.'

'I mean it. I don't know what, how it... I don't know how you...' He broke off, a frustrated sigh escaping on the night air. 'I just don't know any of it. I'm trusting you to tell me.'

'I think...' The words were dancing on my lips, and I heard them in my head the second before they fell, but was powerless to stop them. 'I think I need you to make it go away.'

He went very still, and the only sound was the rain hitting the broad dock leaves and the nettles, and plinking into the newly made puddles. 'How?' he said at last.

'You know,' I whispered. He didn't move, so I stepped closer, putting my hands on his chest. My breathing had sharpened again, and I felt a pull deep in my belly that I had no name for, or understanding of. I only knew that this man loved me, and if he took me now, in that love, then I might be able to look at myself in his light instead of the shadow Drewe had cast over me. My fingers fumbled at the buttons of his shirt, but he caught at my hands and lowered them away.

'Kitty, think what you're saying. What happened back there, in the yard, it *was* real, and it was beautiful, but this? Here?'

'What better place?' I said, my voice trembling. 'Archie, I can't be near you and not touch you. I've lived like that for too long. But I'm terrified.'

'Which is why–'

'No! Listen, please. If I have time to think, I'll frighten myself even more. You'll be gentle, we'll be quick ... and when it's over I won't be scared any more. It doesn't have to be perfect; it just has to be you.'

He spoke very quietly. 'And what if you get pregnant again?'

My heart twisted. 'Then this time I won't wish the baby gone,' I said on a hiccupping sob, and he pulled me to him and wept with me, for a time of darkness and fear, and the legacy it had left us. I'd never known a man cry like that. I'd always thought it would lessen his masculinity somehow, but Archie's tears came silently, and they were for me, and he had never seemed stronger. The only sign of his anguish was a hitch in his chest as he caught his breath, then took my face between his hands.

'Are you sure?' he whispered.

I nodded and stepped away onto the wide verge, aware of him following me, and now that he wasn't holding me a kind of cool realisation dropped over me and I wondered if I were doing the right thing after all. But as soon as he reached me my doubts fled again. He spread his greatcoat on the wet grass, and I shucked off mine too, and we lay down together in the softly falling rain while I eased my trousers down until I could wriggle out of them. His hand moved up inside my shirt, his fingers finding my breast and brushing the nipple so I could feel it pressing against the material of my shirt, and then he kissed me. His lips moved gently over mine, cautious, until I pulled him closer and only then, our mouths parted, and our hands restless on one another, did we lose all hesitation and let the moment take us. He tugged at his belt, and in a moment he was lying beside me, both of us undressed from the waist down, but feeling strangely chaste above it.

'Now,' I whispered against his mouth. 'Please...' I was scared I would panic, and that if I did he would never trust himself with me again. He rolled onto me, and in a moment of bright, joyful clarity, I realised what I was doing. And it was with Archie.

Then he was inside me, and it hadn't hurt, not like when Drewe... I shoved the thought away and captured Archie's face in my hands. 'I love you,' I breathed. 'Oh, please, Archie, I love you...' I didn't know what I was begging for, but he let out a sobbing breath and his hips moved faster. Mine rose to match his urgency, and my hands dropped to grip his waist, and then he uttered a low cry and stopped. I stopped too, the sweet ache he'd given me growing with every second that passed, and then a sudden, shuddering ecstasy overtook everything and I didn't know where I was any more. I was vaguely aware of him pushing forward, slower now, but I couldn't have moved had my life depended on it. Eventually he lowered his face to kiss my forehead, his arms shaking as he fought not to collapse onto me, and then he eased away, letting the chilly air at my skin once more.

He rolled off to lie at my side, and I lay very still, the echo of that glorious pulsing still tugging at my insides.

Then his blindly seeking hand found mine, and his voice was hoarse. 'Are you all right?'

'I'm fine,' I said, then smiled. 'Better than fine. Is it like that for everyone?'

A chuckle drifted out of the darkness. 'How would I know?'

We lay in silence, waiting for our hearts to regain their normal rhythm, and then I rolled towards him. 'Thank you,' I said in a small voice.

He half sat up, propped on one elbow, and touched my face. 'Why on earth are ye thanking me? That was probably the most selfish good turn I've ever done anyone.'

'You're right,' I said, turning to kiss his palm. 'You are utterly selfish. How could you?'

He snorted, and lay back down. 'Now, Miss Maitland, comes the real question.'

'What question?'

His hand flapped at the edge of my rain-soaked coat, and I heard the grin in his voice. 'Well, I may have a wee smudge of yard-dirt on my knee, but I'd like to see how you're going to explain *those* stains to Mrs Adams.'

In the event I didn't have to. I had woken early, still smiling from the warmth of the dream of Archie and me racing donkeys on Blackpool beach – the fact that Archie had kept falling off had made it even funnier; I'd never met anyone less likely to tumble – and as I'd arrived in the kitchen Frances had immediately gestured to the laundry pile.

'I know you want to get off out quickly today, but I've got to go over and see Colin after breakfast, see if he's got that padlock.'

'We can go out later,' I said, trying not to grin at this stroke of luck. 'I'll do it after breakfast.'

She looked at me oddly; laundry was my least favourite chore and she knew it. Then she smiled. 'Do you know, I've never seen you really happy,' she said. 'Not *proper* happy, I mean.'

'I don't know that anyone has,' I said, and the truth of that surprised me too. 'Not for a long time anyway.' It wasn't that I'd felt miserable, as such, just ... adrift, slightly, from everything that other people seemed to find so effortlessly. Now I had this beautiful home, the love of the man who'd lived in my heart all my life, had I but known it, and the care of an eerily quiet, but sweet little girl, who was gradually emerging further from her shell every day she spent among us. And, to shine things off nicely today, I needn't try to explain the telltale smudges on my clothing from last night without having to lie.

I helped myself to a ladleful of oats from the pot, always bubbling on the stove, and welcome in the chilly morning, even in summer. 'Is anyone else up yet?'

'No, you're the first. They've got some sleep to catch up on, I would think, and Amy's slept so well these past few nights.'

'She likes Sally's bed,' I said, pouring honey on my oats, 'but I really think it helps that she's starting to accept she's staying a while.'

'I hope so; she's a dear.'

'Frank won't raise the money to take her for a good while yet,' I assured her. 'Especially if he's sending some of it here for her.'

'Well I'm happy to have her here for as long as she needs a home.'

That reminded me of something I'd meant to ask. 'What's Jessie's mother like? She never talks about her.'

'Just as you don't talk about yours,' Frances pointed out, but her voice had taken on an evasive tone. 'Now, will you fetch Amy down, or let her sleep?'

'But we know why I don't talk about mine,' I persisted. 'She wanted nothing to do with me until she realised I served her purpose. But you're friends with Jessie's mother, and I can't think you'd be friends with someone who mistreats their own–'

'She has *never* mistreated Jessie!'

I blinked, taken aback by the vehemence in her voice. 'That's just what I mean!'

'Never mistreated her,' Frances repeated in a low voice, more to herself than to me. I felt a little uneasy, and subsided. It really wasn't my business, after all.

'I'll let Amy sleep,' I said instead. 'She'll be doing a lot of walking today. She can have her breakfast later, while I do the laundry.'

'That's a good girl.' Something told me she was thanking me for more than acquiescing to a hated chore, and I was glad I hadn't pressed the issue any further. 'Now, you'd better finish that and make a pot of tea. The others will be down soon.'

I was scraping the last of my breakfast from the bowl when I heard Archie's feet on the stairs. I knew right away it was him – not simply because the only other male here was Will, who moved so carefully now, but because of the years I'd spent listening to Archie's footsteps as a child. I'd heard them change, but I still knew them. Gone was the light, athletic but boyish leap down the stairs in our old house, and in its place the firm, steady tread of a grown man, who, when he was happy, still took the last few steps in a little run, as if eager to see what lay at the bottom.

I heard that little run now, and smiled into my bowl. Then the door opened and my heart stopped for a breathless second. He ducked through the doorway, all sleepy-eyed, with a dark stubble along his jaw, and his shirt open at the collar, still fastening it with morning-stiff hands until he looked up and saw me. The tiredness vanished, re-placed by a brilliant smile, and my insides turned to soft cotton.

'Good morning, young Kittlington,' he said, and his voice, unused yet that day, was husky from sleep; I could have listened to it all day. 'Good morning, Frances.'

'And to you, Archie,' Frances said, handing him

a bowl. 'Oats in the pan, tea's in the pot. Be a few minutes though. Did you sleep well?'

'Aye, I can't thank you enough for giving up your bed to me.' Archie spooned some oats into his bowl and sat down opposite me. I could hardly keep myself from reaching across the table and stroking his finely shaped wrist, but contented myself with remembering how it had felt last night, instead. We talked of nothing in particular while we ate, and I saw his gaze going to the pile of laundry, then returning to me with a smile of deep amusement, underlaid by the same memory that made my heart beat a little faster when I looked at him. When he'd finished his breakfast he rose to rinse his bowl and mine, and we heard a light step outside the back door. Lizzy.

Her gaze immediately lit on Archie at the sink, and if I had felt my own breath catch at the sight of him, hers must have locked tight in her throat; she raised a hand to her mouth, then gave a shaky, faintly embarrassed laugh. 'Archie! For a moment I ... sorry. It's wonderful to see you.' I remembered how I'd thought he was Jack too, not so long ago. My heart crumpled at the sight of her disappointment, but she recovered quickly, smiled, and slipped off her coat, turning to hang it on the peg by the door. 'How are you?'

I exchanged an anguished glance with Archie, who looked as though he had accidentally slapped someone and didn't know what to do about it. He gave me another helpless look, then cleared his throat. 'I'm very well thank you, Lizzy.' He dried his hands on the dishtowel, then stepped over to her. He lowered his voice, lost that falsely polite greeting tone, and touched her shoulder. 'I've a message for you. Would you like to walk a moment?'

She nodded. Archie glanced at me before following her out into the yard, and his reassuring smile told me Lizzy had nothing to worry about. While I made fresh tea I watched the two of them from the window; Lizzy's hands were folded in front of her, her slender form held taut, her shoulders squared as if waiting for some kind of blow, and when Archie started to speak I saw her slump in relief.

Frances looked out at them over my shoulder. 'That girl dies a bit more every day he's not here,' she observed, and I felt her hand on my arm. 'It'll be the same for you, when it's Archie's time to go back.'

'How does she bear it, and stay so cheerful?' I already felt the pain of his leaving, and he'd only just arrived.

'She does it because there's no other way to do it,' Frances said. 'And because, so far, he's come back to her.' She stared out of the window, seeing something other than what was there, and it was easy to understand what. Or who.

'I'm so sorry about Harry,' I said quietly. I could still see the shadow his absence had left on her.

'He was so excited about going.' Her voice was distant. 'Joined up the first day, him and half the other lads from the village.' She blinked and turned away. 'Them as are in charge mightn't like Pals Brigades no more, but the boys still go willingly. Still manage to fool themselves it'll do some good.'

'You don't think so?'

'No, love.' Frances squeezed my arm. 'Not any more I don't. But God bless them for going. We'll look out for you, same as we do for Lizzy. Meantime, enjoy the time you've got with him.'

I looked into the yard, where Archie and Lizzy were making their way back to the door, walking slowly and still talking.

Lizzy came in first, wearing a look of wary relief. 'Samuel Wingfield's dead.' She did not seem shocked, nor particularly surprised, but she swallowed hard, as if the next piece of news was stuck in her throat. 'Jack ... Jack killed him.'

Hearing Evie's suspicion confirmed, and knowing the truth had come from Archie, brought my old suspicion bubbling to the surface once again. We needed to talk, but later, away from everyone.

Frances frowned. 'Wingfield? He's that one ran away to Germany after his daughter-in-law shot you?'

I nearly dropped the teapot in shock. '*Shot* you?' I sat down next to Archie, my legs suddenly turned to water.

'It's a long story,' Lizzy said, distracted and concentrating on what Archie had told her, what I'd already heard at Oaklands. 'Apparently he was carrying secret papers. He was found near the border with Switzerland. Jack's...' She shook her head, looking down at the table.

'A government man,' Frances finished for her, her face giving nothing away. Then she looked straight at Archie, and asked the question for me. 'And what about you, Captain Buchanan? You're

300

on loan from the army. Are you a government man too?'

My private fears vanished as he reached for my hand, his face darkening. 'No, I'm not. And even if I was, Uncle Jack's saved more lives than–'

'Oh, hush,' she said. 'I'm not judging anyone. But Lizzy was badly hurt because of that Wingfield wretch; I'm just looking out for my girl.'

'Oh!' Lizzy came back from wherever her thoughts had taken her, and noticed mine and Archie's linked hands. 'At last!'

'I told her it was about time,' said a voice from the doorway, and then Evie and Lizzy were swept up in their own greetings, leaving Archie and me to our silent conversation.

His eyes questioned mine: *regrets?* My smile told him, *none.* My fingers, tightening on his, said, *however long we have, it's not enough.* His breath, now grazing my temple, replied, *I will not waste a second.* Finally, my hand on his chest asked, *are you feeling the same ache I feel?* And his heartbeat, slow and strong beneath my fingers, told me, *yes.*

It seemed the room had grown enormous around us, so that everyone else in it was far away, and there was just Archie, his gentleness and his strength, and his soft voice whispering my name as if it was something magical. I didn't think I'd ever be able to move away from him, but the memory of decent manners found us both at the same moment. We sat up straighter, drawing slowly apart, and gradually the world reasserted itself. I tried not to resent it. Evie sat down on my other side.

'Archie's told me about Samuel Wingfield,'

301

Lizzy told her. 'And I understand you've got the Kalteng Star back now?'

Interested again, I looked at Evie, who shrugged. 'For what it's worth, yes.'

'Uncle Jack arranged to pass it over to me just before I came back, sealed inside a shaving brush,' Archie said. 'I was supposed take it directly to Oaklands and give it to Lady Creswell, but the house was shut up when I got there.'

'She'd already left to go to my grandparents,' Evie said. 'It's just a pity you wasted that extra time going there first.'

Archie shot me a brief smile. 'Well I can't pretend to be disappointed you'd left. The temptation to travel back here was fairly strong, after all.'

I felt the warmth of his hand on my leg, and tried not to give anything away, focusing instead on Evie. 'I'm going to give it to Mother to put back in the Creswell vault,' she was saying, 'but in any event we'll only have it until she can arrange to have it presented it to Sir Joseph.'

'Sir who?' Lizzy asked.

'The president of the British North Borneo Company, according to Uncle Matthew. Sir Joseph Ridgeford. Or Ridgeway, maybe? Whoever it is, it can't happen soon enough for me.'

'Really? Still?'

'More so than ever,' Evie said grimly. 'As soon as Jack told me, yesterday afternoon, I went back into the village and sent a telegram to the company. That stone is no longer ours. Not now that Lawrence is...'

But she couldn't finish. She didn't need to.

'Why tell them?' I asked. 'Why not keep it a

little longer?'

She shrugged. 'They'll know about Lawrence anyway. They'll have been waiting for this news from the minute Lawrence signed up for active service. If we'd refused to give it up Mother would be arrested, but with it being officially declared missing there would have been nothing they could do. Now ... well, now it'll be back where it belongs. They'll send a representative to speak to Mother within a few days, I should think.'

'And what about Wingfield's family? Will they ask questions about Samuel?'

Archie gave a short laugh. 'From what I've heard every member of that family would throw every other member in front of a charging rhino, if it meant a closer look at what little money they've left.' He turned to me, his expression suddenly brightening. 'That's where I'd heard the name before!'

I must have looked completely blank, because he shook his head. 'Sorry, last night. When you were explaining about the wee girl.' He jerked his head to the ceiling, to indicate where Amy still slept. 'When you said the name of her real family.'

'McKrevie?'

'That's the name of the family that near enough bankrupted the Wingfields after they lost the diamond back to the Creswell vault.'

'I knew they had history,' Evie put in, looking interested, 'but I didn't know why spite should have driven Susannah Wingfield to marry into that family.'

'It wasn't entirely out of spite,' Archie said. 'Partly, perhaps, to punish her parents for giving the diamond back to your family. But it was more a desperate attempt to avoid paying what they owed. The McKrevies are a loan company.'

I thought about Louise's reluctance to speak of her family's business – that would certainly explain it. 'I've seen advertisements in the newspapers, for that kind of thing.'

'Aye. Well when the Wingfields had the diamond they borrowed heavily against it, and then, of course, they lost it. They never expected that and neither did the McKrevies, or they'd never have lent the money. Susannah would have inherited the Star, but it'd gone back to the Creswells the generation before, so she married Ballentyne in the hopes he'd write off the debt. Especially if she gave him a child.'

'I doubt if he would ever have done that,' Archie said. 'But no-one will ever know now. When Susannah died McKrevie took everything she owned in a final settlement from the Wingfields, gave Frank away to the Markhams, and cut all ties with both of them.'

'What an almighty mess!' Frances said.

'How do you know all this?' I asked Archie.

He cocked an eyebrow at me. 'Don't forget I'm a Carlisle.'

'And Jack was once engaged to Constance Wingfield,' Lizzy put in.

'That would have been about ten years after Frank was born and it was all over,' Evie said, 'but the Wingfields do like to rake over a grudge long after it's spent.' She looked at Lizzy steadily. 'Part of me was always terrified Samuel would come back. I can't tell you how relieved I am that

304

you're safe now.'

'And so's Jack,' Lizzy added. She visibly shook off the shadows we had brought into the day, and turned to dry the bowls Archie had left on the drainer. 'Right, who hasn't eaten yet?'

Archie sat back in his seat as the conversation melted into everyday matters again. 'Oh, Lizzy,' he said after a moment, 'I forgot to tell you part of Uncle Jack's message. I got all caught up in the Wingfield news.'

'Oh?'

'Aye. Just as we parted, he called me back, and said...' He frowned, making sure to get the wording right. 'Tell Lizzy I said: the small, rattly Ford is still worth a million Silver Ghosts.'

We all looked at Lizzy, puzzled, but the smile that lit her face would not be explained. She shook her head, biting her lip against a laugh, and I suddenly realised she was perilously close to sobbing as well, and I stood up quickly. 'I have laundry to do before Archie and I can take Amy out,' I said to the room at large. 'Please bring everything to me in the next ten minutes, or it will have to wait until next time.'

After lunch, with the washing hanging on the line across the back garden and snapping in a brisk breeze, Archie and I took Amy out in the trap.

'I don't think it's very far past Yelverton,' I said. 'Lizzy says her brothers used to play there all the time, and they had to walk to get there.'

'And it's a rock, you say?' Archie said doubtfully.

'A big rock, apparently. If I ever went into Plymouth I'm sure I'd have seen it.'

305

Archie seated himself next to Amy with great care, so as not to make her feel crushed between us. She looked up at him with wide blue eyes, and her little mouth pursed but silent, so he smiled down at her, and she looked away, content. She fiddled with the spoon that hung to the middle of her chest, and made no sound as I clicked to Pippin to walk on.

He sounded unconvinced. 'On its own on the moor.'

'Yes!' I started to laugh. 'Just wait and see. Lizzy knows what she's talking about.'

Amy tilted her face up to mine, and I realised my laughter was as new to her as it was to me, at least this new, carefree laughter that bubbled up from some deep well that Archie had uncovered. I'd been concerned that he wouldn't want to have his time taken up with caring for a child, but he'd prepared our picnic tea himself, asking me what she liked to eat and what she didn't, what she could take to play with, and did she need spare clothing?

We drew closer to Yelverton, the village that lay between ours and Plymouth, and Archie whistled. 'Some fine houses here.'

I followed his gaze, but then my attention swung back, to a wide open space on our right. I reached over Amy's head and thumped Archie's shoulder. 'Big rock,' I said, somewhat smugly.

He looked. 'Very big rock,' he agreed. 'Okay, I'll grant you this one.'

It rose around twenty feet at either end, though was considerably lower in the middle, and the length took it around a hundred feet from north-east to south-west. No-one was climbing on it today, but I could imagine the attraction for children to test themselves. The central part would be easy enough for Amy, I thought, when we'd gone around and stopped the trap on the far side. The ground there was higher, and the slope from rock to ground much more gentle.

I lifted Amy down from the trap. 'This is *entirely* unseemly for a young lady,' I told her with an exaggeratedly aristocratic accent, then reverted to my own tones. 'But it'll be *fun!* Which is far better for you, I think you'll agree.'

I watched with amusement as the boy in Archie leapt to the fore, proving me right. He scrambled up the side of the rock, stepping onto the higher mass at the end, his hands and feet finding their way easily until he stood on the top, sheltering his eyes from the glare of the sun.

Last night's storm had left puddles in the rock face, and I eyed them carefully as I held Amy's hand and helped her over the lower boulders, wondering with an inward smile how long it would be before she discovered them and the possibilities they held. I looked back up at Archie and felt the now familiar jolt of happy surprise in the pit of my stomach, that he was here, and he was mine. For a moment I didn't move, just admired the tall, strong outline of him up there, one foot braced on an outcrop of rock, his shoulders square against the sky.

He looked down and grinned at me, and my heart lifted even further. 'Be careful!' I shouted up to him, and it had been on the tip of my tongue to say something about breaking his ankle and having to stay laid up for a while, but I bit it back; today was not a day for thinking of returning to the war.

He came back down, leaping the last eight feet to land, laughing at my gasp of horror. Then he stooped to lift Amy, swinging her around so she sat on his shoulders. 'Want to go for a wee ride, lass?'

'Ride. Mulls!'

'Archie's not a pony!' I smiled. 'Go on then, but don't be long.' I sat down on one of the lower rocks, and watched Archie stride away over the grass, his arms raised to grip Amy's hands, her little legs firmly hooked over his shoulders. I could have gone with them, but it was too nice to see Amy's gradual relaxation into complete trust. Archie seemed to understand that she was no delicate flower, that she was unused to flounces and frills, and more used to shouting and dirt. But here in Devon she had softened, smiled more, and although her speech was still well behind that of other children her age, I had the feeling she was taking it all in, nevertheless.

I leaned back against the sun-warmed rock, hoping no-one else would come here today and the three of us would be alone until the sun went down. Wanting Archie to see me at my best, I had dressed in my best skirt and I could feel the gentle tug of the breeze on the loose material. It pulled at my blouse, too, and I let myself remember the strong, gentle touch of Archie's hand at my breast last night, in the rain. I closed my eyes and settled more comfortably, using my hat as a pillow, and took a deep, deep breath. Letting it out, I felt every sour thing, every grain of darkness I'd held inside me, drifting out with it, and when I took another cleansing breath I was smiling.

'God, you're lovely when you smile,' Archie said. My eyes flew open, and I saw him lifting Amy carefully off his shoulders and putting her feet back on the ground. She was a little dizzy, and wobbled, but he caught her and steadied her. Then he came to sit beside me, slipping one arm around my shoulders. I nestled against him with a deep sigh of contentment, and we watched Amy squatting down to pick at the grass, examining each blade closely before throwing it away.

'I meant it,' Archie went on. 'Looking at you there, almost asleep, that little smile on your face... You looked like an angel.' I turned to him with a retort ready, but he wasn't teasing. 'Aye, a tough little red-headed angel, with a heart I'd die for.' He kissed me, not a deep kiss, but a gentle, questioning one. I pressed a little closer and rested my hand at the open collar of his shirt, loving the low vibration of his voice as he spoke again, echoing my earlier thoughts.

'I canna quite believe you're mine. Even now.'

I kissed him again. 'Well, you'd better start, Captain Buchanan, because I'm not going anywhere.'

He smiled and leaned back. My hand drifted down across his chest as a natural result of his movement, and came to rest at his heart; I left it there and he covered it with his own hand. We didn't speak for a long time, just watched Amy picking up stones, putting some in her pocket, and dropping the others in the little puddles in the rock.

'Why is she saving them, do you suppose?' Archie murmured sleepily.

'Keeping them to play with later, I expect. She still forms attachments to the oddest things.'

'We've all collected wee treasures like that, as kids, but with her it's...' I felt him shrug '...it's almost as if she thinks she'll never see these things again.'

'I wish I could make her understand, but she'll be here a good long while before that, I think.'

We fell into an easy, contented quiet, and after a little while we heard voices. I sat up and looked around the side of the rock, to see a group of walkers and their dogs approaching from the Tavistock road.

Archie sighed. 'Time to go?'

I nodded reluctant agreement, and made sure Amy still had her spoon before I popped her back into the cart. This time she was content to ride in the back, and Archie took the reins.

'Where shall we go? I'm not ready to go back yet.'

'Neither am I. Amy?' I turned to look at her. 'What would you like to do now?'

'Splashin' stones,' she said sadly. I realised that, although as usual she hadn't complained when we'd picked her up, she'd been enjoying the simple act of throwing those little stones into the puddles.

Archie heard that sadness, and his voice, while pitched low so she couldn't hear, held the first edge of real anger I'd heard in a long time. 'What the hell did they do to her? I'd give anything to

310

see her throw a tantrum.'

'Me too,' I whispered, fighting an unexpectedly strong surge of emotion. Then I sat up straight and turned a big, cheerful smile on Amy. 'I know! Why don't we go to the river? You know, down by the edge of the woods? Lots of stones down there. Big ones and little ones.'

She nodded, brightening, and Archie flicked the reins. 'We'll take Pippin back, and then we can walk down.'

'Perfect.' I sat back and enjoyed the rare chance to look around as we made our way back to Dark River. Archie leaned forward as he drove, his elbows casually resting on his knees, and he looked so at home I felt a twist of pain in anticipation for a few days' time, when he would no longer be here.

'I have to take Pirate back later,' I said, remembering. 'Do you want to ride him? I'll bring the cart and we'll drive back together.'

'Do I *want* to? Kittlington, you know me. I'd love nothing more. Are you sure you don't want to, though?'

'I'll get another chance, after...' I stopped, but he reached out and briefly squeezed my hand.

'Don't. You'll drive yourself mad thinking about how to avoid talking about it.'

'But not today,' I said stubbornly. 'I won't talk about it today.'

'Agreed.' He smiled, and I relaxed again. 'But now you'll have to think of something else to talk about, or we're both going to be thinking about it anyway.'

'All right.' I leaned forward so our elbows

311

brushed, enjoying the nearness of him, knowing I was allowed to touch him at any time. 'I've been thinking about what you said, about the Mc-Krevies, and what they do.'

'Loaning money? Don't tell me you're thinking of–'

'No! Although...' The thought of Frank, and his desperation to get enough to take Amy away, flashed across my mind. 'How difficult is it to get money like that?'

'It's not the difficulty getting it; it's the paying it back. Interest's the thing.'

'Interest?'

'You borrow a certain amount, say, a hundred pounds, but by the time you pay it all back you'll have paid a goodly sum over and above what you borrowed. And the longer you take to pay, the bigger the debt gets. And let me tell you, some of those companies are not shy in demanding what they're owed, either.'

He sounded grim, and I frowned. 'Do they get ... violent?'

'Oh, I'll say. Some of the stuff Uncle Jack told me about Ballentyne'd make your hair curl.' He grinned at me then, and flicked a stray lock that had crept out from under my hat. 'Well, curl more, in your case. What did you think of him, when you met him?'

'He scared me a bit,' I admitted. 'But he dotes on those granddaughters of his, so surely he can't be all that bad.'

'Don't you believe it,' he said, slowing to turn into the lane at the top of the farm. Midway down, he slowed further, and his eyes went to the verge,

312

with its trimmings of nettles and dock leaves, and its flattened area of grass, and then he looked back at me, his eyes hooded slightly in remembrance. My own breath shortened a bit, and my arm crept around his, holding it close against my side.

He leaned in, butting me gently with his head. 'I'm feeling a wee bit ... selfish,' he admitted, and I broke into laughter. He dropped a kiss on my temple, which was all he could reach, and sat back again. 'So, go on, then. If you weren't asking about borrowing money, what were you wanting to know about it for?'

'I've been thinking about Nathan,' I said. 'I was wondering if perhaps he's hiding down here, away from someone like that. I mean, we know he had debt problems.'

'Aye,' he mused. 'It's likely, I suppose.'

'I wonder if he'd be able to borrow from Mc-Krevie then, to pay back the others? That would give him more time.'

Archie shook his head. 'They all talk to each other. That was the problem the Wingfields had, according to Uncle Jack. Samuel tried to do the same thing – answered an ad in the newspaper, but his name'd been blacklisted. Same thing will have happened to young Beresford; he's sure to have explored that possibility already.'

'But what if whoever's after him finds out he's here? They'd only have to talk to Martin.'

'Who's Martin?'

'The same person who told Nathan that Will was here. The apprentice at Markham's shop. If anyone spotted him going there regularly, as he said he did, it wouldn't take long for them to work things out.'

'We don't know the truth of it yet,' Archie reminded me, but he sounded worried now. 'I'll talk to him and find out. Or maybe get Will to. Either way–' he pulled Pippin to a stop, and jumped down off the cart '–we've got some important stone throwing to do, haven't we, Miss Amy-Anna-Banana?' He lifted her off the seat and put her down next to me. 'Go on, I'll sort out the pony and meet you down by the river in a little while.'

I was about to agree, then I saw the way Amy looked up at him, and felt the hesitation when I took her hand and tried to lead her away from him. I couldn't help a little smile. 'You take her, Arch. I'll see to Pippin.'

'I don't mind–'

I shook my head and looked down at Amy, and he followed the direction of my gaze. She hadn't taken her eyes off him, and would clearly be perfectly happy to wait here all day for him if necessary. I understood how she felt, and stretched up to press my lips to the warm spot at the angle of his jaw. 'Go with her,' I said quietly. 'I won't be long.'

He blinked and cleared his throat, then scooped her up, and she patted his head companionably with her spoon, making him wince. 'I'll see you in short order, I hope,' he said to me, and settled Amy more comfortably before setting off across the field towards the woods.

Still smiling, I turned back to begin unhitching Pippin's harness. Leading him away from the cart, I heard the kitchen door slam and looked up; Belinda started across the yard towards the barn, brandishing a key.

'What a palaver!' she said as she passed me. 'Who on earth would want to steal anything we'd be keeping in that old place?'

'Seth was most concerned,' I said, a little grin tugging at my lips, 'and I'm sure he's not worried about Frances.'

She rolled her eyes. 'Not that again. He's far too straight-laced. Too serious.'

'Not like Nathan, eh?'

Bel sighed and stopped. 'I know what I said to you, but he's changed. We can all see it.'

'Do you know anything about why he's here?'

She shrugged. 'Working, earning a living. Doing some painting when he can. It must surely be better for him than delivering groceries on a bicycle.'

She was probably right. I was creating shadows where there needn't be any. Anyway, today was too precious to waste on any more speculation about Nathan; the quicker I finished here, the quicker I'd be able to join Archie and Amy at the river.

'Give me a hand?' I asked. 'I'll do your chores tomorrow.'

She looked across the field, where Archie was just disappearing over the ridge, and gave me a knowing look. 'Well, since it's you, and since the handsome captain is waiting... Just let me get a box for Mrs Adams. She's putting another parcel together for Mr Pearce.'

I watched her go, amused by the sight of her wrestling with the new padlock on the barn. Her little grunts of increasing annoyance sounded so funny. I was feeling the joy of the day even more strongly now, and my insides leapt with anticipation as I thought about sitting beside Archie by the river, his voice low in my ear, his words making me laugh, and his breath making me tingle...

'I would love to be the one to make you smile like that.'

I jumped. Nathan had crossed the yard from the stable without my hearing him. 'I'm sorry?'

'I'd like to paint you looking like that,' he said, framing my face at a distance with his fingers and thumbs. 'I'd call it: *Who has claimed her heart?*'

'Don't be silly,' I said, embarrassed. 'I'm sure Belinda would be happy to sit for you.'

'Then I'd have to call it: *Where have all her wits–*'

'Don't,' I warned him.

He smiled. 'So, pretty Kitty, why didn't you tell me the truth?'

'What do you mean?'

'You told me there wasn't anyone,' he reminded me. 'That time in the barn, remember? I asked if you'd given your promise to anyone and you said you hadn't.'

'It *was* the truth. Then.'

'But you're no strangers, you and the captain.'

'I didn't lie, Nathan. Unlike you.' He looked hurt at that, but the truth was he *had* lied. To all of us. And he might still be doing it. 'Aren't you glad you've told the truth now though?' I pressed, watching him carefully. I couldn't tell if he was being evasive, but he seemed grateful to see Belinda approaching, carrying the box Frances had asked for. She arched an eyebrow as her gaze went from me to him.

316

'Here,' she said, thrusting the box at him. *'I'm* helping Kitty. You can give that to Mrs Adams.'

I waited until he moved off, and gave her a little punch on the arm. 'You don't have to act all jealous, silly!'

'I'm not,' she said, then shrugged and gave me a sheepish grin as she started to unbuckle Pippin's bridle. 'Maybe a little. He really likes you.' Then, as ever, her butterfly mind alighted on a prettier flower. 'Oh! Did you hear about Evie? She's got her diamond back, the one that was stolen before the war.'

'Yes,' I said, pulling Pippin's collar over his head. 'Archie brought it with him.'

'It's so exciting, isn't it? She must be thrilled.'

I was about to tell her Evie would actually be delighted if she never saw the Kalteng Star again, but we both jumped as we heard what would have been a piercing shriek if we'd been any closer to it. It didn't so much drift up over the field as rip across it. We both winced and turned towards the river.

'You didn't tell him about the spoon, did you?' Bel said with a little grin.

'It slipped my mind,' I admitted. Poor Archie! Since there were no more shouts I guessed he'd learned a quick lesson, and my thoughts remained with him until Belinda nudged me, her arms full of Pippin's harness. 'Buck up, Maitland. You can live without him for ten minutes, surely. You'll have to get used ... oh!' She looked stricken. 'Damn my stupid mouth. I'm so sorry.'

But she was right. 'Buck up yourself, Frier,' I said, picking up the collar and hoisting it onto my

317

shoulder. 'Since I have such a little time left with him–' I smiled at her to show I was teasing '–you'd better not make me miss too much of it, had you?'

Chapter Seventeen

I'd forgotten how annoyingly big the field was. As soon as I'd started across it I'd convinced myself I'd be there in two minutes, but as I went over the ridge to the lower slope, I remembered at least half the field's length was still ahead of me. I'd started off at a run, but now slowed, not wanting to arrive sweating and out of breath – I smiled; he hadn't minded yesterday. I don't think he'd even noticed. At last I hitched my skirt high in order to climb the fence that ran the length of the field, and hopped down onto the path that would take me through the lower edge of the wood, to the river.

The day had not yet begun to cool, and the sun was still high, sending its rays down through the leaves to dapple the path ahead. The dampness from last night's rain had not yet soaked away from here, so the smell was rich and earthy and I breathed it in with deep pleasure. My boots were rather too warm for the day though, and I looked down at the path, considering. It was muddy, but not overly stony, so I stopped to take off my boots and stockings, squelching my feet in the mud and enjoying the coolness on my toes. I hung my boots around my neck and stuffed my stockings into them.

So it was on silent feet that I came upon them, and I watched for a moment, enjoying the chance to observe Amy, unseen. She knelt on the wide, pebble-strewn riverbank, carefully selecting stones and building them one atop the other. After a few minutes, a movement to my left drew my attention and I shifted my gaze to see Archie, shirtless, bending over and grunting. I clapped a hand to my mouth to stifle a laugh; he was muttering under his breath and I couldn't understand a word of it, but he sounded very, very cross.

Then he straightened, and my laughter died. He still had his back to me. I could see a web of scars across the tops of his shoulders and partway down his back, perhaps a year old, but savage-looking. My hand fell away from my mouth, and while I wanted to be able to enjoy the sight of his smooth, muscular back, and broad shoulders, all I could think of was how it must have looked before it had healed.

'Archie,' I breathed, and he heard me and turned. His smile went some way towards quenching my anguish, but he realised what I'd seen, and beckoned me closer.

'Don't fret,' he said quietly, tilting my face so I could meet his eyes. 'It was a while ago, and it's done. Healed.'

'Shrapnel?'

'Aye. You'll remember I named Colonel Sumner last night. My CO, at the time he died.' I nodded. 'Well we were together when it happened; the trench was hit, we all ducked down, and we all got it. But I was luckier than some, Kitty. Be as thank-

319

ful as I am.'

'When was it?'

'November last year. Actually it was just after your birthday, when I told you about the vacancy at Number Twelve.' It looked, for a moment, as if he actually felt some part of the blame for what had happened to me out there, and that he regretted persuading me to come out.

'And just after you'd seen Will safe,' I said, to change the direction of his thoughts and remind him what good he'd done.

I read understanding and gratitude in his expression, and he cupped my cheek in one big hand. 'I'd give anything to have spared you what you went through,' he said softly. 'If I hadn't–'

'It wasn't your fault.' I couldn't think of it now. My mind was filled with horror at the thought of how close he'd come to death, and none of us had had the slightest idea. Not even Oli, or he was sure to have told me. 'Why didn't you let us know what had happened? We'd have visited. Which hospital were you in?'

'I ended up being treated at the dressing station, and sent right back. Didn't even make it out to a field hospital, let alone a Blighty ticket.'

'But you're an officer!'

He shook his head and it was only then I noticed his hair was wet, too, as a drop rolled down his temple. 'It makes no difference. This was easily treatable. We needed everyone who could fight, or dig, or carry ammunition. Come on, Kittlington, you know better than most.'

'I know.' I sighed and rested my forehead against his chest, then twisted my head to check

320

on Amy, but she was still happily building.

'Why is your shirt off?' I asked, remembering the grunting.

I felt him shaking as he laughed quietly. 'Because I'm a bloody idiot. Amy was digging with her spoon at the edge of the water and I was worried she'd bend it, or break it, and tried to take it off her.' His voice turned dry. 'Thanks for warning me never to try that, by the way.'

I chuckled. 'What happened?'

'She let out an almighty shriek and pulled it back, caught me off balance, and in I went, head first.'

'So you were wringing out your shirt when I came down?' I gestured at the crumpled garment, now lying by the river. 'I wondered what you were doing. What were you saying?'

'I can't remember, but it was probably the only bit of Gaelic I bothered to learn. You don't want me to translate it either.' His hand caught at mine, and raised it to gently nip at my knuckle, then kiss it. 'I didn't expect you here so soon,' he said, by way of explanation. 'You should have been another half an hour at least. I'd have been decent again by then.'

'Are you sorry I saw you?'

He shook his head. 'I'm sorry it was a shock, that's all. It doesn't hurt much any more, and I don't really think about it.'

I stepped around him and looked up at the scars. Up close I could see for certain they were no mere scratches. Shrapnel flew everywhere out there. I knew that, and he'd been peppered by the stuff – he'd been lucky indeed. I traced the big-

321

gest of the wounds; it began just inside his right shoulder blade and wound downwards, almost to the bottom of his ribcage, cutting a jagged slice through his flesh and leaving a narrow white rope that would never disappear.

His skin rippled into goose bumps, and I wrapped my arms around him from behind. He tensed, and I spread the fingers of both hands as widely as I could reach over his chest and midriff; he was warm from the sun, and his breathing was shorter now, and light; I could feel each breath in the movement of his back as I lay my cheek against him, and when he spoke I felt his hesitant voice as much as I heard it.

'Kitty, I know we can't, not now, but ... I can't be without you tonight.' He twisted in my arms, to look at me searchingly, then his mouth, lifted in a faint smile of relief, came down on mine in the lightest of touches before we both turned our attention back to Amy. If his heart was crashing anywhere near as fiercely as mine he showed no sign of it, but he kept shooting me little looks that kept up that glorious momentum, and made me hope I'd never breathe normally again.

'Leave Amy here,' Evie said later, as Archie and I prepared Pippin and Pirate. 'She's had a long day. She'll sleep.'

I looked across the yard to where Amy sat on the kitchen step, scuffing the dirt with her feet. She played absently with the spoon on its ribbon, and I couldn't suppress a smile and a wish I'd been there to see Archie tumble into the shallow river.

'I know what you're thinking,' he said from behind me, and when I turned to say I doubted it, he tugged at his shirt and raised an eyebrow. 'Aye, I know exactly what you're thinking, ye wee minx.'

I grinned. 'Do it again? For me?'

He growled and turned away, but not before I saw the smile twitch at his mouth. I couldn't remember ever seeing him so relaxed, and he was clearly looking forward to getting back in the saddle again. He tightened Pirate's girth and checked the stirrups, and I enjoyed watching his easy, assured movements.

'Go as fast as you like,' I told him, buckling Pippin's harness; it wouldn't be fair to make him stick to our pace. 'Take the path across the moors. It's a good, easy track, and smooth enough so you'll be able to give him his head.'

He mounted Pirate with the smooth motion of long practice, and gathered up the reins. 'Up towards Princetown?'

I nodded. 'Turn left in the village, and go down past the station and the prison. It's not far.'

'Right. See you at the sawmill.' He turned Pirate towards the path, and I was whisked back through the years as I watched him urge the horse forward. His riding seat was casual, his hands light on the reins, but his back was arrow-straight in the saddle, and his shoulders square. Every horse I'd ever seen him ride seemed to respond to the combination of mastery and gentleness, and Pirate was no exception; he set off at a steady pace, and I watched until they were out of sight around the bend before turning back to Pippin and patting his short neck.

'Just you and me then, old chap.' I waved to Amy as I climbed into the trap, and for the first time ever, she waved back. My heart gave a little lurch, and I tried to remind myself Frank would be coming for her, but I couldn't deny the affection that had taken hold deep inside me for this strange, quiet little girl.

Out on the main road, with nothing on which to focus my mind, I found my thoughts taking the treacherous path I had sworn not to follow today. Archie had used up three days of his leave by going all the way to Oaklands, before finding the house closed up and travelling down to Devon. He'd been here a day and a night, would have to allow for a day's travel to Dover, and then a night's ferry crossing back to France, and several hours on the rough, congested roads back to Belgium. That left two days. Just two days for us to explore what we'd found, and to make our peace with the fact of our imminent parting...

I sat bolt upright on the seat, jerking on the reins as the thought hit me: I'd had the training, and the experience. They were bound to be able to use me back in Dixmude, particularly now Evie was here. I should go. For Archie, yes, but also because I would be more use out there now than I would ever be here. But what would it do to Amy?

Pippin had stopped obediently at my pull on the reins, and I told him to walk on, my mind turning over everything it might mean, and my heart speeding up as I grew more and more certain of what I must do. It *would* be hard on Amy, horribly hard, and even if I decided to remain at Dark River Farm I still had to explain that she would be losing her 'Mister Arsh' in a day or two. My chest tightened as I thought about that. Had it been a mistake, after all, to have let them become close? But it couldn't have been. Just watching them together anyone could see that, even after knowing each other less than a day, each would hold warm memories of the other no matter how long they were parted for. I couldn't have denied them that. And if I chose to return to my former duties, well, the war couldn't go on for ever. If leaving the farm would be a wrench, leaving Amy would be like leaving my own child, but in all likelihood it would be worse for me than for her; she would still be surrounded by her new family. Lizzy, Frances, and even Belinda, would all be strong, solid and loving.

There was another question that made me hesitate, too. Would I be able to bear knowing exactly where Archie was when there was a push on? Evie said it was easier on her nerves that Will was stationed in France, and she was in Belgium, and that although the opportunity was there to move, she hadn't been able to bear the thought of knowing exactly when he was going over. I'd experienced the same stomach-churning fear before, and understood it. It had been hard enough when I'd been over there working before, aware of the unit's every move, and all through Oli's trial, knowing Archie's battalion was involved in heavy fighting, I had been unable to think of much else. But now, when we had found each other and had so much more to lose, now I had the memory of his touch, and his breath on my skin... Could I really do it?

We were almost at Princetown when I heard a shout, and the thudding of hooves away to my right. Archie had evidently waited for me further back along the path, and I'd been too wrapped up in thoughts of him to notice the man himself. He'd kicked Pirate into a canter to catch up, and now he was close enough that I could see his smile. From the age of sixteen I'd seen and responded to his physical appeal, but now he was so close to going away I had a desperate need to capture a moment that was wholly him, and keep it with me. The image of him on that horse, glowing with good health, his body alert to Pirate's every movement and responding with unconscious grace and skill while his attention was solely on me... That would be what held me to him when he left, until I could be with him again.

Wherever that might be.

'Did you proud, I hope?' Seth asked, taking Pirate from Archie. I held the small box Frances had put together for him, and when he'd looped Pirate's reins over the fence post he took it from me with a smile of thanks. He was like a different man, nowadays. He did look a bit shifty though, as he took the box, as if he desperately wanted to investigate its contents, but didn't like to while I was there.

'I think it's just some extra butter,' I said helpfully, 'and maybe another jar of honey. I hope that's all right?'

'Right you are,' Seth said, looking relieved. He must really like that honey, and I made a mental note to tell Frances and Lizzy, so they could make sure they put some in next time too.

'Pirate's been invaluable, thank you,' I said. 'We got the hay in right before last night's little storm. Might we be able to borrow him once more? Not to work, but just to ride, before Archie goes back?'

'Don't see why not. Let him rest a day, then you can take him tomorrow evening. That suit?'

'It does, thank you.'

Stroking Pippin's nose to avoid making eye contact, he cleared his throat. 'Uh, about the other young miss, do you know if she ... will she be...'

'Mr Pearce,' I said gently, hating to be the one, and cursing Bel under my breath. 'I do understand you've formed a bit of an attachment to Belinda. But she has her sights set elsewhere. I'm sorry.'

'Oh, don't be sorry, maid.' Seth was able to look at me now, clearly glad it was out in the open at last. 'I should have known better. She's a rare beauty.'

'The first time you saw her, her nose was all swollen and covered in blood, and her hair was in her face,' I said, exchanging an amused glance with Archie.

'And that's the only time I've seen her,' Seth pointed out. 'Didn't stop me seeing past it. And she's a dab hand with a bit of rope.'

'She is.' I remembered the expert halter-tying. 'I'm sorry to be the one to tell you.'

He waved a hand, dismissing it. Then he saw me looking nervously at Pirate, and smiled. 'Don't worry, miss. I might not have had the purest of reasons for suggestin' our arrangement, but that don't mean I don't think it's a good one.

I'm not going to stop you borrowing the lad here just because your friend has a bit of sense.'

'Thank you!' I breathed a sigh of relief, and decided I didn't need to push Belinda down the stairs after all.

'Besides, that honey's so good, I'd swap him next week for a lifetime's supply!' It was the first time I'd heard him joke, and guessed it was the relief of talking about Bel that had freed a well hidden, but naturally pleasant nature. He coughed again, and held up a hand. 'Uh, one thing though?'

'Yes?' I'd just climbed up into the trap, and he squinted up at me, shielding his eyes.

'You don't need to worry about how much you can pay me,' he said. The evening sun shone full in his face, and I could see the flush on his already ruddy skin. 'I'd be quite all right about it if you left out them biscuits, next time.'

Archie and I were still laughing a few minutes later, as we drew near the prison. I found more to like about Seth every time I saw him, and it was difficult to equate him with the furious, shouting man who'd terrified Bel and me just a couple of months ago – I wished Bel could see it too.

'Who's that?' Archie said, slowing Pippin slightly, and my eyes followed where he was pointing. Up ahead in the road, a single figure stood, a girl. Staring down at the men still toiling in the fields, she looked out of place here, incongruous even.

'She's very well dressed,' I observed. 'Not a farm girl.'

'No, you're all ruffians and tramps,' Archie

said, and I thumped his thigh. He smiled. 'See? No decorum whatsoever.'

'I wonder who she is,' I said, ignoring him, then started as we drew a little closer. 'I know her!' The hat she wore did not hide her jet-black hair, nor did her smart coat disguise the youth of the figure beneath it. 'What on earth is she doing here alone?'

'Who is it?'

'Helen McKrevie. She's probably here to see her father. Stop a minute. I'm going to talk to her.' I jumped down, and turned back, putting a hand on his knee. 'Better if you wait here. She's only about sixteen. She might not have permission to be here and I don't want to frighten her off.'

'Aye, as you like.' Archie sat back to wait, while I hurried up the road towards Helen. She had heard us approach, but showed no sign of nervousness so maybe her grandfather thought it was all right to send her halfway across the country after all. Or maybe Louise was somewhere close by. I glanced around as I approached, but couldn't see anyone else.

'Helen?' I called, and she recognised me with a jolt.

'Miss Maitland! I thought you had gone to Belgium.'

Following so quickly on my decision to do that very thing, I felt easier in my mind as I said, 'I'm going in a few days.' At least it felt like the truth this time.

Helen followed my quick glance back at the cart, and her expression softened. 'That's him, then? The one you were missing?'

'Yes,' I said, and I remembered how lost and broken my love had been then, when she'd said those words. 'Archie. He arrived yesterday, but leaves by Friday.'

She turned back towards the rocky land below us, where tiny figures still swung their picks. 'And I've seen my father, so all's as we said it should be.'

'Where are you staying?'

'We've taken a room in the village. It's very nice.'

'Your sister is with you? That's good. It will help you both to see your father.'

'Aye, I hope so, although she's not come with me yet. How's the wee girl?'

'She's settling in beautifully.' On impulse I blurted, 'Why don't you visit the farm tomorrow? You'll be able to see what a good place it is, and see that Amy's being well cared for.'

Her face lit up. 'What a lovely idea! It would be wonderful to come to the farm and meet every-one.'

As soon as she spoke I realised my mistake. Neither girl was a fool, and it wouldn't take more than an introduction to show that the Evie and Will I'd mentioned were very much alive and well, and not Amy's parents.

For an instant I tried to think of a way to twist what I'd said against what I hadn't said, so that it might appear a misunderstanding on her part ... but I heard the fresh lies in my mind and knew it had to stop.

'Helen, listen,' I said, and caught her shoulders to make her look at me. 'I wasn't telling you the truth. About Evie and Will. They're not Amy's

330

mother and father at all.'

Helen frowned. 'Then who are they, and why did you say they were?'

'They're good friends of mine.'

'And the man was not killed?'

'No. He was badly hurt, but he wasn't killed.'

She looked as though she didn't know whether to be relieved or angry, but eventually she just nodded, and spoke slowly, taking it all in. 'Well, that's good news, right enough, but why didn't you tell the truth about her parents?'

'I knew your grandfather would not listen to anything I had to say if I did.'

'Why not?'

'I can't tell you now,' I said. 'It's a long story. And it doesn't matter, now Amy's found a home. Will you still come tomorrow? We can talk then if you'd like.'

Helen regarded me for a long moment, then nodded. The distrust in her expression made the guilt twist tighter, and I considered just telling her the truth about her relationship to Amy now, but Frank's face floated in the front of my mind and I couldn't do it. I could have kicked myself for mentioning the farm at all, but she'd been so concerned Amy was being well cared for, and anyway the damage was done.

'I'll come and collect you in the cart at ten. Would you like a lift back to the village now?'

'It's not far; I can walk.'

'No, but we're going that way anyway. Come on, let us help a little bit. Unless you wanted to stay here a while longer?' I added, gesturing at the prison workers below us.

'I've seen enough, and Father's told me what I needed to know, that he's not being mistreated like some of them. I'll take the ride back, and thank you kindly for the offer.'

I helped her climb into the back of the little cart, and Archie turned and smiled at her. She smiled back, but seemed slightly in awe of him until he spoke, and she remembered he was a fellow Scot.

'Glad to meet you, lass,' he said, as informally as politeness allowed. 'I hope your father's well.'

'Aye, he is, thank you, sir,' she said. 'Where are you from, if you don't mind me asking? Not Glasgow.'

'No, a fair bit north of there.' He clicked to Pippin to walk on. 'Wee place up near Fort William, if you know it?'

'Oh, aye. So pretty up there,' she said with enthusiasm, and I smiled my thanks at Archie, who twined the fingers of one hand around mine briefly before returning them to the reins.

When we dropped Helen off at the inn where they'd taken a room, she looked up at me, faintly troubled again now she stood alone in the road. 'I'll see you tomorrow. You can tell us everything then. The truth this time?'

'The truth,' I promised.

Archie didn't say anything as we moved on, evidently expecting an explanation, but after a moment he gave up waiting. 'What was all that about?'

I looked away, my mind once again flashing through all the possible explanations but the right one, but lying to him, of all people, was out of the question. So I told him everything, every

332

detail of the Blackpool trip, my using Will and Evie, and then talking to Helen in the park afterwards. I even told him what she'd said about him living in my head and making me want to be fighting at his side. When I fell away into silence, waiting tensely to defend my actions somehow, he pulled Pippin to a stop and, to my relieved surprise, took me in his arms.

'I can see you feel bloody terrible about it,' he said, 'and that's partly why I love you so much.'

'Partly?'

His soft laugh rumbled in his chest. 'Aye. A bigger part's because you did it to begin with.'

I pulled back, blinking in surprise. 'What I did was—'

'For Amy. And you never came out and said Will was no more, did you?'

'Well, no, but—'

'Stop it.' He drew my head back into the hollow of his shoulder. I could feel the warmth of him through his shirt, and wanted to stay there for ever. 'What you did was completely selfless,' he said. 'You could have come straight home here, where everything was safe and comfortable, and known to you. But instead you went into a strange man's home, a man you knew nothing about.' I felt his hands tighten on my back and across my shoulders. 'Even if that was all you did, it would still be one of the most courageous acts I'd ever known, after Colonel Drewe. But it wasn't all, was it? You gave his daughter your own lunch, walked for miles, made up stories out of nowhere, and then confronted one of the richest men in the city in his own home. All to find a roof and a home for

333

a little girl who's nothing to do with you.'

His sigh went through both of us, and I felt him drop a gentle kiss onto the back of my neck. 'Kitty Maitland, you're the bravest wee thing I've ever known. And the most compassionate. I feel humbled to be living in your head and your heart. I truly do.'

Later that night, sleeping in his arms in Frances's bed, my dreams were filled with peace and contentment for the first time since he'd left for Belgium in 1914. I'd crept out of bed and gone to him as soon as everyone had turned in for the night, and we'd lain in silence, not making love, by mutual understanding, but learning each other the way we couldn't have done last night out in the rain. Our nightclothes had been cast aside in the need to experience the joy of contact, and his hands cupped and pressed, travelled and caressed. Our kisses were not fuelled by urgency, they were born of wonder and growing delight, and my fingers traced the contours of his chest and stomach, making him tremble as they drifted over him.

My head fit perfectly in the hollow of his shoulder, as it had done in the cart earlier that evening, but this time I only had to turn my head slightly to press my lips to his warm, smooth skin. His fingers drifted over my back, and mine traced his ribs as my arm lay across his waist. In this way we fell asleep, and while last night our bodies had come together in mingled fear and need, tonight our hearts and minds became gently but irrevocably entwined and my last thought, before sinking into the bliss of sleep, was that at last we were complete.

If only I had stayed there, everything might have been all right.

Chapter Eighteen

In the very early hours, I woke and reluctantly realised I would have to return to my own bed. It was horribly difficult to ease myself away from Archie, not just because I didn't want to waken him, but because the moment my hand lost contact with his body I wanted to put it back. He lay on his back, one arm hanging off the side of the bed, the other beneath me where he'd wrapped me in his embrace before falling asleep. As my weight shifted off that arm, I saw his fingers twitch, and held my breath, but he sighed and settled again. I carried on, easing myself away from him, feeling the loss of his warmth with every inch. Standing in the moonlit room, looking down at his powerful form, helpless in sleep, I had to clench my fists to avoid reaching out to touch him one last time, and I wrapped my arms across my chest and turned away to pluck my nightgown off the chair. I slipped it over my head, and put one hand over the door latch to muffle the click, but it still echoed around the room and I froze. Archie still did not awake.

Back in my own room, this time trying not to wake Amy or Belinda, I crept onto the bottom of my own bed, and crawled up it to the pillow. It felt cold and empty, but I would have to get used to that. I eased back the covers, and clambered awkwardly in, congratulating myself on my silent accomplishment, but a hiss from Belinda's bed made me groan.

'Kitty! Have you been with Archie?'

'Yes,' I whispered back, 'but not the way you mean.'

'Oh. Have you ever though?'

'Bel! Go to sleep.'

'I'll assume that means yes,' she said with a certain satisfaction. I shivered and snuggled deeper, without answering. The bed might be cold, but I was bone-tired, and it was good to close my eyes again and let my fingers remember the strong swell of Archie's chest, and the way his stomach muscles tightened when he laughed, in his effort to be silent. My fingertips alive with memory, I slipped closer to sleep again.

'Kitty?'

'Hmm?'

'Tell me about the diamond.'

'Not now. Sleepy.'

'Oh, please! Just a little bit.' A pause. I kept very still. 'Kitty!' I squeezed my eyes tightly shut, but I knew she wouldn't give up.

'What'm hwa no?'

'What?'

I sighed, licked my lips, and tried again. 'What do you want to know?' I heard her sit up, but was determined not to do the same. 'I don't know much myself,' I cautioned.

'Well, is it worth an awful lot?'

336

'Quite a lot. Yes. A lot.'

'How did Archie get it?'

'His uncle found it.'

'I do like Jack. He and Lizzy are so perfect for one another, despite their age difference.' I was bemused by the way her mind flitted. It was making me even more tired, but glad she'd changed the subject.

'Good,' I mumbled. But she changed it back again.

'Why do you think Evie never mentions the diamond?'

'She never wanted... It's got to go back to Borneo,' I said on a yawn, not wanting to get into explanations about Evie's hatred of the Kalteng Star. 'Bel, please. I'm tired, and if you wake Amy–'

'Why Borneo?'

'Because... I'll tell you tomorrow.'

'All right.' I heard the rustle of sheets as she settled back down, and breathed a sigh of relief, but she whispered again. 'Kitty?'

'Urghm.'

'I'm so glad you and Archie are happy.'

I grunted, 'G'night, Bel,' but my face, pressed against my pillow, split into a smile.

I'd hoped to spend Archie's last full day with him. I'd pictured the dark, deep green wood behind us, throwing its shadows across the otherwise sun-dappled river, the quiet gurgling of the water providing the score for the familiar mingling of our voices ... but when he'd seen Frances readying herself to go to work in the far fields, he'd exchanged a glance with me, and given me a faint,

337

apologetic smile. I returned it, with encouragement and a little nod, and he told Frances to wait while he fetched some tools and came with her. Her gratitude made the disappointment a bit easier to bear, but it was difficult to hide it, especially when Amy had gone with them. It had been funny and tender to see, when Archie sat on the step to put on his boots, how she had sat next to him and pulled at her already shod feet in imitation. He'd looked down at her with a smile.

'Good morning, Miss Amy-Anna-Banana.'

'Mornin', Mister Arsh. Boots?'

'That's right. I'm away to help Mrs Adams today. She's got lots of things to do before the weather turns nasty.'

'I comin' too?'

He looked back into the kitchen and up at me, one eyebrow raised. 'What say you, young Kittlington?'

'She'll need watching,' I said doubtfully. 'You won't get much done.'

'I'll come and keep her company,' Will said. 'I can't do any heavy lifting, so I can make myself useful keeping her out from under your feet.'

'I comin' too, Mister Arsh?'

'Aye, you're comin' too,' Archie said, and bumped her gently with his shoulder. 'You can make sure Mister William behaves himself, and doesnae try to do too much.'

Evie looked relieved; looking after Amy was about the most she would allow Will to do, after the scare at Oaklands. 'As long as you don't try to lift her,' she cautioned.

'No worries on that score,' he said with a little

338

grin at Amy. 'I might have to ask her to carry me though. Do you think you could do that, Amy?'

She looked up at him, frowning, her little mouth pursed. Then she sighed and shook her head. 'I not carryin' grown-ups. Too big. Mister Arsh carry Mister William.'

'It's all right; I'll walk,' Will laughed, and ruffled her hair. He gestured to where Archie was shouldering one of Harry's scythes. 'Mister Arsh has quite enough to carry.'

And so Archie's new little shadow had gone with him, Frances and Will, out to the far fields, where the last of the long summer grasses were awaiting harvesting for silage. I'd watched them, feeling a little pang of loneliness once they'd gone from sight, but Lizzy had quickly dispelled it by drawing me into a conversation about the two girls from Blackpool. Then, to my disgust, she had called on Jessie to go with me to collect them.

'You two will have to get along eventually,' she said. I wasn't so sure, particularly as my thoughts kept returning to yesterday's idea; perhaps I would be gone from here in a matter of days. A fresh twist of doubt gripped me, but I had no time to give it much thought now. Tonight would be quieter, and I would have the chance talk it over with Archie.

'I wish Frances wouldn't insist on us going in pairs,' Jessie said crossly, as she came into the kitchen.

'It's because of what happened with Belinda,' Lizzy reminded her, but Jessie shook her head.

'No, it's not. It's because of those conchies! She's worried they might see us alone in the trap, and try to steal it and escape. Shirkers.'

'Don't call them that,' Lizzy said mildly. 'They're working hard, just as we are.'

'Some of them are. The ones in the quarries, and the farms,' Jessie said, 'but not the ones out there smashing rocks and building walls nobody needs.'

I'd heard enough; it was still unsettling to hear my vague notions being spoken aloud, but with such venom. 'Do belt up, and let's go,' I said. 'The girls will be waiting.'

'Where are they staying?' It was the first thing Jessie had said, during the whole drive, and while the silence had bothered me, it was still better than the rather wearing snappishness of my enforced companion.

I pointed. 'That's where I dropped Helen last night. The Plume of Feathers.'

'Looks expensive.'

'They can afford it. Even when there's a war on.' I realised they could probably afford it better now than ever, with people desperately borrow-ing, and, from what Archie said, paying back so much more. I didn't like to think how they were finding the money.

'I still don't even know who they are,' she said. 'No-one's bothered to tell me.'

'And you haven't bothered to ask.'

She gave me a steady look, and chose the high road. 'So who are they?'

'Some friends. From Blackpool.'

'And you just happened to bump into them last night?'

'Why is that difficult to believe?'

340

'Just seems … odd that they should be here.'

I turned back to the road to hide the faint blush I could feel heating my face. More lies, but of all people I might have confessed my poor behaviour to, Jessie was the last. 'Not that odd,' I said. 'Their father's working down there.' I gestured to the road that led down to the Work Centre.

Immediately I knew I'd made a mistake; the perceived sins of the father would almost certainly be visited upon the daughters at some point. I sighed, and turned the trap towards the inn where I'd bid farewell to Helen last night. I wondered if Louise would ever offer her father the same understanding her younger sister had, but remembered her eager question about Frank, and realised she still, unbelievably, held a romantic view of a soldier's life. She would be unlikely to be sympathetic to an objector's viewpoint.

The girls were waiting on the little path that led from the inn's front door up through the garden and onto the moor. Louise greeted us both warily, but Helen seemed more relaxed today, and was happy to link her arm through mine as I led them back to the trap. I helped them in, and introduced Jessie, who was polite but nothing more, and I raised my eyes to the sky and gave thanks we wouldn't have to drive past the prison.

The drive back was a surprisingly good one. Jessie gladly swapped places with Helen, and when I'd circled Pippin in the road and handed the younger girl the reins, she smiled, proudly telling the already walking Pippin to 'walk on'. It was refreshing and pleasant to be sitting next to such a cheerful girl, and we talked all the way back to the farm.

When we came to a stop in the yard I couldn't help straining my gaze to reach across the fields, in the direction Archie had taken. Helen saw, and smiled. 'Will he be joining us for lunch?'

'No,' I said with real regret. 'He'll be out there all day. But Amy will be back soon. Will's looking after her.'

'And where's Evie?' Helen looked around with interest, and I saw her nose wrinkling at the smell I never really noticed any more. I smiled, remembering how strong it had seemed when Evie had brought me here for the first time.

'I think she and Belinda are doing the rooms,' I said. 'Come inside and wait there; she won't be long.'

'I'll do the trap then, shall I?' Jessie called, and I didn't like her tone.

'I'll help you in a minute! There's no need to be like that.'

She shook her head, softening. 'No, sorry. You have guests. It's all right. Really.'

Once again, as I left her, I wondered whether I liked her at all, but was soon too busy settling Louise and Helen into the sitting room to waste time thinking about it. We heard Evie and Belinda come back downstairs and go into the kitchen, and I leaned out into the hall. 'Evie! Can you come here a moment, please?'

Both sisters put their teacups down and sat up, and a minute later Evie's head popped around the door. 'What is it, Skittles? I'm just...' Her eyes widened as she saw Louise. 'Oh!'

At the same time Louise caught her breath, and

342

said, 'It's you!'

I blinked. 'You *know* each other?' I was reminded of the night Nathan had arrived, but this time the surprise was a happy one on both sides.

Louise stood up, her face creased into a smile of delight, the first one I'd seen from the more sombre of the two girls. 'I never introduced myself back then, did I? I'm Louise McKrevie. And of course you know Helen.'

Evie looked as stunned as I felt. 'McKrevie?'

'Aye. We were only staying with our grandfather in Blackpool the last time we met, but now we live with him.'

'McKrevie,' Evie murmured. 'Then you're...' She looked past me, out to where Amy had spent the morning, and I gave a tight, urgent shake of my head, and she stopped. 'You're a long way from home,' she finished instead.

'Where did you and Evie meet?' I asked Helen.

'In Blackpool. A few years ago, before the war. There was an anti-suffrage rally in a playhouse there, and Louise took me along to protest it.'

'There was a fire,' Evie put in. 'Only a small one, but it caused a real panic.'

'The people were more frightening than the fire,' Helen said. 'Louise hurt her arm in the rush to get out. I lost sight of her, and climbed up on the stage to see over the crowd. Then something hit me on the head and I fell over, and someone else pulled the scenery down. I was too frightened to move, so I crouched down and waited 'til someone came for me. And someone did.' She gave Evie a look of gratitude, and Evie smiled back.

'He's my husband now,' she said. 'You'll see

343

him soon.'

'I heard he was hurt,' Helen said, and Louise looked stricken; this was evidently the first she'd heard of it.

'He was wounded at Arras,' Evie explained. 'He's getting better though. Soon be good as new.'

'I'm so glad.' Helen looked around the kitchen. 'This seems like a nice place to convalesce in.' She turned to me again. 'Who is she, then? Amy, I mean. Is she yours?'

'No. That man you saw us with, in the park, that's her father.'

'So she's your niece?'

How many more lies had I told? They were swarming out of the woodwork like beetles. This was awful, no matter what Archie said. 'No, he's not my brother. The girl's mother has fallen on very hard times, up in London, and Frank was worried for his daughter's safety. But you saw his difficulties?' I tapped at my own left arm, and she nodded. 'I told him I'd try and find a good home for his daughter, until he could afford to take her away somewhere to start a new life.'

'Then who is he to you? You took a lot of trouble over helping him.'

'He's...' I found a connection that would please her. 'He's Will's friend, actually. Will used to be his apprentice, before the war.'

'It's lovely to see you, of course,' Evie said, curiosity getting the better of her, 'but we're quite a distance from Blackpool. How on earth did you come to be here?'

I wondered if the girls would hesitate to tell her about their father, especially knowing about Will,

344

but although Louise remained tight-lipped, Helen seemed to draw herself up a little as she told Evie about her father. I watched closely, curious to see Evie's reaction, but although her jaw tensed slightly she accepted the explanation with an understanding nod, and Helen relaxed again.

I joined in then, with the same vague tale I'd told Jessie, about seeing Helen near the Work Centre. 'We got talking about Amy, and I invited them to visit the farm and see how she's settling in.'

'I'm glad you did,' Evie said, clearly relieved to have moved on from the subject of conscientious objectors, and I decided her feelings were probably much like my own; knowing it was wrong to condemn, accepting the difficult choices those men had had to make, yet finding it hard to sympathetically compare their suffering with what we'd witnessed at the Front. I was still struggling with it.

Looking out of the window for a distraction, I was relieved to see the outline of a man and child coming across the field, and excused myself to meet them.

'How has she been?' I called.

'Kept me well and truly in check,' Will grinned. 'Took Archie at his word and wouldn't let me lift a finger.'

Amy looked behind her. 'Mister Arsh?'

'He'll be home soon,' I assured her. 'But I've got some visitors who are very much looking forward to seeing you again. Would you like to come and say good afternoon?'

She nodded, her hand going immediately to her

spoon. Now she was coming to know us she was mostly content to leave the now-tarnished silver hanging on its ribbon, but as soon as she felt uneasy about anything, there it was in her hand again. She clutched it now, and gave me her other hand, allowing me to lead her into the house.

Will recognised Louise immediately but only realised who Helen was in relation to her; Helen had been only twelve when she'd been injured in the fire and now she was a young woman. She looked at Will with wide eyes and an expression of awe, and her eyes clouded as she saw him wince whenever he moved too quickly, but although Evie noticed, she didn't comment. Her own gaze lifted to her husband and stayed on him with affection and pride, roving over his beloved face and form, making me ache for the sight of Archie again.

It was a much happier group that sat down to lunch. Even Jessie had lost that pinched, suspicious look and was amusing Amy, allowing me to talk to the others without interruption. Evie and Louise had entered into a lively discussion about women's suffrage, and Lizzy turned to me.

'Will you and Archie be coming down to the cottage tonight? We're having a little get-together.'

'I hadn't heard about it,' I said, my heart sinking. Tonight would be our last night. Archie was due to leave tomorrow afternoon.

Thankfully Lizzy read the dismay on my face and understood. 'No matter. I wouldn't really expect you to. Frances, Evie and Will are popping down, since it's Ma's birthday. But I'll tell her you send your regards.'

346

That left Amy, Jessie, Nathan, Belinda, Archie and me. Belinda would more than likely be hanging over Nathan while he painted, Jessie would be in her room, Amy would be asleep by eight o'clock...

I smiled.

When the meal was over Will offered to take Amy back out to the field, but I shook my head. 'Helen and Louise would like to spend some time with her, I think.'

Jessie's head came up sharply, and her gaze snapped from me to the girls, and then to Amy. 'Why?'

'Well, because ... she's a sweet child, and besides, it will do Amy good to see new people.'

She considered this, and eventually nodded, and I had the annoyed feeling she was giving her permission. I was just biting back a retort when Frances came in, red-faced and sweating, and nodded to the visitors before turning to Belinda.

'You can go out and help finish up this afternoon,' she said. 'You've got younger bones.' Belinda looked as if she was about to argue, then Frances went on, 'And you can fetch Nathan down to help, too. He's been stuck away up there painting most of the morning. Sinful, in this weather.'

Miraculously the protest didn't happen, and Frances rolled her eyes and tried to hide a smile, before wiping her right hand on her trousers and holding it out to Louise. 'Very nice to meet you both, misses. I hope you're enjoying your visit.'

'Oh, we are,' Louise said. 'I'm afraid we're not

347

dressed to look around your lovely farm, but what we've seen has been terribly interesting.'

'How long are you staying in Princetown?'

'We leave tomorrow morning.'

'Well, it's been nice to meet you.' Frances shook their hands again. 'Kitty, why don't you show them the creamery? Let them see we're not all muck and chickens.'

'And rats,' Jessie said, as soon as Frances had left the room.

'Rats?' Louise looked horrified, and even Helen frowned.

I shot a glare in Jessie's direction, then forced a smile at Louise. 'Don't mind Jessie. That's just what she calls the hens.'

I was startled to see Jessie's mouth twitch in a grin. 'We have small brown hens here, with long tails,' she said, and winked at me. While I was annoyed with her for throwing a light on an unsavoury aspect of farm life, I couldn't help feeling my smile becoming more natural as I remembered that first day, when we'd worked so well together in the barn.

I gave a brief shake of my head, turning back to the McKrevie girls. 'She's just being silly. Come on, I'll show you the creamery.'

Louise glanced at her sister. 'That would be lovely. But we'd just like to have a little look around outside first, alone, if that's not too rude?'

'Not at all,' I said. 'We've rather launched you into everything, haven't we? You've not had a moment's peace. I'll wait for you here, and Amy and I will clean up the lunch things.'

Later, as they followed Amy and me out to the

little add-on that lay alongside the parlour, I thought they seemed a little uncertain about something, but let them continue exchanging glances and nods, each one silently urging the other to be the first to speak. Amy climbed onto the stool where she often sat to watch Frances churn the butter, and, unable to bear it any longer I turned to face the two sisters.

'What is it? You clearly have something to say.'

They looked at each other again, and I sighed, but before I could say anything more Louise spoke. 'We love Dark River Farm. We really think it's a wonderful place, but...' another glance '...we wonder if it's right for Amy?'

I looked at them, stunned. 'What on earth do you mean? Don't listen to anything Jessie says. In all honesty yes, there are bound to be a few rats where there's animal feed, but really, there are hardly any. Amy has the best of everything here, including attention–'

'Oh, yes,' Helen said hurriedly. 'We can see that. But she's a young lady, Kitty. She shouldn't be, well, we feel she shouldn't be working in the fields.'

'Working in the...' I gave an incredulous laugh. 'She wanted to be with Archie, that's all! She and Will would have been playing, not working.'

'All the same.'

There was a tense silence, and the atmosphere in the dairy, always cool, now dropped several more degrees. My voice was tight when I spoke again. 'And what would be your solution to this problem?'

'We think ... that is, we're *sure* we would be able

to convince Grandfather to take her, after all.'

'No.'

They looked at one another, frankly astonished. 'But it's what you wanted! Amy would have the best of everything. She'd be raised as a lady, and no-one would ever have to know about her ... unfortunate start in life. Don't you want that for her?'

My heart lurched as I thought about my own family's rejection. But this wasn't the same. 'Her father was actually relieved when your grandfather turned us away,' I said, my voice matching the chilly air. 'He may not be able to give her everything just now, but he's made plans to come and get her when he can.' I struggled for a more polite tone. 'But thank you for your kind offer.'

'Please, Kitty, we didn't mean to upset you.'

My rising frustration was reflected in my voice, echoing off the rough stone walls. 'I would have been so grateful if you had accepted Amy when we came to you! If you'd offered her a home then and there, or even asked for time to think about it, you might have her now. But it's too late. She's settled here, and she's staying here.'

'We understand.'

'No! I'm not sure you do.' Seeing Amy's head start to draw down into her shoulders, I lowered my voice. 'You must remember what she was like when we came to your grandfather's house? Not a word, barely a look ... and you can see she's not as other children of four are. But she's found her home now, and I know even Frank will see that when he comes for her. He told me he'd rather settle nearby, and see her when he could, than take her away from somewhere she feels safe.'

'I'm sorry,' Helen said. She reached out and touched my arm, and her eyes met mine. I began to believe her, and relaxed my posture.

'I'm sorry too, I shouldn't have shouted. You do understand, though?'

'Of course.' Louise hesitated and bit her lip. 'Whatever I say next, Kitty, I want you to promise me you will accept in the spirit with which it's spoken. We want to help, somehow. We have...' She stopped, and Helen nodded for her to go on. 'We have more money than we need. We'd like to give you some. For Amy. To put away for her future.'

I looked at them in turn, unable to think of a single thing to say. 'Why would you do that?' I managed at last.

'She's such a sweet thing. And so sad,' Helen said softly. 'We want to think that one day she'll be able to choose the life she wants for herself. To go to school, and maybe even university if she wants to, or simply to buy her own horse, or her own house. To never worry about debt.'

The word rang around the room, and suddenly everything made sense. Louise stepped away from us both and folded her arms tight across her chest. Until now I'd always felt as if Helen were the oldest, in maturity if not in actual years, but now Louise looked every bit as old as Evie and Lizzy, and every bit as capable.

'Kitty, our family has seen some awful things. I don't know if you realise, but–'

'You organise loans, yes.'

'Well then, you'll know. We talked about it after lunch, and we can't bear the thought of this poor

351

child suffering in the way we've seen some families do. Especially since the war.'

'We'll look after her,' I said, but it was pride and good intention talking, not practicality. I knew that as well as they did.

'But what about if her father does collect her after all?' Louise pressed. 'He might save enough to take her away, but do you think he'll have thought to save enough to sustain them after that? If he's as devoted as you say, he'll be here and whisking her away the moment he has the train tickets, or the steerage fares. But what then?'

Frank was sending what he could, and saving what he could, but the memory of his expression whenever he looked at his little girl made it painfully clear that Louise was right. She came over to me, and her hand gripped mine. 'Please. Let us do this. For Amy and her father, and for your own peace of mind.'

I found myself nodding. Part of me hated myself for it, but a glance at Amy, flushed, now happy again, and cross-eyed as she peered into her spoon, banished that. 'Thank you.' It was hard to speak, but I tried to keep my voice steady. 'We'll put it away in the bank, and make sure she writes to you as soon as she's able, to thank you herself.'

'Well good,' Louise said, and her sudden smile broke the thin veil of ice that had hung over us. She slipped her arm through mine and led me back into the main part of the house. 'We have it safely locked away at the hotel, so we'll give it to you when you drive us back.'

'Thank you,' I said again. It seemed inadequate,

but for them it was enough.

An hour later I went to find Jessie. She was scrubbing vegetables for tonight's dinner, and Lizzy was making pastry, and they were chatting quite happily. It was an unusual sight, and it gave me hope for my next request.

'Jessie, I know you don't like it, but would you please come with me to take the girls home?'

'Do you really need someone else?' Jessie looked beseechingly at Lizzy, who considered.

'It won't hurt you to go alone this once, Kitty. Frances is writing some letters at the moment, so I don't want to disturb her just to ask.'

'I'd be more than happy to go alone,' I said, 'but I'm going to bring Pirate back. It's Archie's last half-day tomorrow, and I'd love him to spend some time doing what he loves most. Mr Pearce is expecting me this evening and I need someone to drive the trap home. Please, Jessie?'

She seemed gratified that I was asking nicely, and was able to acquiesce with good grace, thereby preserving the pleasant atmosphere, and convincing me she'd turned as much of a corner as Amy had. Indeed, the drive out to Princetown passed agreeably enough. Amy sat in the back with Louise and Jessie once again, and now there was more chatter drifting up to where Helen and I sat. Amy's words were as few and far between as ever, but now and again her quiet giggle would settle into my heart and I'd find a smile on my face that grew wider every time.

Pippin clattered to a stop outside the Plume of Feathers, and I jumped down to help Louise and

Helen; their fashionable skirts looked very nice, but they made climbing in and out of a pony trap something only other people ought to do.

'Wait here,' Louise said, and she and Helen went indoors quickly, leaving me standing in the road, and Jessie clicking her tongue impatiently.

'What are we waiting for?' she wanted to know after a few minutes. 'I want to get back.'

'You can go if you like,' I said. 'I can walk over to Mr Pearce's.'

'Fine, we will.' She called back over her shoulder, 'Hold tight, Amy; we're off.'

She had just turned Pippin around to face back down the road towards Plymouth, when Helen and Louise came back out. Curious, she pulled the trap to a halt again, and waited.

I tried to swallow the feeling that I was doing something awful; this was for Amy, and how was it so different, after all, from asking for a roof over her head and food on her plate? Besides, they had offered... Still, it felt wrong, and I wanted it done and over with. I went to meet them.

Louise gave me a package wrapped in brown paper and tied with string. I had no idea how much might be in there, but it felt substantial. I thanked her once again and hugged her close. Then Helen put her arms around me too, and I felt that Amy, if not myself, had found two real, everlasting friends.

'Come on,' Jessie called. 'I might as well take you down there, now.'

I climbed back onto the front seat, and waved the two girls out of sight before tucking the small package into my pocket.

'What's that?'

'It's for Amy.'

'Yes, but what is it?'

'What does it matter?'

Jessie clicked to Pippin. We drove for a few minutes in silence, then, as we passed the railway station she took a deep breath. 'Is it money?'

'Why ever would it–'

'*Is it money, Kitty?*'

Taken aback, I could only blurt, 'Yes!'

A second later I almost fell off my seat, as Jessie flicked the reins hard, sending Pippin into a startled canter. My heart thudding, I twisted to see Amy's white face staring at me in terror, her mouth open in a wordless cry, and I grabbed Jessie's hands and pulled, slowing Pippin to a fast trot.

'Don't worry, darling,' I said to Amy, when I could speak properly. 'That won't happen again.' I turned back; Jessie's face was set and stony, no apology forthcoming. 'What the *hell* was that?' I hissed, not wanting Amy to hear. 'What does it matter if they want to give her some money?'

She turned to me in a fury. 'You are *such* a liar!'

'What?'

'Get out! Go on; get out! I'll take Amy home. She doesn't need you.'

'Jessie!'

'She'll be quite safe with me. Get *out!*' She gave me a rough push, and it was only by jumping that I managed to avoid a nasty fall. Even so I stumbled as I landed, and fell, skinning my knee. The apple I'd brought for Pirate dug into my thigh as I pitched awkwardly sideways. Stunned,

355

I watched her turn Pippin and the cart in a tight, practised circle, and drive back the way we'd come.

'Jessie!' I yelled, angered beyond belief. I couldn't think of anything to say that might make her stop; I was still reeling from the accusation she'd flung at me. It was true, I'd lied a lot over the past week, but nothing that warranted this. And in any case it was the money that had pushed her into this fit of madness, not my lies.

I climbed stiffly to my feet, and began the short walk to the sawmill. By the time I got there I was hot, and even angrier than before, until Seth appeared, and nodded. 'Miss. Your soldier not with you?'

'No, he's working for Mrs Adams today.'

'Ah. That's good of him. He seems like a nice sort, if you don't mind my saying so.'

Despite myself, I felt a smile crossing my face. *A nice sort.* He was certainly that. 'Thank you, I'll tell him you said so.'

'Hurt your knee, miss?'

'Just a graze,' I said, pulling the material of my trousers away from where they had stuck, with a little wince. 'I'll patch it up when I get home.'

'Right you are. You'd be used to that.'

'Sorry?'

'You know, Red Cross.'

'Oh, you remembered that?'

'I didn't say at the time, miss, 'cos I was so blood ... uh, so angry with the two of you. Beggin' your pardon. But, well, it's a good thing, isn't it, fixing broken people? Best you can, anyway, like.'

'Yes,' I said slowly. 'It is, isn't it?' And just like

that, I made my decision. A tightening in my belly, and a faint, queasy roll, told me it wouldn't be easy, but I would do it because it was a 'good thing'. The right thing. The only thing. My heart picked up pace, and I felt myself straightening, my shoulders squaring.

'Anyway, you'll be wanting Pirate,' Seth went on, oblivious to the way his words had affected my future, and that of untold others. 'He's ready and waiting. Bring him back in a day or two.' He led Pirate out of the stable, and the long white face nuzzled me in recognition. I fished out the apple, and let him pluck it from my hand while I gathered up the reins with the other, then I was up, and waving goodbye, feeling the cool wind tug at my hair and cool my hot face.

Once past the village I took the moorland path, pushing Pirate into a canter, and letting all the tension and anger flow out of me as the ground sped by beneath us. I remembered Archie's look of relaxed happiness yesterday, and knew my expression would match it now; something about the horse's smooth strength, and the ease with which he responded to the lightest touch on the rein reminded me of the day I'd ridden the horse we'd named Woody. If we hadn't done that, I wouldn't be here riding Pirate now... It was odd how things turned out.

I drew closer to Dark River Farm, and a glance to my right revealed the pony and trap, ambling along the main road. I looked long enough to satisfy myself that Amy was safe and happy, now sitting alongside Jessie, and then veered off and took the long way around once again. This time I came out at the field where the others were working. I heard Nathan's shout, and Belinda's laughter and reply. I didn't know what they were saying, but the sounds of people working companionably together in these fields, underlaid by the distant sound of sheep and the call of the wood pigeons in the trees, gave me a sudden pang; could I really leave this, now I knew I loved it so much? And then, lower and stealing all the strength from my legs, Archie's voice joined the others and I knew I'd go wherever he went, for the rest of my life.

I didn't go over to them; they didn't know I was there. I just turned Pirate towards home, and hacked him quietly the rest of the way, out to the road and then down the lane. I passed 'our' patch of grass, now no longer flattened, but easily distinguishable from the rest of the path, and the pleasant ache deep in my belly flared. Tonight we would be together again, and even if we didn't make love, I would be able to touch him, talk to him, and read his immediate response to my decision to go back to Flanders.

But first, there was Jessie.

Chapter Nineteen

I found her upstairs, walking towards her bedroom. My voice cracked out. 'You!' She turned, her eyes wide, then saw it was only me and carried on walking. *'Jessie!'*

She stopped and sighed. 'What?'

'Where's Amy?'

'As if you care!' She whirled on me. 'You have the money.'

'Why are you so angry about that?' I was honestly puzzled. Surely it couldn't be jealousy, not this time.

'Who are those girls really?'

'Jessie–'

'Tell me!'

I sighed. 'Helen and Louise McKrevie. Will and Evie met them in–'

'Yes, I believe that. What I don't believe is that you met them purely by chance yesterday. And I want to know why they're suddenly giving you money for a little girl they've never met before.'

Something about her face stopped my fury in its tracks; she looked stricken, not angry, and I eased my voice down into a softer tone. 'What's wrong? Why don't you trust them?'

'You can't trust anyone in this world,' she said, her own voice catching suddenly. 'Not *anyone*.'

'Jess–'

'Stop saying that!'

'Well what do you want me to call you? Your real name's Frances, isn't it?'

'Yes. Call me that.'

I looked at her for a moment, wracking my brain for something that would explain this strange behaviour. 'It's going to get confusing,' I said at last.

'Then call Frances Mrs Adams.'

'Oh, not that again!' My irritation crept back. 'You've never liked that, have you?'

She ignored that. 'Why did Lady Creswell throw you out of Oaklands, Kitty? Same reason as your

359

mother doesn't want to know you?'

I hurt with the need to make her stop. 'You don't know anything about that.'

'Then tell me.'

'No.'

'Why can't you go home?'

'Why can't *you*?'

She stopped then, and her mouth opened and closed, then she shrugged. 'I can. If I want to. I just don't want to.'

'What's your mother done to you?' It was my turn to throw the barb, and it struck true; she lashed out, thumping the wall.

'Stop it! I told you, nothing.'

'Shall I write to her, like you wrote to mine? Would that be fair?'

'What?' Her face went blank with surprise. Had she forgotten already?

'You did your best to send me away, and it nearly worked, so perhaps I should do the same to you.'

'You think *I* wrote that letter?'

'You ... you didn't?'

'No!' She laughed then, and it wasn't wholly unkind, but neither was it the slightest bit mirthful. 'You idiot, that was Belinda!'

'Don't lie; Bel wouldn't.'

'Oh, wouldn't she? Not even if she thought the handsome stranger had taken a shine to you?'

'Nathan? Don't be–'

'I didn't write the letter, Kitty.'

I spoke, not with disbelief now, but with a sort of bewildered betrayal. 'Why would Bel want to send me away? We're friends.'

'Why do you think? It's always men with you girls, isn't it?'

'What do you mean, us girls?'

'You flighty, pretty types.'

I almost laughed too, then, but it would have been through humour, at least. 'Are you poking fun at me?'

She ignored my question. 'Look, ask *her* your stupid questions. I'm more concerned about those girls, and what they want with Amy.'

'They don't want anything with her. They just want her to have a good start in life.'

'I don't believe you.'

I was really cross again now. 'Well what do you think they want?'

'I ... she...' Jessie stopped and closed her eyes for a moment, then opened them again and looked at me steadily. She seemed to come to a decision, and took a deep breath. 'Kitty, what do you know about Amelia Dyer?'

'Who?'

She glanced past me down the landing, and then opened her bedroom door. 'Come in here. I want to talk. It's time.'

'What about Amy?'

'She's with Lizzy. She's safe.'

It was an odd thing to say, but curiosity got the better of me and I followed Jessie into my old room and sat down on the bed. Jessie sat beside me, but wouldn't look at me. We remained silent for a while, and although I was desperate to ask her something, anything, to get her talking, it would only upset things. So I waited.

Eventually Jessie took a deep breath and began.

361

'Just over twenty years ago a woman called Amelia Dyer was hanged. Her daughter Polly was arrested too.' She fell silent, but again I bit my tongue against the obvious questions, sensing her need to get her thoughts straight before she voiced them.

'They were baby farmers.'

I flinched. *'Baby* farmers?'

'Didn't you hear about the "Reading Horrors" then?'

I shook my head, tight with apprehension at the thought of what I might hear next. Jessie's voice was calm enough as she explained, helping to steady my rising horror.

'Amelia used to take in children. Unwanted children. She used different names over the years, and she'd take payment from some poor girl who'd been caught out, ten pounds, something like that, and offer to give the child a good home. Save the girl the disgrace, and the cost, of bringing up a child.'

'That's ... well, it's awful, but surely it's good for the child?'

'It might have been. Except they never brought those children up. The children died, Kitty. Almost every one. Hundreds, they said, by the time those women were stopped.'

My mouth suddenly dry, I couldn't swallow for a second, couldn't breathe. I waited for my heart to start beating again, and when it did it hurt. But the air moved through me again, and I was able to speak.

'Why are you telling me this? Do you think I'd give Amy up to someone like that?'

She looked at me then, and her face was like that

of a ghost; not just pale, but blank and lost. 'Not deliberately, no. But what if you didn't know?'

'But they're dead. You said so.'

'Amelia is. Her daughter Polly was alive as of '98, and still up to her old tricks.'

'Tricks...' The flippant phrase made me feel sick. 'But the McKrevie girls ... they're respectable. I've been to their home!' Her knowing look made me realise another lie had come to light, but it didn't matter any more. 'I promise you, Jessie, I would have never let her go to them if I didn't trust them.'

'That's really my point, isn't it?' Jessie said. 'It's like I said, you can't trust anyone.'

'But if I refused to let her go, why would they give me money, instead of the other way around?'

'That's what worried me,' she admitted. 'I didn't know for sure that you *had* refused them, did I?' She shrugged. 'Perhaps you'd sold her instead of paying them to take her.'

The shock of her accusation was like a slap. It pushed aside the distress at the thought of all those unknown children, and brought my anger back with a flash. 'How the *hell dare* you suggest I'd do that!'

I stood up and moved towards the door, my heart pounding, desperate to get out, and away from Jessie and her cruelty. But she leapt up too, and caught at my arm.

'Kitty! Sit down. Please. I haven't finished.'

'I don't want to hear anything you have to say.'

'I might have been one of those children!' she shouted, and this time it took a lot longer to find my breath again. I stared at her, and she stared back at me, and then she gestured to the bed. I sat.

'My mother, Elizabeth Shorey, made ... a mistake. A big mistake. She fell in love with the hotel owner she worked for. He got her pregnant. He was married, of course.' She cleared her throat, and went on, her fingers twisting together in her lap, 'He arranged for the baby ... for me, to be passed to someone called Mrs Palmer. He paid, and it was even all done through a solicitor.'

'But didn't the solicitor know?'

'How could he? Mrs Palmer was supposedly married to a respectable poultry farmer. All was quite above board. The solicitor drew up the agreement and they arranged to meet at his offices in Gloucester. My mother's aunt, who'd gone with her, suggested my mother go back with Mrs Palmer for a day or two, to let the ... let *me*, get used to my home. Mrs Palmer said no.'

'What reason could she possibly give to refuse that? It sounds perfectly sensible.'

'She said she and her husband were in lodgings, and it wasn't convenient. So they went to the railway station, mother was allowed to hold me for one last time, while Mrs Palmer bought the tickets, and that should have been it.'

When I spoke it was with a kind of breathless wonder. 'What happened, Jessie?'

'Mother had a box all ready for me. Pinafores, nightdress, socks. A brush, I think, that kind of thing. And a hat.' Her voice took on a sad tone. 'Mother kept talking about that red hat, as if it meant everything. Excused everything.' Jessie swallowed hard and continued, 'She gave it over to Mrs Palmer, and just when she was about to let me go too–'

'I shouted to her.'

We both jumped and turned to the door. Frances stood there, her face as white as Jessie's. 'I've been listening a while,' she said. 'I wanted you to be able to tell it your way.' She came in and pulled up the little wicker chair that lived by the window. She was far too tall for it, and sat hunched over her knees, and her heels jerked in a restless tattoo against the thin carpet. 'I knew her, you see, or thought I did. I didn't really think she'd go through with it, and I didn't want to bully her into a decision, so I waited for her to come to her senses by herself. But when I saw her give over the box of clothes I knew I had to stop her.'

'Go back to the beginning,' I urged. 'How did you know Jessie's mother?'

She looked at me, then at Jessie, and then back down at her tightly linked hands. 'I left Tavistock when I was old enough to go away to work, and went to Gloucester. That's where I met Elizabeth. We got to be good friends, as good as you can be, working all day. When she told me she was in trouble by Mr Aldridge, the hotel owner, I said I'd try to help, and I did. But when the time came she went off alone, to the union workhouse, for the birth. I found her again, after.'

She glanced at Jessie again, her long, homely face filled with pain. 'You were such a dear little thing. I took to you right away. I tried to make your mother come back down to Devon with me. But by then Mr Aldridge had made his arrangements and paid his money to Mrs Palmer. He had

365

no idea, of course. Thought he was doing right by everyone, and so did Elizabeth. I was glad she had her aunt to help her, but I ... well, I didn't trust Mrs Palmer. And rightly, as it goes, 'cos she turned out to be Amelia Dyer's daughter.'

'So you stopped it all just in time!' I was forgetting, for a moment, that these were real lives I was hearing about; it all sounded so tense and exciting it was like reading it in a book.

'Thank goodness, yes,' Frances said. 'I watched, and waited until I was sure, then I stepped in. Eventually Elizabeth saw sense, and came back with me to Devon. We only meant to come home for a little while, but I met my Harry, and we wed. We put together a story of widowhood for Elizabeth, and she went back up to Gloucester with little Frances here.'

'So that's why Elizabeth named you after Frances,' I said.

Frances nodded. 'She was so grateful, especially two years later, when the full story came out. I think it was only then she realised how close she'd come to losing her little girl for ever.' She touched Jessie's still furiously twining fingers and spoke softly. 'Is that why you came down here to work? Because you found out?'

She didn't reply, but her fingers stopped twisting. Frances cupped her hand over them and raised them to her lips. 'Sweetheart, you can't blame your—'

'Don't defend her!' Jessie shouted, ripping her hands out of Frances's gentle grasp. 'It was only thanks to you that I'm not dead! *She* wouldn't have cared!'

'Of course she would!' Frances curled her own hands back into her lap in a clear effort to stop herself reaching out again. 'She was horrified when she realised I was right about Amelia and Polly.'

Jessie went very still. 'How *did* you know?'

Frances blanched. I felt a sick heat sweeping through me as I watched her face slacken into defeat. 'Because I lost a child to them,' she said at last, in a low, hoarse whisper.

The silence stretched. The clock ticked away the minutes, while the reality of what had passed between us settled like a thick, choking layer of ash.

Eventually Jessie spoke, and her voice was hard and cracked. 'You sold your baby.'

'It wasn't like that! I wrote, and sent money, and clothes ... and ... and ... I got letters back. Filled with news about how she was learning to walk, how she couldn't say certain words and how charming it all was. I believed them...' Frances caught her breath in a sob, and I felt my own throat thicken with anguish. I reached to touch her hand, and Jessie slapped my arm. Hard.

'How can you be kind to a woman who would let someone kill her baby?'

'She didn't mean it to die!' I shouted back, and at the awful, bald word, Frances broke down. Her face dropped into her hands as she wept, and I didn't know what to do to help her. My arm was stinging from Jessie's slap, but I couldn't be angry with her. 'She wanted what was right for it,' I said, more quietly.

'Just like you do for Amy?'

367

'I haven't sold her! I told you, I refused them.'

'So you say.'

'You're going to have to trust me. What else *can* I say?'

'It's just as I said, you can't trust anyone. Now do you believe me?'

I kept my voice even, but the anger was making my throat hurt. 'If you had a single ounce of decency in you, Frances Jessie Goulding, you'd see your behaviour is unbelievably selfish. You're lucky you have a mother who loves you, and has done all your life. And Frances *saved* your life, for goodness' sake! What possible good can it do to punish someone who only wants to help? Not that you deserve it!'

There was a faint flicker in Jessie's eyes, but she didn't answer. She went to her drawer and started to pull out clothing. She threw it onto the bed, and Frances looked up at her in dismay.

'Don't leave, Jessie! Let me tell you how it happened. You'll understand–'

'I understand why you feel this need to take in every waif and stray who comes to your door,' she said, shooting a dark glance at me. 'You feel guilty.'

'No! I feel...'

'What?'

Frances choked on the word, 'Empty,' and my own tears spilled over. I moved to hold her, and Jessie, also crying now, dragged her suitcase out from under the bed. She dashed her hand across her wet, shining eyes.

'Kitty, be truthful: do I need to take Amy with me?' Numb, I shook my head. 'Good, because I don't know where I'm going yet.' She fixed me

368

with a strange, half-furious, half-understanding look. 'I'll come back for her if I have to though. I believe you love that little girl, but–'

'At least as much as your mother and Frances love you.'

'No. I mean really *love* her. Not just feel responsible for her.' She glanced at Frances as she said it. 'And I believe, if you've done the terrible thing I think you've done, you'll take it back.'

'I haven't!'

'Just as you say.' Her voice was calmer, but she sniffed. 'Whatever it was that made Frances cling to you like her own, I hope it's over now. Look after Amy.'

'Stay tonight, at least,' I said desperately. 'Let this settle. We can talk about it properly.'

She ignored the hankie I offered; the sleeve will always be the nose-wiper of choice for the truly heartbroken. 'No. I've had enough of being lied to.'

'No-one has lied to you.'

'Nor have they told the truth! I believed Frances saved me because she was a good person, not because she wanted to get back the child she sold to the grave.'

'Stop it! She might not even be dead.' I turned to Frances. 'Jessie said not all the children died. Maybe yours was one of the lucky ones, a new name, a new home... You don't know, Frances!'

'Don't be naïve, Kitty.' Jessie looked oddly sympathetic. Then she turned away. 'It's your turn to replace her lost child now. Apparently I've been doing it for twenty-one years.'

If I'd had something heavy in my hand at that

moment I might have indeed done a terrible thing, but all Frances and I could do was watch her pick up the case with the few bits she had thrown into it, and walk out of the door. There had been so many times I had wanted her to do just that, but not at the expense of Frances, who had always seemed so strong, and who now sat broken and bereft in a too-small chair, listening to the child whose life she had saved clumping down the stairs with her pathetically small suitcase.

I remembered something then, and bent to pull the heavier case out from where she had pushed it under the bed. I loosened the buckles and lifted the lid to see, not just books, as she had said, although there were some, but probably every other thing Jessie owned and had ever cared for. The weight was mostly due to several large, framed photographs, some obviously her and her mother, but many more of Frances, and a woman I didn't recognise but I thought might be Elizabeth Shorey's aunt.

'She wasn't ever going home, was she?' Frances said in a low, hurt voice. 'She left her mother, and never told her she wasn't going back, and now she's left me.'

'Then she's as much a liar as she's accused you of being,' I said shortly. Frances sighed, a heavy, tearing sound, and I crouched beside her. 'Go to Lizzy's house tonight, put your smile back, for those who need you, and we'll talk tomorrow about how we can patch things up with Jessie. She's bound to see sense, given time.'

'I'm worried about her,' she admitted. 'What if she can't find nowhere to go?'

'It's summer; it won't hurt her to sleep under a hedge once or twice.'

Frances sniffed and stood up, bringing me with her. 'You don't blame me, do you? For what I did?'

'How can I? I might have just done that very same thing, believing I had Amy's interests at heart.'

Frances drew me against her in a hug. 'I'm not trying to replace ... her,' she said, her voice low.

'What was her name?' I don't know why I asked, and Frances stiffened slightly, then sagged, as if the name had been lying heavy on her heart all these years and now she could finally speak it aloud and banish its weight. 'Alice.'

'Tonight, when you raise a glass to Lizzy's mother, say Alice's name in your head too, and I'll do the same. We'll give her that same peace we sent our fallen.'

Frances nodded and pressed the heels of her palms to her eyes, blotting the last of her tears. 'You're a good girl, Kitty,' she said, a little roughly. 'Now go on with you. If I'm going out I'll need to wash and tidy myself. And don't forget those tools haven't been cleaned yet.'

Frances, Evie, Will and Lizzy had already gone by the time the others came back in from the field. I didn't know whether to tell them about Jessie, but Bel and Nathan probably wouldn't spare her a thought in any case, and it might open up awkward conversations. So I made sure her bedroom door was shut, and let everyone assume she had gone to her room for the night. Amy sat at the kitchen table with her drawing paper, and I looked down to see if the random straight marks she made were starting to look as if they represented anything. Not yet, but they were less heavy. I looked closely and even saw a curved line here and there.

I smoothed my hand over her head as I passed. 'Mister Archie will be back soon,' I promised. 'Maybe he'll take you up the lane to look at the rabbits.' The family of brownish-grey wild rabbits were as much a source of fascination for her as all the other animals she'd seen; late in the evening, just before bed, she would crouch down and stare at them as they came out to hop around the corner of the field at the top of the lane.

I'd expected her to repeat *rabbits*, but instead she said, 'Mister Arsh,' and I swallowed a lump in my suddenly tight throat as I tried to find the words to tell her he was leaving, and so was I.

I heard the three of them coming across the yard, Nathan coughing a little after his exertion, and Belinda chattering away as she peeled off her hat and let her hair fly free. Only Archie was quiet, but not through a sombre mood; he walked with the lazy, comfortable stride of a hard-working man at home in his surroundings, his movements strong and graceful as he swung his jacket from where it lay across his shoulder and hung it on the peg by the door.

When he ducked into the kitchen his gaze found me immediately, and the smile that lit his face was reflected in my own, but I nodded at Amy and he switched his attention to her.

'Why, it's Miss Amy-Anna-Banana!' he said,

and held out his hand. She giggled and shook it, and he ruffled her white-blonde hair before turning, again, to me. He seemed to fill the large kitchen with his presence, and as he crossed the room and took my face in his hands to kiss me, I realised that he'd been waiting for this moment as long as I had. It was a strange feeling, exciting and frightening, and it gave me a warm, liquid sensation in the pit of my stomach. I kissed him back, feeling the heat of his work-warmed skin grazing mine, and I slipped my arms around him to pull him closer.

But he held back a little, and broke the kiss with a little grimace. 'Sweetheart, I'm all sweat and muck. Don't dirty your apron.'

'Might I remind you of the evening you arrived?' I countered, sliding my hands up his back and stepping closer again. 'I'd just finished a day's work too.'

'Aye, and you stank of horse,' he said with a grin. 'Still, it'd been so long since I'd seen you I wouldn't have minded if you'd been up to your shoulders in swill.'

'Well then, you'll know,' I said, and stretched up and nipped lightly at his throat, tasting the cool, salt sweat on his skin. He groaned, and I smiled against his neck, which made him groan again and turn his head to take my mouth with his. Locked in his arms, feeling his damp shirt through my thin apron-top, I breathed deeply. Muck and sweat be blowed, I had never smelled anything sweeter.

When we released each other from the initial tight grasp, our arms stayed around each other and Archie twisted to look around. 'Where's everyone?' he asked, belatedly realising we were alone but for Amy.

I told him about Lizzy's mother's birthday. 'I don't suppose they'll be back much before midnight,' I said, with slow insinuation in every word. The well-bred young lady I had once been couldn't believe I was speaking like this, but with my hand resting on Archie's hip, and his cupping my side, his long fingers playing silent, absentminded tunes on my ribcage, it didn't seem the slightest bit forward.

He turned to look down at me, and a smile pulled at one corner of his mouth. 'Well then, best we get the rest of the jobs done early.'

'We can clean the hand tools together,' I suggested. 'That'll get them done faster. And I've told Amy you might take her up the lane to look at the rabbits.'

'Rabbits?' Archie swung back to Amy. 'Will you show me the rabbits, Amy?'

'Rabbits,' she confirmed solemnly. 'Inna lane.'

'Right, well then I'd better get cleaned up, then Kitty and I will do our last jobs of the day, and as soon as we're finished, you–' he tapped her little hand where it lay curled on the table, clutching her pencil '–can take me to where the rabbits are playing, before it gets dark.'

He dropped a last kiss on my forehead and went upstairs to wash, and I sat down opposite Amy. For a moment I didn't say anything, but watched her pencil move across the paper, and saw more curved lines appearing; I couldn't have said exactly why, but it gave me hope to see it. They seemed so much gentler than those harsh

374

black diagonal lines that slashed the paper from corner to corner.

'Amy, did you like those girls you met today?' She nodded, but showed no particular interest; I might as well have asked her if she liked the table at which we sat. 'Do you like living here?' Another nod, slightly more enthusiastic this time. I waited a moment, then tried again. 'Do you remember the man who took you away from your mother?'

'Da.'

'Yes.' He must have told her, but she'd never before said the word out loud. The tingle of hope grew; if she was taking in more than we thought even back then, she had probably stored up all kinds of knowledge she had yet to share. It both helped and hurt since I was, in all likelihood, going to miss it when she did.

'Sweetheart, your da will come and find you one day, and you must tell him if you're happy here, and don't want to leave. He won't make you go if you don't want to. It's just ... I might have to go away too, in a day or so. For a little while.'

'Kitty goin'?'

'Maybe, yes.'

'I comin' too?'

I swallowed hard and wondered again if I had chosen the right path. 'No, darling, not this time. But you will have Evie, and Lizzy, and all the others.'

'Mister Arsh?'

'Mister Archie has to go too,' I said gently. 'He's a soldier. And he has other soldiers to look after, just like he looks after you.'

'Da's a soldier.'

375

'Yes, he was,' I said, surprised again.

When she looked at me with wide, worried eyes, I saw the connection she had made before she said, 'Da got no arm. Gone.'

I didn't know what to say, but I desperately wanted to ease her fear. 'Your da is a brave, brave man, and he was badly hurt. But Archie will be too busy looking after the other brave men to go anywhere dangerous.' Of all the lies I'd told these past few days, this seemed the most innocent.

'Kitty not a soldier?'

'No. They don't let ladies be soldiers. But I help them, just like Archie does. I take them to the doctor when they need one. Like someone took your da when he got hurt.'

This seemed to satisfy her about both mine and Archie's safety, and she went back to her drawing. But as I stood up, relieved, and started to clear the table for our evening meal, I saw her draw a thick black line right across the page.

Amy didn't repeat any of our conversation to Archie when he came back down, and I was relieved; I wanted to tell him myself about my decision to return to Belgium. Happy to be with us both, she swung between us as we walked towards the barn, her hands gripped in ours as we lifted her over the muddiest parts of the yard. I unlocked the door and we went inside, and I dragged Pippin's harness across to prop the door open and let in the daylight.

Archie nearly tripped over the box of tools. 'Bit of a daft place to leave them, right in the middle of the floor.'

'Sorry, that was me,' I admitted. 'I was a bit ... cross with Belinda, at the time.'

He raised an eyebrow, but I changed the subject quickly. 'Speaking of Belinda, she's already planning what she's going to wear to the Harvest Festival dance.'

'When's that?'

'The end of September,' I said, then remembered, and a cool feeling swept over me and made me feel a little bit ill; Archie would definitely not be here, and there was a strong chance I wouldn't be either.

'What a pity I'll miss it,' he said calmly, then smiled at the look on my face. 'But I plan to be here for the next one – Kaiser Bill will have had enough by then, I'm sure.'

'I hope so.'

'And then I'll be able to show you all a wee thing or two about the dance.'

'You can dance?' It shouldn't have surprised me though; for his size, he had always moved smoothly and well.

'Aye,' he said, in wounded tones. 'Don't sound so shocked. I'll have you know I was famed for my sedate and elegant foxtrot back in Fort William.'

'Show me,' I challenged, and stood up straight, for once thankful for the torturous hours spent at dance lessons in the large sitting room at Ecclesley. He gave me a haughty look and placed one hand against mine, resting the other behind my shoulder, then cleared his throat, lifted his chin ... and pulled me into an energetic and horribly executed Scottish reel, flinging me around the barn and leaving me gasping for breath and doubled over laughing.

'What was *that?*' I managed eventually, still giggling and trying to regain my equilibrium.

He gave me a pitying look. 'It's no my fault you can't dance. I'll teach you, don't worry. Right, come with me, Miss Banana,' he added to Amy, picking up a bucket. 'Let's get some water.'

They went outside, and, still laughing, I emptied the box of hand tools onto the long worktable that ran down the side of the barn. Covered in mud and bits of grass, they'd been sitting in their box for too long for this to be the quick, easy job I'd hoped. Still, being with Archie out here would be almost as good as being with him in the privacy of a quiet room, with nothing between us but a promise. Almost.

He and Amy came back in, and Amy went to sit on the hay bales we'd brought in. I handed Archie a stiff-bristled brush, and we set to work scrubbing at the dried mud on the assortment of tools. It turned into a race, and we made short work of the first few.

'What on earth's this?' Archie held up the next in the line, a perplexed look on his face.

'Ah. That's the reason I was angry with Belinda,' I said. 'It's a dibble.'

He laughed, 'A *whattle?*'

'Dibble. It's for making holes in the ground, for seeds and bulbs and things.'

He looked at the narrow spike, with its handle that looked like a small spade handle. 'Bloody funny name for a useful little thing,' he observed. 'So tell me then, why did the dibble make you so angry with Belinda?'

378

I told him how I'd found Amy playing with it, and then the subject of the broken wine bottle slipped out before I realised. Hoping he hadn't noticed, I pressed on, 'She could have hurt herself badly. Belinda was just so keen to throw herself at Nathan, she didn't think.'

'Wine bottle, eh?'

I felt the flush stealing up my neck until my face burned. There was no way to say it that would sound acceptable, so I just blurted it out. 'Bel and I were drinking it when we were out picking up Jessie. Bel threw it in the back when it was empty, and we forgot it was there.'

'You *are* a minx, young Kittlington,' he said, and the smile in his voice made me feel better.

'If I hadn't drunk it, I never would have ridden the horse,' I pointed out. Then I remembered he didn't know about that either. But it was too late.

'Pirate?'

'No, Woody. Well, we named him that because we found him at the sawmill.'

'Found him? I don't know that I like the sound of that. Besides, I didn't know there was another horse there.'

'There isn't, now. Woody was a ... an Army Remount Service loan. He was just there, and, Archie, he was so beautiful! And Bel can be very persuasive–'

His laughter was so spontaneous, and a relief to hear, that I couldn't help joining him, and even Amy looked up from plucking stray bits of hay out of the bale, and her giggle wove among ours as if it had never belonged anywhere else.

'Wait a moment,' Archie said, putting down the

dibble and leaning back against the table. He folded his arms across his chest, and laughter still bubbled in his voice. 'Let me just see if I've got this story straight: you and Belinda were sent on a serious errand, to collect a lone female traveller very dear to your employer, and the two of you left her to her own devices, because you got drunk on illicit wine and stole a ride on an army stud horse?'

'Well, I did,' I said, admitting it sounded even more awful when he said it. 'Bel didn't get around to riding him. Seth Pearce yelled at us, and Woody shied and threw her. After he more or less broke her nose, that is.'

'But you were both drunk?'

I blushed again. 'No. Just me.'

He chuckled, and held out his hand. I took it and he drew me against him, and I could still feel the mirth rumbling in his chest. 'Kitty Maitland, if I didnae love you so madly already, I'd have fallen for you now.'

I dropped the brush and trowel I was holding so I could put my arms around him. 'I love you too,' I said, and the words reminded me of two nights ago, when I'd first uttered them, crying them to the night as Archie had chased away the terror. He seemed to remember that too, and grew very still, his humour not dying, but settling into a sigh that shook a little bit.

'Will we have a chance to ... be together again, before I go?'

I tightened my hold. 'Yes. Tonight. Please?'

He pushed me gently away from him and held my shoulders, looking squarely into my eyes. 'We will be wed, won't we? Soon.'

380

'Yes. As soon as we can.'

He nodded. 'Right.' He moved off across the barn, in search of something but I didn't know what, and after a moment of watching him not find it, I turned back to my task. I listened to him muttering under his breath, then ripping something, and I peered through the growing gloom to see him pulling at one of the sacks in the corner. Curious, but patient, I picked up the dibble, grinning at the way he'd found it such a funny name – and him a country-born Scotsman! By the time I'd got halfway through scraping the dried mud off it, Archie had returned to my side, brandishing a strip of sacking. Without explanation, he lifted my right hand and gripped my wrist. My fingers automatically wrapped around his forearm until we looked like two battle chiefs in some ancient greeting.

Archie kept his eyes on mine, but called out, 'Amy, sweetheart. Come here a moment?' Of course she immediately did so, and Archie smiled down at her. 'Now, your job is just to remember this,' he said. 'Do you understand? Just remember it.' He wrapped the sacking strip around our two wrists, and by then I knew what he was doing, and why he'd questioned my agreement to marry him. Just to be sure. I looked up at him and blinked back sudden tears, but seeing his own eyes equally bright, I didn't know how I didn't break down, floored by the emotion that thundered through me.

His voice was hoarse. 'I, Archie Buchanan declare my deep and abiding love for you, Katherine Maitland, and so do legally take you to wife. 'Til death us do part. And thereto I plight thee my troth.'

Somehow I stumbled through a similar vow, and all the while I was aware of Archie's pulse thumping against mine as the tightly wrapped sacking pressed our wrists together. When my voice had died away the tears were pouring freely down my cheeks, and Archie's left thumb gently brushed them away before he bent his head and kissed each eye.

'Now,' he said softly, 'we're handfasted.'

I couldn't speak for a moment, then managed, '*Is* that legal?'

'It is in Scotland, and that's good enough for me. You're mine, young Kittlington, and I'm yours. Heart, body and soul. And if *I* ever catch you drunk and riding a valuable stud horse, I'll tan your bloody hide.'

I locked up the barn half an hour later, the tools laid out neatly, and gleaming, and the knowledge of my new status, legal or otherwise, making my blood sing. Archie had taken Amy up to see the rabbits a few minutes earlier, when we'd noticed the sun starting to dip. Soon he would bring her back from their little walk, I would put her to bed, and then Archie and I would ... well, we would begin our honeymoon. My insides were tight with anticipation as I went into the house and replaced the padlock key in the little dish on the sideboard.

Outside the sky was turning a beautiful gold colour, and my thoughts went to Jessie, and where she might be now. On impulse I went to the jar where Frances kept our wages, and groaned; yes, she had taken it. Frances would be glad she would have enough money to find a room for the night, but where did that leave the rest of us? I pushed aside the thought of Amy's money with a little shiver, but I couldn't deny that's where my mind took me... I must be a truly awful person to even consider it, and it would probably be a good thing for everyone when I went back to Belgium. In the meantime, my first trip in the morning would be to the bank, for the removal of temptation.

The door to Nathan's room, the little room at the back of the house, was shut when I went upstairs; he must be in there painting again. Perhaps his fame would grow, locally at least, and he might make enough money to pay his creditors. I hoped so. I was still worried about them finding where he lived and coming after him.

But all those dark thoughts faded as I went to my own room, and my mind turned to better things. I pressed the fingers of my left hand against my right wrist, remembering vividly how Archie's heartbeat had echoed there. Levering open my own bedroom door with my elbow, not wanting to let go of my wrist, I was surprised to see Belinda in there, her eyes red, her face pale.

'He's gone,' she said, her breath hitching.

'Gone? Nathan you mean?'

'Y-yes. I went into his room and his things are gone. No sign.'

I sighed. 'Bel, you know he had his problems. It's probably a good thing he's gone. I'm sorry. I know you were attached to him, but–'

'That's not it!' She began to cry again. 'It's much, much worse. Oh, Kitty, I've done something terrible!'

Chapter Twenty

I sat in silent dismay, while Belinda told her story.

It had begun that afternoon, when she'd gone to find him and tell him they must both help Archie in the fields, in Frances's stead. He'd been gratifyingly keen, and they'd walked out there together, and Belinda had kept sneaking glances at him; he'd looked so handsome, so smart. And when he spoke he sounded so well travelled. She asked him if he was looking forward to the Harvest Festival dance, and he had expressed mild interest, but hadn't said anything about her reserving a dance for him, as she'd hoped. She felt small and a little stupid beside him, and couldn't think of anything clever to say, until she remembered the diamond, now back in Evie's possession.

'Have you heard of it?' she asked.

'No, is it valuable?'

'Kitty says so. But Evie says it's got to go back to Borneo, where it came from.'

'Why?'

'Because the family line has come to an end. You know, since her little brother was killed. He was the last named Creswell.'

'God rest him,' Nathan said grimly. Conversation had moved on to the war then, and Nathan had not shown any further interest in Evie's wealth. He was more concerned for her husband. Belinda hadn't been able to tell him much more than he already knew, so he'd been glad of Archie's companionship as they worked, and for the chance to learn more about what had happened to his old friend.

Disappointed, and feeling foolish, Belinda hadn't thought about the diamond again either, until earlier that evening. Nathan had found her in the creamery, checking the cheeses, and he'd leaned against the door to watch her, his hazel eyes soft and smiling. 'You look very pretty doing that. Like a painting by Vermeer.'

Belinda had nearly blurted that he looked wonderful too, doing absolutely nothing, but the way he'd dismissed her eager talk earlier in the day still rankled somewhat, and she chose to just smile. Besides, she didn't know if this Vermeer person painted pretty people or not. Nathan might be teasing her, using her lack of knowledge for some private joke at her expense.

'I've been thinking about what you said,' he went on. 'About the diamond, and it having to go back to Borneo.'

She perked up, pleased she had piqued his interest after all. 'Yes, it's a terrible shame. Poor Evie.'

'Well, how about if I was able to paint it? As a gift for her and Will, I mean? It'd be one way to start to make amends for what I did to him.' He gave a little laugh. 'Who knows, one day after I'm long gone it might be worth something.'

Belinda wiped her hands on the cloth hanging from her belt. 'That's a wonderful idea!'

'It's to be a surprise, so would have to be tonight, while they're out,' he said. 'Do you know where she keeps it?'

'No,' Belinda said, 'but I'm sure we could find it.'

'Best if you look for it. If anyone's caught in her room it'd be better you than me. I'll go and set up everything while it's still light enough to sketch by the natural light.' He glanced behind him, through the kitchen towards the open back door. 'There should be enough time if you hurry. Bring it to my room. And remember–' he lifted a finger to his lips, and she saw his beautiful smile behind it '–not a word, lovely Bel.'

'I found it easily enough,' she said to me now. 'It was as if Evie didn't care about it at all, and just dropped it into a box on her dressing table. So I took it, but I made sure I knew exactly how it had landed, so I could return it before she got back.'

I felt ill, knowing what was coming. 'Bel–'

'He let me watch him sketch it, and it was just wonderful. He did a perfect circle without even drawing around anything! Then he added just the right types of shadow.' For a second she was lost in bright, appreciative memory, then her face fell again. 'But he said I couldn't stay while he painted it; he needed to be alone. I offered to put it back, since he'd finished the sketch, but he said he needed it a little while longer, to mix the colour.'

'You didn't–'

'I believed him!' she cried. 'And all because he

drew it so beautifully! Oh, Kitty, how could I have been so stupid?'

I stood up and went to the window. 'How long ago did you see him?'

'About half an hour. I went back to his room a few minutes ago, and...' She dropped her face into her hands again and couldn't finish.

'Stay here,' I told her. 'If he's out there and knows you've told someone, who knows what he might do?' I didn't want to frighten her, but she had to understand the danger.

'I'll stay,' she promised. She looked up at me with new hope, as if she really believed I might be able to do something, and I went out and slammed the door behind me, feeling worse than useless. The worst thing was she wasn't to blame; I, in my sleepy happiness, had told her about the diamond, how valuable it was, and how Evie would soon lose it... Yes, Belinda had let Nathan turn her head, and she'd tried too hard to impress him, but it was my treacherous mouth that had, once again, done the damage.

If only Archie was back from his walk. I would have given anything to be able to turn to him and lay this catastrophe in his lap, knowing he'd at least say something soothing, even if we'd lost the Kalteng Star for ever. But he was nowhere in sight as I went out into the yard. Pippin still stood looking over the field gate, and Pirate watched me through the shadows, from the stable. There was no sign of Nathan either. I looked around, at the cart that stood in the corner of the yard by the gate, even at the water trough that could easily conceal a man desperate enough not to be found, but there was no sound that gave him away. He'd gone. Probably over the fields to the woods, if he had any sense and, I reluctantly admitted, he'd already proven himself resourceful in avoiding those he wished to avoid. His scarred lungs might prevent him from running fast, but he'd be able to hide well enough once he reached the woods. We had to stop him getting that far.

Archie would be faster on his feet than me, and stronger. I had to find him, and tell him. I started towards the path, thinking quickly: I'd give him the bare bones, and then take care of Amy while he went after Nathan. A movement caught the corner of my eye – the barn door swinging slightly in the breeze. They were already back, thank goodness!

'Archie!' I yanked the door open and went in, blinking to let my eyes adjust to the fading light. Nathan was at the worktable, a bag over his shoulder, holding it open with one hand and picking up a newly cleaned trowel with the other. He'd frozen at the sound of my shout, but now dropped the trowel into the bag.

'Nathan,' I said in as calm a voice as possible. 'Put them back; it will all be all right.'

It was only when he spoke that I realised he was weeping. 'It won't be. You don't understand, Kitty... Please, go away. Pretend you haven't seen me.'

'Don't be silly, you know I can't.' I took a step closer. 'At least give me Evie's diamond.'

He sagged. Had he really hoped Bel would say nothing about that? Or perhaps he was hoping she hadn't even discovered he'd gone.

'Nathan?'

'Move away from the door, Kitty. Please.'

I stood firm, but my knees were shaking uncontrollably, and I didn't know how long I'd be able to stand up without grabbing something for support. 'You can go,' I said, 'but give me what belongs to Evie. She'll be the one blamed if it goes missing again.'

'I need it!' His voice was higher pitched now, and I could hear panic setting in. 'Tell her I'm sorry. But they'll find me, they...' He let out a shuddering breath, and my conversation with Archie came flashing back; he must have talked to Nathan while they'd been out working together, hoping to help, but instead putting this new fear into Nathan's mind. The idea of what he might do about it had come neatly wrapped from Belinda's eager lips. It seemed we'd underestimated both Nathan's troubles, and his terror.

'We'll do our best to protect you.' I took a few steps towards him, and he backed away. I eyed the distance between him, me and the door, and wondered if I'd be able to catch him if he suddenly ran for freedom. To my despair I realised not, and he reached the same conclusion at the same time. He ducked away to his right, slipped around me and past my outstretched arm, and ran towards the door.

I spun around, crying out in frustration, and then the light from the doorway was blocked by a tall, square-shouldered shape. 'Stop him, Archie!' I cried, but Nathan had already stopped. He stood very still, the bag of tools at his side, and I wanted to step forward and take it back; now Jessie had

389

taken our wages, these tools were more necessary to us than ever, but I daren't just yet.

Archie stooped to set Amy down. 'Run outside, Amy-Anna,' he said in a forcedly cheerful voice. But she didn't. 'Sweetheart,' he said, more urgently, 'go into the house. We'll come and find you in a wee while.' Amy gripped his trouser leg, and he bent to prise her fingers loose. 'All right, just go into the yard and wait for me.' Finally, to our relief, she went, and Archie came right in and held out a hand to Nathan, palm up, friendly. 'Whatever it is that's going on here,' he said quietly, 'we can sort it out.'

'We can't,' Nathan insisted, looking from him to me. 'Let me past, Archie.'

'What's in the bag?'

'It's our tools,' I said. 'Nathan, we need those. You know that. They're bread and water to us.'

'And they're life and death to me,' he said, gulping as his own words hit him with their truth. He bent to pick the bag up again, and one hand dipped in and came out holding the newly shined dibble, gripping its spade-like handle in a white-knuckled fist. Then he broke and ran towards the door.

Archie's normally quiet voice suddenly bellowed across the dimly lit barn. 'Stop it! Don't be an ass!' He moved towards Nathan, and my breath stopped as I saw Amy running back, drawn by her beloved Archie's shout. Archie followed my gaze, and, as Nathan reached him, he moved to stop Amy coming any farther in, but Nathan's foot ploughed into the back of his knee, spilling him to the ground. Amy stopped still, in wide-eyed fear,

390

and, before either of us could do or say anything else, Nathan had moved past Archie and reached out to grab her hand.

'Let her go!' Archie scrambled to his feet, already lurching after them before he was fully upright. He seized the arm that held Amy, and Nathan spun, openly sobbing, and his other arm moved in a blur. A high, downward-slashing motion. Archie stopped dead still, and Nathan gave a moan of horror – he dropped the dibble, and it thudded against the ground, bouncing and rolling away.

Archie staggered back a couple of steps, almost fell, and his hands came down on his thighs to steady himself, then he tried once more to grab Amy but Nathan whisked the child up and into his arms. 'I'm sorry,' he stammered. 'I'll let her go. I promise. Archie, I'm...'

I couldn't move. I should have tried to take hold of Amy too but I was too far away, and all my attention was on Archie, who had now pitched onto one knee, and was pleading in a low, shocked voice for Nathan to leave the bairn behind.

By the time I could take a single, shaking step towards him, Nathan had reached down and seized Pippin's harness, dragging it out with him. The door creaked shut. Then he was gone, and Amy with him, and in numb disbelief I vaguely recognised the sliding sound of the bolt, and then the padlock, and finally I was able to reach Archie's side and drop to my knees beside him. He turned to me, his face white in the semi-darkness, and as my hands came up to catch him, he sagged against me. I eased him onto the ground, my heart tripping wildly in terror, and tried to see the extent

391

of the injury. The spike had caught him just below the collarbone and slashed diagonally down across his chest – a good six inches, maybe more. Blood was seeping through his shirt, and the left shoulder, where the tool had struck first, looked to be the deepest point; Nathan seemed to have realised the danger and instinctively pulled back, even as his hand had continued its unstoppable motion.

Archie's eyes came back into focus, and his right hand went to the wound. To my amazement his mouth, though tight with pain, twisted in a rueful little smile. 'Maybe I shouldn't have made fun of that wee dibbly thing after all.'

'Maybe not,' I agreed, trying to match his tone, but the sight of him lying there filled me with a white-hot fury, and if Nathan had been standing before me now I wouldn't have pulled the dibble back. I'd have driven right through–

'Amy,' Archie mumbled, and tried to move but hissed a sharp breath and subsided.

'He might really leave her,' I said with a half-hearted hope. 'He's not a bad person. He ... he wouldn't hurt her, would he?'

'Wouldn't have thought he'd hurt anyone,' Archie said, and his breath shook as he sighed. 'He's a desperate man or he wouldn't have done this, and desperate men are unpredictable.'

'He'll be all right now. He's got Evie's diamond,' I said grimly. I stood up and went to the door, rattling it experimentally, then harder. I put my mouth to a knothole in the wood, and shouted, without much hope. 'Amy! Are you there?'

I turned back to see that Archie's head, which

he had been holding up so he could talk to me, had dropped back. In that position it was easier to see the blood leaking from between his fingers. I knelt beside him and touched his neck gently to make him look at me. 'I'm going to try and find something to bind that with.'

'Aye, nurse,' he said, but he didn't lift his head again, and only swallowed hard as a groan shuddered up through him. 'Better hurry. Feel a bit ... strange.'

Trying to stop my hands from shaking, I wriggled out of my pullover and placed it beneath his head, then looked around for something to use. All I could find was the strip of sacking he had bound our wrists with, and it wasn't long enough to wrap around him so I wadded it instead, and pressed it to his chest. It wouldn't soak up the blood, but the pressure would help. 'Hold that. I'm going to try and get us out.'

I went to the door again, and a sound from outside made my heart leap. 'Someone's there! Help!' I banged on the door again. 'Please, Archie's hurt!'

There was no response, and I pressed my eyes to the knothole instead. 'It's Nathan. He's taking Pippin.' I drew a deep breath and yelled through the hole. 'Nathan! It's not too late! Let us out and we can help you!'

I peered through again; he had stopped, one foot on the board ready to climb up, his head half turned towards the barn. Hope flared, and I held my breath, watching with one eye until it burned. Then his voice, cracked and filled with tears, drifted across the yard.

'You can't. I... Archie, I'm...' Then he shook his

393

head and pulled himself onto the seat.

'Stop! Please! Archie needs help!'

'Kitty,' Archie said suddenly. I looked back, and he had managed to get onto one elbow, which I took as an encouraging sign. 'Did you say he's got the Star?'

'Yes.'

'Then you have to stop him. *Have* to.' He tried to rise farther, but was overcome by dizziness and shook his head. 'They'll kill him for it.'

I could hear the tremor in my own voice too now, as I shouted again. 'They'll kill you if you take the diamond!'

There was no answer, and then I believed I was capable of killing him myself, as I heard a tiny voice say, 'I comin' too?'

'Leave her!' I screamed, in a fury so intense it became pain in every part of me.

'I'm sorry! I need to know you won't follow. I'll let her go when I'm safe.' Then Pippin, for the first time in his life, felt the whip and moments later they were gone.

Still in a mindless rage I cast about for one of the bigger tools, and found a heavy spade that nevertheless seemed to weigh nothing, and I raised it as high as I could and then smashed it, edge first, against the door. It just slid down, and the wood didn't even tremble. I did it again, concentrating where the new padlock had been fitted, and then at random, with the same result. My voice became as cracked and sore as my hands, as, shouting and sobbing, I rammed the spade into the small gap between door and frame, and first pushed, then pulled back on it, time and time again. Nothing happened except a slight splintering at the edge of the door, and eventually I threw down the spade and came back to sit beside Archie.

He had managed to get into a sitting position, with his back against the hay bale on which Amy had been sitting, and he was still pressing the little strip of sacking to his chest. I examined my own hands, the blisters already rising, the skin burning, and with the movement I realised my arms ached horribly. But it stopped mattering when Archie reached out with his left hand and touched my face, turning it up to his.

'I'm going to be all right, Kittlington. It's not as bad as all that.'

'Are you sure?'

'Well, it's bloody painful, and I might let loose some of that shirt-wringing-out language you stumbled upon yesterday, but I don't feel so dizzy now.'

'But you're still losing blood.'

'Not so much. I'm all right.' He lifted my hand, bringing it to his lips and kissing my blistered palm. 'I'm concerned about Nathan though.'

'Well I'm not wasting my worrying on that little thug,' I said. 'I just want Amy back, and I want to get that wound seen to properly. Someone will come soon. Frances and the others will be back before long.'

'You said they'd probably not be back until midnight,' he reminded me, resting his head back against the hay bale. He wasn't as fine as he pretended, and I frowned, about to say as much, but he went on, 'I meant it about Nathan. He's a rogue, granted, but he's not a bad person. You know that. He doesn't deserve to die.'

'He won't die. He'll just get all his debts paid and then go back to being a grocery boy. It's Evie and her mother I'm worried about.'

'No, Kitty, listen.' Archie's voice was lower now, and I didn't like the way his breathing had changed. 'He has no idea what that diamond is. It's famous in ... certain circles. Money-lending circles, aye? If he gives it over to someone who knows its worth, that person is not going to let him live, knowing he could point to them at any moment.'

He raised his head again, and his skin looked waxy in the last of the light that crept through the cracks in the barn roof. 'If they kill for that bloody stone, they'll no stop at Nathan.' His head fell back, and he caught his breath at the jarring movement. 'They'll no stop. D'you understand?'

'Archie, you're slurring...'

'D'ye *understand?*' His accent was growing sharper even as his voice was becoming weaker, and I felt the cold finger of panic.

'Yes!' His words drove me to my feet, and I seized the spade once more, feeling my hands shriek in protest. I tried to ignore the slick feeling of fresh blood as the skin broke, and I smashed the spade into the door again. 'It's hopeless, Archie!'

I threw the spade down, and turned in time to see his eyes close, and I was back at his side in seconds. 'Don't you dare drift off now. Stay awake!' I caught at his face as it slipped to the side, and brought it back around, both hands supporting his head, forcing him to look at me. He blinked, and stared, and a tiny sound escaped on his breath that might have been a groan, but from the exasperation and affection on his face I thought was probably actually a laugh.

'You're a fierce wee thing, Kitty Buchanan,' he said. 'Just the kind of bossy wench an officer's wife ought to be.'

I gathered him close, pressing my cheek to the thick dark hair at his crown, not knowing whether to laugh or cry. His right hand still gripped at his shoulder, but his left crept around my waist, his fingers spread over my back and pressing me gently closer to him, his breath heavy, dampening my shirt. We stayed like that for a long time, and it was fully dark by the time I heard a sound outside. Someone was scuffling in the dirt around the hen-houses. I scrambled to my feet and flew to the door, and hammered on it.

'Help us! Please!'

'Kitty?' came the startled voice from outside.

'Jessie! Quick, Archie's in here, and he's badly hurt!'

'Oh, God! I'll get the key!'

'It's gone, just break the lock. Anything!'

'Gone? Who–'

'Just *do something!*'

'Right, just, uh … wait there.'

The preposterousness of that wrung a quick, barking laugh out of me, but a good part of that was relief; the door was still just as hopelessly locked, but she was *outside!* Where the world went on. It must be all right now. Somehow. I stumbled back in the pitch dark to where I thought Archie was, but I couldn't find him. Panic gripped me tight, and I forced myself to stop where I was. It

397

wouldn't help him for me to go tripping up on him on top of everything else. Maybe the noise had woken him.

'Archie,' I said. 'Can you hear me?' I crouched down, patting the floor with both hands, wincing as the blisters flared and the cracked skin began to bleed again. At last I found a boot, and, with a little gasp of relief, patted up his leg and his hip, and then across his stomach until I was huddling into his side again. From outside I could hear the sound of Jessie smashing at the door with something she'd found, but it didn't sound as though it was helping.

Archie twitched under my hand, and I sat up and put my hand to his face, feeling his cool, clammy skin. There was a tiny movement as his eyes opened. *Oh, thank God...*

'Archie,' I whispered. 'Jessie's here. She's trying to help us.' He nodded, once, but didn't speak, then his head slipped again and he was away into darkness.

'What happened?' Jessie was shouting through the door now. I heard the crashing give way to scraping and levering, and a renewed hope leapt in my chest.

'I'll explain later. Why are you back?'

'Would you like me to go away again?'

'Don't be stupid!'

'That's no way to talk to someone who's trying to help.' She flung her shoulder at the door and grunted. It shook, but the padlock only rattled. 'I saw Nathan on the road. In the trap.'

'Was Amy with him?'

'No.' I heard the accusation crash back into her

voice then. 'What have you and those girls done?'

'Nothing! It wasn't the McKrevies who did this. It was Nathan. I told you!'

'*What?*'

'Belt up and go and get Bel to help you!'

'Belinda?' Jessie gave a short, breathless laugh as she swung again at the door. Then she paused. 'Well, between us we'll be stronger, at least. We might be able to break that lock. I'll be back in a minute.'

'Hurry, Archie's ... just hurry.' I put my hand on his forearm, the one he had so recently bound to mine, and it felt warm and strong beneath my fingers; it seemed I was not the only one who could lie.

I heard another voice joining Jessie's out in the yard. Jessie's was muffled, but as Belinda stepped closer to the door I heard her clearly. 'What's he done to Archie?'

'*He's* opened his chest from shoulder to bloody breastbone!' I shouted, infuriated by all the talking, when Archie lay at my side barely breathing. '*Do* something!'

There was a shocked silence, then Belinda said calmly, 'Get Pirate.'

'What?'

'Do it!' I screamed, my throat hurting with the effort. All it had taken had been two words from the flighty, hopelessly scatterbrained Belinda, and I knew exactly what she had in mind. I wanted to hug her, but all I could do was scramble over to where we kept the rope for tying things into the cart. And for making halters for illicit horse riding... I made a strangled sound that was half laugh, half sob as I remembered Archie's reaction. I fed one end of the rope out beneath the door, and felt it snagged immediately, and pulled, and then it snaked past me at a terrific speed, the very last coil whipping around and snapping against my leg. I yelped, and Belinda shouted, 'Sorry!' But my heart was leaping with relief.

A moment later I heard Pirate snorting, protesting at being dragged out of his nice warm stall and made to stand still in the chilly darkness of the yard. Jessie didn't say anything. She had obviously seen Belinda's plan as well, and I knew that later we'd both be reminded whose idea it was, and made to suffer accordingly ... but Bel would have earned that moment of glory.

Belinda had tied the halter as quickly as she had before, and now she took the trailing end and, instead of looping it into a rein, I heard her slip it beneath the barrel of the bolt where it crossed the tiny gap between door and jamb. Then, talking gently, she began to coax Pirate into walking backwards. He made a whickering sound, and didn't move. Bel spoke to him again, and I could hear his hooves shifting in the dirt by the door, and then, to my relief, he began to move back. The rope pulled tight against the bolt, and I could hear Bel patting Pirate's powerful neck as she talked to him, and he pulled again. And again.

I crawled around in the darkness by the door, until my hand fell on what I was searching for and I jerked back in instinctive revulsion at the greasy feel of blood on the spike. Then I grabbed it again and shoved it under the door. It snagged a little at the widest point, but I pushed harder, and the bottom of the door splintered enough to allow it to pass under.

'Jessie,' I shouted, 'get that under the bolt and lever it off!' Pirate jerked at the sudden sound of my voice, and the rope slackened, but soon tightened again as Belinda urged him on. I heard Jessie sliding the dibble beneath the bolt, and pulling hard on it, groaning with the effort.

'Should have let Colin put this bolt on,' she muttered. 'Frances did too good a job.'

And then it happened. Between Jessie's levering and Pirate's pulling, the screws tore loose from the wood, and bolt and padlock flew off together. The door creaked open and a lantern flashed, and two voices began to speak at once. I ignored them both and crawled back to Archie, and they followed; Jessie crouched at his other side, and Belinda knelt beside me, and touched my arm. She was trying to say sorry, I knew, but she had saved us. I shook my head and turned my attention back to where it wanted to be.

He was stirring again, and when he opened his eyes he blinked against the light, and instinctively tried to raise his hand, but I thought he looked stronger. Or maybe it was hope that made me think it.

'How do you feel?' I asked. 'We need to get you out. Can you stand?'

'Aye,' he croaked. 'Give me a minute though.'

'He keeps rallying, and then slumping again,' I said, worried.

'That's bullheaded Scots determination for you,' Jessie murmured, and I couldn't help a tiny smile. But I knew I couldn't stay here, and at least Archie wouldn't be alone now.

'I'm going to get Amy back, somehow,' I told him, squeezing his hand in farewell.

His confused mind was gradually untangling, and he looked at me worriedly. 'For God's sake be careful, but ... Kitty, you *have* to tell him. He mustn't let anyone see he has that stone.'

'You can't go, Kitty,' Bel protested. 'It's too dangerous. I'll go for the constable instead.'

Archie shook his head. 'No, you'll panic him. And it'll take too long.'

I turned to Jessie. 'How long ago did you see the cart?'

'About an hour, I suppose.'

'Going towards Princetown,' I confirmed, and she nodded.

I took Archie's face in my hands and kissed him, and before he had the chance to do or say anything else, I was back on my feet and running towards the door. 'Look after him,' I said, and it was a struggle not to cry. 'Please, look after him for me.'

Chapter Twenty-One

I bent and untied the end of Belinda's home-made halter, wincing as one of my blisters broke, and flicked it up to fasten it as a rein. There was no time to tack him up properly, so I led Pirate to the mounting block in the yard, and a moment later I was on his back and urging him into a walk. I wanted to be able to ride fast and hard over the moors, but although it was mid-August, it was well past ten o'clock and almost pitch black, so instead I let him pick his way up the lane and out onto the main road. There were few stars, the sliver of moon gave very little light, and we made slow progress, but at least I wasn't walking or running and wearing myself out.

I talked to Pirate as we plodded towards Princetown, telling him everything that was in my heart, but despite my calm voice I could feel the panic growing. Amy was not at the farm or one of the others would have seen her, yet Jessie hadn't seen her in the cart ... perhaps Nathan had told her to lie down? But that was a cause for worry too, because if he still had her she was in as much danger as if he'd turned her loose on the road. I remembered Archie's words: *they'll no stop at Nathan...* Surely they wouldn't hurt such a sweet, quiet child, even if they... I shuddered and shook the thought of Nathan's possible fate aside. It would help no-one to think about that. They might let her go. They might.

Or they might find someone like that awful Dyer woman Jessie had told me about, and give her over, just to be rid of her. My breath hitched at the thought, and I only realised my knees had tensed as Pirate shifted into a fast trot. I let him go; the thought of Nathan and Amy getting onto a train to an unknown destination but for the sake of a few minutes was eating away at my sense of caution.

Before long The Plume of Feathers loomed on my right, and with it the realisation of my utter

403

stupidity. I'd had the answer all along – I could have prevented this! One word to Nathan about Amy's money would have stopped him; if I hadn't been so panicked, so terrified... If it had helped at that moment, I might have thrown myself off Pirate and lain on the ground, screaming at the sky. As it was I just slapped hard at my leg, welcoming the distraction of the thin, self-inflicted pain in my hand as I turned down towards the station. I had been stupid, yes, but as long as I found Nathan I might still be able to stop him from running off again. I spared a quick glance back at the inn, and was humbled by the knowledge of the friendship that lay behind its walls. I would have need of that friendship soon; I hoped they would understand. It was for Amy, after all.

The station was deserted; no trains were due, and none had recently departed and left behind the usual clutch of passengers waiting for further transport. I slid off Pirate's back, wondering vaguely how I would get back up again if I needed to, and hooked the halter over the rail, tying a quick knot and snugging it over the post. I patted the warm, gleaming neck that steamed gently in the low light that shone through the window of the stationmaster's office, and decided to go in and ask if a man and a little girl had been spotted nearby. It was possible someone may have pointed them in the direction of a hotel, at least. Turning to climb the steps to the platform, I felt a surge of relief as I caught sight of the farm trap. It stood behind the station, near the big sheds, and Pippin was standing patiently in the traces –

he couldn't have been there very long either, or he'd have been pulling and complaining by now. I'd made better time than I could have hoped.

Now my mind was freed of that worry, I allowed Archie back into my thoughts. Had he been able to leave the barn under his own strength – and what Jessie had accurately described as bull-headed Scots determination – or was he waiting for medical help? Was he still in pain, or had he been cared for and was now resting comfortably in bed? When I thought about what Evie had gone through earlier in the year, I wondered how she had survived the terror and the grief without being driven mad by it. I felt as if I were coming apart inside. The need to be close to Archie was a physical ache that only the sight of him could cure. Until I was back at his side I would be useless to everyone.

My anger towards Nathan was returning now, but I fought to keep it under control as I walked over towards Pippin, who whickered gently in recognition. 'Where are they then, my friend, eh?' I said gently. He blew down his nose and shifted in the traces, making his harness rattle. I smoothed him down and patted his shoulder, and looked around, my fear for Amy a growing, cramping thing in my belly.

'Amy!' I shouted, and my voice sounded furious and loud in my head, but out here in the cool night it just sounded small and scared. I tried again, finding a little more strength. 'Amy!' Pippin tossed his head and snorted, and I heard an answering whicker from the fence where Pirate was tied. No sound came from anywhere else. If

405

Amy had heard me, surely she would answer? I tried to deny the picture of a small, still body somewhere nearby, a bloodied patch matting white-blonde hair ... but my imagination had always been one of my biggest enemies, and it would not easily be banished.

'Amy, it's all right. Nobody's cross.' I tried a different approach. 'Mister Archie's waiting for you. Don't you want to come and see him?'

I waited, breathless, feeling sure that would do it. 'Amy, if you want to see Mister Archie you must tell me where you are...' Then I lost control. 'NATHAN! YOU BRING HER BACK RIGHT NOW!' Both horses stamped and whinnied, and the door to the stationmaster's office flew open.

'What the 'ell's goin' on out 'ere?'

I swung around in relief. 'Have you seen a little girl with very light blonde hair? She would be travelling with a dark-haired man. Just one bag between them.'

'That their pony cart?' The stationmaster jerked his head, and I nodded.

'Tell 'em to get it off this land. It's trespassin'.'

'I told you, I can't find them!'

'Well *I* ain't seen 'em. And that other 'orse belongs down't the sawmill, not tied up on my rails. Does Seth know you've got 'im?'

'Yes.'

'Oh, uh?' He peered at the writing on the side of the trap. 'You from Dark River Farm then?'

'Yes.'

'No children down there,' he said, with the firm authority of one who knows he's right. 'Trespass is a serious business,' he added as he turned to go

406

back into his office. 'Fine you six shillings, I could.'

And then he was gone. For the second time that night, tears and laughter battled it out, and I leaned my head against Pippin's patient neck, and let the soft, disbelieving laughter have its way. It relieved some of the tightness in me, and let me think clearly again. I straightened, realising it was pointless trying to make Amy respond if her years of enforced silence had come to the fore again. My ever-helpful memory showed me a small girl crouched in a farmyard, her thin little arms covering her head, and not a sound passing her lips despite her obvious terror.

I crossed to the sheds, and was about to pull open the door before I remembered how panicked Nathan had been, and how Archie had borne the brunt of that panic. Nathan still had most of the hand tools, and if I was hurt now there would be no-one to help Amy at all. Besides, the memory of the deep puncture and long slicing wound in Archie's chest, and the thought of it happening to me, made me feel faint with terror. My hands grew sweaty with it.

I wiped them on my trousers, wincing at the sting, then took a deep breath and knocked on the side of the shed. My voice was low, reasonable. 'Nathan, if you're in there, just let Amy go, please? I ... I have money. I can get it for you.' When no reply came I banged again, this time much harder, and my voice rose in volume to first match the noise, and then beat it.

'NATHAN!'

The stationmaster's door crashed open again,

and he marched down the platform to the gate, his eyes on me all the while. 'I've 'ad just about enough, miss! Do you want me to call the constable?'

It was the last thing I wanted. Archie was right; it would only serve to panic Nathan. 'Please, can you help me?' I said, in as calm a voice as I could. 'I'm telling the truth; I've lost the little girl I was caring for. I think she might have been taken in here.' I gestured at the shed. 'Could you shine a light for me?'

He eyed me narrowly for a moment, then went back to his office, returning with a rather small flashlight. It wouldn't light the whole shed at once, but it would soon show me if Nathan and Amy were hiding in there ... and all I could hope was that it didn't also show me the same picture my imagination had taunted me with. The light briefly played across me as he turned it towards the shed, then it swung back. I looked down; my shirt was covered in what could only be blood. There was no point in pretending otherwise.

'Difficult calving,' I stammered, seeing the stationmaster's mouth draw down sharply, and his brow furrow. 'That's why Amy was able to run off. I wasn't paying attention.' I could see my hesitation was giving him cause to doubt me, and tried to use it. 'It ... it was my fault,' I said in a small voice. 'She wanted to go out in the cart, and I think she climbed in when this man wasn't looking. He's probably scared to bring her back. He ... took some of our tools when he went.'

The stationmaster bit the inside of his lip for a moment, then nodded. 'Well no wonder he'd be hidin' then. Lots of that goin' on lately, there is.' Decision made, he pulled open the door and shone his torch inside, sweeping it from side to side. 'No-one in there, miss,' he said, less brusquely now. 'Do you want me to call the constable?'

I shook my head, finding yet another lie. 'I think Mrs Adams has done that already. Is there anywhere else they might be ... sheltering? Waiting for tomorrow's first train, perhaps?'

'All the other sheds is locked. But I'll keep a good watch out; don't you fret.'

I found a smile and tried not to sound too worried. 'Thank you, sir.'

At the cart Pippin turned to nuzzle my shoulder, and bit gently at my coat, and I absentmindedly rubbed his nose, trying to think of a place that would afford shelter for Nathan that wasn't too far from the station. Jealous of the attention, Pirate snorted and tossed his head, and that's when the answer hit me: the sawmill. Sheds and stables, and hay and sawdust that would make for a comfortable night. He must have left the trap here to make anyone who might come after him think he'd already left ... which he might well have done by the time we caught him up, if it hadn't been for Jessie coming back. I felt my breath shorten, and my fingers shook as I began to gather up the long rein ready to climb into the trap. Then I stopped. I couldn't let him know I was coming. I had to find him first if I didn't want him to slip away and find another hiding place.

Regretfully I dropped the rein and turned to the stationmaster. 'Please can I leave this here a little while? It'll be gone by morning, when the passengers start arriving.'

He huffed a moment, then shook his head and threw a hand up in defeat. 'Just see it is.'

'Thank you.' I refastened the rein to the rail and turned to go, and he put that same hand on my arm. When I looked back his face was solemn.

'I 'ope you find the little maid,' he said. 'B'aint right for a little one to be out at night. Not with that lot–' he nodded towards the prison '–allowed out and about, free as you like.'

'I think I know where she might be,' I said, and was trying to think of a believable reason why I'd prefer to walk, when I remembered Pirate. If we approached from the back field, where Woody had taken me, no-one would hear us. 'I'll take Mr Pearce's horse.'

'Ah, well, as you like.' He turned back towards the warmth of his office, but I called to him, a little embarrassed. 'Would you possibly be able to give me a leg up? He's not saddled, you see.'

'Go on then.' And he chuckled, surprising me. If nothing else I had provided some light relief during his night's work.

Once up on Pirate's back again, I turned him towards the moorland path that led parallel to the road. I would have to trust his sure-footedness, but he moved carefully and steadily towards the sawmill, and in less than half the time it would have taken me on foot, we arrived at the top of the back field. I slid down and hugged him, thanking him silently for bringing me safely here, then unlatched the gate and led him through. I let him graze, while I climbed the wall and dropped down into the field where Belinda had taken her tumble. My foot twisted as I landed, but I was able to clamp down on the exclamation and turn it into a sort of hissing gasp instead.

After a few steps the ache faded, and I blew out a sigh of relief, feeling it lifting my fringe away from my sweating face. I crossed the field more carefully from then on, reluctant to risk even the slightest injury that might slow me down, peering through the darkness at the sheds in the yard, rising black and imposing against the night, and utterly silent. Which one might he have chosen?

My intention was to go to the house, and look in all the windows to find whichever room Seth was in, so I could attract his attention without making any noise and alerting Nathan before I was ready. It only took a moment for that idea to be driven flat; the house was in darkness. There was no sound other than the wind rustling the trees overhead, and my own hammering heart, as I passed through the yard. The two workers had long since gone home for the night, and Seth must have gone out. I fought back a groan of frustration, accompanied by a little thrill of re-newed fear; I would have to do this alone after all.

Whichever shed I chose at random would leave the way clear for him if I was wrong, and no-one to block his escape. So I stayed in the middle of the yard, and called out, as I had at the railway station, but this time with a calm voice. 'Nathan, you can't take the diamond. You'll be killed for it. I can help. I have money. Just come out and let me talk to you.'

No movement, no sound. I tried again, my certainty that he was there never wavering. 'I'll give you all of it, if you'll come back to the farm with me!' The silence bounced back at me, and frustration started to build. 'Don't you trust me?' But of course he didn't; where would I get money from, when I'd just told him how desperately we needed those few tools?

'Nathan, the money was a gift for Amy, from those two girls who came today. You can have it all if you let her go!'

Still nothing. Well then, I'd simply wait until he came out. I moved across to the wide, open gateway, and sat down, my back against the post so I faced into the yard. If he came out of one of the sheds or stables I'd be sure to see him.

I don't know how long I sat there, staring into the night, but I felt my eyes growing heavy; the fears and tensions, and the hard work of the past few days were starting to tug at the last of my strength, leaving me light-headed, and floating dangerously into slumber. I blinked hard, and renewed my attention on the dark, silent sheds, one by one, listening out for the slightest movement from within, but there was none; Nathan and Amy must be asleep. It couldn't hurt, then, for me to... My eyes drifted shut and I snapped them open. I mustn't. He knew I was here now, and would be extremely cautious; if he crept by me while I slept I might not wake up. The night walked on, touching me with chilly fingers as it passed, and brushing my skin with its soothing quiet. I heard Pirate's hooves in the grass over in the field; sound carried more clearly than I'd realised. I heard the grass protest and finally tear free as he pulled up mouthfuls and chewed them, and I heard him whicker softly in the darkness, a lazy, contented sound.

How wonderful it had been for Archie to have had the chance to ride him, and not just to hack him gently along the lane, but to let him have his head, to remember the glorious combination of a powerful horse and the open moors after so long. I could feel a little smile on my face at the memory of Archie's breathless laughter, and my mind's eye drifted over his tall, strong form as he sat upright in the saddle, his graceful hands light on the reins, his thighs gripping Pirate's flanks and urging him on, and on, and on...

I jerked upright. How long had I slept? Maybe less than a minute, maybe much longer. My head had fallen to the side – that's what had awoken me, and I raised it now to find the tiny crescent moon. Not as much as an hour, but probably a good deal more than a minute. I scrambled to my feet, reluctantly letting go of the idea of waiting Nathan out; the risk was too great. My thoughts turned, once again, to how to get him to reveal himself so I could block his escape.

I looked around, as best I could in the weak moonlight. There were four large sheds. They would be thickly laid with sawdust in places. A row of stables, from before the war when there had been horses to fill them. Amy might be in any one of them, asleep, I hoped, but maybe wide awake and terrified to make a sound. I was still sure Nathan wouldn't hurt her, but she didn't know that. She had only her past experiences to go by, and a noisy child in the same place as a street-girl trying to make a wage would soon be silenced by any means to hand. All her life she'd have been threatened if she made a sound, and ignored if she didn't. Lucky to find a meal, no home comforts, no toys to play with. No wonder she...

The idea bloomed. I caught my breath, and thought it through quickly. Was it too dangerous for Amy? I didn't think so; in fact I was counting on the opposite to be true, and Nathan's reaction to this would prove it one way or the other. If he wouldn't answer, then I had to break Amy's silence instead, and there was only one way to do it.

I moved into the middle of the yard, and tried to keep my attention on all four sheds, and the stables, at once. 'Nathan,' I called, putting a new urgency in my tone, my fingernails cutting into my palms as fear and readiness took hold together. 'This is important. I know you don't want to hurt Amy, so I need you to listen. If she has a ribbon pinned to her dress, with a silver spoon on it. You have to take it off her. It's...' I thought frantically, but could think of nothing convincing. 'It's dangerous,' I finished lamely. There was a silence. I waited a moment, then was about to throw some fantastical but desperate explanation that it had been used to spread rat poison in the barn, but, thankfully I didn't need to; a moment later an outraged wail cut through the night air. My feet launched me across the yard, and before Amy's cry had died away, my sore and blistered hands were pulling at the end stable door.

Inside I blinked rapidly, and, as the thin moonlight shone into the stable I saw movement, and heard Nathan's tired, defeated voice. 'Go to her, Amy. Go on. It's all right.'

Small feet rustled the hay, and a moment later Amy was standing beside me and I dropped to my knees. I could hear Nathan still talking, but ignored him, and folded Amy into my arms, dropping kisses on her head and listening instead to her quiet, calm breathing, as if it were the most glorious symphony ever heard. After a moment I felt her hands drop away from the spoon and slowly, sweetly, wrap themselves around me in return.

When I could bear to ease away from her, I sat down and gathered her into my lap, blocking the door, although Nathan could easily have knocked me aside. I didn't think he would, and I was right. His babbled words started to make sense, and I gave half of my attention to them while the other half was on the solid, comforting weight of the child in my lap, and the small sounds of concentration she was making as she pushed stray bits of hay into the lace-holes in her shoes.

'I don't know why I did it,' Nathan was saying. 'I wasn't thinking. Is he... Will he be...' It sounded as though the words had been dragged from his throat with barbed wire, and he was terrified of hearing the answer.

My anger flared again, hot and tight in my stomach. 'I don't know,' I said with complete honesty. Archie had rallied so often, each time falling into an increasingly weaker state immediately afterwards... Fear wormed its way through me again, and I could hear it reflected in Nathan's voice.

'Kitty, if I've hurt him–'

415

'Of course you've hurt him!' Amy stiffened slightly, and I dropped my voice, but sounded no less furious. 'If that thing had been two inches higher you'd have stuck it in his neck!' He gave a sob, and I fought the natural urge to try and ease his terror; how could I, when I shared it?

His voice cracked. 'What can I do?'

'You can come back to the farm. Show some remorse, put things right.'

'No! I can't. They'll find me, and when they do, they'll kill me.'

'They still will, even if you give them that diamond. Especially if you do.' I told him what Archie had said. 'I didn't care what they did to you,' I finished. 'All I cared about was getting Amy back. But Archie seemed to think you deserved our help too. I thought he was wrong.'

'And now?'

I studied his outline, faint moonlight touching only on the shoulder of his jacket and the side of his head, but his slight stature made him look like a child. He sounded like one, too, and I couldn't reply to his question because I didn't know the answer. 'Why did you take Amy?' I said instead.

I saw that one shoulder lift in a helpless shrug. 'I wasn't thinking,' he repeated. 'I had to make you stay there long enough for me to get away. I meant it when I said I'd let her go. I thought you'd believe me.'

Believe him? 'So why didn't you?' The ache to get back to the farm, to Archie, was still pulsing in me, but I needed to play Nathan's line very carefully or he'd wriggle off my hook and be gone.

'I got to the top of the lane, and tried to make

her get down off the cart, but she wouldn't. So I lifted her down, and told her to run back home.'

'You used those words? "Run home?"'

'Well, yes–'

'Nathan, if you'd spent any time around her at all, instead of locking yourself away in your room, you'd know she has no idea what a home is.' Amy must have heard the sadness in my voice, and I felt the solid movement of her head, twisting against my chest to look up at me.

'Kitty cryin'?'

'No, darling, it's all right.' I bent and kissed her forehead, and she went back to her work, satisfied. 'So, she wouldn't run back down the lane,' I prompted Nathan.

'I couldn't make her move,' he said. 'She just stood there. I started to move off up the road, thinking it might make her go back ho ... somewhere more familiar. But she started following me instead, and I didn't like to think of her on the road alone.'

I didn't know whether to slap him or hug him; he'd been desperate, terrified for his life, making worse and worse decisions every step of the way, and yet he had still been moved to risk everything to protect this child he barely knew. Yes, Nathan was a rogue, but he didn't deserve to die.

'Archie was right,' I said gently. He sniffed, and the part of me that felt sorry for him grew a little bigger, edging aside the anger and frustration. 'Will you come back to the farm? Just long enough for me to get you the money,' I hurried on, as he started to shift backwards – an instinctively defensive movement that took him farther into the darkest part of the stable.

'You were telling the truth?' he said, his voice taking on a hopeful note.

'For once, yes.'

He came closer again. 'Why didn't you say something when we were in the barn?' He didn't sound suspicious, more pleading, and I shrugged but my voice was dry and somewhat unforgiving when I answered.

'I have asked myself that very same question. I believe I might have been slightly distracted by the fact that you had just stabbed my husband.' A silence fell, and as the seconds slipped away I felt the urgency to leave like a painful tug in my chest. 'Will you come?' I said, when the wait became too much.

He stirred from whatever thoughts had him in their grip. 'Yes, I'll come.'

'Good. The trap is still at the station.' I eased Amy off my lap and stood up, then held out my hand to her. 'Come along, sweetheart, we're going to see Mister Archie now.'

'I's tired,' she said. 'Can't walk no more.'

'Let me carry her.' Nathan moved towards her, and I had to stop myself from snatching her up into my own arms. But while he might not be very strong, and the wheezing sounds he made reminded me he needed to be careful of exerting himself, he was still stronger than me. When Amy didn't balk at his approach, but lifted her arms to be carried, I let myself relax.

As we started back up the road to the station Nathan glanced behind us. 'I was going to leave her there, as soon as dawn came,' he said quietly.

'She would have been asleep, and Seth Pearce, or one of his lads, would have found her and brought her back to you.'

'She'd have been comfortable, yes,' I allowed, brushing sawdust from my trousers. 'But what you did, Nathan—'

'I know.'

Pippin had begun to pull at his harness when we reached him. Guilt niggled at me for leaving him for so long, and I murmured my apologies and unhitched the long rein from the fence. As we rolled along the dark road, Pippin picking his way carefully back towards Dark River Farm, Nathan asked what had clearly been on his mind since he'd learned I'd been telling the truth about the money.

'How much did the girls give you for Amy?'

'I don't know,' I said. 'I didn't want to accept it, and now it feels wrong to sit and count it. I was going to take it to the bank tomorrow.'

'Then how do you know it'll be enough?'

'How much do you owe?' He didn't answer at first, and I slowed Pippin until we were barely moving. 'How much, Nathan?'

'Seven hundred pounds.'

I snatched a horrified breath. 'Seven *hundred?* How on earth did you borrow so much?'

'I didn't. I borrowed one hundred and twelve. Almost enough to pay Will back, but not quite. Then...' He trailed away again, and I remembered what Archie had said about paying back so much more than the original loan. Still ... seven hundred?

'Then what? Come on, you might as well tell me everything.'

'Then I found a job as a chauffeur. A business-man with an appreciation for art, which is why he took me on despite my lack of experience. I thought I would be able to pay back the loan, but it kept growing, faster than I could earn. They found me, those who'd set up the loan, and offered to remove the responsibility of cutting my finger-nails, one by one, unless I made a substantial pay-ment by the end of the week.' He flexed his fingers. 'As an artist, I felt compelled to accept their terms.'

Despite the wry humour in his words, I shuddered, with no small degree of sympathy. 'What did you do?'

'I stole the money from my employer.' He said it in a small voice, so unlike the confident, cheer-ful Nathan I'd first met. I had to remind myself it was the same man. He cleared his throat, and carried on, in matter-of-fact tones. 'Unfortun-ately I didn't do it very well, and I was caught, convicted and imprisoned. The debt mounted up while I was in Walton Gaol, and by the time I came out, complete with pneumonia–' he thumped his chest '–I owed just over four hundred pounds.'

'When was that?'

'In July of 1915. Two months later I heard about Will, how he'd married into money, and so I went back to Breckenhall. That was the day I met Evie, in Will's old shop.'

'And Martin told you where Will was living,' I finished.

'Yes, and that he was wounded, but not how badly. I would never have–'

'Yes, you would,' I said. 'Of course you would. In your position you'd have been a fool not to try.' Something else puzzled me. 'How did you know to get talking to Belinda in the bank?'

He leaned down and patted the side of the trap, where the name of the farm was painted. 'This was waiting in the street. The only people I saw in the bank were two old men, a very fat nurse-maid, a woman with three children in tow, and a pretty young woman in trousers and boots. It wasn't hard to make the connection.'

'Poor Bel,' I murmured. 'Go on.'

'When I settled into Dark River, it felt like the safest place in the world,' he said. 'I thought, I can stay here, make a new life. No-one would ever find me. Then I got talking to Archie out in the fields. I'd never seen him really angry, not like this. He told me if I brought violence to Dark River he'd...' He broke off.

'He'd what?' I said, intrigued to hear of this new, harder side, especially since he'd been the one to send me after Nathan to try and save him.

'Doesn't matter. Wasn't very nice though. Any-way, I remembered how easy it had been for me to get Martin to trust me, so it would probably be even easier for them.'

'It was easy to trick him by friendliness, because he's a gentle soul,' I said. 'But he's also loyal; he might not give in so easily to intimidation.'

'No,' Nathan said, 'but would you want to be the reason he was in that position?'

Once again I felt the complication of combined

421

anger and affection. 'You're a waste of a very nice man,' I said at last.

He gave a little laugh. 'Pretty Kitty ... what on earth do you see in that tall, strong and handsome Scotsman, when you could have me?'

I laughed too, and it felt surprisingly good. 'It was a hard choice,' I said, and nudged his arm. 'But you make a very nice friend when you forget to be such an arrogant oik.'

He remembered something then, and sat up straight. 'Did you call him your husband?'

'I did,' I said, pride unfurling inside me. 'We're handfasted.'

'I'm glad,' he said softly. 'Really, I am. You're made for each other.'

'And what of Belinda?' I asked.

'I like her. I thought perhaps there might be something there for us, until I saw Evie and Will, and then you and Archie.' He fetched a deep sigh, and shrugged. 'I want what you have, or nothing at all. What would be the point in settling for less?'

We had reached the top of the lane now, and as I turned Pippin down it I realised I had almost forgotten everything that Nathan had done, but his mention of Archie brought it all vividly back again. I became once more aware of my shirt, stiff with Archie's blood, and of the pain in my hands where the reins cut into the sore spots and blisters. With Amy safely in the back of the cart, and home growing closer with every turn of the wheels, it had been easy to let my mind release the fear that had consumed it throughout the night. But now it returned; what if the money was not enough to tempt him to exchange it for the diamond? After everything that had been risked for it, everything that had nearly been lost... Evie hated the thing, but it was no longer hers to hate, and it was Lily we had to think of now. If only Evie hadn't already sent that blessed telegram...

'Leave the cart here,' Nathan said, interrupting my thoughts. 'We'll walk the rest of the way.'

'Why?'

'No-one else must know we're back. Those who know what's happened will be awake, and waiting for you to come back.'

'And what if they hear us? The money's up in my room.'

'They won't. Amy won't make a sound, and if someone's in the kitchen you'll just have to think of an excuse to go straight to your room.'

But the house was all dark; it was predawn and there would have been no sense in Jessie and Belinda worrying Frances and the others into a sleepless night. Belinda was probably asleep by now too, and even if Jessie were awake I could be quiet enough that she wouldn't hear me.

The lantern Belinda had brought out was still on the ground in front of the barn, and I picked it up and turned to Nathan. 'Matches?'

He fumbled a silver box from his pocket, and gave it to me before pulling open the barn door as quietly as the broken latch would allow. I stepped inside before I lit the lantern, and in its light I saw his face had taken on a pinched look; things had grown taut between us again, the pleasant interlude of the drive home was no more.

'You must understand, if anyone but you comes

423

out of that house, I will run.'

It was on the tip of my tongue to say, 'Do it, and be damned; it's your life,' but I didn't. I could see the fear in the set of his brow, and in the tremble of his lips. Besides, it was Lily's life too.

'I'll keep Amy with me,' he said, and held up a hand as I started to protest. 'No, listen. She's in no danger. But you'll be quicker and quieter on your own.'

I eyed him closely, then realised the only real hostage was the Kalteng Star. The lantern swung, illuminating the blood-soaked strip of sacking on the floor, and my stomach clenched at the sight of it. One minute it had bound my arm to Archie's, our heartbeats finding each other through the thin skin of our wrists, the next it had been pressed tight against Archie's chest, glistening with blood, and held there by that same hand.

I saw Nathan's gaze follow my own, and a muscle jumped in his jaw. He took a long, deep breath and I could hear it shaking when he let it out again. 'Don't go to him,' he said, and I'm sure he meant it as a warning but we both heard the desperation and pleading in his voice. He turned to me. 'I mean it, Kitty, no-one can know I'm here.'

I nodded, and left him the lantern, then bent and kissed Amy's soft, rounded cheek. 'Soon be time to go to bed, sweetheart,' I said. 'I just need you to stay here and look after Nathan for a minute while I go and find something. All right?'

She nodded and sat down on her favourite hay bale, the same one Archie had leaned against earlier. I saw my folded pullover on the floor...

424

How could I go into that house now, knowing he lay in Frances's bedroom, and not go to him?

'Mister Arsh?' she said, as if she'd read my mind.

I choked back a little sound of distress, and smoothed her hair. 'He's sleeping, but you'll see him at breakfast.'

As I crossed the yard to the kitchen I couldn't help wondering, with a low feeling of dread, if I'd just told yet another lie. The biggest one of all.

Chapter Twenty-Two

In our room, Belinda lay face down, with one arm hanging off the edge of her bed, snoring lightly. I found myself glad for once, that she slept like the dead; if it made for a ridiculously difficult job waking her for work, at least it meant that the harsh squeak of the top drawer, where I'd put the money, did no more than make her snuffle and twitch her fingers.

I let out a relieved sigh, tucked the packet into my pocket and crept from the room, pulling the door closed carefully. As the metal arm of the latch clicked into its notch, I held my breath and peered down the landing, waiting for the telltale flicker of someone lighting a lamp. Nothing happened, and I cast a longing glance at Frances's bedroom door. Behind it, Archie would be lying, either sleeping or trying to sleep, no doubt worrying about me, and about Amy. And also, I realised with a flicker of exasperated affection, worried about Nathan. It would be the quickest, easiest thing in the world for me to go in, tell him we were all right, and then go down to the barn.

My fingers hovered by the latch, my thumb extended ready to press down on the flattened metal, but I couldn't do it. Archie would want to know everything, and when I told him about the money the girls had given Amy, and that I was giving it away, he would try and stop me. He'd believe it was possible to keep the money and still persuade Nathan to stay, but he'd be wrong. And he'd hurt himself even more proving it.

My hand drew back slowly, reluctantly, and I curled the fingers into my palms so they wouldn't be tempted to return to the cool metal that would simply clunk gently, and then let the barrier between Archie and me swing away. It was painfully difficult, but I stepped back from his door, and turned to go downstairs, Amy's future bumping against my thigh.

I couldn't tell how long I'd been in the house; it felt like hours and I fumbled my way back across the dark kitchen, hitting the edge of the table with my hip in my frantic hurry to return to the barn, in case Nathan had grown impatient. I was almost there, when the door to the hallway opened and I saw Jessie, fully clothed and with a paraffin lamp in her hand.

'What are you doing?'

I wanted to just tell her to go to bed, but my heart overtook my impatience. 'How is Archie?'

'Sleeping. No thanks to you and your noise.' She relaxed slightly, and put the lamp on the table. 'He's well, Kitty. He's tired, and sore, and

426

horribly worried about you, but he was too exhausted to stay awake, particularly after Belinda force-fed him the last of Frances's best whisky. The others don't know anything yet. What happened? Where's Amy?'

'With Nathan, in the barn. I'm ... I'm taking him Amy's money so he'll go.'

'Her money? For goodness' sake, Kitty, that's–'

'I have no choice!' I moved towards the door again but she grabbed my arm. I wrenched it free. 'He won't give back the diamond unless he has something to pay his creditors with.'

'So you're using Amy's money to buy back a rich woman's trinket? Why? Call the constable!'

'If he sees anyone but me he's going to run. And he still has Amy.'

'He won't hurt her, will he?'

'I'd like to think not, but look what he did to Archie when he was scared. Jessie, if the police come, Nathan knows he will be put back in prison and it'll make him–'

'*Back* in prison?'

I almost howled in frustration, but tried, unsuccessfully, to keep my voice lowered. 'It doesn't matter. I'll tell you later! Just let me go, will you? For goodness' sake, I know you've had a terrible time but you have to learn to trust *some*one, *some*time!' I stopped, breathing hard and wondering how loudly I'd shouted.

There was a pause, then she gestured at my bulging pocket. 'How much is there?'

I took out the packet. 'I don't know.'

'Then neither does he.'

'No.'

427

'Well then, if he's promised to go away with whatever you give him, take most of it out.'

I blinked. Why hadn't I thought of that? 'I ... I'm ... right!'

'Honestly, Kitty, you are a bit thick.'

'I've been a bit distracted,' I pointed out acidly, as I had to Nathan. 'Why are you back, anyway? Our wages have run out already, have they?'

'Wages?'

'The ones you took from the jar, before you stormed off leaving Frances in pieces.'

'I do wish you wouldn't keep accusing me of things I haven't done! I didn't take any wages, you little idiot. If money has gone missing, don't you think it more likely to have been Nathan when he was fetching the key to the barn?' I groaned; of course it was. I felt dreadful, and wanted to say so, but she was still talking. 'Now take out most of that and put it somewhere safe.' She separated the money into two vastly uneven piles, and gave me the smallest one.

I looked at the thin pile of notes doubtfully. 'I don't think this will be enough to make him leave.'

'It's going to have to be.'

'No, give me some of that back.' I glared at her in the jumping light of the lamp, and she sighed and gave me half of the remaining pile. 'Thank you.'

She finally stepped to one side and let me pull open the door. I looked back to ensure she stayed put, and she folded her arms and fixed me with a cool look. I wondered why she was back; was it just to collect some of her belongings? I hoped not, but at the moment I had more important things to think about, and I shook my head to clear it of everything but Amy.

I welcomed the faint light from the kitchen as I crossed quickly to the barn, and pulled open the door so I could see in the light from the paraffin lamp that stood on the worktable. I looked at that table for a moment. Could it really have been such a short time ago that Archie and I had stood there and pledged our lives to each other? Since he had shown me just how badly he danced? Since Amy had been playing happily with the hay, the day's work had been almost done, and Archie and I had been thinking no deeper thoughts than the anticipation of an evening together. Tenderness and conversation, and the bliss of two bodies made for each other. It seemed impossible to imagine now.

'Have you got it?'

I jumped and turned. Nathan's hands rested at his sides, his fingers curling and uncurling, as if he didn't know what to do with them. At least he had no weapon this time. 'Yes,' I said. I proffered the packet and he stepped forward and took it, and I could feel his hands shaking. He pulled out the pile of notes, and I held my breath; it was a long way from being enough to pay off his debt, but perhaps he would take it and offer it to his creditors, to show his intention to repay when he could.

'Oh, *I* see!' The voice from behind me made my heart stutter, and I whirled to see Jessie, standing in the doorway. 'You'll give it to *him*, but you won't give it to me!'

'What? I told you–'

'You know how badly I needed it!' she went on, coming farther into the barn. I could see her face alight with betrayed anger, and belatedly realised what had lain behind her insistence on removing most of the money from the packet. I felt half faint with fury at myself – how foolish could I have been? Decision after decision tonight had been rushed, panicked and lethally wrong.

I saw a chance, with the doorway unobstructed. 'Amy!' I said. 'Go into the house, quickly. Run and find Miss Belinda. She's in the dorm.'

I half expected Jessie to grab at the little girl as she passed her, and was ready to lunge if she did, but she stood aside, too interested in the real prize in Nathan's trembling hand. 'I always knew you were a little sneak,' she told me, though still not looking at me, 'but I thought you'd have been glad to see me go.'

'I was,' I said tightly. The relief that Amy was safe was making me reckless, and I stepped forwards. 'Nathan, give me Evie's diamond. You two can fight over the money all you like.'

He put his free hand into his pocket, and withdrew a tobacco tin. 'It's in there,' he said, tossing it to me. Somehow I caught it, and fumbled it open. Fragrant tobacco spilled out, curls of dark brown that drifted to the floor in the light of the lantern, and then my fingers withdrew the hard, perfectly circular gold band in which the famed Kalteng Star was set. I was struck breathless by its beauty; simple and stunning, in daylight it would look even more so, but even in this flickering light it was like holding the night sky in my hand.

I was momentarily transfixed by the sight, and only vaguely aware of the sound of the kitchen door slamming closed behind Amy, and a movement from the corner of my eye, but a second later a viciously hard hand was in my hair, hooked fingers pulling my head back. I saw a blur, then felt the sharpness of metal pressed beneath my jaw, and my heart stopped beating as I closed my eyes and waited...

'Give me the money, Nathan,' Jessie said. Her voice was tight with malice, and if I could have moved I'd have torn the skin from her face. 'Don't think I won't do this. You know there's no love lost between us. They'll blame you anyway; everyone knows what you did to Archie. And no-one else knows I'm back.'

I opened my mouth to refute this obvious lie, but felt the spike of what I now realised was the dibble press into the skin of my neck and I could feel tears of terror prickling at my eyes – what if it all ended here? After everything, all the danger in Flanders, the midnight dash to rescue Amy, my terror for Archie... What if it all ended right here in a smelly barn, with that cursed diamond still in my hand?

I raised the hand that somehow still clutched the Kalteng Star. 'Take it,' I managed, my eyes still closed. I was glad I hadn't told her about the danger of trying to sell it, although I probably would if she let me go; I didn't want to see her dead any more than I wished it on Nathan.

'I don't want *that*,' she said, and pulled my head back harder. I couldn't prevent a tiny cry from escaping, and was relieved when her grip slack-

431

ened, just a little bit. But the dibble never wavered and I could feel a drop of blood rolling down the side of my neck. 'The money, Nathan, or you'll be arrested for murder before you get to the end of the lane.'

I heard a small thud at my feet, and then I was free, stumbling to the side, away from her reach, my fingers going to my neck and coming away bloody. I heard Nathan's feet pounding as he broke and ran for the door. Jessie bent to pick up the packet and looked briefly at the contents, and I wondered if I'd be able to rush her and knock her off balance. She came over to me, and I was horrified and ashamed to feel myself shrinking back, despite my brave intentions, my heart hammering in terror. She still held the dibble in one hand, and looked down at it, frowning. Then she turned to the door, flipped the twice-bloodied tool over in her hand so she held it by the spike, and threw it out into the yard, watching it spin end over end until it left the circle of light from the paraffin lamp. I heard it hit the side of the water trough with a ringing scrape of metal on stone, and then fall to the ground.

Then, to my stunned disbelief, she turned back to me, hefted the packet of money, and shoved it into my pocket. 'For goodness' sake, Kitty. You've got to learn to trust *some*one, *some*time.'

'You–'

'Sorry about the scratch,' she added, and tilted my head to the side. 'It really is just tiny, though.'

'Why didn't you warn me?' I managed.

'Because you'd have been waiting for me, and it wouldn't have worked.' Jessie gently wiped away

432

a fresh bead of blood from my neck with her thumb. 'I'm sorry I frightened you.' Her voice had softened now. 'And Amy too.'

I looked at the door, through which Amy had disappeared, and a cold hand clutched at my heart, for a second. What if Nathan had caught her again?

'I waited 'til she had gone into the house,' Jessie said, reading my thoughts with uncanny accuracy. 'Anyway, he wouldn't. He's a bad one, but he's not that bad. Besides, he'll just run now. He has no choice.'

I looked down at the Kalteng Star, still clutched in my hand. Relief was setting in now the shock had worn off, and I had time to appreciate the value of what I held, and its short history here in England. The Creswell family, Evie and Lizzy's friendship ... and Oaklands Manor. Although the house would no longer have the benefit of the diamond's ownership, it had Lawrence's own legacy of care for the wounded. And it would have life, and even children running through its rooms again, if Evie and Will chose to live there after the war.

I turned to Jessie, who had folded her arms and looked awkward now, and even shy. 'Why are you back?' I asked her again quietly, hoping she would stay, for Frances's sake. I would find a way to live with her for a few more days, until I left for Belgium again.

Jessie blew her fringe away from her eyes. 'As much as I hate to admit it, it's because of what you said. About what I was doing to the people who love me. You were right, that's all.' She looked at me almost defiantly, waiting for me to play the superior no doubt, but I was absurdly touched by her honesty.

'And you'll stay?'

'If Frances will let me.'

'Of course she will.'

'What about you?' she wanted to know, and now she sounded timid again.

'What about me?'

'How would you feel if I stayed?'

It was on the tip of my tongue to ask why she cared, but her expression was one of genuine, anxious hope, and I bit back the words. Instead I reached for her hand. 'I'd like it.'

'Truly?'

'Truly. I like you, Jessie. I never understood you, but I like you. You frighten me, but I like you. You annoy me no end...' she grinned at that, and I grinned back '...but I like you.'

'Good,' she said, 'because I like you too. Even though you are a pompous know-it-all.'

'Then we're agreed.'

'It seems so.'

'You're the prickly, annoying daughter, and I'm the pompous know-it-all one.'

'Frances is very lucky to have us,' Jessie said solemnly, as we left the barn behind and walked towards the house, where lights were coming on in various rooms.

Crossing the yard, past the henhouses, I remembered the noises I'd heard when I'd been locked in the barn. 'What were you doing, scrabbling around the henhouses?'

I heard her laugh softly in the darkness. 'The

house was locked. I was going to sleep in one of them.'

I raised an eyebrow, although she couldn't see. 'Lots of rats around there, you know.'

'Not really. Just small brown hens. With long tails.'

Epilogue

Harvest Festival Celebration, Sunday 30 September 1917

Evie and I had left Archie and Will reminiscing over their strange and difficult first meeting, and everything that had happened since. They were the only men not dancing, apart from two soldiers in hospital blue, and Amy was sitting on Archie's lap, playing with the lapel of his coat and pushing the handle of her spoon through his buttonhole. I'd watched for a while, fascinated, and the concentration on Amy's face was only broken once, when someone danced too close and knocked her arm. The spoon tumbled from her grasp, but I felt a glow of warmth and quiet pleasure as I noticed that her face didn't melt into the familiar look of dismay, followed by relief when she found it still attached by the ribbon; this time she found her interest taken by the dancer, instead, and her eyes followed as the woman was once again swallowed up by the crowd. Only after she'd gone did Amy pick up her spoon again and return her attention

435

to Archie's buttonhole.

I stood in the village hall doorway, looking out at the bright, full, harvest moon. It hung in the sky, looking almost close enough to touch, and I tried to remember if it had ever looked like that out there. Flanders. Then I pushed the thought aside; tonight was precious, and in Lawrence's words I wanted to wring every bit of joy out of it I could, for tomorrow I would be leaving it all behind. Archie would travel with me as far as Number Twenty-Two, where Elise would be waiting for me, before continuing to rejoin his unit who were currently still at Dixmude but likely to move soon.

'Penny for them?' Evie joined me at the doorway, but I didn't want to tell her which way my thoughts had taken me.

'I was just wondering if they've raised much money tonight.' I gestured at the tins placed in various spaces among the harvest. A week ago there had been a terrible accident at Bere Ferrers railway station, just across the River Tavy, and the village was collecting with the vague notion of erecting some kind of memorial. Mostly it was just felt it was the 'thing to do', and perhaps the money would be sent to the families of the dead instead, or used to pay for their burial.

'People haven't got an awful lot to give,' Evie said. 'But it was such a horrific thing, I think everyone's just doing what they can.' She shivered. 'Nine dead, wasn't it?'

'And three who went to hospital. I don't know if they're still alive.'

'Did Seth say how it happened? I haven't heard any details other than that it was the New Zea-

436

land lads, and a train coming down from Water-loo.'

'All I know is that the men had got out on the wrong side of the carriage to collect rations, and were on the track when the London train came through.'

We were silent for a moment while we both struggled with the image of how it must have been – still light too, at only ten to four in the afternoon. Suddenly the room felt close and far too warm.

'Let's go outside for a minute,' I suggested, and Evie agreed, but we were stopped by a breathless Belinda, who bounded up and seized our arms.

'Wait! You can't run off; you have to dance with Brian and his friend!'

I looked beyond her, where two flushed and exhausted young men were having a well-earned break and watching the dancers. I recognised them from the sawmill. 'They can choose any one of fifty partners,' I protested. 'Men *are* in rather short supply.'

'But I'm sure they'd want to dance with you two. They'd ask you themselves, but said they "don't want to tread on no soldiers' toes".'

'It won't be the soldiers' toes they'll be treading on,' I pointed out, and Evie laughed. It was a wonderful sound, and it made me smile too – and the wraiths of the nine dead soldiers faded slightly.

Belinda shook our arms urgently. 'Please! Then, if you're dancing with them, I'll be able to dance with ... with Seth.'

We stared at her in amazement, and turned to look at the men again. Seth Pearce had just come off the dance floor, where he was in even greater demand than most of the others. The girl whose hand he was holding was looking hot and excited, and laughing at something he was saying. He gently released her, and went to stand with his workers and friends. Belinda's eyes followed every movement, and I saw him through her eyes at that moment – not handsome, but strong and pleasant-looking, friendly and dependable. And he was still as smitten with her as ever; his gaze accidentally found hers, and he rubbed a hand over his hair and turned away, no doubt remembering my assertion that her heart lay elsewhere.

'Bel,' I said gently, 'you don't need us to give you an excuse. Go and ask him.'

'But Archie and Will won't mind if you...' Then she sighed and admitted, 'He'll think I'm fickle and a dreadful tease.'

'I'm sure he'll put up with it,' Evie said, and removed Belinda's hand from her arm. 'Go on, love. He's never going to put his heart out where you can kick it again. You'll have to be the brave one this time.'

'Brave. Yes,' Belinda said, nodding. 'You two have been unbelievably brave. I'm sure I can do this.'

She turned back into the room, and Evie and I went out into the cool night. A gentle rain had started falling. It felt cool and refreshing after the heat of the village hall and I turned my face up to it gratefully.

'Are you all right?' Evie said, with quiet concern, and I nodded.

'I think so. I didn't know if I would be, but ... yes, I really think I am.'

'At least you'll have Archie nearby. For a while, at least.'

I turned to look at her, to watch her reaction carefully; I had to know. 'Was it terribly difficult, day-to-day, you know, when you knew Will was out there?'

She considered a moment, her blue eyes catching the light of the moon and looking, for a second, a lot like the Kalteng Star. 'Yes, sometimes. But by no means all the time. You know what it was like – so much to think about, your work carries you. Being home was harder. Having time to think.'

'Like Lizzy and Jack,' I said. 'It must be heartbreaking for her, and for you too, when he goes away, right into...' I glanced around and dropped my voice, although I couldn't see anyone nearby '...you know, into the thick of things.'

'I don't know how she copes,' Evie admitted. 'I rather thought she might be here by now, but perhaps her brothers are making life difficult tonight.'

'I hope she manages to get here,' I said. 'I don't think I'll have time to see her before we leave tomorrow.'

Evie nodded. 'I'm sure she will. She said she would use this as her own personal birthday celebration since it's only two days late. I'm glad Archie was able to stay, too.' She paused, then added casually, 'I suppose we ought to thank Nathan for that, really.' She laughed at the horrified look I threw her, and put her arm around my shoulder. 'Skittles, you are so easy to tease!'

'And you're far too good at teasing!' I said, with

439

a light punch on her arm.

'Lawrence certainly thought so.'

We were quiet for a moment, and I felt an oddly strong need to see and talk to my own brother, to remind myself he was alive, if not free; Evie's grief was well hidden for our sakes, but it was there and at least I had been spared that with Oliver.

'Speaking of Lawrence,' Evie said, 'I had a letter from Mother. She's honouring his wish to turn Oaklands into a convalescent home.'

'I'm so glad.'

She gave me a shrewd look. 'I don't really see Lawrence coming up with that idea on his own, do you? I mean, he was the sweetest boy. We knew that...' She broke off and cleared her throat, then went on, her voice growing steadier again. 'But he really never thought about the house at all, never considered it as his own, certainly not to do something like that with.'

'Well, I might have mentioned it,' I confessed. 'But he really took to the idea. He didn't need any persuading.' I realised now that Lawrence's eager acceptance of the idea had been more to do with Will's close call, than the fact that I had suggested it. 'I suppose Lady Creswell would think twice, if she thought the idea was mine?'

'She might,' Evie admitted. 'For a while, anyway. Common sense would win through in the end, I'm sure, but her first reaction would be disappointment that it hadn't been Lawrence's notion at all, and her second would be irritation that it had been yours. But she'd still do it.'

'Well I shan't be in a position to let anything

slip,' I pointed out. 'She won't let me near the house again.'

'I wouldn't be too sure,' she said. 'Mother was in a ... very fragile state when you left. She's not the type to let what happened to you form a lasting opinion. I promise.' She turned to look towards the hall. 'Besides, she has a fondness for any relation of Uncle Jack's, and for your Scottish captain in particular.'

I followed her gaze; Archie and Will had noted our absence and guessed we'd come outside to enjoy the cool of the evening. They emerged now, Amy nestled securely against Archie's shoulder, and Evie's face lit up as I'm sure mine had. Archie put Amy down on the step, and she promptly scooted away until she sat on the damp ground, and began her favourite game of digging.

'Are the doctors sure Will won't ever go back?' I asked in a low voice.

Evie shrugged. 'Maybe if the war goes on another five years, which, please God, it won't. But for now, no.'

I was glad to hear it. He tired quickly and was prone to infection, and it was easy to tell when he'd overdone things; his usually brisk walk would slow, and his hand would stray briefly to his waist. But his smile still had the power to melt hearts, and his good humour rarely wavered; he was an adoptive big brother to be proud of, and I gave thanks that he would be so much safer now.

Archie's own wound had healed well. The torn pectoral muscle had taken the longest, but he had been pronounced fit for active service again. I felt cold whenever I thought about it, but I remem-

441

bered that first day I'd seen him in his uniform, and my childlike conviction that he would emerge unscathed. He made it easy to convince myself I'd been right. His confidence and quiet competence shone through every movement; his men would walk through fire for him. His reaction to my own decision to return had been less sure, but it had been confined to a darkening of his eyes, and a tremble in his hand as he'd touched my face – not a word of it had fallen from his lips.

He raised his hand now and I went to meet him – Evie and Will nothing more than shadows behind me as my world shrunk once more. He still had a way of doing that; I could be the busiest I'd ever been, could be tired, or laughing at something, or furious, or weeping, have a hundred things on my mind, but as soon as Archie's grey eyes caught and held mine there was only him. Everywhere. He drew me against him, and I rested my head on his chest, feeling the warmth of him through his shirt, and the slow, steady beat of his heart against my cheek. My arms went around him and held him tight, and I felt his lips against my hair.

'Young Kittlington, you are the most desirable thing I have ever seen,' he whispered. 'I'm so proud to call you my wife. Have I told you that lately?'

'Every day since August,' I said, and looked up at him with a smile, 'but please don't let that stop you.'

He smiled back, then sobered, pushing a lock of my hair away from my eyes. 'Are you ready for it all?'

My chest tightened for a moment, and I didn't know how I'd feel when we had to part tomorrow evening, but for now I was as ready as I could ever hope to be, as ready as Evie had been when she'd travelled with Will to their separate trains, as ready as anyone was in these cold, uncertain days.

'Yes,' I said, and reached up to kiss him. My hands slipped around the back of his neck and into his thick dark hair, and as our lips touched I felt his calm strength flow into me, and it told me that this, at least, was no lie.

The sound of an approaching car, still rare enough here in the village, caught our attention and Archie and I drew apart and turned to look. Jack Carlisle's Model T Ford clunked to a halt in the road next to the hall, and Lizzy, never the lady, leapt out and ran around to the driver's door. She pulled it open, and grabbed Jack's hand, and he emerged, chuckling at her eagerness.

'Look who arrived just as I was about to leave!' she cried. As they came over to us the moonlight shone on her dark hair, where a carefully applied clip had come loose and let her thick curls escape, and I tried not to notice how her dress had been buttoned up wrong. I exchanged an amused glance with Evie; now we knew why she had been late, at least.

Jack, looking so much younger than when I had seen him last, and more like Archie than ever, embraced Evie, shook hands with Will, and then turned to his nephew. 'How are you?' he said quietly, and touched Archie's arm with the tenderness of a father.

'Fighting fit,' Archie said, and Jack pulled him

443

into his arms. The hug was brief, but when they parted their two dark heads remained close, their foreheads touching, and Jack took a ragged breath and clasped Archie's shoulders.

'Be bloody careful, lad,' he said roughly, and I felt a wholly unexpected sting of tears. I looked at Evie and Lizzy, and saw they'd been struck by the same sharp emotion, and even Will had turned away. Through the open doorway of the village hall I could see Belinda and Seth – I was too far away to see their faces, but their hands were linked and her attention was firmly on him. My smile returned. And there, making it even broader, was Frances Adams being pulled away from her conversation with Jessie, and towards the dancers, by an insistent Colin Trebilcock. She was not protesting at all.

I looked back at the people who had come into my life so recently, and then at Archie. It didn't matter whether I'd known them for a few months, or most of my life; the fierce joy I felt in that moment, at simply being with them, would be what kept me going through whatever was to come. I would leave Dark River Farm and return to the war, and if and when I came back I might not be the same person I was now, but these people – these complicated, generous, courageous and deeply loved people – would be with me for ever.

My thanks to everyone whose brains I have picked, stories I have read, and opinions I have solicited during the writing of this book. Also, to those who have told me they enjoyed the previous books in the series, giving me the confidence and impetus to continue.

A massive 'thank you' to Sarah Tweedle, for allowing me to use her ancestor Frances Jessie Goulding as a character, and for providing me with all the biographical information and research material to build on her tragic history and to give her a life she never had.

I would especially like to thank everyone who has smiled and nodded, and patted me on the head when I've gone into the twilight zone, and has waited patiently for my return to some kind of normality. I hope it's been worth it!

The publishers hope that this book has given you enjoyable reading. Large Print Books are especially designed to be as easy to see and hold as possible. If you wish a complete list of our books please ask at your local library or write directly to:

Magna Large Print Books
Magna House, Long Preston,
Skipton, North Yorkshire.
BD23 4ND

This Large Print Book for the partially sighted, who cannot read normal print, is published under the auspices of

THE ULVERSCROFT FOUNDATION